The Jade Lioness

Christina Courtenay

Book 3 in the Kumashiro series

Where heroes are like chocolate – irresistible!

Published 2015 by Choc Lit Limited
Penrose House, Crawley Drive, Camberley, Surrey GU15 2AB, UK
www.choc-lit.com

A CIP catalogue record for this book is available
from the British Library

ISBN 978-1-78189-237-4

MIX
Paper from
responsible sources
FSC® C018072

Printed and bound by Clays Ltd

*To the Romantic Novelists' Association
and all my RNA friends*

Acknowledgements

This book was partly inspired by the time I spent in Japan as a teenager and the wonderful people I met there, in particular my fellow pupils at the American School in Japan (ASIJ). Some of them, as well as one of my teachers, Mr Jose Luis Velasco (the best Spanish teacher ever!) have stayed in touch through the years, which is wonderful since our shared experiences in Tokyo were unique and unforgettable. I would like to thank them all for their friendship and support, especially Anna Rambäck (who helped me enormously when I first got to Tokyo), Margie Miciano, the 'Gai-jin Bosozoku' gang (you know who you are), and in the case of Jacqueline Oishi Tapper (now my sister-in-law), James Wade and Nozomi Shinoda-Wade, thanks also for help with Japanese words and phrases. I do hope I've got it right now!

Huge thanks, as always, to the wonderful Choc Lit team and Choc Lit authors, and special thanks to the Tasting Panel members (Jennifer S, Rosie, Claire W, Megan, Sarah H, Jennie A, Jennifer S, Betty, Adele, Izzy and Betty C) for liking this novel – that always gives me confidence and makes me feel I'm on the right track!

Thank you to my writing buddies and my lovely family for always being there – love you all!

Chapter One

Sitting in the shade on a small balcony overlooking the bay of Nagasaki, Temperance Marston watched her surroundings through half-closed eyelids. The blazing sun sent piercing shards of light bouncing off the water like the flashing of a lustrous diamond, making it impossible to do anything other than squint. And although the stifling heat of the August afternoon distorted the view into a shimmering haze, it was mesmerising nonetheless.

She ought to have been resting on her *futon*, but the air indoors was even more oppressive and her mind, as always, was too alert. She shifted slightly and sighed. The sea breeze didn't make the tiniest bit of difference. Her young servant, Akio, who sat a few feet away from her, looked up and commented, 'Very hot today, *neh*?'

'Indeed. I feel like the air is strangling me.' In fact, the humid air around Temperance seemed an almost tangible entity, its moist fingers invading every pore and causing perspiration to soak her clothing at the slightest move.

'*Nan desu ka?*' Akio frowned. His English was improving each day, but such abstract descriptions were as yet beyond his understanding. Temperance could have repeated the sentence in Japanese, as her linguistic skills were much better than those of her servant, but officially she wasn't supposed to understand or speak the native language at all, so she kept quiet. Instead she told him to go and rest if he wanted to.

'I don't have any tasks for you at the moment. I'll call for you later.'

'*Hai*, Marston-*san*.' Akio didn't need much persuading and took himself off.

Temperance was glad to be alone. Here in Japan she played a dangerous game, having to pretend to be a boy at all times since foreign women weren't allowed. Although Akio wasn't the most observant of youths, the only time she could truly relax was when no one else was around. After a year of acting the part it came naturally to her, but she was always afraid she might slip up. Slouching in her seat now, she put her breeches-clad legs up on a small table, rather than sitting upright like a lady. She smiled to herself – there were definite advantages to being a boy, but she'd better not become too used to them as, sooner or later, she'd have to go back to England and resume being a woman.

Across the harbour, on the mainland of Japan, there was constant movement despite the sweltering conditions. In a bid to distract herself from the discomfort, Temperance surveyed the comings and goings of the port and the surrounding coastline. From her vantage point she had an excellent view and there was always something of interest to gaze upon. Today was no exception.

Sailing vessels of every kind cluttered the bay, with two large foreign ships looking incongruous among the smaller native ones, their rounded bulk so different to the angular shape of all the rest. Tiny rowboats flitted between them in a never-ending stream, their crews seemingly risking life and limb, but so nimble and quick there were never any accidents. Chinese junks, with their colourful sails, vied for space with the similar-looking, but more subdued, Japanese vessels. There was shouting in all manner of languages flying through the air, which Temperance tried, and failed, to interpret.

She'd been told that Nagasaki's natural harbour, in the deep but narrow bay at the mouth of the Urakami river, was perfect for ships of any size. Here Dutch traders were allowed a precarious foothold on the tiny island of Dejima, while the Chinese had established a thriving business community in the town itself. Temperance had arrived on one of the Dutch ships the previous year and she could still remember the excitement of that day.

'I can't believe we're here at last!' She'd laughed, celebrating with the rest of the passengers and crew. Having sailed halfway across the world – from Plymouth in England via Amsterdam, Africa and the Spice Islands – she had been ecstatic at the thought of arriving at their destination at last and hardly noticed the debilitating heat as she stood by the railing, taking in the scene around her. The different climate was just part of the adventure then, something new to experience. Stepping ashore on Dejima, she'd felt like the luckiest person in the world ...

'All alone, young Marston? Is that wise?'

She was jerked out of her reverie by a familiar, but unwelcome, voice. Pieter Haag, an employee of the Dutch East India Company just like herself, had appeared next to her on the balcony, seemingly out of nowhere. Of late, he'd developed an uncanny ability to waylay her at every opportunity and it annoyed her, especially since she went out of her way to avoid him. There was something unwholesome about him, something she couldn't quite put her finger on, which made her want to run and hide, but of course she didn't. That would have been both impolite and absurd.

'*Mijnheer* Haag.' She acknowledged his presence with a slight nod and took her feet off the table. His English was accented, but otherwise good. Most of the foreigners on Dejima spoke Dutch – and indeed were supposed to be Dutch citizens – but Temperance hadn't yet become proficient in that language. She'd been more interested in learning Japanese. 'Why shouldn't I be by myself?' As a boy, she didn't need a chaperone so she had no idea what Haag meant.

Without asking permission he sat down beside her on the small bench. Temperance sidled as far away from him as possible.

'No reason ... if you really were who you're pretending to be.'

Haag smirked and Temperance stifled a gasp. Surely he couldn't mean ...? But his next words made her heart leap into her throat.

'Mistress Marston, I've seen through your disguise.'

Temperance was stunned into momentary silence, paralysed with shock. No one had called her 'mistress' for a long time and she had thought she'd fooled everyone on the island with her male clothing and mannerisms. How had he found out? She tried to stop the panic from rising inside her and scowled at him. Short of ripping her clothes off, he couldn't prove anything. Perhaps he was just guessing? She'd have to call his bluff. 'What are you talking about? Have you been out in the sun too much? I'm a—'

'Don't!' One word uttered in a harsh, uncompromising voice which made Temperance's stomach turn to icy knots of fear. 'I know you're a female so there's no point denying it. For the sake of keeping you here, we'll have to go on pretending you're a boy. We don't want anyone else to know, after all. Trust me, your secret is safe with me ... as long as you do as I say, of course.' Another smug smile, which made Temperance long to smash her fist into his mouth or, at the very least, box his ears.

She glared at him. She'd known it was a possibility that someone would unmask her, but she'd never dreamed it would be in this way – furtive and accompanied by an implied threat. 'And what exactly is that?' she asked, trying to keep her temper under control. It was vital to stay calm and rational if she was to extricate herself from this. She would need all her wits about her.

'You're going to become my wife, in secret of course, then once we're married you can just agree to share my quarters and no one will be any the wiser. After all, some of the other men share accommodation.'

This time Temperance did gasp, she couldn't help it. 'I don't wish to live with you, *mijnheer*.' She refrained from saying the word 'marry' as that would imply she admitted being a woman, which she hadn't as yet.

Haag smiled again, but it was the smile of a predator who has well and truly cornered his prey – gloating, victorious. 'I'm sorry, did I not make myself clear? Your wishes don't come into it. Unless you'd like the Japanese authorities to find out about your little deception? I hear they can be quite cruel to those who break their laws.'

Temperance gritted her teeth and swallowed the sharp retort that rose to her lips. She needed to discuss this with Nico Noordholt, her step-cousin and temporary guardian who was also the man in charge of the Dutch Factory here. He had agreed to her coming, albeit against his better judgement.

But as if he'd read her mind, Haag gripped her wrist with hard fingers. 'Don't even *think* of running to the Chief Factor. He won't be able to help you. Consider the position you'd be placing him in – the Japanese will see him as dishonourable since he's responsible for bringing you here and then they'll refuse to do business with him. He'll be sent home in disgrace, his career in tatters. Is that what you want?'

Temperance tried to wrest her arm away from his grip, but he held on tight, his fingers digging into her flesh, hurting her. *Hateful man.* There was nothing very wrong with either his looks, which were fairly ordinary, or his birth, since he came from a noble family, but she simply couldn't imagine ever being married to him, letting him touch her and have the right to bed her every night. She shuddered at the thought. The truth was he made her skin crawl.

He laughed at her puny efforts to free herself. Finally, he let go. 'I can see you need a little time to get used to the idea,' he said. 'Fair enough, but I shall expect your favourable reply very soon. You have two weeks, not a moment more.' He rose, as if about to go, then stopped and turned to her again. 'I do hope you have a sizeable dowry, seeing as you come from a rich merchant family? It will make the match so much more palatable to my relatives when I inform them of it. After all, I'm the eldest son and I can't be expected to marry just anyone. Though they won't be best pleased I've chosen an Englishwoman.' With that, he gave her an ironic bow and left.

Temperance could only stare after him. The sheer effrontery … Words failed her and her mind was in a whirl. There was a rumour going round that Pieter Haag was in dire need of funds, having spent every last penny of his salary on the courtesans that often came to entertain the foreigners. But to imply that his family would only accept her on the grounds of what she could bring in the way of a dowry? That was low. Still, it was the least of her problems.

He'd been right – how could she tell Nico about this without ruining his career, his life? And not just his, but his wife Midori's as well. Midori was Temperance's cousin too and the person she loved most in the world, apart from her brother, Daniel. She simply couldn't hurt her this way, even though they'd all discussed what they would do in the event Temperance was ever unmasked.

'We will all just leave,' Nico had stated. 'I can always go back to being a sea captain. I have enough money to buy my own ship now.'

They were bold words, and no doubt he'd meant them at the time, but Temperance knew he loved being the Chief Factor of Dejima, loved Japan and enjoyed trading here immensely. No matter what he'd said, he would be devastated to have to leave and in disgrace no less.

She groaned out loud. 'Damn Haag!' He wasn't used to being thwarted, that much she knew, and she believed he really would carry out his threat if she didn't comply with his demands. She rubbed at the arm he had touched as if trying to erase the memory of him, but it was impossible. What on earth should she do?

She'd rather die than marry him, but this wasn't just about her, she had Midori and Nico to think about too. It would seem she was well and truly trapped.

Chapter Two

Temperance cast a longing glance towards the sparkling sea. How she wished she could throw herself into its cool waves. Then she could wash away the mere thought of the repulsive Mr Haag and the imaginary stain of his touch.

How had he found out? Had he been spying on her? He must have done since the only two people who knew would never betray her.

She'd been so careful, only undressing when she was alone and insisting on taking her baths by herself without help from Akio. She wore men's clothing at all times – breeches, hose, shoes and an oversized shirt and roomy waistcoat. Although she had womanly curves, they were well hidden, and her blonde hair had been cut to just below her shoulder blades and kept in a simple queue. Nico had said she made a very credible, if pretty, boy.

During the voyage, Nico had given her lessons. She'd improved her reading and writing skills, and learned how to keep accounts. From the moment they'd arrived, Temperance had acted as a junior clerk and assistant, working alongside Nico for the most part, and no one had questioned her work since she'd proved to have an aptitude for it. To her surprise, she also enjoyed it immensely.

So what had given her away to Haag? Presumably he'd tell her after they were married, but by then it would be too late. Perhaps he had bribed Akio and spied on her by opening her door a crack when she was taking a bath? She wouldn't put it past him.

'The utter bastard,' she muttered.

Restless, she paced the wooden boards while staring across to the mainland once more. Only seven years before, in 1641, all foreigners except the Dutch had been expelled from Japan on the orders of its ruler, the powerful *Shogun*. It was a minor miracle that he had allowed this one nation to continue their trading. However, his permission had come at a price – seclusion.

There were no two ways about it, Temperance and the other foreigners were virtual prisoners here on Dejima island and today it felt more like a gaol than ever. It wasn't just its size – a mere one hundred and thirty by eighty-odd yards – but also the fact that the only way onto the mainland was through a gate and across a small bridge, which was guarded at all times. Neither Temperance nor anyone else would dare to even attempt to cross it. All they'd get for their trouble was a rebuke from the stern guard who was posted there day and night. The only thing she could do was to observe from afar, while frustration built inside her.

She itched to go across and explore the winding streets leading up the hillsides that ringed the bay. Wooden houses with *shoji* windows and sliding doors – some with thatched roofs, some with tiled ones – climbed in tiers up the steep slopes. They gave the whole an air of orderly chaos that was charming and exotic at the same time. The tip-tilted corners of most of the buildings added local flavour, as did the flashes of bright red from some of the temples. Around the town were heavily wooded areas, a lush green now that the summer rains came frequently. Temperance could detect the scent of pine borne across to her by the wind, but she couldn't wander in the shade of those trees.

'This wasn't what I came for,' she'd complained to Midori.

For years she had dreamed of seeing the wonders of this faraway land after Midori, who was half Japanese and had grown up here, had told her endless stories about her homeland. Temperance had begged her cousin and Nico to be allowed to accompany them when Nico was offered the position of Chief Factor. Never had she imagined that she wouldn't be able to go any further than this miserable little island, so near the mainland, yet so far.

It was a sad let-down after coming all this way.

In fact, it was almost as unbearable as having to marry Haag would be.

She glanced once more towards the sea and an idea came to her, an idea so daring it almost made her gasp out loud. There may be no way she could cross the bridge and enter the town, but perhaps she could at least steal – no borrow – a rowing boat before dawn, when it was still dark? Then she could go in search of a small, secluded cove where she could bathe in peace, with no one the wiser. The coastline hereabouts was mostly wild, or so she'd heard. There wouldn't be anyone to see her, no one to care, and she'd keep well away from any habitation.

Surely that shouldn't be too difficult?

She closed her eyes and imagined diving into the welcoming waves, immersing herself in the soft brine, floating in carefree, blessedly cool abandon for hours on end. She could forget her dilemma for a while and put off making a decision.

Why not?

The sea was calling to her.

Dejima had no less than four sets of guards dotted around the island, each in their own little house, to keep an eye on the foreigners. There were also numerous interpreters, other officials and servants, all constantly watching and listening.

'Damned spies,' cousin Midori muttered whenever she saw them, but they were just doing their job so couldn't really be blamed for being conscientious. It was rather unsettling to know that every tiny detail of their lives was probably reported to some official or other on the mainland, but they were all used to it now. It wasn't something they could change.

The gates were manned at all hours and Temperance knew it wouldn't be easy to escape the men's vigilance. Her only chance would be to create a diversion of some sort, in order to distract the guards long enough for her to slip past them, but she had no idea how she was going to achieve this.

Tiptoeing out of the house just before dawn, she looked about her for inspiration, determined to escape the island – and her worries about Haag – somehow, at least for a day. Her gaze fell on a goat standing nearby munching on a small bush with evident enthusiasm and she smiled to herself as an idea sprang into her mind.

'The very thing,' she muttered.

There were many types of livestock roaming the island, but she decided this shaggy animal would be perfect for her purposes. Grabbing the goat by one horn and pulling off a branch of the tasty bush, she enticed the animal along between the houses. She headed for the guardhouse nearest the sea gate and approached it from the back where there were no windows. There was no one about and silence reigned as Temperance and her captive crept forward. She hoped the guards were half-asleep, lulled into complacency by the long, boring hours of the night watch. As she cautiously rounded a corner and peered in through a half-open window she saw that her luck was in. Out of the four guards in the room, only one had his eyes fully open, and he was staring at the wall.

Tugging at the goat again, she propelled the animal towards the door of the guardhouse, keeping the branch just out of reach of its nose. The goat was becoming frustrated with this game and tried to snatch at the treat. When Temperance threw the branch in through the open door and pushed the goat in after it, the animal didn't hesitate.

It bleated loudly and disappeared inside, and pandemonium broke out in the tiny house. The guards erupted into shouts and curses, but Temperance didn't stay to listen. She shot past the house and through the sea gate, and threw herself into a tiny rowing boat tethered to the little quay. Quickly she untied it and pushed off, rowing round the corner out of sight of the guardhouse while she waited for peace to descend on the island once more. As Dejima was surrounded by walls she was able to lurk in the narrow channel between the island and the mainland, without being seen from any of the four guardhouses. She stayed there, waiting for what seemed like an eternity.

Finally silence returned. Not even the seagulls stirred and she set off along the harbour, rowing as fast as she could. Having grown up in Plymouth, Temperance was a competent rower and had no trouble steering her little craft. Once on her way, she simply followed the coastline until she rounded a headland and emerged from the bay. Still staying close to the coast, she rowed for what seemed like ages until she deemed it safe to go ashore, and then looked for a small, secluded cove or a beach. As the sun began to crest the horizon, she found the perfect spot and headed for land. The prow of the little boat hit sand and, as it wasn't heavy, Temperance managed to pull it up the beach and hide it behind some bushes. That way no one would be able to spot her if they happened to sail past.

Temperance waited until the sun was blazing down from a cloudless sky, then shed most of her clothes and ran into the sea. She sank beneath the waves and breathed a sigh of pure satisfaction, turning expertly underwater to watch as the bubbles she exhaled made their way to the surface. It was every bit as wonderful as she had imagined, and now that she'd finally achieved her ambition she revelled in the feel of the water as it caressed her near-naked body. Nothing but a man's shirt covered her previously over-heated skin and although this felt very sinful, the relief was immeasurable.

Coming up for air at last, she drew in several deep breaths, steeped with the tang of brine, and savoured the salty taste on her tongue. Revitalised, she swam with sure strokes back and forth across the little bay until her muscles quivered with the effort. Then she lay motionless on the surface, letting the waves carry her in any direction. It was sheer bliss to be cool at last and she simply couldn't get enough of it.

'By all the gods, a water sprite in broad daylight!'

The voice, low pitched but strong, carried across the water and made Temperance flip to an upright position instantly while she searched for its source. She found it on a large, flat rock on one side of the bay, where a young man stood gazing at her with an astonished expression that swiftly changed to one of delight. He leaned forward for a better view and Temperance reacted instinctively by covering her chest with her hands and attempting to tread water at the same time. Her insides turned cold with fear and she cast an anxious glance towards the shore where her clothes lay discarded, so near yet impossible to retrieve. She'd been so careful before removing them, making sure she was alone, but now suddenly here was this intruder.

'*Hanarero!* Go away,' she ordered, too shocked to care whether she sounded rude or not.

The young man's eyebrows rose. 'You can speak?'

'Of course I can speak.' Her Japanese was far from perfect, but she could make herself understood well enough even if the finer nuances of grammar still eluded her. 'Now leave, please, this is a private bay.' She had no idea whether it was or not, but the lie was worth a try.

He looked around slowly. 'I was under the impression that this stretch of the coast was wild, no matter which *daimyo* owns it. But perhaps it is reserved for water sprites?'

'Yes, no, I mean … oh, please, just leave.' Temperance tried to imbue her words with imperious command to hide the fact that she was panicking, but it didn't have any effect. The young man smiled and shook his head. He seemed very much at ease and Temperance realised it would have been better if she'd kept quiet.

'If you don't mind, I think I'll stay for a while. It's not every day I come across a water sprite, and one who talks to me no less.'

Was it a trick of the sun or were his eyes twinkling? Temperance wasn't sure, but she suspected the latter.

'Please, won't you tell me why you are here?' he continued. 'Are you the guardian of this bay? Is there something special, perhaps holy, about it, or are you one of the unfortunates who have drowned hereabouts?'

'I am *not* a water sprite, as I'm sure you are fully aware. I am a perfectly normal human being and if you are an honourable man, you will turn around and walk away now. I shall dive under the water and when I come up again, I expect you to be gone.' She turned and did just that, hoping against hope that the man would do as she asked without arguing further.

Having spent her entire life living next to the sea, Temperance was an expert swimmer and could hold her breath for a long time, thus giving the man ample opportunity to leave. When she surfaced at last, she was much further out than before and resolutely stared out to sea for a while to give him even more time to depart. She heard nothing, so she finally turned around to make sure he'd gone. She had to put up a hand against the glare of the sunlight in order to scan the shore and a sigh of relief escaped her when there was no sign of him. The feeling of dread subsided.

'Phew, that was close,' she muttered, then gave a little shriek as the man's head suddenly popped out of the water not three feet away from her. Her heart went into panic mode again.

'I thought I would join you instead.' He smiled. 'That way you don't have to feel embarrassed.' He looked pointedly at her hands, which she had raised automatically to shield her near-nakedness from his view.

Temperance stared at him, momentarily lost for words, then scowled fiercely while trying to put some distance between them. 'How on earth did you reach that conclusion?'

He followed. 'Well, if we are both without clothes, you are not at a disadvantage.'

'But you are a man and I'm a —'

'Female, yes, I know.' He grinned. 'Surely you have bathed with other people before? Or do water sprites not mix with humans?'

'For the last time, I'm not a spirit of any kind and no, I am not in the habit of bathing with others, especially not men. Why do you think I'm here in this bay by myself?'

'I was hoping you would tell me that. If you're not a magical creature, what pray are you? And why is your speech so strange?'

The man was staring at her hair now, the silvery blonde strands that floated all around her shimmering in the sunlight even when wet. She noticed him studying her blue eyes with an expression of fascination too. Anger took hold of her, pushing the fear aside temporarily. He was teasing her again, he had to be.

'I'm a foreigner, as you must know, still trying to master your language, and I am not allowed to mix with your people. We *gai-jins* have to remain on the island of Dejima and not set foot on Japanese soil. I was desperate for a swim, so I borrowed a rowing boat before first light and made my way here. There, are you satisfied now? I warn you, if you are thinking of reporting me to the authorities, I will not come willingly.'

'Why would I want to do that?' His grin broadened. 'I'm a *ronin*.'

'An outlaw? Dear God ...' She looked around frantically for some means of rescue, but found none.

'Don't worry, I'm not a threat to you and I should think the authorities would be much more interested in me than in a foreign woman. After all, you can always pretend you fell in the water and were swept over here. I have no such defence. I shouldn't be here at all.'

It was Temperance's turn to be curious and she forgot about her more or less naked state and his proximity for a moment. 'Then why are you?'

'I'm on a secret mission, but I'm afraid you distracted me. Won't you tell me your name? I am Kanno Kazuo.' He tried to bow to her in the water, after the formal Japanese fashion, and a giggle almost escaped her at this ludicrous sight. She hesitated for a moment, then decided it couldn't do any harm to give him her name.

'I am Marston Temperance.' A year of living in such close proximity to Japan had taught her some of their customs, and she knew that to introduce herself she had to give him her surname first, as he had done.

He frowned. 'I don't think I can say that.' He tried and managed the Marston part fairly well, but had great difficulty with Temperance. 'Ten-pe-renu-su? Temmu-pu-renni-su?' It sounded so comical she took pity on him.

'Most people call me Temi, it's easier.' She didn't add that in order to keep up her disguise as a boy on Dejima, Nico and Midori called her Tom, while everyone else just referred to her by her surname.

'I see. Well, if you ask me, you ought to be named *Gin*, or perhaps *Shinju*.'

'Silver or pearl?'

'Yes, like your hair.' He swam closer and reached out a

16

hand to touch it, as if unsure whether it was real. 'What happened to make it fade thus?'

Temperance shivered as his fingers touched some of the lighter strands and brushed against her shoulder in the process, but laughed at his ridiculous question. 'It didn't fade. I was born with it that colour. Lots of foreigners are.'

'Oh. I have never met one before. I know nothing of such things. Is that why your eyes are not dark either?'

'Yes.'

He fell silent, just gazing at her in wonder, and Temperance became aware of the awkwardness of her situation once more. He was so close, she could see his upper body clearly – a smooth, tanned chest, as well muscled as the arms that floated near the surface, and further down, his stomach and ... *Oh dear Lord!* Temperance averted her eyes and let herself sink beneath the waves to cool her flaming cheeks. This would not do, really it wouldn't.

She had been raised as a Puritan, closely guarded from sights such as the one now before her. Morality was instilled into her very soul, and although she had often secretly wished to rebel against all the rules that governed her life, she'd never done so openly.

Until now.

She came up for air, her cheeks no less heated. 'You must leave, please,' she begged him. 'If anyone saw me with you like this, I would have to marry you.'

Kazuo chuckled. 'I doubt it. I have no prospects, no one would want me for a son-in-law. I told you, I'm a *ronin*.' He looked her in the eyes. 'But if it is your wish, then I will leave. Will you not swim with me first? I saw you earlier, your prowess should more than equal mine.'

His nearness still disturbed her and her conscience screamed at her to refuse, but the prospect of having someone to swim with, if only for a while, was too tempting to turn down. Besides, what did it matter if she spent a little while longer with this man? The damage was already done, a treacherous voice whispered inside her head. Temperance had been wishing for a companion, so eventually she said playfully, 'Very well, catch me if you can,' and shot off. She knew she was fast, and the thrill of the chase added extra strength to her limbs, making her blood sing as it pumped through her veins.

She vaguely heard a whoop of delight behind her, but paid him no heed, concentrating on her strokes. The water swirled by and she was almost on the other side of the little bay before he caught her feet, effectively stopping her so that she had to turn around to try and free herself. A mock fight ensued, at the end of which she found herself held captive, her back against his chest, while he trod water for both of them. Her Puritan conscience ordered her to break free and put some distance between them immediately, but her body seemed to have a will of its own and refused to obey. Temperance felt herself go limp, his arms supporting her, while her breath came in small, sharp bursts. The oversized shirt billowed slowly around her, but was as see-through as if she'd been without a stitch. Somehow she didn't care. She suddenly realised that she felt truly alive for the first time in weeks, perhaps in her entire life.

He nuzzled her neck, just below her right ear, and she tried half-heartedly to pull away. 'You mustn't do that,' she murmured, but she wanted him to all the same.

'I know, but I just had to breathe in your fragrance so that I can remember this day.'

Temperance shivered and his arms closed around her more tightly. 'If anyone should see us ...'

'They won't. This is a desolate spot, which is no doubt why you chose to come here. There is no one else about.'

His words both thrilled and alarmed her and she wondered

if she had taken leave of her senses. She knew she ought to be afraid – held fast by a stranger in such an isolated place – there was nothing to stop him doing whatever he wanted to with her, but it wasn't fear that coursed through her.

Perhaps the heat had fried her brain, to the extent that she was now permitting a man to hold her close, touch her, and with her the only one wearing any clothing. Every part of her body was aware of his, the skin so soft and warm where it touched hers, despite the chill of the water. Although she had never been this close to a man before, she knew that he desired her, the proof of this was difficult to ignore. It didn't frighten her. She felt lost to all propriety and strangely uncaring, suspended in the soft cradle of the ocean like a cloud floating in the sky.

'I won't hurt you,' he whispered, as if he had read her thoughts. His voice sent another shiver through her. 'I just want to hold you a while longer to convince myself that you are real. Will you turn around?'

Temperance knew she definitely shouldn't do that, it might just be her undoing, but it was as if some force compelled her to do as he wished. His hold on her loosened slightly and he spun her around. His gaze held hers and she was spellbound, scarcely able to breathe. He was beautiful, there was no other way to describe him. Smooth skin stretched tight over high cheekbones and a rather blunt nose that was small for a man, but suited him admirably. Eyes as dark as the deepest well, shaded by slanted lids and short but dense lashes. A mouth so perfectly sculpted it seemed made for smiling, kissing. She wondered how it would feel pressed to hers, kissing her softly, caressing … Temperance blinked, totally dazed, then tried to put some distance between them.

'This is wrong, completely wrong,' she muttered. 'My soul will be damned for all eternity.'

'Your soul will not begrudge you a moment of enjoyment,'

he stated confidently. 'Even the gods take their pleasure whenever they can. It is the natural order of things.' He smiled and pulled her close, leaning backwards to float with her on top. With a laugh, he sank under the water, his laughter turning to a gurgle. Temperance could now feel every inch of him again and she knew she couldn't let this go any further, no matter what he said. She pushed at his chest and rolled off him, striking out for land, her limbs shaking. She heard him follow, but to her relief he didn't try to catch her again. When her knees hit sand, she stopped swimming and floated stomach down in the shallow water, digging her fingers into the bottom. Kazuo came to rest next to her.

'I suppose we had better part then for I must be on my way.' They looked at each other. 'Thank you for a most enjoyable interlude. I shall remember you always, Temi-*san*.'

'And I you, Kanno-*san*.'

'Kazuo,' he corrected. 'I don't wish to be formal with you.'

'Kazuo,' she repeated, knowing it was a name she'd never forget. She hesitated, then couldn't help asking, 'Will you ever come this way again?'

He grinned. 'I might. When I have finished my mission I shall make it my sole purpose in life to search for water sprites. This bay will be the first place I look.'

She smiled back. 'And if you don't find any?'

'Then I shall leave a special sign – perhaps carved on that tree over there – and go on to look for land spirits, *kami*. I hear they dwell on the island of Dejima. Watch for me after dark. *Sayonara*, Temi-*san*.'

He put out a hand to stroke her cheek almost reverently, then rose swiftly out of the water, shaking out his long hair. It reached halfway down his back and gleamed blue-black in the sunlight. He strode over to the rock where he had left his clothes, seemingly unconcerned that she was staring at him all the while, taking in every last detail of his physique.

Temperance had never seen a man completely without clothes before, but she knew instinctively that they didn't come much better than this. She revelled in the sight, storing the images in her memory with guilty pleasure. Kazuo dressed swiftly, raised his hand in a quick salute, and was gone.

Temperance stayed in the water until her heart rate had resumed more or less its normal rhythm, then stood up and made her way slowly to her own clothes. She stretched and dried herself carefully with a linen drying cloth before exchanging the wet shirt for a dry one and pulling the rest of her garments on. She wondered if perhaps Kazuo had stayed to watch her dress, the way she'd watched him, but she didn't care.

Even if he had, she had nothing to fear from Kazuo, of that she was sure. *Ronin* or not, he was an honourable man and she very much hoped he would come back.

Chapter Three

Kazuo Kanno strode away from the bay with a spring in his step. He could hardly believe his luck. No sooner had he landed on the coast than he'd come across the foreign girl, his very own water sprite, and he felt it was a good omen.

Although she had protested against being called a spirit, he still thought of her as one, albeit a benevolent *kami* come to give him luck for his mission. He would need help from all the gods and other unearthly beings, that was for certain, and this auspicious beginning to his secret quest gave him confidence that they were on his side.

'You must be on your guard at all times,' his father had warned him for the hundredth time before his departure. 'There are those who will seek to kill you, should they find out that you have set foot on the mainland. They won't hesitate, they have too much to lose by my return.'

The older Kanno-*san* had been a *daimyo*, a warlord, and a highly respected member of the *Shogun*'s inner circle in Edo, when disaster struck and the family was all but destroyed. Someone had accused him of stealing a valuable item from the *Shogun*'s personal quarters – a small object, but ancient and highly prized by the ruler – and when a search was made, the missing piece was found to be in Kanno-*san*'s possession.

'I have no idea how it came to be there,' the older man had protested, but the proof of his supposed crime was there for all to see, and with several people backing up his accusers, Kanno-*san*'s fate had been sealed. Banished to one of the smaller islands of the Oki group, he'd been declared an outlaw and his entire family with him. Their properties and possessions were confiscated and all honours rescinded. It was as if the whole clan had never existed at all.

'Well, we'll see about that,' Kazuo muttered as he walked on with purposeful strides. His father had been adamant that he'd been set up. There was someone at court who obviously hated him or was jealous of his former power, and that someone had engineered his downfall. Kazuo had vowed to find this man and bring him down in turn.

'There were three signatures on the warrant for my arrest, although none of those men were present when the item was found at our house,' Kanno senior had told his son. 'They sent others to do their dirty work for them, but they couldn't hide when it came to signing the official papers. Now unless they were in collusion, one of them was the instigator and the other two were merely asked to sign as a matter of formality as there have to be three. You must visit all of them and infiltrate their households and try to find out whatever you can. There must be someone who knows something.'

The chances of success were minimal, but it was all they had to go on and so Kazuo had set out on his mission. Now he was even more determined to succeed, because once he had cleared his father's name, he would be able to think of other matters.

Such as searching for water sprites with silvery hair.

After Kazuo's departure, Temperance ate the food she had brought with her then slept for a while in the shade before going for another swim. There was no point in returning before nightfall since she didn't want to be caught trying to sneak back onto Dejima – that would ruin everything.

As darkness fell, however, she became uneasy and wished that she'd thought of bringing a weapon of some kind. There was no knowing what might be lurking in the forest all around her and she started at unfamiliar rustling noises and the sharp crack of a branch being stepped on by some unknown creature. In the end, she went and sat in the little boat, counting the minutes until she could safely leave.

Just as she was about to get out and push the boat into the water, a voice came hissing out of the shadows. 'Temi-*san*? Are you all right?'

She jumped, but recognised the speaker as soon as he came out of the undergrowth. 'Kazuo! I thought you far away by now.' She stared at him while he walked towards the boat with rapid strides.

'I was, but then I came across some suspicious-looking men. It struck me that I shouldn't have left you here unprotected, so I decided to come back, although I wasn't sure you'd still be here.'

'What kind of men?' She glanced around, the flicker of fear in her belly suppressed by his nearness.

'Who knows? Other *ronin* perhaps?' He shrugged. 'I think they're long gone, but in any case, I will see you safely back to your home.'

'That's very kind, but won't that be dangerous for you? You told me you're an outlaw and I wouldn't want you to be captured.'

'Wouldn't you?' He smiled teasingly and her stomach flipped over with an entirely new kind of sensation that had nothing to do with fear.

'Well, no. I mean ...' She ground to a halt, realising that to all intents and purposes she was consorting with a criminal and she *ought* to want him captured. But she didn't and surely that was wrong of her? Although, come to think of it, she was a criminal herself, here in Japan under false pretences.

He reached out a hand to stroke her cheek, the way he had before he left the water earlier. 'Don't worry about it. I can take care of myself. It's dark now, no one will see me clearly and I doubt I'm known hereabouts anyway. Now let us be on our way or they will send out a search party for you.'

Temperance had thought of that and had taken some

precautions, but things could go wrong. Midori would be worried if by any chance she'd noticed her cousin's absence and might raise the alarm. More often than not she was preoccupied with her children though, so hopefully Temperance hadn't yet been missed. She prayed this was the case.

'Let me do the rowing,' Kazuo said and pushed the boat out before jumping in.

'How about we share?' Temperance was already seated on the middle bench and moved over to make space for him. 'It will be faster that way, although I suppose you'll have to row lightly since you're bound to be much stronger than I am.'

He didn't protest, but sat down next to her and took one oar. Their bodies began to move in a silent rhythm, raising the oars and dipping them into the water at exactly the same time with barely any splashing. It was as if they had worked together like this all their lives and Temperance marvelled at the ease with which they co-operated. With her older brother, there had always been a tussle and complaints about her lack of strength, but Kazuo simply matched his rowing to hers.

'Had you gone far?' she ventured to ask when they had travelled some way down the coast. She found the silence unnerving since it made her focus too much on the way their thighs were practically joined together and the feel of his arm as it brushed against hers inadvertently every so often.

'Yes, but it doesn't matter. Although my mission needs to be accomplished fairly swiftly, it's not so urgent that I can't rescue water sprites if I want to.'

She heard the teasing note in his voice again, but protested nonetheless. 'Kazuo, I told you—'

'I know, I know.' He chuckled. 'But you seem magical to me, so that is how I will always think of you.'

'I'm just a woman like any other.' Temperance wasn't sure if she wanted to be a fairy tale creature. She would rather he treated her the way he would a real woman. A woman he cared for. *No!* What was she thinking? She barely knew him.

He stopped rowing for a moment and turned to gaze at her. The moon was rising and she could see clearly that his expression had turned serious. 'No,' he said firmly, 'to me you will always be unique.'

She stared back, not knowing what to say, then acted on impulse and leaned forward to brush his cheek with her lips. 'Thank you,' she breathed. 'So are you.'

He looked startled, as if no one had ever kissed him before, even in such a chaste manner, but then he smiled again and nodded. 'Perhaps we can be unique together one day, but for now, we must row.'

They remained silent the rest of the way until they reached the harbour and began to make their way across to the island of Dejima.

'How will you enter the gate without being seen?' he whispered.

'I don't know. I'll think of something. After all, the guards don't have any orders not to let me in, I'm just not allowed *out.*'

He laughed at this. 'Very well, good luck. You should be safe enough now. Jump out of the boat when we reach the steps and I will return it later, then swim ashore.'

'Thank you.' She hesitated, then blurted out, 'I wish you didn't have to go.'

'I told you, I'll come back to the bay. I have a feeling you'll be going there again too, am I right?'

'The thought had crossed my mind, but we may not go at the same time.'

'Then I'll leave a sign as I said – carved on a tree – to let you know that I've been there and when I'm coming back. Else I'll find you here. Don't worry, you will see me again, I promise, but I have to fulfil my mission first.'

She nodded. '*Sayonara* and thank you again.'

'Where on earth have you been?'

The question came hissing out of the darkness, making Temperance start guiltily as she entered the Chief Factor's residence. To her surprise, there had been no one about and she'd been able to sneak into the house without anyone seeing her. As she came in through the sea gate she'd been challenged by a guard, but she told him she had only slipped outside for a minute to look at the sea and he believed her. Obviously he'd been under the impression that another guard had allowed her out earlier. It was a relief to reach the house unseen, but now here was her cousin.

'Midori! You startled me. I ... I've just been out for a while.'

'All day?'

'Well, no, not exactly.' Temperance's brain worked with lightning speed, trying to come up with some plausible excuse for her absence.

'I've been worried sick about you! I thought you'd been taken by pirates or something.' In the faint light from the moon that shone in through the window, Temperance could see Midori cross her arms over her chest, glaring at her.

'I was in my room earlier. I had a headache.' Temperance had asked Akio to tell everyone his master was resting because of illness and didn't want to be disturbed. Had the stupid boy misunderstood?

'Yes, that's what Akio said, but when I went to check, you weren't there.'

'You must have come just when I was out getting some fresh air.'

'Tom, I'm not stupid.'

Temperance could hear the warning in Midori's voice and decided it was time for the truth. She took a deep breath and turned to face her cousin. 'Oh, very well, if you must know, I went swimming. I borrowed a rowing boat this morning and found a small cove up the coast, very secluded, and I swam for most of the day. I'm sorry if I worried you, I didn't think you'd notice I was gone. You've been so busy.'

It was true that Midori had been preoccupied lately, as her baby son Casper had been ill with a fever. In her anxiety she seemed to have no time for anyone else, spending every waking moment watching over the child.

'Of course I noticed. I may have been worried about Casper, but I still see what's going on around me.'

Temperance shrugged. 'Well, I'm back now and no harm has befallen me.' She knew she sounded defiant and defensive. Knew also that Midori had a right to be angry, but she didn't care. She'd had a most wonderful experience, nothing could spoil that.

They stared at each other for a moment in the darkness, then Midori heaved a sigh. 'You should never have come here, should you.' It was a statement, not a question, so Temperance didn't reply. It was true after all, as she knew only too well now. 'Would you like me to arrange passage back to England for you? I could send Akio with you to keep you company.'

'No!' Temperance was startled by her own vehemence, but she didn't think going back to England would solve her current problems. By the time all had been arranged it would be too late, for she doubted Midori would be able to find her passage immediately so the threat of Haag's ultimatum still remained. She'd have to find some other way of getting out of that. 'I mean, no, thank you. I'd like to stay a while longer, if you don't mind? Really, I'm fine. It was just the heat. It's been unbearable these last weeks and I couldn't stand having all this water around me and not go in it, do you see?'

'Yes, I can understand that, but please, don't do it again.

It's too dangerous.' Temperance didn't reply, and her cousin seemed to take that as an affirmative. 'And what were you thinking, going dressed like that? You should at least have worn Japanese clothing.'

They both looked at Temperance's outfit. She was wearing her usual English men's clothes and, thinking about it, perhaps it was a miracle that so far the Japanese didn't seem to have noticed that she was a girl. She supposed all foreigners looked so strange to them, it never occurred to them that she could be a female. Midori was right though, outside the island Temperance should have worn something else.

Midori herself wore Japanese garments at all times. In order to be allowed on the island, she had to pretend to be her husband's concubine, and this had been accepted without question since she was half Japanese and therefore looked the part. She was also very beautiful in an exotic way with large, slightly almond-shaped green eyes under perfectly arched brows, sculpted cheekbones and flawless skin. Her dark, straight hair was so long it reached to her knees when not twisted on top of her head and she had the grace and figure to tempt any man. Temperance knew that playing the role of a courtesan, when in fact she was Nico's wife, had bothered Midori at first, but as she wanted to be with him at any cost, it had soon ceased to worry her. It was a strange situation for both of them, but after a year of practising these deceptions, they were used to it.

'It was dark, no one saw me,' Temperance muttered.

'They could have done. Never mind, let us go to bed, I'm exhausted. I must tell Nico you're safe, he's been worried too, although he did tell me you were probably off on an adventure of your own.'

As her cousin linked her arm with hers, Temperance suppressed a shiver of excitement. Adventure was the right word and how could she possibly leave Dejima now that she'd met Kazuo? He had said he would return, hadn't he? Implied it anyway.

She had to find a way to stay without marrying Haag.

Pieter Haag skulked in the shadows and watched Mistress Marston hurry down the main street towards the Chief Factor's residence. He'd noticed her absence all day and wondered where she'd gone and how she had escaped the island. Did she have a lover on the mainland? Someone she bribed with her luscious body? The thought made him want to smash his fist into the nearest wall but he restrained himself for now and waited.

It annoyed him that he didn't know her Christian name. Obviously it wasn't Tom, as he'd heard Noordholt call her, but he guessed it must be close – Thomasine or Tamsyn perhaps? He'd find out when they married as she'd have to give her real name then.

He heard low voices and guessed that either the Chief Factor or his concubine had lain in wait too and was giving Mistress Marston a telling off. *Good!* She deserved it. Soon it would be his privilege – and pleasure – to take her to task and keep her under control. He'd given her two weeks to get used to the idea, which he thought was generous in the extreme, but he knew she had no choice really. Not if she didn't want to be handed over to the Japanese authorities. Nor if she cared for her step-cousin at all, and it was clear to everyone on the island that she did. Haag was counting on it.

It never occurred to him he wouldn't get his way. Being the eldest of four sons, he'd always ruled the roost at home. If the others dared to protest, he'd simply resorted to underhand measures to prevail until they stopped opposing him. If all else failed, he'd administered a beating in secret and with no witnesses nothing could ever be proved against him. His brothers had learned that he wasn't someone you crossed, not if you didn't want to regret it. Mistress Marston would soon learn the same lesson.

After a while she came out of the Chief Factor's house and crossed the street to her own abode, a small room on the ground floor of the building opposite. Her servant boy slept in an anteroom, but it was unlikely he was still awake. Haag made his way round to the back of the house where her windows were situated. She made sure to keep them shuttered at night and whenever she undressed, but he'd found a way around it. The walls of the buildings were made of wood and by borrowing a drill from one of the carpenters when the man wasn't looking, Haag had managed to make a hole big enough to look through, but not large enough to be visible unless you knew it was there.

And what he'd seen had almost taken his breath away.

As he put his eye close to the hole now he was rewarded with the same vision – Mistress Marston shedding her mannish clothing and giving him tantalising glimpses of her beautiful body. Soft, creamy skin and a figure that could drive any man half-crazed with desire; high, full breasts, a flat stomach and perfectly curved backside. How everyone else on the island had failed to notice that she was a woman he'd never know, but they all just thought her a very handsome, if effeminate, youth.

As such, there were those who desired her, and at first he'd been afraid he had discovered such tendencies in himself, which had never happened before. Once he began to spy on her, however, he was relieved to find his instincts had been perfectly normal and all male. He'd just been the only one to subconsciously see through her disguise, which admittedly was very good. The extra large and loose shirt and waistcoat hid her curves admirably and covered her behind as well. The baggy breeches concealed the perfection of long, shapely legs.

He watched her free her lovely, blonde hair from the queue she always kept it in. Let loose it caressed her shoulders as she brushed it out with sure strokes. The sight of those amazing breasts before she pulled on a clean shirt made Haag draw in a hasty breath as lust hit his groin like a lightning bolt. He couldn't wait to touch them, knead them, make her moan ...

Breathing heavily now, he had to close his eyes and lean his forehead against the rough wood for a moment. He wanted to rush in there this minute and just take her, but he knew his victory would be all the sweeter if she came to him willingly. Or as willingly as blackmail would permit. Submissive was how he wanted her. She had to be aware she had no choice, that she must acquiesce to his every demand. Then and only then would he have her completely in his power, just as he wished.

He couldn't wait.

Chapter Four

Two years previously, Temperance had sailed with Nico and Midori halfway across the world to Japan in search of adventure. She'd been sixteen years old when they left and had just survived four long years of civil war in her staunchly Puritan home town of Plymouth, which had been besieged by Royalists for most of that time.

'Is it any wonder I dreamed of escaping to wondrous foreign lands?' she'd commented to her cousin, and Midori understood only too well, having lived through the same.

It had been a difficult time for them all and Temperance was sure she hadn't been the only one wishing herself thousands of miles away from the harsh life of a country at war. Once it was over, Temperance couldn't get away fast enough and had pleaded with Nico and Midori to let her come along. By that time her mother had succumbed to congestion of the lungs and her father had died defending the town so the only other family she had left was her brother, Daniel, six years her senior.

'Do you really want to go traipsing round the world pretending to be a boy?' he'd asked, obviously trying to take his new role as head of the family seriously. 'I really shouldn't allow it.'

'Oh, please, Daniel, don't say that! If this war has taught me anything it's that you have to live life to the full and staying here in Plymouth will seem so dull compared to what Midori and Nico will be doing. I don't think I can bear it! And it's only for a few years.'

Although Daniel, being a very kind brother, had given in, Temperance realised now that she'd been totally unprepared for the realities of what lay before her. Nico did try to warn her that it may not be as thrilling as she imagined it, but she had refused to listen, preferring to think that anything would be better than being left behind. Now she wasn't so sure.

Having come all this way, however, Temperance had had no choice but to accept her situation. The first few months were exciting, but soon the monotonous routine and lack of space began to irk her. She tried to dispel the boredom by learning as much as she could of the native language – in secret since the official interpreters would not approve as their jobs would be at stake – and both Midori and Nico had also given her lessons in self-defence and fencing, which they said could prove useful.

In addition, Temperance and Nico studied the mysteries of the strange Japanese writing, again in secret as the foreigners weren't supposed to learn. The rest of her time was taken up with acting as Nico's clerk, helping him with letters and ledgers. She didn't mind that, but the enforced confinement on the island frustrated her beyond belief.

'Never mind,' Midori soothed her, whenever she noticed Temperance's irritation with the situation, 'we'll go and visit my brother soon, then you'll see a bit more of the real Japan and all the wonderful things I've told you about.'

Midori's English mother, Hannah, Temperance's aunt, had been married to a Japanese warlord, Taro Kumashiro. She'd lived in a castle in northern Japan until her death and that was where Midori had grown up, together with an older half-brother named Ichiro. Midori's brother was now the *daimyo*, a powerful man, and he had promised to arrange a secret visit to his castle for Midori and her family. They had to be very careful, however, and therefore the promised outing was slow in materialising. Temperance grew tired of waiting and was beginning to wonder if it would ever happen at all.

She knew the foreigners, or *gai-jin* as they were called by the Japanese, were viewed with suspicion and the *Shogun* had decreed that there was to be no contact between the foreigners and his subjects. Most especially there was to be no spreading of religious beliefs. Any Christians found in Japan were dealt with swiftly and severely, and as all foreigners were thought to be Christians, they were apprehended on sight. Temperance thought this appalling.

'If only there was some way I could persuade the Japanese authorities that not all *gai-jin* are the same,' she said to Midori. 'I'm not here to convert anyone, I merely want to visit their country.'

Her cousin shook her head and smiled. 'That's impossible. Why should they listen to you? You are a foreigner, that's all there is to it. Sorry, but you're just going to have to be patient.'

Temperance tried her best, but it wasn't easy and now that she'd had a taste of freedom, their confinement seemed an even greater burden. It was an impossible situation.

'Can you please take Emi for a short walk while I put Casper down for his nap?' Midori asked, the day after Temperance's little excursion. As her cousin looked exhausted, Temperance felt guilty for having added to her worries and gladly agreed. Childcare wasn't really part of her duties, but everyone had been told Temperance was Nico's step-cousin, and therefore family, so no one would question the fact of her spending time with his children occasionally.

'Yes, of course. Come, Emi, let's go outside.'

Five-year-old Emi wasn't their natural daughter, but Midori and Nico loved her as if she were their own. The child's father had been an employee of the Dutch East India Company whose long-term liaison with a Japanese courtesan resulted in pregnancy. When the mother died giving birth to a second child, who also died, and the father succumbed to a tropical fever soon after, Midori and Nico adopted Emi. No one else seemed to care what became of her and the child, being so young, quickly accepted them as her parents. She was a sweet and biddable little girl, no trouble to look after apart from expecting answers to a seemingly endless stream of questions, but Temperance heaved a sigh of impatience anyway as they left the room. Both Emi and little Casper were a delight, but as they were not hers, their antics didn't fascinate Temperance to the same extent as they did their doting parents.

She wished herself far away instead, in a small sunlit bay, swimming in the cool water, perhaps with a companion whose dark eyes teased wordlessly ... With another sigh, she forced herself to concentrate on the present instead.

It had been raining all morning, as it had done on and off almost every day for weeks, but now the sun was out once more. The heat from its rays turned the air into humidity so thick it felt like walking into a moist wall. Temperance almost turned back, hating the sticky sensation on her skin, but one look at Emi's expectant face made her continue.

'So, where shall we go today?' she asked the little girl.

'The pigs.'

Emi was fascinated by a large sow who wandered freely around the island, her brood of piglets following in a squealing, disorganised group. Temperance thought it an ugly beast, but she had to admit the piglets were sweet and they were not averse to being picked up and petted, to Emi's delight.

'Very well, let's see if we can find them. Can you hear them?' Emi nodded. 'Then you lead the way.'

They walked past two storey buildings in the Japanese style, some with storage areas on the ground floor and living quarters above, some where both floors were used by the Japanese officials and translators who worked on the island. The main buildings were arranged along what Temperance jokingly called the 'main street', a wide pathway that ran from the Chief Factor's residence, where Nico and Midori lived near the sea gate, to the other end of the island where there were gardens and a cattle pen. There were further houses containing kitchens and merchants' offices round the edges of the island as well, but Temperance seldom ventured there.

It was a very restricted environment and Temperance was heartily sick of it. She wanted to be on the mainland, to see the wondrous castles, forests, lakes and valleys that Midori had described to her. She wanted to mingle with the people of Japan and partake in their festivals and customs. Above all, she wanted adventure. In the little bay she'd found it, but it had been short-lived and only made her long for more.

Kazuo had gone to accomplish his mission, and no doubt it would take some time, but perhaps when he returned she could persuade him to accompany her on a secret journey? He'd seemed the type of man who wouldn't baulk at minor difficulties, such as foreigners not being allowed in his country. Temperance wondered if he could find a way around it – a disguise of some sort perhaps? Midori's brother seemed to be having difficulty with this whereas Kazuo appeared to be a man of action and he would be the perfect travelling companion – cheerful, resourceful, able to defend her.

Playing half-heartedly with the piglets, Temperance allowed herself to daydream.

'So, you're going to the mainland, did you say?'

'Uh-hm.' Kazuo stared straight ahead and tried to sound nonchalant. He was sitting in the prow of a small boat, having paid for passage across the Kammon Strait. He could have gone by boat all the way along the Inland Sea to Kobe, but he'd decided to take the long way round the coast on foot in order to throw any potential pursuers off the scent. Not that he thought he was being followed, but it was just possible that someone could notice his absence from the Oki Islands and he wasn't taking any chances.

The islands lay west of the Japanese mainland, Honshu, and he could easily have reached his destination between Kyoto and Kobe by going straight across due east. However, his father had advised him to travel a long way south first so that no one would know where his journey had originated. It seemed like a good plan.

What he didn't need, though, were nosy fishermen asking too many questions.

'You on a mission for your employer?'

'No.'

'Ah, a man of leisure seeing the sights, eh?'

'No.'

'Then let me guess – you're being transferred from one of your employer's properties to another?'

The fisherman was nothing if not tenacious and Kazuo swallowed a sigh and decided he'd better make up some story. 'No, I'm an artist. I'm looking for beautiful views to draw,' he improvised. He *was* able to draw, quite well in fact, so that part was true at least.

'*Honto?* Well, you'll find plenty around here.'

Thankfully the man didn't ask to see what Kazuo had drawn so far and the talk turned to more general matters. Kazuo was able to steer the conversation onto the topic of the man's own family and business, and this lasted until they reached land.

'Good luck with your drawings!' the fisherman called after him as he hurried to jump out of the boat. 'Perhaps you'll come back and show us, eh?'

Kazuo nodded and smiled, bowing his thanks for the journey, but he had no intention of ever seeing the man again.

'That's another load on its way then. Should make a tidy profit if they reach Batavia and Amsterdam safely,' Nico said as he swept into the dining room just in time for supper.

He seated himself next to Midori, after first bending down to give her a tender kiss. The couple sat close to each other, their bodies touching wherever possible, and it was apparent to any onlooker that they were sublimely happy together. Temperance suppressed an unexpected stab of jealousy.

She was old enough to be wed but had never met anyone who'd taken her fancy as yet. At home in Plymouth it would have been Daniel's task to find her a suitable match, although she was sure her brother would have allowed her a say in the matter. If she'd been here as a woman, there were several of Nico's employees who could have made offers for her hand in marriage, just like Haag. But she didn't like any of them and found their lecherous talk about women disgusting. In her guise as a boy, they spoke freely around her and she'd learned to hide her blushes whenever they mentioned fornication and such things. If they'd tried to court her, however, she would have felt nothing but revulsion or indifference for them, and having seen the outright love between Midori and Nico, she was determined not to settle for anything less herself. Most girls couldn't afford to be so choosy, but Temperance was far from home and not in a position where she needed to marry at the moment. She'd thought she could take her time and wait until the right man came along.

The Dutch employees gathered in the dining room of the Chief Factor's residence twice a day for lunch and dinner, so there were quite a few people around the table. Apart from Mr Haag, who was the *Coopman*, third in rank to Nico after the Deputy Factor – or *Weede Persoon*, as he was called in Dutch – there was the warehouse foreman, the bookkeeper, the physician and several assistants. Sometimes they were joined by Japanese officials as well, but on this occasion there were none present.

Haag sat on the opposite side of the table to Temperance and whenever she looked up he seemed to be sending her meaningful glances. She tried not to feel intimidated and ignored him as best she could. She didn't need to give him an answer yet and hopefully by the time she did, she'd have found a way to thwart his schemes.

The Chief Factor's house was the most imposing building on the island and consisted of a storage area on the ground floor and several large reception rooms on the first floor. Most of these were covered with *tatami* mats, a type of flooring woven from rice stalks, which was soft and slightly springy to walk on and which gave off a lovely fragrance reminiscent of a summer meadow. Temperance loved it. The walls and ceilings were papered with a patterned paper and European furniture had been placed on the *tatami* mats, which looked slightly odd. Temperance was used to this incongruous sight now, but for her own sleeping quarters, in the building opposite, she had opted for a traditional *futon* and a few Japanese low tables and cushions instead. This looked more in keeping with their surroundings.

'It looks like I'll have to go to Edo soon,' Nico told them over supper. 'As you know, we have to pay our respects to the *Shogun* from time to time, and I have been given hints that my predecessor was remiss in attending to this. I really don't know what he was thinking. The man was an idiot.' Nico shook his head in disbelief. 'Haag, you'll have to come with me as I can't take my deputy. He'll need to take command in my absence.'

Haag bowed slightly. 'As you wish. And what about young Marston, will you bring him?' The question was accompanied by another look which made Temperance want to shudder, but Nico didn't seem to notice anything unusual.

He shook his head. 'No, the mainland is no place for young boys. Tom can stay here and keep my ledgers up to date.'

'How long will you be gone?' Midori looked unhappy at

the prospect of being separated from her husband. 'I don't suppose I could go with you as interpreter?'

'No, sorry sweetheart, only men are allowed. I believe we may be gone as little as three months so you won't be on your own for too long.'

'Three months? That's ages!'

'It will pass quickly, you'll see.'

'I suppose so. I do hope he receives you graciously.'

'As to that, we shall have to wait and find out. In the meantime, I must look out some suitable gifts to bring with me. It won't do to arrive empty-handed, of that I'm sure. Will you help me choose something, my love? You will know better than I what the *Shogun* might like.'

Temperance smiled inwardly. By asking Midori's advice regarding suitable presents, Nico had neatly deflected his wife from worrying about the proposed trip and how long he would be gone. And when that subject had finally been exhausted, he turned to Temperance. 'So, no more outings today then, young varmint?' he joked, although in a low voice so that the others present wouldn't hear. They had always dealt well together and he treated her the same way her older brother Daniel had always done.

'Not today,' she affirmed with a smile.

'Not ever again,' Midori added with a frown, but she was distracted by something the physician said and didn't see Nico raise his eyebrows at Temperance, seeking her promise to do as her cousin asked. She looked away and pretended to help Emi with a piece of fruit. Nico saw far too much and Temperance felt sure he wouldn't approve of the plans that were taking shape inside her head. She suppressed the feeling of guilt that surged through her. She was an adult now; she would make her own decisions.

'Please don't do anything so foolish again,' he whispered to her. 'I understand why you went – I felt the same as you when I first came here, wanting to fight the boundaries, but it's too dangerous. These people are not like us, they won't hesitate to kill you. Pleading ignorance might work once, but it may not. This isn't a game, do you understand me?'

Temperance did. What she couldn't tell him though was that she was sure she'd be perfectly well protected if only she could persuade Kazuo to help her. All she had to do was find him again.

Chapter Five

A week passed and nothing happened – Kazuo didn't come to find her or contact her as he'd promised. Temperance wasn't stupid and doubt began to cloud her mind. As the vivid memories of her day of freedom receded slightly, she was able to look at what had happened with more perspective. She acknowledged that she'd probably allowed herself to be taken in by a charming rogue who had found in her a pleasant diversion, but who had no intention of returning. She should think herself lucky he hadn't taken advantage of her in any way.

She sighed. Kazuo had seemed so sincere, his dark gaze promising all manner of things. When he told her that he would come back, she believed him wholeheartedly, but now she wondered forlornly if this was only because she'd been so desperate for something like that to happen. Was she seeking adventure where none was to be found? It was a sobering thought.

She didn't want to give up on her dream completely, but if he never came back, what choice did she have? And apart from anything else, she'd come to realise he was her only hope of escaping marriage to Haag as he could take her away from Dejima.

Daydreaming about Kazuo and the possibility of freedom, Temperance wandered aimlessly round the island in the late afternoon, too restless to stay indoors despite the heat. Her steps took her in the direction of the little quay and, after persuading the guard to allow her outside the gate while he kept her under supervision, she stood staring longingly across the water.

'Going for another excursion, Mistress Marston?'

Temperance jumped and turned with a frown to face Mr Haag, who was standing only a few feet behind her, blocking her way back to the gate.

'I beg your pardon?' She tried to infuse her words with as much icy politeness as possible. How could he know of her adventure? She hadn't told anyone and she was sure Midori or Nico wouldn't have either.

'I saw you returning the other evening,' he drawled, a self-satisfied smile on his lips that made her want to slap him.

'You were spying on me?'

'Not at all. I was merely passing by.'

Temperance didn't believe that for a moment. 'Well, it's no concern of yours where I go or how I choose to spend my time.'

'Perhaps not yet. Anyway, I was merely asking if you were thinking of going again. Only, I wouldn't be averse to a little outing myself. It's so tedious being confined to this island, is it not?'

'Well, I won't be going anywhere. It's too dangerous. Now, if you could be so good as to let me pass?' Temperance took a step to the left and lifted one eyebrow superciliously, but he followed suit and blocked her way.

'Not so fast, my dear Mistress Marston. I am enjoying our little talk. Can't you spare me some of your precious time? That would be the Christian thing to do, wouldn't you say?'

'The *gentlemanly* thing to do,' Temperance gritted out from between clenched teeth, 'would be to step aside when a lady asks you to.' No point denying it any longer as he clearly wouldn't be dissuaded from blackmailing her.

'Ah, but are you a lady, Mistress Marston? That is the question.' He stared pointedly at her attire. 'Any young woman who thinks nothing of dressing as you do, nor going off by herself, can surely not be too careful of propriety. It makes one wonder—'

'Mr Haag, as you well know, I have no choice in the matter of clothing if I wish to stay here. Now if you don't step aside this instant, you will regret it.' Temperance had had enough of his insinuations and the thought that he might denounce her to the Japanese authorities right now made a tendril of fear coil inside her. No, surely he would at least wait until he'd received her reply?

'I don't think so.' He continued to smile in that infuriating way and Temperance saw red.

Without further thought, she feinted quickly to the right, then stepped left and gave him a push while he was still stepping in the other direction to block her path. Off balance, he was unable to stop himself from continuing and fell heavily into the water next to the quay. He floundered around, yelling in outrage before hauling himself to where there was a sort of ramp for unloading goods that he could use to pull himself out. Temperance didn't stay to watch. Instead, she made a dash for it, running as fast as she could towards the safety of her cousin's house, her heart beating fast with relief at her temporary escape.

'Odious man!' she muttered. Why wouldn't he leave her alone?

Pieter Haag stormed into his quarters, slamming the flimsy door shut so hard it almost jumped off the frame. For a moment he stood in the little entrance hall, dripping seawater onto the stone floor, then he began to tear off his sodden garments, flinging them down into a heap.

'Clean only this morning and now look at them.' He swore under his breath. 'She'll pay for this, the little bitch.'

'Haagu-*san*?' The sliding door to his *tatami* covered bedroom opened and a woman's face peered out.

Keiko or Reiko? Haag couldn't remember the courtesan's name, but it didn't matter because he'd had enough of her anyway. Her simpering annoyed him and she didn't have much in the way of a figure. 'What are you gawping at?' he barked. 'Get out. I'll pay you next time.'

'But must eat.' She blinked in consternation, her face falling.

'Out!' he shouted. 'Now!'

She must have seen in his expression how furious he was, because she quickly withdrew into the bedroom and emerged soon after pulling on her robes. Throwing him a fearful glance, she stepped into her strange wooden shoes – the ones the natives called *geta* – and scampered away, giving him a wide berth.

'*Sayonara.*' She bowed politely, but not until she was outside the door, safe in the street. Haag didn't bother to return her goodbye.

'Stupid whore,' he muttered, but he knew deep down it wasn't her fault that she didn't have beautiful ash blonde tresses and blue eyes. Like Mistress Marston, damn her. *That* was what he wanted. A proper European woman with delicious curves under that male clothing she was forced to wear.

And that was what he'd have very soon. He'd make sure of it.

'It was too bad of you, Temperance, really it was,' Midori chided, but she didn't look as stern as she should have done. There was a distinct twinkle in her eyes and a smile tugged at the corners of her mouth. 'You ought to apologise, you know.'

'Never. He's a toad and he deserved to go swimming. I don't know what he was playing at, blocking my way like that,' Temperance lied. She couldn't tell Midori the real reason, obviously. At least not yet. 'I really can't stand him.'

'No, he's not the most likeable of men, is he? I've noticed

he's quite boorish to everyone.' Midori sighed. 'Would you like me to ask Nico to have a word with him?'

'No, don't worry. I can handle Mr Haag.'

Temperance's words sounded braver than she felt. She'd seen the iron determination in Pieter Haag's eyes and she knew he was hell-bent on forcing her into marriage. He wasn't afraid to use foul means instead of fair, and she was sure he wasn't making empty threats. She sensed he was a man who would stop at nothing.

But she had to thwart him somehow.

A few days later, after supper, Temperance was standing by the wall facing the mainland, which was separated from the island by only a narrow canal of about twenty yards or so. She was watching the comings and goings of the natives on the other side, so near yet so far, when suddenly two arms came around her from behind and pulled her round the corner of the building, out of sight. Temperance struggled, but the hard grip didn't lessen. Quite the opposite.

'Be still and don't cry out or it will be the worse for you,' Pieter Haag hissed in her ear.

'How dare you?' Temperance whispered back. 'Let go of me at once. My servant will be back any moment.' She continued her struggles, panic rising inside her, making her unable to think clearly.

'No, he won't. I've sent him on an urgent errand for you.' He chuckled, his mouth much too close to her ear. 'We have some unfinished business, you and I, and I wanted to get you alone.'

'We have absolutely nothing to say to each other, Mr Haag, and if it's an apology you're after, you can forget it. I'm not the slightest bit sorry I pushed you into the water. You deserved it.'

He tut-tutted as if she were a naughty child. 'Such

vehemence, but I like it. Spirited women are so much more exciting, I find. Now if you could just channel some of that energy into being nice to me, we'll come to an understanding. You don't have much time left before giving me your answer, so what will it be? Dishonour for your cousin and a painful death for you at the hands of the Japanese, or a secret marriage to me? Seems like an easy choice.' He stroked the side of her right breast with his fingers, without letting go of her arm, and Temperance stiffened. He had gone too far.

'Understand this,' she hissed. 'I wouldn't be nice to you if you were the last man on earth. That is all the answer you're getting for the moment. Now let go of me!'

He chuckled again, an evil sound that should have made her blood freeze, but suddenly Temperance was too angry to be frightened. Her mind was busy trying to remember everything Midori and Nico had taught her during their self-defence lessons. Closing her eyes for concentration, she went through the moves in her mind, before executing them – hooking one foot behind his right leg, twisting her arms upwards quickly to free herself from his grip, and then grabbing one of his arms and pulling on it, while using her shoulder as leverage. Before he knew what was happening, he went sailing through the air and landed face first on the dirty ground with a howl of pain.

Temperance watched him for a moment, her legs shaking so much from delayed reaction that they refused to move. But when he pushed himself up onto his knees, sending her a glare of pure hatred and launching himself in her direction, she somehow found the strength to flee. Drawing in shallow breaths, she ran all the way to Midori's room and collapsed in a corner.

When Midori found her some time later, she was still shivering.

'Tom? What on earth happened?'

'It-it was Haag. He tried to attack me.'

'Attack you? Whatever for? Oh, revenge for pushing him into the water? I did tell you to apologise.'

'No. No it wasn't that.' Stuttering slightly, Temperance finally confessed the truth to her cousin. She didn't see that she had any other choice now. They were all in jeopardy because of her, and Nico and Midori needed to know.

Midori went slightly pale, but she was made of stern stuff and immediately went storming off to find her husband, while muttering imprecations in Japanese. They were soon back and Nico ushered them into his private office, making sure no one was outside listening.

'Tell me from the beginning, please,' he demanded. 'I want to know Haag's exact words.'

Temperance complied, then watched as Nico paced the *tatami* floor with a massive scowl on his face. 'This is a damnable business,' he muttered. 'A pox on the man!'

'What on earth are we going to do?' Midori said. 'We'll all be disgraced if he tells the authorities and they might even be so angry they won't let any Dutch people trade here at all!' She crossed her arms in front of her chest and looked at Nico for support. 'We must find a way to threaten him in return.'

'I agree.' Nico nodded, his expression severe. 'But how? We could beat him senseless, I suppose …'

'Or I could ask my brother to hire some *ninja*,' Midori interjected. 'Yes, that would be the best way, just make him disappear.'

'No, don't, please. At least not yet.' Temperance was sure this would only make matters worse. 'The authorities might become suspicious and investigate further, then our deception could come to light after all.' She sighed. 'This is my fault for wanting to come here in the first place. I've put you in danger so it should be up to me to extricate us all. I have a few more days to think of something, so please wait. I promise I'll stay close to you at all times. There will be no opportunity for Haag to attack me again.'

'Don't be silly, what can you do?' Midori was scowling fiercely. 'The man must be made to see reason or be silenced for good.' Temperance knew her cousin wasn't one to recoil from violence. She'd even fought in some of the civil war battles back in Plymouth a few years earlier. But was violence really the answer here?

'Just give me a little more time to come up with a plan,' she begged. 'I feel responsible and want to make things right.'

Neither Midori nor Nico looked convinced, but after further pleading on Temperance's part, they finally acquiesced.

'Very well, we'll keep this quiet for now, but if he tries anything more then I'll personally thrash him within an inch of his miserable life,' Nico concluded.

Temperance had had no word from Kazuo and was beginning to give up hope of any help from that quarter. She was also wondering how he was supposed to reach her, even if he wanted to. He'd said he would look for her in the bay first, and if she wasn't there, he would come to Dejima, but how could he? No one was allowed onto the island except certain Japanese officials.

What if he had tried and failed? Although she had no idea how long his mission would take, she imagined he could have completed it by now. She had a growing conviction that she simply had to go back to the bay and see for herself whether there was any sign of him. Just in case he'd been in earnest, she could at least check, couldn't she? And if she could only find him, she was sure he'd help her disappear for a while and thereby thwart Haag's evil plans.

Temperance was nothing if not impulsive and no sooner had this idea taken root, than she was planning her escape.

However, it wasn't as easy to sneak away a second time. Not only did she have to think of a new type of diversion in order to pass by the guards, she also had to watch out for Pieter Haag. And Midori's eyes seemed to follow her everywhere as well so that Temperance had to force herself to act normally. It was impossible.

'No, I can do this,' she told herself, determination firing her blood. All it would take was some careful planning.

The last time she left the island she'd gone just before daybreak. This time she decided she would have to leave even earlier. Surely Haag wouldn't be spying on her all night? At some point he had to sleep. And two could play at that game – she'd ask Akio to keep an eye on the man for a while. She began to accumulate a secret stash of items she would need, hiding them at the bottom of her clothes chest. Remembering Midori's comment, she gathered together Japanese clothing. Her cousin had given her some *hakama,* a type of loose trousers to wear over a male belted robe when they practised self-defence, and she also had a straw hat, some *geta* – the strange clogs that looked like a piece of wood with two smaller pieces attached to it underneath – and a large cloth to tie her hair up with. From the kitchens she stole some rice biscuits, *sembei,* and dried smoked fish, and she decided to bring a small knife, just in case she needed to defend herself against anyone.

Her preparations complete, she waited for night to fall,

Akio had agreed to keep Haag under observation all night, fortunately without questioning why this should be necessary.

'Please just come and tell me if Haag-*san* leaves his quarters,' she'd told him.

'*Hai.*' Temperance had often been grateful for the fact that the boy wasn't terribly bright and tonight she was extra thankful for his obedience.

She dressed quickly in the Japanese garments. The clothing was easy to put on in the dark and she made hardly a sound. Tying her hair into a scarf on top of her head proved more difficult. It was thick and straight and had a tendency to escape every attempt at confinement, even though she'd cut it to just below her shoulder blades in order to pass for a youth. She managed it at last and then crammed the straw hat down on top of it. It was a wide-brimmed, cone-shaped one, bought for the purpose of shielding her from the fierce sunlight, but if she tilted her head forward, it also served well to hide her pale face and blue eyes.

Satisfied with her preparations, Temperance picked up the little bundle of food she'd prepared earlier, tied into a piece of wrapping cloth called a *furoshiki*, and made her way stealthily out of the house. She had also brought a bucket, a blanket and a lantern, which was lit but shuttered so that no light escaped it at the moment. Once she'd drawn close to the guardhouse, she rolled the blanket into a tight bundle and placed it inside the bucket near a window, together with some dry grass gathered nearby. Then, after listening carefully to make sure there was no one else about, she opened the shutter of the lantern and extracted the candle, which she applied to the edge of the blanket and the grass. Both caught fire almost immediately and flames began to rise upwards, past the window, as well as a billow of smoke.

Temperance waited around the corner until she heard the warning cries of the guards as they spotted the fire from inside. Then she sprinted round the other side of the house and out through the gate while they were occupied with putting out the flames. She appropriated the smallest of the boats as before without hesitation, and quickly cast off and began to row. Like the last time, she waited out of sight until all was quiet, then set off with sure strokes along the mainland.

As she looked back towards the island of Dejima, she was pleased to see no signs of life, nor any pursuit. Contained in the bucket, the fire would have gone out by itself as soon as the blanket had finished burning, so darkness had returned as well.

Temperance smiled to herself. She had succeeded.

Chapter Six

There were plenty of other vessels floating in the bay outside Nagasaki, but Temperance dodged them easily despite the darkness. If anyone keeping guard on board the larger ships saw her, they didn't pay much attention to what looked like a servant in a small rowing boat. She kept her head down and sculled for all she was worth, heading for the opening of the bay and then around the headland in a northerly direction. Once away from the busy harbour, the shore quickly became deserted and wild, with only the odd fisherman's dwelling to be seen. It was just a dark blur which she kept at approximately the same distance.

Temperance continued doggedly up the coast, her arm muscles burning with the effort, until at last she spotted the small bay surrounded by pine trees and cut off from the rest of the sea by a long promontory that shielded it from view. It was very distinctive and even with only moonlight to guide her she knew it was the same one as before. She headed towards the shore, landing her little craft on the beach, then jumped onto the sand. Pulling the boat up as far as she could, she tied it to a nearby pine tree for added security.

Taking the bundle out of the boat, she made her way onto the large, flat rock near the shore where Kazuo had stood, and she lay down to wait for dawn to break. It was eerily silent, the only sound to be heard the shushing of the waves as they hit the shore, but Temperance wasn't afraid. Excitement kept her from imagining any dangers lurking in the forest around her, and she lay still, staring at the sky. There were no clouds and stars twinkled far above her. Temperance felt as if it was magic. God had brought her here. He would keep her safe until Kazuo came.

Before she knew it, she was fast asleep.

When she woke, the sun was already beating down, despite the early hour. As soon as Temperance had finished eating a few of the *sembei*, she walked along the shore, looking around to see whether she could find the sign Kazuo had said he would make if he came back to the bay. She didn't find anything, despite checking all the trees in that area, and finally had to acknowledge that perhaps he would never come. She'd been deluded, naïve, trusting a man she hardly knew. Her spirits sank further as she also realised what this meant – her only hope of evading Haag was gone. She'd been unable to come up with any other plan or proposition, so the alternatives were to do as he'd asked and marry him or let Nico and Midori arrange to have him silenced.

She couldn't have that on her conscience.

'I acted wilfully, insisting on coming here,' she muttered. 'Now I have to accept the consequences of my actions. It is obviously God's will, my punishment.' So much for her grand adventure.

There was nothing for it but to row back to Dejima again, but since she couldn't go until after dark, she decided to pass the time by going for a swim. The water was as refreshing as last time and for a while she forgot about everything except the wonderful feeling of cool water against skin. It was definitely not as enjoyable to be swimming on her own though, so she soon made her way to shore and dried herself before putting her garments on once more.

Just as she had finished tying the belt of her jacket, she noticed movement to her right among the pine trees. Her heart began to beat faster in anticipation of seeing Kazuo again, but its rhythm soon changed to one of intense fear when she realised the man coming towards her was not him.

'*Konichi-wa.*' The stranger stopped a few feet away from

her and looked her insolently up and down. 'What have we here then?' he mused in Japanese. 'A *gai-jin* lady dressed as a boy? Interesting, most interesting.'

Temperance found that her tongue refused to form any coherent words and she couldn't return the greeting. When at last she managed to make her vocal chords work again, she stammered out, 'Wh-who are you?' answering him in his own language. She wondered fleetingly if Kazuo had sent someone to give her a message, but if so, the man seemed in no hurry to deliver it. Then she remembered him telling her about other outlaws roaming the area. How could she have forgotten? She mentally kicked herself but it was too late now.

The man was short – no taller than herself – but he was broad-shouldered and obviously strong, and a pair of lethal-looking swords hung at his side. She didn't like his face. It was oblong and thin, with a large, slightly crooked nose and a small mouth which did nothing to add to his attractions. The man's eyes were decidedly unfriendly.

'Yamato Ryo, *da yoh*,' he said. She noticed that he didn't bow; he obviously didn't think her worthy of any politeness. That wasn't a good sign and she felt her stomach turn into knots. 'Not that it's any of your business.' Temperance stifled a gasp at his tone. 'Give me your name.'

It was an order, not a request, and Temperance thought for a moment about refusing or giving him a false name, but she realised that it made no difference whether she told him or not. 'Temi,' she said, not bothering with her surname or the longer Temperance. He didn't seem to care.

'*Ah soh*, Temi. Well, gather up your things, you're coming with us.'

Us? Temperance had until that moment focused solely on the man in front of her, but she now realised he wasn't alone. Several other men materialised from behind tree trunks and large boulders, all staring at her with menacing expressions. To a man, they were armed with swords or knives that reflected the glare of the sun onto the perfectly honed blades. She shivered violently, her eyes flickering from one possible attacker to another. Her own puny knife, the only weapon she'd brought, would have availed her nothing, even if she hadn't left it in the boat.

'I ... I can't. I have to go back or I will be missed.' She inched towards her boat, but one of Ryo's henchmen moved to block the way.

'It wasn't a request,' Ryo sneered. 'Now pick up your belongings if you want to take them with you, otherwise we'll leave them behind.'

Temperance reluctantly did as she was told, and the moment she had the bundle in her hand Ryo grabbed her arm in a vicious grip and tugged her into motion. 'Go!'

'Where are we going?' Temperance asked.

'Never you mind.'

They began to walk inland, through the dense forest, leaving the sea behind. The scent of pine trees and steaming greenery enveloped them, and the ground, which sloped upwards, was soft underfoot, a profusion of mosses growing in the oppressive humidity. If she hadn't been so frightened, Temperance would have found it fascinating to explore this foreign landscape, since there were only a few trees on Dejima and not much else. Pines, majestic cedars and what she took to be beech trees passed in a blur. Clumps of bamboo as well, taller than she had imagined, but as she was hauled along willy-nilly by Ryo she barely registered anything of her surroundings at all. She concentrated on keeping up with the man holding her arm while thoughts and conjectures swirled around inside her brain. Where were they taking her? What would they do with her? Her mind shied away from the answers, but still kept on asking the questions.

How could she have been so stupid as to come here alone again?

If only she had listened to Midori and Nico. She should have let them deal with Haag, not run off on a fool's errand.

Temperance was used to wearing *geta*, as they were practical footwear during the summer, but she had never walked any great distances in them before. She found the fast pace of Ryo and his men difficult to match for any length of time and stumbled frequently. The only replies were some muttered oaths instead of assistance. When they came upon a clearing where a number of small horses were tethered, she breathed a sigh of relief. At least she wasn't going to have to walk all the way to wherever they were taking her.

'Thank the Lord for small mercies,' she muttered to herself in English.

Ryo himself pulled her up behind him, on the horse's rump, and Temperance made no protest. She knew that resistance was futile, at least for the moment. Even if she managed to escape from him, she would soon be caught by the others. She had no choice but to go along meekly and try to lull them into complaisance while waiting for an opportunity to present itself.

'Don't try anything,' Ryo warned, as if reading her mind. 'You are being watched all the time.'

He kicked the horse into motion and Temperance glanced back the way she'd come, wishing once again that she had listened to Midori. This was definitely not the kind of adventure she had been looking for.

'No, I don't believe it – gone again? Damn it all!'

Pieter Haag pricked up his ears and stopped just outside the door to the Chief Factor's office, listening shamelessly to his employer's conversation with his concubine. The man sounded extremely cross.

'Well, I haven't seen him all morning. I was busy with the children and when I finally had time to look for him, Akio told me he wasn't there. He must have gone swimming again. Honestly, he doesn't listen to a word I say.' Haag heard clearly that Midori's voice veered between exasperation and anxiety, but he was impressed that she still remembered to refer to Mistress Marston as a 'he' for surely she must be in on the secret?

'I thought I'd made him understand how dangerous it was. I warned him expressly.' Nico Noordholt sighed. 'Foolish!'

'What are we to do? He'll have to be severely punished this time in order to make him understand. I know he's an adult now, but really, he's gone too far.'

Haag smiled to himself. He liked the sound of that and it might be to his advantage. If he could persuade Noordholt that the girl was better off married, her relatives would perhaps coerce her to accept his suit as punishment for disobeying them and he wouldn't need to implement his other threats. He could say that as his wife she'd be his responsibility and even though she would have to continue to be disguised as a boy, he'd keep a close eye on her. He would demand her services as clerk for himself – Noordholt could find someone else.

'I agree,' he heard the Chief Factor say. 'I'd better go and find him though. It's too risky for him to come back at night like last time.'

'But what if someone sees you? You're not supposed to be going up the coast either.'

'I'll be careful. I can always say we've lost some cargo or something. It floated away and we're looking for it.'

'At least take someone with you. Please?'

'Very well, if that will make you feel better, my love.'

Haag didn't stay to hear any more. He planned to be the first man Noordholt set eyes on so that he could go along.

It would give him great pleasure to see Mistress Marston humbled when they caught her in the act of swimming. And the sight of her wet wasn't one he'd be averse to seeing either.

He smiled to himself. It was turning out to be a good day.

They rode for hours, up and down winding paths that zigzagged the sides of the steep hills and crossed the valleys in between. They stopped only once to eat. Temperance was given some food and allowed a brief time behind some bushes, but other than that she was kept under constant surveillance. The looks she received from some of the men made her feel distinctly queasy. They must have been watching her while she swam since they clearly knew she was a woman, as Ryo had said, and her male clothing made no difference now. Her stomach churned unceasingly as the disquieting thoughts continued to plague her, giving her no respite, and her legs had a tendency to shake whenever she had to stand up or walk. She tried to bolster her courage, telling herself that she would find a way to escape, but she was afraid of what might happen to her before then. What if her chance came too late?

They stayed well away from all villages and settlements. From time to time they saw or heard the sea in the distance, and Temperance surmised that they were skirting the coast, albeit slightly inland. Judging by the position of the sun and the fact that the sea always seemed to be on their left, they were heading north and then east. Just before nightfall, Ryo signalled for the men to halt and make camp. A few oiled sheets of material were rigged up to form an awning, in case it rained during the night, and after another quick meal of dried food Temperance was ordered to lie down and go to sleep.

'Can we not have some sport with her first?' one of Ryo's men asked with a leer, but to Temperance's huge relief Ryo snarled an emphatic 'no' at him.

'She'll be worth far more to us as a *shojo*,' he said. 'Besides, do you really want to bed someone who looks like an evil *kami*? She may put a curse on you.' Ryo laughed and it wasn't a nice sound.

Temperance knew that *shojo* meant 'maiden' or 'virgin' and sent up a prayer of thanks to God for Ryo's greed. At least if she was not molested immediately, that would give her more time to devise a plan of escape before any harm befell her. She didn't care that he thought her as ugly as a spirit. She realised that with her blonde hair she must resemble a ghost to these people. What she couldn't figure out, however, was who would want to buy her from Ryo? If everyone thought as he did, then surely she wouldn't be worth much even if she was a maiden still.

The leering man must have been thinking along the same lines because he asked, 'Who're you planning on selling her to anyway? Nobody'd want her.'

'That's where you're wrong, Saburo. I know of just the right person, name of Imada. He owns a very prosperous tea house and inn just outside Kobe. Does a little business on the side, buying and selling girls for men who want unusual mistresses, something out of the ordinary.' He jerked his head in Temperance's direction and chuckled. 'Now you can't get more extraordinary than that, can you? I reckon he'll pay a good price for such an unusual female. So hands off!' He shouted the last words and they echoed round the small clearing, bouncing off the trees. His men blinked, but no one seemed inclined to argue and they all settled down for the night.

Saburo threw Temperance one last look, but lumbered off to his place without further rebellion. She drew a sigh of relief and, wrapping herself in her drying cloth since she didn't have a blanket, she lay down on the ground with her food bundle as an uncomfortable pillow. Ryo lay down next to her and took hold of her arm, tying a piece of rope around it and securely knotting the other end around his own wrist. It would seem he wasn't taking any chances and he gave her a long, hard stare before closing his eyes and falling instantly asleep.

Temperance stared back at him in the darkness, hating him more than she had ever hated another human being. She swore she would escape, if it was the last thing she did.

Chapter Seven

'He can't have gone much further. It's hard work rowing and he's a lot weaker than I am.'

Noordholt was scowling while scanning the shoreline for any signs of the fugitive. Haag did his best not to show his mounting excitement. His imagination was running riot, picturing the scene they might come upon at any moment – Mistress Marston bathing, gloriously naked, wet ... Desire flamed inside him, almost painful in its intensity, and he shifted on the bench, uncomfortable in his suddenly very tight breeches.

He tried to calm down and concentrated on rowing for a while. As he'd hoped, he had been the first person Noordholt ran into when exiting his house and Haag was asked to accompany the Chief Factor on what he'd called 'a delicate expedition' to recover 'the varmint' who'd sneaked off for some illicit swimming somewhere up the coast.

It took a while for Noordholt to persuade the guards by the sea gate to allow them out, but they finally swallowed his tale of needing to row out to the mouth of the harbour to check for some goods which he claimed had floated away. It hadn't sounded very plausible to Haag, but the two of them were on their way now, alone.

This seemed a good time to show his hand, since there was no chance of them being overheard out here on the sea. Besides, Noordholt would find out soon enough anyway so Haag said casually, 'No need to pretend with me, *mijnheer*. I know she's a woman.'

Noordholt's head whipped round and he scowled ferociously. 'A woman? You have proof of this?' There was frost in his voice which made sudden chills run down Haag's back, but he stared back. He was the one who had the upper hand after all.

'Yes. I've, er … seen her.'

'You mean you've been spying on your fellow workers on Dejima? I could have you whipped for that.' Noordholt's expression was severe, something which would normally have Haag quaking, but he knew the man was bluffing so he tried not to let it affect him.

'Let's just say I had my reasons and they don't matter now. The fact is I've asked her to marry me and seeing how disobedient and wilful she is, doing things like this,' he gestured vaguely towards the sea, 'I'd think you would be glad to be rid of the responsibility. I can deal with her for you.'

'And if I prefer to do that myself?' the Chief Factor's eyes held a challenge which Haag accepted with alacrity.

He shrugged. 'Then I'm afraid I'll have no choice but to denounce her to the authorities. I'm sure you realise the implications for your own position if I have to do that …' He let the sentence hang between them, but to his surprise Noordholt didn't look as intimidated as he'd hoped.

'I don't take kindly to threats,' the Chief Factor hissed. 'We'll discuss this further when we have found her, but believe me when I say there are options other than those you've outlined. In fact, I could push you into the water right now. You can't swim, can you?' A grim smile curved the man's mouth and Haag shivered.

It was true, he couldn't swim, but he didn't take Noordholt for a murderer. He guessed he was probably trying to stall for time. Very well, he could afford to give him that and the man was right – first they needed to find the lady in question. He was about to say something to that effect, when his attention was diverted by an object on the shore.

'There, look, a boat.' He'd spotted a small rowing boat

pulled up on a little sandy beach. There didn't seem to be anyone either in the water or on shore though. Haag frowned. 'Although perhaps it's not the right one?'

'Only one way to find out.' Noordholt pulled on the oars and rowed towards land.

Haag jumped out first and tied the boat to a small tree after helping to pull it up next to the other one.

Noordholt went to investigate. 'Nothing here,' he commented. 'If this was hers, why isn't she here?' Worry lines appeared between his brows and Haag felt his gut clench. Where had the silly girl gone? Had his suspicions been right and there was more to her outings than she'd let on?

They searched all along the shore of the little bay, but there wasn't anyone there and no sign of the woman. Haag's temper was reaching boiling point, but he didn't want his employer to see how desperate he was to find Mistress Marston so he tried to maintain an outwardly calm facade. Finally, Noordholt sat down on a large, flat rock and sighed, running his fingers through his hair. 'Surely she wouldn't have gone inland? Swimming is one thing, but that would be pure madness.'

'Maybe this isn't the right place?' Haag suggested. 'There must be other bays like this along the coast.'

'Yes, perhaps, but ... oh, hold on!'

'What is it?'

Noordholt was leaning forward and pulled something off the edge of the rock. 'Look!'

'I don't see anything.' Haag stared at Noordholt's hand, which seemed to be holding up thin air.

'Look closer. See? Long blonde hair.'

'Ah.' There were indeed a couple of very long strands of silver-blonde hair between Noordholt's fingers. 'So she *was* here.'

'It would seem so. Was being the operative word.'

Noordholt got to his feet and went to look around one last time. 'I could be mistaken, Haag, but doesn't this look like a lot of footprints just here?' He pointed to a part of the sandy beach. 'It's all scuffed up, as though there's been a tussle.'

'You're thinking she's been attacked? Abducted? But why? Who? I mean, she's a foreigner. They don't even like us.' Haag didn't like the implications of this – that she was out of his reach temporarily and he wouldn't have her in his bed quite as quickly as he'd counted on. *Godverdamme!*

'Well, maybe that's just the officials. We never meet any ordinary people so we don't know what they think of us. Damnation! If she's been taken, how the hell are we ever going to find her?'

'I've no idea.' Haag felt disappointment and fury swamp him. This wasn't turning out at all how he'd envisaged it. Did the stupid girl have any idea how much trouble she'd caused? If he ever got his hands on her again, he'd make sure she understood.

'Let's walk inland a little way, just to see if there's anyone nearby. We can't leave anything to chance.'

Haag nodded, too angry to care where they went. She was gone and his day was ruined. The day when she was supposed to have accepted her fate. Grinding his teeth, he snarled, 'So what is her name really? I'm guessing it's not Thomas.'

Noordholt stopped on the path in front of him and turned round, eyes wide with astonishment. Then a grin split his face. 'You don't even know and you're wanting to marry her?' He laughed, a harsh sound that echoed round the forest nearby. 'Why should I tell you?'

'Because if you don't, I'll tell the authorities *your* kinswoman is missing, the one you've illegally kept on Dejima for a year,' Haag shot back. To his satisfaction, Noordholt's smile died away.

'Very well, her name is Temperance, but don't think for a moment I'll allow you to go squealing to the authorities. From now on, I'm not letting you out of my sight and if you utter so much as a word about my step-cousin, you'll find yourself with your throat slit and your tongue cut out. Do I make myself clear?'

The Chief Factor was a big man, muscular and well-trained, towering over Haag in a way that made him feel distinctly weak and insignificant. Impotent rage threatened to drown him. For now, there seemed nothing he could do, but he would bide his time and somehow he would triumph. He'd make sure of it.

Ryo and his group continued their journey the following day, mostly in brooding silence which Temperance found unnerving. She was dying to ask him questions about their destination and his plans, but after a few attempts at conversation she had to give up as he threatened to beat her black and blue if she didn't keep her mouth shut.

'Can't bear chattering females,' he muttered and threw her a murderous glance over his shoulder. Since he was the only thing that stood between her and certain rape by the members of his gang, she deemed it prudent to obey him. The further they travelled, however, the more desperate for answers she became.

It seemed they had left the sea behind now, as there was neither sight nor sound of it all day. Temperance knew that without it she had no hope of finding her way back to the cove. Travelling inland, on barely noticeable paths, she soon became lost and her spirits sank. Even if she was able to escape eventually, how would she return to Dejima? She had no money with which to pay a guide and in any case she would probably be apprehended on sight as her disguise wouldn't fool anyone for long. It was a distressing thought, but Temperance vowed to find a way round it. She wouldn't give up hope yet.

On the afternoon of the second day, Temperance thought she could detect the scent of the sea once more. Sure enough, Ryo led his little group down towards the shore soon after, where they came upon a small fishing village. They halted on the edge of it, next to the first dwelling, and Ryo dismounted, pulling Temperance off the horse as well. He threw the reins to one of his henchmen.

'I'm going to see the headman. I won't be long,' he said. 'Don't let her out of your sight.' He nodded in Temperance's direction before striding off.

The other men kept her under surveillance, some with surly expressions, some leering like the vile Saburo. Temperance ignored them. It was obvious that she couldn't escape on foot, while they were all mounted, so she didn't even think of trying. Instead she looked at the few houses dotted around a clearing near a small bay with a sandy beach. Most of the dwellings looked old and weathered and were of very poor quality, made of wood with steeply sloping thatched roofs. Only one was large enough to contain more than one room, and she guessed that must be where the headman lived.

True to his word, Ryo returned shortly afterwards with two village men in tow. 'These people will look after our horses and lend us a boat for a small fee,' he said. 'Everyone dismount. Take her to the shore.'

Temperance found her arm gripped once more and another of Ryo's men marched her off in the direction of the beach.

'Where are we? What is this place called?' she ventured to ask, hoping this knowledge would come in useful if she managed to escape at some point.

The man hesitated, then shrugged. 'This is the Kammon Strait, leading into the *Seto-naikai*, the Inland Sea.' He volunteered no other information, and Temperance didn't ask for further enlightenment because what he had told her was enough. She knew that the Kammon Strait was to the north and east of Nagasaki. Nico had spoken of it once. If she could only escape, all she had to do was follow the coastline west and south in order to go back. It would be difficult, but not impossible and she would have to try soon, before it was too late.

As they embarked, Temperance had the misfortune of being placed next to Saburo, who gripped her wrist with strong, dirty fingers. She cast him a glance of pure loathing, but sat meekly while waiting for the right moment to make her move, trying to ignore the feeling that he was cutting off the blood supply into her hand. There were butterflies dancing in her stomach, but she tried to remain impassive so as not to arouse any suspicion.

The moment the little boat reached the mouth of the bay, she took her chance, knowing that she may never get another opportunity. She turned suddenly and hit Saburo across the nose with as much force as she could muster. He yelped with pain and let go of her arm temporarily. Temperance flung herself into the water and began to swim for all she was worth. Sounds of confusion and bellows of rage reached her dimly through waterlogged ears, but she ignored them and concentrated on swimming as she had never swum before. She used every muscle she possessed to propel herself forward as fast as possible. She must reach the shore before Ryo and his men were able to turn the boat around. Her only chance was to hide among the trees until they gave up looking for her.

For a while it appeared that she had succeeded. She continued doggedly through the waves, looking up from time to time to make sure she was on course, but all too soon she became aware of the sound of pursuit. She'd forgotten that the boat was equipped with oars as well as the sail, and Ryo had obviously wasted no time in setting his men to work. They bore down on her with a speed she had thought impossible, and despite her best efforts, they soon caught up with her.

A glancing blow to the head from something heavy – an oar perhaps – stopped her in her tracks, and this gave Ryo and his men the time they needed to draw up alongside her. Almost blinded by pain, she nevertheless struggled to escape the arms that reached out to pluck her from the sea, kicking, biting and screaming like a woman possessed, but it was to no avail. They were simply too strong for her and she had the added disadvantage of feeling dazed from being clouted on the head.

She was swung over the side and dumped at the bottom of the boat in a wet heap, like a fish caught on the line. The breath was knocked out of her lungs and she lay there, winded. She gulped for breath, coughing and spluttering out the water that had entered her mouth and lungs during her struggles.

'*Baka jaro!* Idiot! Foolish woman, what were you thinking? You can't escape from me. *Chikusho!*' Ryo was almost beside himself with rage, his face contorted with the force of it. He continued with a long tirade against women in general and her in particular until at last he ran out of breath.

Temperance ignored him. Her head pounded and she put up her hand to feel gingerly for the lump she knew was forming at the back of it. Warm blood oozed onto her fingers and she winced, then closed her eyes, admitting defeat. Ryo was right. What had she been thinking? There were a dozen of them and only one of her. She had no chance of escape, none whatsoever. If she was ever to return to her cousin, she would have to place her trust in God.

Only he could save her now.

Chapter Eight

'So you wish to apply for a position in my household, do you?'

Kazuo was kneeling in front of one of the men whose name had appeared on the document that sealed his father's fate. 'Yes, my lord,' he replied without looking up or rising, his head down, forehead almost touching the floor.

He heard the rustling of paper as the man no doubt read the letter Kazuo had brought. It was a document which purported to come from a lord whose holdings were in the far northern part of the country. The man in question, Ebisu-*sama*, was old and ill and seldom travelled, and Kanno senior had therefore thought it safe to use his name on the fake letter. The old *daimyo* would never know and, in any case, Lord Ebisu had always been a good friend of Kazuo's father and would no doubt have colluded with them had they had a chance to ask him.

'By the time anyone has been able to verify your credentials, you will be long gone,' Kazuo's father had said. 'I don't want you staying above a few weeks at each place, my son. That would be too dangerous.'

Kazuo agreed and prayed that the man in front of him didn't suspect foul play. He knew his life would be forfeit if he was found out and his father's chances of obtaining justice non-existent.

'And why have you come to me, of all people, young man?' The voice was peremptory, abrupt, lashing Kazuo like a whip, as if the man were trying to crack open a flaw.

'Because I have been told that you are a man who has the high esteem of our ruler, the *Shogun*, my lord. What better way to advance in the world than to work for such a man?'

'Hmm. Flattery, eh?'

Kazuo held his breath. Had he gone too far? His lordship was a clever man after all and it was almost unheard of for someone to seek to work for a different clan to the one he'd been born into. If his own lord couldn't employ him any longer, for whatever reason, he ought to become a *ronin*.

'There is also the fact that I am related to your clan on my mother's side,' he lied. 'Albeit distantly.'

That appeared to settle it. 'Very well, you may join my guard and if you work hard, I will promote you. I do not tolerate any laziness or shirking of duty, mind. And I have a good memory. I will remember to watch your progress. Understood?'

'Yes, my lord. Thank you, I am very grateful.' Kazuo bowed once more, touching his forehead to the floor while bile rose in his throat. He wanted to kill the man, not bow and scrape in the dirt before him, but he wasn't here for mere revenge. He needed proof of the man's treachery if he was to help his father.

He had, at most, four weeks to find it.

For several days Temperance, Ryo and his men sailed along the northern coast of the *Seto-naikai*, pulling into quiet coves with sandy beaches every so often to rest, eat and find water supplies. The Inland Sea appeared to be dotted with hundreds of little islands and was quite breathtakingly beautiful, especially at sunset when the sky turned a glorious red, orange and amber. It was precisely the kind of sight that Temperance had wished to experience, but under her present circumstances she was completely uninterested in any scenic beauty.

Most of the time she sat huddled near the stern next to Ryo, who had delegated the job of steering and taking care of the sail to the others and was not letting her out of his sight.

As leader it was obviously beneath him to do menial tasks anyway, Temperance thought, or perhaps he didn't know how. Either way, she was stuck with him, and each time they boarded the little craft he tied her to his wrist again.

'Just in case you're thinking of jumping a second time,' he said with a scowl. 'You may be a good swimmer, but believe me, you don't want to try it here. There are currents that can pull a man under in seconds, never mind a mere woman.'

Temperance just glared at him in reply. She no longer cared, and for the first few days her head hurt so much she was barely aware of her surroundings. During the hours that followed her ill-advised attempt at escape, she also had the added discomfort of sitting in wet clothes that clung to her skin, the salt-heavy material itchy beyond belief. No one had any spare garments, or if they did, they didn't volunteer to lend them to her. Later, when hers had finally dried, they felt hard and unyielding, as well as slightly sticky, coated as they were with a thin layer of salt.

She assumed they were going to this place called Kobe that Ryo had spoken of, but she had no idea where that might be or how long it would take to reach it. If they were going by boat, it must be because it was either faster or it was situated on the other side of the strait or along this Inland Sea. She would just have to wait and see.

Ryo ignored her for most of the time, but after a few days his temper cooled and she sensed that he grew bored and restless. He began to glance at her, as if he was contemplating speaking to her, but held back until he couldn't resist any longer.

'So why did you come here?' he suddenly said, obviously by now in desperate need of some kind of distraction.

Temperance, who'd been lost in her own thoughts, turned slowly and focused on him. 'Here?'

'To Japan,' he clarified.

She shrugged. 'I'd heard a lot about your country and wanted to see for myself. I didn't realise I would be cooped up on a tiny island the whole time, locked away on Dejima.'

'Well, you're seeing it now,' he said with a mocking grin. 'Does it please you? Is it how you imagined it?'

'There's nothing wrong with the country,' Temperance muttered, 'it's the company I object to.'

'Are you saying we're not good enough for you?' A superior look down his crooked nose accompanied this question and Temperance wasn't sure if he was teasing her or not.

She sent him a withering glance, then looked pointedly at the piece of rope tied round her wrist. 'I think I would prefer not to be tied to my guide. Somehow that would make the experience so much more enjoyable.'

'And would you swear on your honour not to try and escape?'

'No.'

'Ah, well then, I can't remove your bonds, can I?'

They were silent for a moment, but as he'd been in such an expansive mood, Temperance decided to try and engage him in conversation for a while longer. 'Please will you tell me about your country? I have no idea how big it is or anything.' That wasn't strictly true, as she'd asked Midori, but she thought Ryo might know more about it since outlaws presumably travelled around a lot.

He looked slightly surprised at the question, but complied nonetheless. 'Japan is comprised of four very large islands and thousands of smaller ones. We have just left Kyushu behind and are now going to the largest island, Honshu. The place we're heading for is called Kobe, and it's not too far from the great city of Kyoto, where the Emperor lives, which is further inland. South of this Inland Sea is another large island called Shikoku, and I've been told the fourth one, Hokkaido, is far to the north, although I have never been there.'

'Your country is very large then?'

He nodded. 'Yes, but mostly it's made up of mountains so almost everyone lives around the coast or in the deep valleys in between the peaks. There are also many huge forests and numerous lakes and rivers. The easiest way to travel is by boat, and much the fastest too.'

'I see. Thank you.'

'Will you not tell me of your own country in return? Where do you come from and how far away is it?'

He seemed genuinely interested, or perhaps he was still bored and wanted to pass the time, Temperance thought, but she couldn't see that it mattered whether she told him about herself or not.

'I come from an island country as well. It's called England and we had to sail for nine months to get here, across huge oceans and past many other countries. I lived by the coast too, although England doesn't have as many mountains and so it is populated almost everywhere.'

They continued to talk about their respective countries for quite some time, comparing the merits of each and the differences in culture and conditions. Temperance could almost forget the circumstances of their being together. She found it fascinating to talk thus to a real Japanese person, but whenever he gesticulated to demonstrate a point, the rope tugged on her wrist and she was reminded of her captivity. Although Ryo had proved interesting and had shown her a different side to himself, he was still her captor, her gaoler, and in the end she couldn't ignore this fact.

'Why are you doing this to me?' she asked at last, exasperated. 'You seem like an intelligent man. Surely you could find some better way of earning money?'

He seemed taken aback by her question, then he looked away. It was as if a wall had sprung up between them once more and Temperance almost regretted questioning him.

'There are things about my country you don't understand,' he said.

'Then explain, please. I really want to know.'

He shook his head. 'No. My motives for capturing and selling you are none of your business. I have no choice; this is how it has to be. I am sorry for it, but I cannot take you back, if that's what you are asking.'

'What if my countrymen would pay to have me back?'

He gave a mirthless laugh. 'And inform the authorities at the same time? No, thank you. As you said, I'm not stupid.' He turned his head away, as if terminating the conversation once and for all. 'Now cease your chatter, I need some peace and quiet.'

Temperance did as she was bid and held her tongue. She felt she had made some progress, so perhaps it behoved her to tread carefully then maybe she could make him see sense. For now, she had to be content.

Ryo relented the following day, obviously bored again, and they talked some more.

'You speak our language very well. Where did you learn?' he asked.

'My cousin taught me. She's fluent in Japanese and I wanted to be able to understand what everyone was saying.'

Fortunately he didn't ask how her cousin had learned and Temperance reckoned it was probably better not to mention Midori by name. She didn't want to get her into trouble for teaching her. She changed the subject and Ryo was happy to tell her about his country and its customs, as long as she reciprocated with tales of England and other European nations. But he refused point-blank to talk about what was to happen to her.

'Never you mind,' was all he'd say.

Consequently, Temperance's fear of what awaited her

grew daily. Her mind conjured up all sorts of dreadful fates, none of which she could see any way of extricating herself from. And the more she tried not to think about it, the more her brain ran round in circles returning to the few hints Ryo had let slip.

He was going to sell her, as if she were a slave. He knew of a man who would be interested in buying her. What sort of a man would buy women and what would he want from her? She knew of only two things – hard work or her body. Hard work held no fears for her, as she was strong and healthy and had never been used to idleness before sailing to Japan, but the thought of someone owning her body and being able to do with it what they wanted made her feel physically sick.

She wished Ryo would at least tell her – if she knew what was going to happen, she could prepare herself for it in her mind. But whenever she tried to fish for information, he clammed up and went to sit elsewhere in the boat, tying her instead to a man called Jiro. He had a vacant expression which showed Temperance clearly that there wouldn't be any point engaging him in conversation. She wondered what Ryo was afraid of – that she would make him see sense? That she would prick his conscience? Or that he might actually like her enough to want to set her free? She had no idea, but it was obvious he wasn't going to give her the opportunity to work on him.

Despite her nervousness, Temperance became so bored she almost cheered as they finally reached their destination. It was bliss to walk on land again, although she felt as if the ground moved for quite a while after disembarking while her body adjusted to not being rocked by the waves. They didn't go into Kobe itself, but skirted the city and continued along smaller roads into the countryside to the north-west.

Temperance's feet began to ache. 'Why can't we have horses here too, Ryo-*san*?'

'I'm not made of money,' he replied, which made her realise he must desperately need whatever sum selling her would bring him. It was true he and his men were dressed in old, worn clothes and only ate meagre amounts of food so clearly they weren't well off. It didn't make things any better, but at least she understood that what Ryo was doing was a necessity rather than mere greed on his part. She walked without complaint after that.

They walked past neat rice paddies, where the ears of rice were heavy, showing that harvest time approached. There had been much rain during the last two days, which undoubtedly weighted them down as well, and the humidity seemed worse here inland without the slight sea breeze Temperance was used to. She struggled on past houses like the ones they had seen in the fishing village, huddled together in small settlements, and everywhere they went the people they encountered looked tired and downtrodden. The life of a peasant was obviously a hard one here, and Temperance felt for them. She wondered how much of their produce they were allowed to keep for themselves – none seemed to be starving but appearances could be deceptive.

When Temperance had begun to think her feet would never survive another hour of walking, they arrived at a slightly larger settlement, which seemed to have grown up around a crossroads. There was much coming and going, carts and horses, and men milling about, and a large, sprawling building stood in the centre.

'What is this place?' Temperance dared to ask Jiro.

He stared at her as if she was a complete idiot. 'An inn, of course,' he replied, as though it was something everyone knew. And perhaps it was common knowledge if you were Japanese, Temperance thought rather crossly, but how was she to know when she had never seen one before?

'There's a tea house at the back,' Jiro added with a leering sort of grin. Temperance wondered why a tea house should make him look like that, but didn't get a chance to ask.

'Come.' Ryo took her arm in a gentle grip and led the way into the inn, which upon closer inspection seemed somewhat ramshackle and not in very good repair. He didn't seem in much of a hurry; in fact, if she hadn't known better Temperance would have sworn he was dragging his feet, which was odd. Was he having second thoughts? She sent him a hopeful glance, but he refused to meet her gaze. Instead he swore under his breath and pulled her along a corridor. They were ushered into a private room, where Ryo and two of his men sat down on cushions, while the others were told to wait outside. Temperance was left standing in a corner, her stomach once more harbouring butterflies as she realised this was where she would meet her fate.

The innkeeper bustled in and Temperance took an instant dislike to the little man whose fat fingers and jowly appearance made her shudder.

'Imada-*san*.' Ryo stood up and the two men greeted each other like long lost friends. Temperance's heart sank even further. 'I have brought you something extraordinary this time, something I believe one of your clients will value highly. You know of whom I speak.'

'Of course, of course.'

Ryo indicated Temperance and Imada walked over to inspect her, recoiling slightly as she raised her blue eyes from under the brim of her hat and gave him a malevolent stare. '*Chikusho!* What is this, my friend?'

Ryo removed her hat, then released her hair from its confinement with a flourish so that it tumbled around her shoulders in silvery disarray. Temperance was pleased to see Imada-*san* practically wrinkle his nose at the sight of it.

'A *yuki onna*?' the man whispered, his eyes wide open.

Ryo shook his head. 'No, she's not a snow ghost, but

a *gai-jin*. She comes from a country far, far away, and I thought your client would be interested in adding her to his collection.' He lowered his voice. 'Naturally, the authorities must not be allowed to find out about her existence. Strictly speaking she shouldn't be in our country at all, but once she's ensconced with her new master, I doubt that will be a problem.'

'Indeed, no. She'll be safe there.'

Temperance was growing increasingly annoyed at being discussed as if she wasn't there and, if her future was to include this surly man, extremely frightened as well. 'And where is it I'm going?' she demanded. 'I have a right to know.'

Imada scowled at her. 'You have no rights at all, girl. Now keep a still tongue in your head or it will be the worse for you.' He turned back to Ryo and the two men began to discuss remuneration.

'How much? You can't be serious!' Imada-*san* looked thunderstruck at the amount Ryo was asking and Temperance had the distinct impression he was reluctant to sell her after all, as he'd clearly quoted a sum well beyond the norm. He kept glancing her way with a frown, squirming on his cushion as if he were ill at ease. But really, did he have a choice? She knew that if he didn't sell her, he and his men would be without funds. Without food. And the others would surely be angry if they'd come all this way for nothing.

Temperance tried to keep calm, but panic threatened to overtake her at the prospect of having to stay here. Being captured by Ryo and his men had been bad enough; being left here with this coarse stranger was far worse. She looked around her to see if there was any way of escaping, but the door was barred by Ryo's men and she couldn't see any other way out. All too soon the haggling was over. Imada had agreed to a preposterous sum, which seemed to stun Ryo.

The innkeeper went off to fetch the money, muttering under his breath, and Ryo fixed her with an almost defiant stare.

'Do as he tells you or he'll beat you,' he warned. 'I'm saying this for your own good. Imada-*san* is not a man to be trifled with. He wants a good price for you, so he'll treat you well if you behave, but he will not hesitate to punish you for any wrongdoing.'

'And you're leaving me with this monster? What kind of man are you, Ryo, that you can do this to a defenceless woman?'

'One in need of money and who can't afford sentimentality,' he retorted. '*Sayonara*.' He gave her a curt bow and turned to collect his money from Imada, who came back into the room.

'You'll pay for this, Ryo!' Temperance shouted after him and thought she saw him flinch, but he didn't so much as look her way. Within moments he was gone and she had to fight the urge to run after him.

Imada walked up to her and backhanded her across the cheek. 'Shut up,' he said. 'Now come with me. It's time to begin your training. You're way past the usual age.'

'Training? What training?'

Another slap. Temperance felt as if her ears were ringing. 'I told you to shut up. Are you deaf as well as ugly?'

This time she'd learned her lesson and said nothing. Instead she let her eyes speak for her and had the satisfaction of seeing him turn away. He muttered something about a 'damned *yuki onna*', and this gave her a ray of hope. She prayed that he was heartily afraid of ghosts as she intended to send him malevolent glances at every opportunity from now on.

Chapter Nine

'You are now a *shinzo*, even though you're a bit old for that,'
Imada told her. 'You'll be trained in the arts of a courtesan. I
expect you to learn fast as really you should have started at
the age of fifteen.'

'A *shinzo*! I'll have you know I'm a decent woman,'
Temperance protested, shocked to the very core at this
prospect, although she had suspected something of the sort
the moment she set foot in Imada's establishment.

She'd heard the Dutchmen on Dejima joking about the
loose women that frequented the island, and their comments
were definitely not flattering. Courtesan was just a nicer
word for these women's profession. And this man expected
her to become one? 'I'll not submit to any man except my
husband,' she stated, trying desperately to sound as if she
actually had a choice in the matter.

Imada sent her a scornful glance and said sarcastically,
'Don't try my patience, fool. Husband, indeed. Hah! Where
would such as you find one of those? No, if you wish to
survive, you'll do as you're told. I don't want to hear another
word out of you. And as I said, you'd better learn fast. I
don't want you here eating me out of house and home for
weeks on end with no profit to show for it. Count yourself
lucky I don't put you to work immediately. I have other plans
for you.'

He gave Temperance a none too gentle push in the small
of her back, which made her stumble into one of the houses
that were built at right angles to the back of the inn itself.
'This is the tea house, where my girls live and work.'

Temperance looked around her as she finally understood
why Jiro had been smirking about the word 'tea house'.

Apparently it was just another term for brothel, or at least in some instances.

Imada interrupted her thoughts. 'You're to listen and follow instructions, nothing more. Even a foreigner should be able to manage that. Nyoko!'

He bellowed the last word and a pretty but slovenly-looking girl appeared through a doorway and sashayed towards them. Her clothing was rumpled, her hair mussed, hanging in uneven tresses around her face and down her back, and her skin was sallow with traces of face powder. And yet Temperance had no doubt that when scrubbed clean and wearing her best clothes, the girl was probably devastatingly attractive, especially to the opposite sex. She fairly oozed confidence and her eyes seemed to speak of some secret knowledge, which made Temperance feel very uncomfortable. Would she herself end up looking like that? It was a sickening thought.

'What?' Nyoko asked, coming to a halt in front of them with a frown. She looked Temperance up and down. 'By all the gods, what have you brought me this time? Have you taken leave of your senses?'

'Don't talk to me in that tone of voice. I've warned you before,' Imada snapped at the girl, but she merely stared him down. 'This is ... what's your name?'

Temperance decided not to use her own name any longer, since she most certainly didn't feel like herself. 'They call me Shinju,' she lied, remembering how Kazuo had said she resembled a pearl.

'Very apt,' Nyoko drawled and grabbed some of Temperance's hair and yanked hard.

'Ow!'

Nyoko shrugged. 'Just checking it's not a wig. Dreadful colour, looks dead. We could dye it perhaps?'

'No,' Imada cut in, forestalling Temperance's own protest.

'You're not to change her in any way. Just teach her what she needs to know in order for me to sell her. You know what needs to be done. A few mannerisms, proper walking, the basics. She knows nothing, like those little peasant girls they keep bringing us, although she's much older to be sure. How old are you exactly?'

'Eighteen,' Temperance answered, reluctantly. After all, what business was it of Nyoko's how old she was?

'Untouched?' Nyoko asked with eyebrows raised as if she didn't believe it for a moment.

'Yes, of course!' Temperance felt her cheeks flame at discussing such intimate details about herself in front of this pig of a man, but he took no notice.

'You'll have to check,' he told Nyoko.

'What? No, you can't do that!'

'I thought I told you to shut up unless you were spoken to?' Imada snarled, raising his hand as if to strike her again. 'Don't learn very fast, do you?'

Temperance glared at him, but said nothing. Instead she ground her teeth in silence, anger warring with fear inside her. What a whoreson. She would pay him back somehow.

'Well, come with me then, I haven't got all day,' Nyoko said and turned to go. 'I'll have to get old Mai to help me, I think. I'm too busy to babysit all the time.'

'Do whatever is necessary,' Imada growled. 'I want her ready in two weeks.'

'Two weeks?' Nyoko stared at him as if he was mad. 'Three at the very least, if not four.'

'Two and a half and not a day more.' And he turned on his heel and left.

Nyoko regarded Temperance with acute dislike. 'You'd better learn fast or else …'

Temperance glared back defiantly, albeit shaking inwardly

with suppressed dread. 'I'll do whatever it takes to get away from here. Lead on.'

Imada's inn and tea house was called the Weeping Willow, presumably because there was such a tree outside or overhanging the nearby river, but Temperance was never given a chance to verify this fact since she wasn't allowed outside. She had exchanged one prison for another.

'You're to stay indoors,' Nyoko told her, and added that Imada had guards posted outside the front door at all times. 'They protect us girls from intruders,' she said, her smirk making it clear that wasn't their main purpose.

'You can sleep in here.' Nyoko pulled open the sliding door of a small room already filled to the brim with girls, some of whom looked to be as young as five or six. 'There's a spare *futon* in the corner and someone will fetch you a blanket later.'

Temperance stared at the worn mattress, which looked lumpy and uncomfortable and sported several stains of indeterminate origin. Revulsion engulfed her and she had to suppress a shudder. It was a far cry from the soft *futon* she'd left behind on Dejima, conscientiously aired by Akio every morning. She supposed she ought to be grateful for something to sleep on at all in the circumstances, but she couldn't summon up one iota of gratitude. Instead, she railed inwardly at the cruel fate which had brought her to this, although the rational part of her brain knew it was her own fault.

The room itself had a musty, enclosed smell and its walls were of plain, unadorned wood which was scuffed and marked from years of wear and tear. The *tatami* mats covering the floor were decidedly shabby.

'Is there nowhere else?' she asked Nyoko, hating herself for the pathetic sound of her voice, but unable to resist uttering the question.

Nyoko looked at her as if she couldn't believe her ears. 'No, there isn't. Is this not good enough for you, your high-and-mighty-ness?'

Temperance didn't reply. What was the point? Instead she glanced around at the faces of the other girls. Most had an air of resignation about them, as if they had been beaten into submission and now accepted their lot. Only the prettiest, the ones who were obviously in demand from clients, had any kind of vivaciousness left in them. Some, like Nyoko, looked merely calculating and no doubt affected a falsely cheerful demeanour whenever clients approached. It all made Temperance feel nauseous in the extreme.

She clenched her fists at her side. There was no way she would ever accept this as her life.

She had to find a way to escape and fast.

'Is there no one we can ask? Not one person who might have seen her?'

Haag watched Midori, Noordholt's concubine, wringing her hands as she argued with him yet again. She'd been in a state of anxiety ever since they returned from the bay to tell her that Temperance was gone without a trace, proving that she'd been in on the secret all along as well – a fact verified by Noordholt when he'd told her that Haag knew all about Temperance's gender. Another excursion hadn't yielded any further results and Midori looked as though she was reaching the end of her tether. Haag stood silently next to Noordholt as the man replied patiently.

'No, I told you, not a single one and there were no dwellings anywhere near the area. Just forest. There were lots of different trails but we'd have no way of knowing which way she went. Or rather, was taken.'

Midori paced the room in front of them. 'This is intolerable! What was she thinking? And how do we get her back? We must make a complaint to the officials here in Nagasaki. Perhaps they can send out a search party?'

The Chief Factor shook his head. 'You know we can't. We'd have to admit that Temperance is a woman, otherwise they'd be looking for a youth. I doubt her captors will stay ignorant about her true status for long.'

'But we have no choice. What else can we do? We can't just sit and do nothing!'

'It could jeopardise the trading rights of the Dutch nation, Midori. You know I can't do that.' Noordholt looked pained, but his mouth was set in a firm line. He glared at Haag as if to emphasise his determination not to allow anyone to talk to the Japanese about the matter. The Chief Factor had stuck to his word and had had Haag under observation ever since their return from the cove, which was a damned nuisance.

Haag deemed it time to intervene. He was happy to keep quiet for the moment as long as something was being done to find Temperance, although he had his own plans for her. He'd deal with Noordholt later. 'Is there no one you trust on the mainland who could help? Any relatives of yours, perhaps? Or someone who can be bribed?'

Midori turned to look at him, hope dawning in her eyes. 'Of course! Thank you, why didn't I think of that? The very thing. If anyone can help us it will be Ichiro.'

'Who's he?'

'My, er ... relative.'

Noordholt nodded and gave Haag a tight smile. 'Good idea. Thank you.' He turned back to Midori. 'You must write to him at once, my love, and I'll go and hire the fastest messenger I can find.'

Haag smiled back, not caring who the man was as long as he did something about finding Temperance. At last, they were making progress.

* * *

After a week Temperance gave up looking for a means of escape. To her despair, she had discovered that the front door was the only way out, as the back of the building was enclosed by an extremely high wall. This was impossible to scale and none of the side windows were big enough to climb out of.

'Once you're here, you stay until they have no further use for you,' one girl whose name was Cho muttered when Temperance tried to ask whether anyone else had ever escaped. 'Even if you managed to get away, they'd hunt you down and kill you as an example. Imada-*san* has spies everywhere.' This was said with such bitterness that Temperance assumed the girl had lost a friend in this way.

'How long have you been here?' she asked Cho, who looked to be in her early teens and happened to have the *futon* next to Temperance's.

'Not sure. I think my parents sold me to Imada-*san* when I was about seven?'

'Your own parents sold you?' Temperance was horrified. How could any parent do such a thing?

Cho shrugged. 'They had no choice if they wanted the rest of the family to eat. I had too many sisters and I might do well here so that I can help them more. Old Mai says I show great promise.'

Temperance envied the girl her stoicism and optimism. She'd obviously embraced her fate and didn't suffer from any of the moral qualms that bedevilled someone brought up as a Puritan. Temperance didn't know how she could ever reconcile her conscience to what was expected of her at the Weeping Willow. It was impossible. She decided her only hope now was to watch out for a chance of escape once she was sold. For the moment, all she could do was to learn whatever they wished to teach her as quickly as possible.

This was easier said than done, however, as she'd soon found out.

'Hold your back straight, as if you had a pole stuck up your behind. No slouching. Bend gracefully. No, no, no, *gracefully* I said, not like a clumsy yokel! By all the gods, how you've managed to survive this long I don't know.'

Old Mai proved to be an ancient lady with a face like a dried currant and eyes that were barely visible, so deeply embedded were they in the folds of wrinkled skin. She was as tiny as a sparrow, but her voice could have carried across mountains. Temperance's training in how to walk and move elegantly while wearing a *kimono* had been entrusted to Mai, and she was a hard taskmaster. She wanted perfection, nothing less, and although Temperance tried her best, it never seemed good enough.

'Your hands are like the wings of a tiny bird, not the great big flapping appendages of a goose. Move them slowly, carefully, as if they are being blown gently by the wind, not buffeted by a storm. Have you no imagination? Again, try it again, girl.'

With a sigh Temperance did as she was told. If the truth be known, she actually liked the irascible old lady for, although she wasn't easy to please, she never looked at Temperance as if she were a freak or an oddity. Everyone else at Imada's establishment did. Most of the other girls, apart from Cho, avoided her or made signs as if to ward off evil whenever she looked at them, and it annoyed Temperance no end.

'They should be used to me by now,' she'd muttered at one point, and old Mai heard her.

'They're superstitious ninnies,' she said, shaking her head. 'Not a rational thought between them, but then that's just as well, isn't it? In their profession you don't need to use your brain. You, on the other hand, think too much.'

It was disconcerting to have someone read your mind to that extent and Temperance tried to protest, although she was pleased that she hadn't been lumped together with the other girls in Mai's mind.

'But I wasn't—'

'Yes, you were. I can see it in your eyes. You're itching to escape from here, but you won't succeed, believe me, so you'd best reconcile yourself to your fate.'

'I know I can't escape.'

'Well, perhaps you do, but I can see your mind hasn't accepted it yet. Don't try to bamboozle me. I'm three times your age, girl,' the old lady snapped. 'Now let's try those moves again, shall we? You need to concentrate.'

Temperance was afraid Mai spoke the truth, but she simply couldn't stop searching for a way out of her predicament, even though she knew the best thing to do would be to bow to the inevitable.

But how could she?

It proved even harder when her lessons with Nyoko began. The girl was a whore, there was no other word for it, and she set out to teach Temperance the tricks of her trade. True to her word, she began by ordering four other girls to hold Temperance down while she examined her to determine whether she was still a maiden or not.

'She is,' was the verdict. 'Won't last long now though, will it?' Nyoko smirked in her usual fashion and the others sniggered. 'I'd better teach you what to do about it then.'

'And if I don't wish to learn?' Temperance had never been so embarrassed in all her life and she knew that her face was virtually on fire.

Outright laughter greeted this question and Nyoko merely shook her head. 'Follow me. I'm going to show you some drawings first, then we're going to watch something.'

The upstairs rooms of this part of the building could be reached via the main staircase from the hall, but there was also a secret staircase hidden behind a screen downstairs. Nyoko took Temperance up to the second floor and into one of the rooms used by the courtesans to entertain their clients.

'Sit down,' the girl ordered.

Temperance sank onto a cushion and waited while Nyoko pulled something out of a cupboard behind a sliding door. 'Here we are. Have a look at these.'

Two hand scrolls were dumped on Temperance's lap and she began to unroll one of them. There were drawings of couples, about a dozen of them, and although in the first two the figures were clothed, the rest featured semi-naked bodies copulating in various ways. Temperance blinked and felt her stomach tie itself in knots. Although she'd been vaguely aware of what men and women did together, the men in the pictures had appendages the size of a bull – she'd seen one once when it was about to mate with some poor cow – and they were depicted in minute detail. Temperance found the sight revolting. For some strange reason the women in the drawings looked to be enjoying what the men were doing to them though, which she found hard to believe. Surely having anything that size inserted into your body must be extremely painful? She shuddered at the thought and tried to give the scrolls back to Nyoko. 'I'd rather not look at these, thank you very much.'

'The gods give me strength,' Nyoko muttered. 'Do as you're told or I'll have you beaten. If you don't look, I can't explain what you have to do, now can I? Not unless I bring a man in to show you.'

'You wouldn't. I mean, you can't ...' Temperance was appalled and completely at a loss as to what to do. All her life she'd been taught that fornication out of wedlock was a great sin and that one's desires were to be controlled by willpower at all times. She knew there were women who didn't adhere to such rules – whores of Babylon her father had called them – but never in her wildest dreams had she imagined she'd have to learn how to become one herself.

'Don't be an idiot. Now listen,' Nyoko said, and proceeded to explain exactly what was happening in the drawings, picture by picture.

Temperance listened in silence, hoping the ordeal would be over quickly, but as soon as she'd finished talking, Nyoko put the scrolls away and pulled Temperance to her feet. 'Now come on, it's time to watch.'

'Watch what?'

The girl didn't reply, but led the way to a small, dark cupboard at the end of the corridor.

'Shhh, now. Look through there,' Nyoko ordered, pointing to a couple of small holes in the wall in front of them. Temperance did as she was bid, but immediately drew back with a gasp.

'I can't! I don't want to see that.'

There was a man and a woman in the room next door, clearly visible through the peepholes, and they were doing exactly the same thing as the couples in the scroll pictures. The only difference was that the man's appendage appeared to be much smaller and both parties were making strange noises, like grunting pigs. Temperance swallowed hard. This was unbearable.

And this was what Imada wanted her to do?

In the darkest moments after her kidnapping she had thought that perhaps she would be ravished by Ryo and his men, which would have been unspeakably vile. But to think of having to actually submit to a complete stranger, and take part in the act while pretending to like it as the woman next door was doing, made her feel seriously ill. 'Is Imada-*san* going to sell me to men like that every day?' she asked, her voice a hoarse whisper.

'No, stupid. You'll belong to only one man, but you'd better learn how to please him or he'll give you to his servants for sport.' Nyoko tittered, then shoved Temperance's head back towards the spyholes. 'Now look and learn. It's really quite easy.'

Revulsion and her father's words of warning warred with sinful curiosity and the need to obey so that she could leave this place soon. The latter won. Temperance reasoned that just to watch couldn't possibly damage her own piety in any way, and as long as she managed to escape before she actually had to do any of this herself, then her soul shouldn't be in jeopardy.

Later, when she had seen more of the physical act of lovemaking than she had ever thought possible, Nyoko took her back downstairs.

'Listen to me. There are many ways of pleasing a man and your future master will expect you to know them well,' she said and began to explain in more detail what would likely be expected of Temperance.

'I'd rather kill myself,' Temperance muttered and turned away, putting her hands over her ears. She could feel her entire body grow hot, then cold, at the thought of having to learn such things. Surely ordinary women were never expected to act thus with their husbands? She'd been told only that she must submit to his needs, as and when the time came for her to marry. There hadn't been talk of anything else.

'Don't be a fool.' Nyoko grabbed her chin and forced her hands down. 'You get used to it, trust me, and you'll be amply rewarded. Who knows, your master may even fall in love with you – there's no accounting for taste – and make you one of his consorts.'

'Never. I won't do this.' Temperance stubbornly kept her eyes tightly shut, no matter what Nyoko said, until the latter finally lost patience.

'Very well, if you insist on learning the hard way, that is your choice.'

Before Temperance knew what was happening, Nyoko had called for Imada-*san* and some of the other girls to come and help. He came striding into the room, already angry at having been disturbed during an afternoon nap. When he was told that his latest acquisition was proving difficult, he didn't hesitate for a moment, but lashed out instantly with both fists. Heavy blows rained down on Temperance, everywhere except her face, and Imada bellowed a string of epithets at her while panting with the effort of hitting as hard as he could.

The beating seemed never-ending to Temperance, but probably only lasted a short while. Whenever she tried to duck or step aside to avoid the worst of it, the other girls pushed her back into Imada's reach. At first, she tried not to cry out, but the pain soon became unbearable and she couldn't help it. This was far worse than any punishment she'd ever received from her father.

'Are you going ... to stop ... being so ... stubborn?' Nyoko's words penetrated Temperance's befuddled mind in snatches.

Temperance held out for as long as she could, but in the end she realised that it was futile and she was only making matters worse for herself by delaying the inevitable.

'Very well,' she cried at last. 'I'll do whatever you say.'

Nyoko stopped Imada by pulling him away, and they both stood glaring at her, his chest heaving. 'See that you do, or I'll have to do this again,' Imada panted. 'I've got better things to do with my time.' Without a backward glance he strode off, closely followed by Nyoko and the others. Temperance noticed that there was no sign of sympathy in their eyes. She was the odd one out, in more ways than one.

When she was alone, she sank down and lay on the floor, curled into a ball, every part of her body throbbing with pain. She cried silently, tears coursing down her cheeks, but not for long. There wasn't any point and if she wished to survive at all, she would have to accept her fate stoically.

A gnarled hand gripped her shoulder and she looked up into the wise old eyes of Mai. 'Come, child,' she said. 'I will take you to the bathhouse. A good long soak in hot water is what you need. There will be bruises, but they'll heal in time. I hope you have learned your lesson? I did warn you.'

Temperance nodded mutely. She had indeed learned her lesson and something inside her had hardened in the process. This was her life for now and she would submit, but she would bide her time. There had to be a way out of this.

Chapter Ten

Nyoko threw herself into teaching her reluctant pupil with gusto, triumphant now that she had the upper hand, and this time Temperance paid attention, albeit listlessly. Her entire body still ached every time she moved and she was as stiff as an old woman with gout.

'Are you listening to me? These things are important if you wish to please your master.' Nyoko frowned.

'If you say so.' Temperance's reply was sarcastic, but the more she listened to Nyoko, the more she began to wonder if perhaps she wasn't overreacting just a little. After all, the other girls here seemed content enough with their lot, apart from the very youngest who, like Temperance, had yet to come to terms with it. Maybe it wasn't such a dreadful thing after all, especially if she would only have one man to please?

'It won't be so bad,' Cho said, when Temperance questioned her again about why she didn't mind being one of Imada's girls. 'If the man you're with is skilled in the art of love-making I'm told it feels heavenly.' She giggled. 'I hope I attract the handsomest of the men.'

'Really?' No one had ever mentioned that to Temperance, but then she hadn't asked.

She had to admit that her father had been rather overzealous with regard to many things. It could be that this was another matter where his views had been a trifle extreme. Temperance cursed herself for never daring to ask Midori about matters of the flesh. Her cousin seemed not to mind when Nico touched her. In fact, they were forever close to each other as if they couldn't bear to be apart. An image of Kazuo came into her mind – Kazuo holding her close in the water, his body soft and warm against hers. She knew that if he were the man she was sold to, she didn't think she would object all that much to giving him her body.

She sighed. There was no chance of that. In fact, she doubted she would ever see him again now. If he came back at all, he would look for her in the little bay and on Dejima, but he would no more find her than Nico and Midori would.

She was lost.

Almost exactly two and a half weeks after her arrival at the Weeping Willow, Temperance was led into the best room in the house. She was teetering on lacquered *geta* sandals so high she thought she would surely fall flat on her face in front of her prospective buyer. She thought of him thus, not as her future master, since that would imply she wanted to work for him, whereas she knew she was nothing more than a chattel to be sold to the highest bidder.

She'd been scrubbed and polished from head to toe, her hair oiled and pulled into an intricate hairstyle which was held in place by pins and combs made of carved wood with little silk flowers and tassels attached to them.

'It's a shame it's so short,' old Mai had muttered. 'But I suppose it will grow. At least it's soft as goose down.' She'd combed it almost reverently, but Temperance wasn't in the mood to even reply to the old lady.

Her face had been powdered to remove any trace of colour and her eyes and mouth carefully outlined with paint. She was wearing a borrowed *kimono* of pink silk, a so called *furisode* with long hanging sleeves, which she'd been given to understand was the fashion for young unmarried women. There were several layers of thinner robes underneath, making her feel overheated. The *kimono* was embroidered to within an inch of its life with a riot of flowers and other nature motifs. Temperance thought it would have been much nicer had the seamstress kept it simple instead of loading as much onto it as was humanly possible. The *kimono* dipped low at the nape of her neck, which had also been powdered, exposing it to view. She'd been told that this was considered attractive to the opposite sex. Why, she had no idea, but it was certainly better than having any other parts of her displayed.

Nevertheless, her stomach roiled, a sick feeling making her want to spew its contents onto the beaten earth floor, but she knew there was nothing much inside her as she'd been unable to eat all day due to nervous tension. A headache nagged the top of her head, stabbing every now and then behind her eyes, but she tried to ignore it. She needed to keep her wits about her now.

A corner of the room had raised flooring covered in slightly grubby *tatami* mats, and Imada was seated there on a cushion next to a man whom he addressed as Tanaka-*sama* or simply *o-tono*, 'my lord'. The latter was dressed splendidly, in clothes of shining azure silk with his clan motif embroidered on the shoulders, back and sleeves. The customary two swords of a *samurai* hung by his side, gleaming with deadly promise. Temperance knew they were kept razor-sharp at all times; so sharp they could cut the head or limb off a person effortlessly in the blink of an eye. A shiver ran up her spine, but she knew she had nothing to fear in that respect as long as she acted the meek maiden. The question was, could she make herself submit to this man?

'Ah, now here she is, my latest acquisition, Tanaka-*sama*.' Imada swept a hand to indicate Temperance, as if the other man couldn't see for himself. She almost snorted. What a buffoon the landlord was.

She studied Tanaka covertly, from under her lashes. There was nothing physically repugnant about him, apart from the fact that he must be old enough to be her father. He was neither too fat nor too thin, and his features were pleasing enough, although she considered his eyes too deep set and narrow. Their calculating gaze made her uncomfortable. His hair was worn in the customary topknot, his forehead shaved to make it appear larger as was the fashion among the *samurai*. He had a moustache and a beard, trimmed and groomed into tidiness, and the rest of him appeared both clean and neat. Why then did he make her skin crawl, Temperance wondered?

If he decided to buy her from Imada, she would in effect be his possession, his slave, to do with as he wished. Unless she could somehow escape and return to Dejima she had no recourse to justice – not being Japanese, her fate would be even worse should she be apprehended by the authorities. It would seem she was well and truly caught in a trap, and if she wanted to live, her choice was clear. She took a deep breath and tried to make herself accept her fate, but couldn't quite manage it.

Standing nearby were Tanaka's servants or guards, while some of Imada's maids scurried round serving refreshments as gracefully as they could. One of the powerful man's retainers moved slightly, shifting from one foot to the other, which drew Temperance's gaze. Something about him seemed familiar and at first she couldn't think what that could be. Then suddenly he looked up briefly from under his straw hat and caught her eye, shaking his head just enough to warn her without anyone else noticing. Temperance swallowed a gasp and almost choked on her own breath.

Kazuo.

She felt as if she had been doused by a bucket of cold water, her lungs constricting in shock. What on earth was he doing here? And at this time? Had he come to save her? Or was he part of the deal? *Dear Lord, what am I to do, to think?*

She looked away from him quickly, having caught the

warning glance that accompanied his gesture, but her limbs began to shake and she had to grit her teeth together to recover her composure. Her thoughts whirled and she blinked to try to focus her attention on the men in front of her instead. She would have to think about the implications of Kazuo's presence later; now was not the time. Not by so much as a flicker of an eye must she reveal that she'd met him before. She didn't know how she knew, but she was certain it would mean instant death for both of them. Taking another deep breath, she made her way slowly towards her present master. She stopped in front of him and his guest and bowed as gracefully as she could, exactly as she'd been taught. Imada smiled.

'You see, my lord,' he said to his guest, 'strange-looking she may be, but she has manners, I've seen to that. Taught her myself much of the time.'

Temperance remained silent, not bothering to refute this blatant lie. It made no difference anyway. Her main problem was that Tanaka was looking her over with what appeared to be some interest. She had hoped he'd be put off by her foreign looks, but he beckoned her closer and she obeyed, after only a slight hesitation. Standing up, he touched her hair and then turned her face towards the light to study her eyes.

'Extraordinary,' he muttered, running his hand up her exposed neck, before poking a finger into her left eyeball. Temperance jumped and blinked back the tears that formed instantly, biting down on her tongue to stop from crying out. Her eye smarted, but he hadn't poked very hard so there wasn't any actual damage, only discomfort. It almost made her laugh that the man obviously trusted Imada so little he had to make sure there was no trickery involved. She derived some small satisfaction from the fact that she wasn't the only one to think Imada a vile, lying toad.

'So how much?' Tanaka was saying, having resumed his seat.

Imada named his price, and Tanaka began to laugh, making Temperance wonder if there was hope after all. She was soon disillusioned as this turned out to be a mere prelude to fierce haggling that went on for what seemed like ages. At last, when Temperance felt she really couldn't bear it any longer, a price was agreed and she became the official property of Tanaka.

As she was led out of the room, she wondered what was in store for her, but when two of her new master's servants were called forward to escort her out towards a waiting palanquin, she was slightly reassured as the one on her left breathed, 'Have faith.'

Kazuo.

What in all the world was she doing here? His water sprite. The woman he'd been dreaming of each night since he left her on Dejima. It beggared belief.

Kazuo kept his head down and his gaze lowered, so as not to give away by so much as a glance that he'd met her before. He'd heard her referred to as Shinju, the name he'd teasingly given her, but how could that be?

Perhaps she'd been tricking him all along? Had she been sent to that bay expressly to attract susceptible males? But it was hundreds of leagues from the place they now found themselves. It made absolutely no sense for her to have travelled that far for such a purpose.

Kazuo shook his head, needing to clear it. Something was wrong. Every fibre of his being sensed it and Temi – or Shinju as he'd better think of her now – had looked cowed, almost desperate. Nothing like the laughing, happy woman he'd met all those weeks ago.

She must have been captured, taken prisoner, and now she

was sold to the very man Kazuo had sworn to bring down. It seemed the strangest of coincidences and it was a damned nuisance. He needed to concentrate on the task at hand, not worry about a woman who wasn't really his concern.

But how could he not? Just one look from those blue eyes made him want to protect her. He had to find a way.

Riding in a palanquin proved to be a strange mode of transport, comfortable and nauseating at the same time. Temperance had cushions to lean on and could while away the hours by looking at the countryside around them, but the swaying motion took a long time to get used to and her stomach refused to settle. It didn't help, of course, that she was worried about what her duties would be once they reached their destination. Having listened to some of the other girls at the Weeping Willow, she was under no illusions. She would not remain a *shojo* for much longer.

Would she be able to bear Tanaka's touch? She knew if she angered him he may well kill her on the spot, but perhaps that was preferable.

She caught only fleeting glimpses of Kazuo during the journey, but spent much of her time thinking about him. It was impossible not to wonder whether he'd had a hand in her capture. Perhaps he'd even sent Ryo and his men to keep watch on the little bay where he'd found her? He had, after all, lured her back with his promises, or so it seemed to her at the time. She couldn't decide whether to believe that he'd been laying a trap for her, or if it was merely coincidence.

Have faith, he'd whispered, but perhaps they were only empty words, uttered to placate her so she wouldn't give away the fact that she'd met him before. It made her angry to think how naïve she'd been, if indeed she had been ensnared. Young, inexperienced with men and ripe for adventure – how he must have laughed to himself to have found such an easy prey if this was his doing. Still, it didn't make sense that he had refrained from taking their dalliance further, unless he too knew her value was higher while untouched?

'Damnation!' she muttered, berating herself yet again for her stupidity. This whole mess was entirely her own fault and she didn't know what to believe any more. In the end, she decided only time would tell.

'I've had a letter from my relative at last.'

Midori walked into the office waving a rolled up piece of paper. Noordholt and Haag, who had been busy with their ledgers, looked up.

'And what does he have to say?' Noordholt put down his quill, as did Haag. He resented being made to do the work of a junior clerk, but the Chief Factor was adamant he wouldn't let him out of his sight and someone had to do Temperance's tasks while she was gone.

'He's sent out spies to see if anyone has heard of a foreign lady, but he thinks we ought to go and report her disappearance to officials in Edo. Although he knows we shouldn't have brought her here in the first place, he thinks that because she's been going around pretending to be a youth we could get away with saying she had us fooled as well. If we made up a story that we'd only just found out she was a woman, and this made her run away, then no blame can attach to us.'

Noordholt rubbed his chin. 'Hmm, I suppose that could work. It would at least serve as mitigating circumstances if they think we'd been duped too. I've never said we were closely related after all. I've been thinking I should bring my visit to Edo forward in any case. It's the capital, after all, and it would be the best place to conceal someone among so many inhabitants. What do you think, Haag, can we be ready in a couple of days?'

As Haag knew, it was the duty of the Chief Factor of the Dutch trading post on Dejima to go to the capital, Edo, every so often to pay his respects to the *Shogun*. And Noordholt had been planning to go soon – a few weeks early wouldn't make much difference. As it was a lengthy journey, however, it was something that needed careful planning and the preparations were nowhere near ready. If it meant finding Temperance sooner though, Haag would be happy to work much faster. He nodded.

'Yes, if we get everyone to help.'

'I'll help too,' Midori offered. 'My maid can look after the children. What would you have me do?'

'If you could look out suitable presents, please, as you'd promised, that would be wonderful.' Nico sent her a grateful smile. 'I'll go and hire bearers and horses now. And obtain the necessary permissions from the mainland officials. Haag, can you find supplies for the journey and plan how many people we need to bring? I'll send Bert with you to assist.'

Haag hurried off to the stores, for once not slacking, even though he was annoyed about having another clerk along with him. It was obvious the man was there to make sure Haag didn't speak to any of the interpreters about anything other than supplies, but right now he didn't care. He was as eager to reach Edo as the Chief Factor, but he'd make sure he was the one who found Temperance. Then perhaps she'd be grateful enough to agree to marry him, or if not, he would persuade her by other means.

Tanaka's estate, when they finally reached it, proved to be situated near the shores of a lake, which Temperance was later told was called Lake Biwa. It was an enormous expanse of water overlooked by distant mountains and impenetrable forests. His holdings comprised thousands of acres of land and a vast compound of buildings of various sizes and shapes, including an imposing central tower four storeys high. High walls of grey stone with white painted render at the top enclosed his domain and they crossed a bridge over a deep moat before entering through an impressive gate flanked by two watch turrets.

Inside were courtyards and gardens, inner gates and walls and a veritable rabbit warren of buildings, all cross-timbered and painted white in between the beams, and all with the characteristic grey tiled roofs with tilted corners. Temperance was much impressed by the sheer size of some of them; indeed Tanaka's home seemed more like a palace to her. He was obviously a man to be reckoned with, and as if to emphasise this fact, scores of men and women scurried back and forth between the houses and a large contingent came running to deal with their master's arrival.

By the time their cavalcade stopped next to the largest building, which was fronted by an ornate entrance porch decorated with intricate carving and gilding the like of which Temperance had never seen before, it was pouring with rain. Tanaka dismounted swiftly, throwing the reins of his horse to the nearest retainer. He disappeared inside without so much as a glance in her direction and Temperance wasn't asked to go with him. Kazuo too had vanished, presumably to attend to his duties, and Temperance was left sitting in the palanquin, trembling with nerves.

She didn't have to wait long. A serving woman carrying a large, oiled paper parasol to shield her from the torrents of water, opened the little sliding door of the conveyance and beckoned for Temperance to follow her towards a building on the opposite side of the compound. A temporary reprieve, but a reprieve nonetheless and she drew a sigh of relief. They squelched their way through deep puddles and mud, quickly becoming soaked to the skin despite the protection of the strange parasol. Temperance was very happy to enter the building at last as the servant bowed her inside, bidding her welcome.

'*Dozo, onegai-shimasu.* Please, enter. *Irasshaimase.* Welcome.'

As was the custom, they removed their shoes by the entrance and proceeded down a long corridor made of smooth, wide wooden planks that squeaked slightly as they trod on them. One side was covered with latticed windows made of rice paper, not see-through but still very thin. These let in a lot of light, making it a bright space where beautiful paintings on the walls opposite were shown to advantage. Doors led into various rooms and Temperance glimpsed yet more paintings, hangings and other embellishments. It was truly sumptuous and even the ceilings were highly decorated with symmetrical shapes picked out in gold leaf.

They turned several times before stopping by an open sliding door. As Temperance gazed inside, she couldn't stop her eyes from widening at the sight. Several large rooms lay before her, all connected by sliding screen doors that were gilded and painted with lovely motifs from nature. The floors were all covered by fresh *tatami* matting which still emitted the sweet fragrance akin to new-mown hay.

One room had a large window like the ones in the corridor made of pieces of white rice paper fitted between squares of wood – a *shoji*. The servant went over to open it a fraction to show her that outside was a verandah and a small private garden. It was all breathtakingly beautiful in its simplicity, with smooth pebble stones immaculately raked into patterns around the edge of an arrangement of larger stones, interspersed with shrubs and flowers. Temperance marvelled that her new master thought her worthy of such fine accommodation.

But what will I have to do to earn it, she thought miserably to herself. She closed her mind to such musings and concentrated on her surroundings instead.

'*Irasshaimase.*' Several more serving women came into the room and chorused their welcome, bowing to her and trying their best not to stare, but not succeeding very well. She smiled.

'I am called Shinju,' she said and bowed back.

'I am Ko, at your service,' said the servant she had first met. 'Would you like to change your clothing, Shinju-*san*?'

'Or take some refreshment perhaps?' added another maid.

'Both would be nice, thank you,' Temperance told them. 'But I have no other clothes so could you just give me a blanket or something to wrap around me while this dries?' She indicated her *kimono*.

'We will give you dry clothes. Please, come this way.' Ko led her into one of the smaller rooms and slid back another screen door, behind which lay a great number of rectangular wicker baskets on shelves. Ko opened the lid of each one to reveal one beautiful garment after another. 'Please, choose a gown and we will help you put it on.'

Temperance's eyes widened again at the sight of at least ten silk kimonos in all the colours of the rainbow. Most were embroidered with seasonal motifs – cherry blossom for spring, red acer leaves for autumn and so on – but some were plainer, perhaps for everyday use. If all these were indeed at her disposal, she was spoiled for choice. Despite the temptation of the gaudier ones, she chose one of midnight blue silk with a sprinkling of silver embroidery and a light grey lining. She didn't feel like dressing up as if it were a special occasion. Then it occurred to her to wonder if that was precisely what she was expected to do.

'Will I be seeing Tanaka-*sama* today?' she asked.

Ko shook her head. 'Not today. You will need to be properly prepared, that takes time. Also, our master has business to attend to. There were urgent messengers waiting for him.'

Another reprieve. Temperance sent up a swift prayer of thanks to God, then stood still while the serving women helped her out of her wet clothes and into dry ones. Despite its plainness, she felt like a princess in the blue *kimono*, but she knew her status was very far from that exalted state, no matter how gilded her cage.

The future looked bleak.

Chapter Eleven

Temperance ate a solitary supper and went to bed early, sleeping soundly now that she knew Tanaka was occupied elsewhere. She fell asleep listening to the rain drumming on the roof and whispering on the foliage outside her verandah, an extremely soothing noise that calmed her spirit. She'd insisted on leaving the sliding door to the garden open so that the fresh scents of rain-soaked earth and greenery from outside mingled with the soft smell of the *tatami* mats. It made a pleasant change from the stuffy odours of Imada's inn and the constant noise and bustle she had experienced there.

When she woke the following day, the rain was still coming down in a steady downpour and she lay on her *futon* for a while, enjoying the sounds of nature. She felt supremely well-rested and delighted in the comfort afforded by such a simple bed, its softness enveloping her and moulding itself to her back. It was a far cry from the hard mattress she'd been given at Imada's house, and a lot cleaner too.

'O-*hayo gozaimasu*.' The serving women, led by Ko once more, came bustling in with a breakfast consisting of rice, soup and pickles.

'Good morning.'

Temperance found that she was surprisingly hungry and devoured every morsel. The meal was served on an exquisite black lacquer tray with a flower motif inlaid in gold leaf, and the dainty bowls containing the food were arranged in a pleasing pattern. They were of matching lacquer ware and so fragile Temperance was almost afraid to hold them. Yet more proof of Tanaka's high status, if proof were needed.

'If you have finished, lady, we will take you to the

bathhouse.' Ko deftly removed the tray and passed it to someone in the corridor outside Temperance's room. 'Follow me, please.'

Temperance was secretly pleased to be given this opportunity to observe the rest of Tanaka's domain with a view to finding an escape route. She looked around with interest, although she tried to do it surreptitiously so as not to rouse suspicion. Ko and the others led her past numerous buildings and along smooth pebble paths through the most incredible gardens Temperance had ever seen in her life. Not a leaf or blade of grass appeared to be out of place, and every bush and tree had been trimmed and placed in its position for a purpose – to give maximum enjoyment to the viewer.

Rocks were scattered in seemingly random arrangements which achieved a harmony with the surrounding area that could not be anything other than man-made even though it looked natural. They also passed several ponds, some with large orange fish in them, some with lotus flowers. Others had tiny waterfalls at one end and were sometimes spanned by bridges of wood or stone. There was something to delight the eye at every turn and Temperance was so entranced, she almost forgot to look for a way out.

The bathhouse was set in a corner of the gardens, and instead of the tiny tub she had been pushed into at Imada's inn, here was a large pool with tendrils of steam hanging just above the surface. Temperance and her ladies whiled away the best part of the morning in this wonderful place and she had never felt so pampered in all her life. Every inch of her was scrubbed clean before she was allowed to enter the pool, and her hair was washed and a sweet-smelling scent added to it. Ko combed it, patiently teasing out every last knot, until it shone like polished mother-of-pearl. Although she knew it was vain, Temperance had always secretly been very proud of her thick tresses and was sorry to have had to cut them.

Before going to Japan her hair had reached past her backside. Perhaps now she could let it grow again.

'Your name suits you, lady,' the servant ventured to say with a shy smile. 'This is like nothing I have ever seen before, and so incredibly soft, like the hair of a baby.' She looked up, a hand over her mouth. 'Not that I meant ...'

'It's all right, Ko-*san*, I'm not offended,' Temperance reassured the maid. 'It is a good thing, having hair like a baby, isn't it?'

'To be sure, lady. That was what I meant.'

'You don't find it frightening or ... ugly?' Temperance was genuinely interested in how these people saw her and took the chance to ask.

Ko shook her head vehemently. 'Of course not, lady,' but she didn't look her new mistress in the eyes.

'I don't mind if you do, I was merely curious.' Ko's reaction to her words led her to ask another question. 'Is Tanaka-*sama* a hard taskmaster then? You all seem loath to voice your opinions.'

'Servants do not have opinions, unless they are specifically asked. Our lord is no harsher than any other. He has to be obeyed.'

'Hmm, I thought so.' Temperance stifled another sigh. Ko's answer didn't reassure her nor bode well for the future. Butterflies began to dance in her stomach once more. She'd managed to suppress all thoughts of her coming ordeal during the morning, but now her fears returned tenfold. If only there was a means of escape.

On the way back to her rooms, she paid more attention to her surroundings and kept an eye out for any possible way out, but to her frustration she saw guards posted everywhere. Anyone wanting to pass through a gate obviously had to explain their business. With her strange looks, there was no way she could hope to leave unnoticed, even if she managed to come up with a plausible excuse.

Tanaka's exquisite palace was nothing but a fortress designed to keep his enemies out and his women in.

The afternoon passed pleasantly enough as the ladies taught Temperance an easy board game.

'You have played before?' Ko asked, when Temperance caught on quickly.

'No, not this particular game, but something similar.' For some reason the simple pastime made her feel terribly homesick, missing Midori and her family. She should have been content with her lot, staying in Plymouth with Daniel instead of traipsing halfway across the world only to end up in this predicament. Midori and Nico must be thinking the same thing right now and cursing themselves for allowing her to accompany them. What had happened back on Dejima when she was found to be missing? Her relatives would be extremely worried and they had no way of tracing her. Even if they guessed that she'd gone to the cove again and were lucky enough to find it, there wouldn't be any sign of what had happened. They might even think her dead. And they couldn't involve the Japanese authorities for obvious reasons. Their hands were tied and Temperance had no hope of rescue whatsoever.

Dear Lord, what a mess.

She couldn't banish the knot of nerves nestling in her stomach as she wondered when she would be sent for. There was no doubt but that she had been dressed for her master's benefit. The *kimono* she wore had been selected for her this time and was one of the gaudier ones, made of bright green silk with gold, red and orange embroidery in the shape of acer leaves. It seemed fitting now that autumn was approaching. A matching *obi,* as the belt was called, had been tied around her. The robe's neckline dipped low in the back, in the manner of a courtesan, which Temperance supposed was apt. It was what she would soon become after all.

Her hair had been combed yet again and swept up on top of her head in an intricate creation. Jewelled and lacquered combs and ornaments adorned her hair – as many as nine or ten if she hadn't miscounted. Her face had been powdered with rice powder and her eyes and mouth painted.

'Must I be painted like this?' Temperance dared to ask, but the perplexed expression on Ko's face was all the answer she needed. 'No, forget I asked.' It was simply the done thing, obviously. She took one look at herself in a small hand mirror and wondered whether to laugh or cry. The face staring back at her definitely wasn't her own. It belonged to a stranger.

She explored her little garden briefly, while there was a short break in between rain showers. Although it was lovely – a miniature version of the main garden with symmetrically arranged paths and perfectly trimmed plants and shrubs – it was surrounded by a six foot high wall and there was no gate to the outside world. The end wall had tiny slits through which one could admire the view towards Lake Biwa, but this only served to emphasise Temperance's feeling of being locked up. Her gilded cage was in fact nothing but a glorified prison and she wasn't allowed to go anywhere without leave.

Once she attempted to stray into the corridor, ostensibly to look at a particularly fine wall hanging which could be seen through the door, but she was gently asked to remain in her room. 'For your own safety, lady,' Ko said, but Temperance didn't believe that for an instant. At the end of the corridor outside her suite of rooms she had glimpsed several guards, and although Ko told her that they were merely for her protection, Temperance doubted this very much.

'At what time does Tanaka-*sama* usually eat?' she finally asked, unable to stand the suspense any longer.

Ko and the others looked at each other with puzzled expressions, then outside into the darkness. 'Well, he should have sent for you by now, but perhaps he has been detained. Would you like me to make enquiries?'

'Yes, please.' Temperance tried not to let her impatience with this cat-and-mouse game show in her voice. It wasn't Ko's fault after all that she found herself in this situation. The poor woman was only doing her duty. Having waited this long, however, Temperance now wanted the dreaded encounter over and done with. She'd been steeling herself all day, telling her mind to try and detach itself from what was happening to her, but it was difficult to keep up this bravado. If the wretched man didn't request her presence soon, she would break down and that would never do. She would lose face completely.

Ko came back with a smile. 'You may come with me now,' she said, and held open the screen door for Temperance to pass through. She cast a critical glance over her charge then nodded to herself as if pleased with her handiwork. 'The master is waiting.'

Kazuo ducked into a doorway when he heard voices and steps approaching. He'd been sneaking around, trying to find a way into the women's quarters without being seen. He had to find out what had become of Temi, talk to her, make sure she was all right, but it had proved impossible so far.

There were guards everywhere, damn them.

He'd seen her being led away by a servant the day before, treated with politeness and respect the way a treasured object would be. As the concubine of a powerful lord that would be her right. Kazuo guessed that she was to be prepared for her first encounter with the man who'd bought her. Pampered, dressed in fine clothing, showered with gifts – although the latter perhaps not until she had fulfilled her part of the bargain. And fortunately his lordship had been too busy the day before to give his new plaything any thought.

Today, however, was different. The knowledge of what Tanaka would probably do to her this evening made Kazuo's blood boil, but he took deep breaths to quell the fury. He had no right to this anger. None whatsoever.

But that didn't make it any easier to bear.

Perhaps she wasn't as innocent as he'd thought though? Tanaka had bought her from that vile tea house and it seemed clear she'd spent some time there. Who knew what she'd learned or been made to do while she was there?

Yet somehow Kazuo couldn't imagine Temi tainted in such a way. And he'd sensed her desperation.

Gazing out from behind the doorjamb now, he saw two women walking along the corridor and ground his teeth. He was too late. *Chikusho!*

'This way, Shinju-*san*,' the servant who led the way murmured, but Kazuo's gaze fixed on the woman behind her – Temi. It wasn't his Temi any longer though, the naturally beautiful water sprite, but a doll-like imitation of her. Face painted, hair dressed and bedecked with fine ornaments, fancy silk clothing. A concubine worthy of a very rich man. The only difference was her lustrous pale hair and, if she'd looked up, her strange eyes.

Kazuo wanted to reach out and pull her through the door as she walked past. Spirit her away and keep her safe from the old lecher towards whose room she was heading. But he knew he couldn't. It would achieve nothing except his own and Temi's certain death. Gone would be any hope of revenge for the wrongs done to his father. Any hope, however slim, of ever being with Temi again.

He had to let her go. It was her fate and she wasn't for him.

But by all the gods, it was the hardest thing he'd ever done in his life.

Temperance followed Ko reluctantly. The knot in her stomach had solidified and she found it hard to breathe, but she was determined not to let her nervousness show. At least she could hide her feelings behind the painted mask that was her face. There would be no betraying blushes to give her away with all that powder covering her skin.

They crossed several courtyards before reaching the back of the main residence, where softly lit lanterns swung slightly to and fro in the evening breeze outside a smaller, less grand, entrance.

'*Dozo onegai shimasu.*' Ko-*san* bowed and indicated that Temperance should now follow the lady who was waiting inside and then disappeared into the darkness. Temperance swallowed hard and took off her shoes before hurrying after the servant, who seemed somewhat impatient.

The corridors in this building were much larger than in the one where Temperance was lodged, and every surface, wall and ceiling alike, was decorated with exquisite paintings of birds, trees and animals. Gilded metal decorations adorned handles and wooden posts, and the floors in the rooms they passed were covered in the softest of *tatami*. The whole gave a feeling of sumptuous opulence that was at the same time beautiful and overbearing, making Temperance feel small and insignificant. The serving woman stopped before one of the screen doors, knocked, then pulled it open and prostrated herself on the floor just inside. Temperance followed suit, unsure of the correct etiquette, and surmised that she had done the right thing when the woman merely announced her presence. 'Shinju-*san*, my lord.'

'Excellent. Come over here and be seated.'

Temperance looked up into the face of Tanaka and

suppressed the urge to recoil. He was sitting on a cushion, looking stiff and formal in a luxurious black robe, but there was a look of satisfaction in his glittering eyes that was far more unsettling than the thought of what he was about to do to her.

'You speak our language very well, I have been told,' he commented as she scurried forward and kneeled on a cushion opposite his own. There was a table in between them, laden with food, and to Temperance it seemed like a blessed safety barrier, shielding her from his onslaught for the moment.

'Yes, my lord,' she replied. 'I'm still learning, but I can understand most words now.'

'Good, good. You can tell me of your country while we eat.'

Temperance forced herself to eat whatever was put in front of her, but it all tasted like sawdust and she could never afterwards recall what it was. Nor could she remember any particulars of their conversation, which consisted mostly of Tanaka asking questions that she answered to the best of her ability. He was interested to hear about the recent civil war in England, but couldn't understand the reasoning behind it. Temperance couldn't either, if she was perfectly honest, but she did her best to explain that many of her countrymen had been unhappy with the way their king had been governing and had taken it upon themselves to challenge him.

'Ah, so now you have a *shogun* perhaps, just like us,' Tanaka said. 'He is the true ruler, not the king?'

'No, no *shogun*. At the moment the country is ruled by Parliament, a sort of council I suppose you could call it.' Temperance had never thought about it and cared even less. Her disinterest must have shown in her voice, for it was at this point that Tanaka clapped his hands for the servants to remove the food, then indicated that she should proceed him into an adjoining chamber.

'Let us not discuss any more politics, we have better things to do,' he said with a wolfish smile that made Temperance want to disgorge the contents of her stomach then and there. She hung onto her dinner and her composure by sheer force of will and walked through the door with her head held high, determined not to show weakness.

As she'd suspected, they had entered his sleeping chamber, another magnificently decorated room, albeit on a smaller scale. There was a huge *futon*, at least twice the size of Temperance's own, spread out in the middle of the floor, with a coverlet of jewel-hued silk in different shades of red, ochre and yellow. Tiny lanterns were suspended around the walls, giving off a subdued light that was no doubt intended to create an even more intimate mood. The air was perfumed by incense sticks which burned slowly on a low table in one corner, the smoke curling lazily upwards in an ever increasing spiral.

In another corner of the room a cupboard door had been left half open, and Temperance glimpsed a small alcove with staggered shelves built into its recess. These held a few precious ornaments, no doubt collected together for their beauty, which drew the eye. One in particular caught Temperance's gaze – on a plinth of pure gold sat a little lioness, exquisitely carved out of the purest pale green jade. It had to be a female as in front of her an equally beautiful jade lion cub seemed to be playing with a ball made out of a huge natural pearl, lustrous and creamy. The lioness wasn't looking at her offspring, however, but straight at Temperance and her mouth was open in what looked like a mocking grin. A shudder passed through Temperance at this sight. Although she knew it was ridiculous, she felt the lioness was laughing at her. It seemed a bad omen, but there was no time to ponder such matters.

'Lie down,' Tanaka ordered, and Temperance felt panic spread through her. He'd turned away, obviously certain in the knowledge that he would be obeyed without question, and was busy undoing the belt of his black tunic. Temperance searched the rest of the room with her eyes for something, anything, with which to stop this happening, but apart from the swords hanging at his side, there was no weapon of any kind. Nothing to defend herself with.

A numb sensation unfurled inside her veins as Temperance tried once more to resign herself to her fate. With heavy steps, she made her way over to the bed and lay down on her back, fixing her eyes on the lovely ceiling, but seeing none of its beauty. This was it, this was the end. *Accept your fate, accept*, she chanted silently to herself, but when he came towards her wearing only an open robe with a loincloth underneath, she had to clench her fists inside the sleeves of her *kimono* in order to stop from crying out in fear.

'You are wearing too many clothes,' he complained and fumbled with the knot of the rope which held her *obi* in place. 'I'm sure I gave orders for you to wear something light,' he muttered. In his haste, the knot defied him and he turned to grab the smaller of his two swords and used it to slash the rope neatly in two. 'There, that's better.'

The *obi* was pulled off and Temperance had a vision of herself as a parcel being unwrapped by a greedy child, which made hysterical laughter bubble up inside her. She quelled it and her thoughts sobered once more when he succeeded in opening the three layers of robes underneath and bared her to his gaze. He stared at her for a moment, then grunted.

'A bit fleshy, aren't you?' he murmured, putting a hand on one of her breasts and squeezing painfully. 'Well, no matter. Turn around. At least you have a neck like a swan.'

He rolled her over and pulled the robe away from her back, exposing her neck and shoulders. This time his grunt sounded more satisfied, and he began to caress her soft skin, his rough fingers sending shivers of disgust through her. With another huge effort of will, she kept still, bending her neck slightly forward to show it off to its best advantage, as Nyoko had taught her. At least if he concentrated on that, she didn't have to look at him and see the hateful lust she'd glimpsed in his eyes.

His hands continued to roam, pulling her garments off entirely so that he could spread his palms across her behind. He pressed himself against her, and she felt the evidence of his desire through the loincloth while he nibbled his way down her neck and shoulder, the harsh beard on his chin rasping her sensitive skin. She shuddered, but it was not with any matching desire.

'Show me some of your whore's tricks, then,' he urged. 'Don't just lie there.'

'It ... it's my first time, my lord,' she stammered, swallowing a sob that tried to push its way out of her throat.

'Hmm, yes, I forgot. I paid extra for that, did I not?'

His right hand reached the most sensitive part of her and she tensed, wanting to run for her life, but he held her fast with his other hand with a not too gentle grip on her arm. She thought of begging for mercy, of asking him to ransom her to her family instead, but knew it would be futile. He was too worked up, too far gone in his intent, to stop now. Only a miracle could save her, unless she took matters into her own hands. But how?

She registered the glimmer of metal out of the corner of one eye and realised that the smaller of his swords was still lying close by. Desperation welled up inside her, and for a brief moment she wondered what would happen to her if she killed him. No doubt she would be executed in a painful manner, unless she took her own life as well. *It doesn't matter. Anything is better than this, surely?* Blinking back tears that refused to stay contained any longer, she reached out a hand towards the shining object.

Just as her fingers hovered over the hilt, however, there

was a loud knocking on the door. 'My lord, urgent message,' someone shouted.

'Go away,' Tanaka ordered, his voice quivering with indignation and as yet unfulfilled desire.

The knocking became more insistent. 'My lord, this cannot wait. I swear on my life.'

A string of expletives came tumbling out of Tanaka's mouth, but he let go of Temperance and stood up, wrapping the loincloth around himself in haste. He pushed her down onto the *futon*. 'Stay there, I'll be right back.'

With angry strides, he walked over to the door and jerked it open. 'What is it?' he thundered.

'H-here, my lord. This arrived just now and I was told to deliver it immediately, on pain of death.'

'I'll kill you myself if it isn't as urgent as you say,' Tanaka snarled and broke open the seal of a document. Temperance dared a glance over her shoulder and saw him frown as he read, then turn an angry shade of puce. Finally he let out a bellow of rage that echoed round the room, making Temperance cower among the bedclothes, but fortunately his anger seemed to be directed elsewhere.

'*Konyaro!* The son of a *yujo*! He dares to lay his hands on what is mine, does he? Well, we will just see about that. Saddle my horse, bring me clothes for travel, gather the men. We leave as soon as I'm ready. *Move, imbecile!*'

Temperance appeared to have been forgotten, but she didn't dare move and stayed where she was while the sounds of shouting and stomping reverberated round the room next door. Some time later, when all had gone quiet, she sat up and pulled her discarded robes on, holding them together with her hands instead of tying on the belt. She waited for what seemed like ages then, gathering up her *obi*, she tiptoed into the adjoining room. There was a manservant there who looked surprised to see her. She bowed low.

'*Gomen-kudasai.* I am sorry to disturb you,' she said, 'but do you know if my presence is still required? Only I was told to wait.'

He shook his head. 'No, lady, the master has left for Edo. He will not have further need of your services tonight.'

Temperance felt quite light-headed with relief and had to put out a hand to steady herself against the wall. 'He's gone?' she asked incredulously. 'To Edo?'

'Yes, lady.' The servant was staring at her blonde hair in fascination and seemed to forget who he was talking to. 'There was bad news. The lady Akina, his wife, well, apparently she has been unfaithful to Tanaka-*sama*. She stayed in Edo, while he came south to see to his estates, and it would appear she was caught with another man in her rooms. His lordship's brother found them.'

Temperance's head whirled. God really had worked a miracle and she couldn't believe her luck. 'So Tanaka-*sama* has gone to Edo to confront her?'

'Oh, he'll punish her all right,' the servant said. 'Then she'll be sent back to her family in disgrace, no longer his wife. His main concern, however, will be the lover.' The servant shook his head with a rueful smile. 'I wouldn't want to be in his shoes, that's for certain.'

'Poor lady.' Temperance could imagine Tanaka in full fury and didn't envy his wife the coming confrontation.

'She brought it on herself. She has greatly dishonoured her family and that of Tanaka-*sama*.' The servant suddenly seemed to remember who he was talking to. 'Anyway, it's none of our business. You had better return to your quarters. Do you know the way?'

'Yes, yes, I think so, thank you. Goodnight, then.' A thought occurred to her and she stopped by the door to ask one final question. 'How far is Edo from here?'

'That depends on the speed at which one travels, but I

should think our master will be gone at least a week, even though he rides fast. In fact, he will probably be gone for two weeks.'

Temperance wanted to dance and cheer, but knew that wouldn't be appropriate so she held herself in check, although with some difficulty. She had been granted yet another reprieve, now all she had to do was find a way out of this place.

She had two weeks at most.

Chapter Twelve

The rain ceased at last and the following afternoon Temperance was able to spend more time in her little garden. She had asked for something to occupy her hands with and been given some embroidery threads and materials, as well as a tiny basket to carry it in, and this she brought outside. There was a small stone bench, with two ornate lions as supports, standing against the back wall, and as there was a cherry tree shading that particular spot from the sun, Temperance sat down and went to work.

'Would you like a motif for your embroidery, lady?' Ko asked.

'No, thank you, I'll make something up myself. Do you have a piece of charcoal I could draw a pattern with, please?'

'Yes, of course.'

Temperance looked around and her eyes fastened on a clump of bamboo planted nearby, where a tiny butterfly hovered. She quickly sketched this out on the piece of material on her lap, then showed it to Ko. 'Will this do, do you think?'

'It is lovely. You have a flair for drawing.'

'Thank you, so I've been told.' Temperance knew that she'd inherited this trait from her aunt, Midori's mother, Hannah, who had been very good at drawing. Hannah hadn't had the patience for sewing and instead painted on parchment or canvas, whereas Temperance always found embroidery soothing and something she enjoyed very much.

She set to work and lost herself in the various shades of green needed for her composition. The silk threads were of the finest quality and a joy to work with and at any other time Temperance would have been very content to be occupied in this way. Here, however, it was impossible to forget where she was and why.

Ko and the other ladies drifted in and out of the open door, occasionally leaving her on her own while they went to fetch refreshments or were busy with other household matters. Temperance observed them surreptitiously, but didn't move from her place. She thought it best to appear outwardly resigned to her fate, even if her thoughts were in constant turmoil.

It was hot, even in the shade, and Temperance was almost lulled to sleep as the heat became more stifling around midday. The droning of bees and the sound of voices in the distance gave her little oasis an almost dreamlike quality, and she had to put her embroidery down for a while when her eyelids became heavy.

'Will you not come in for a rest, lady?' Ko called from the doorway. 'We can pull down the bamboo blinds to keep the heat outside.'

'Yes, in a moment, thank you.'

'I will make your *futon* ready then.'

Ko disappeared inside and Temperance began to gather up her things, putting the materials away in her new basket. She was just looking around one last time to make sure she hadn't dropped anything, when she heard a whisper nearby.

'Temi-*san*.'

She froze, then waited to hear more. Only one person had ever called her that – Kazuo. Even if he hadn't, she would have known his voice anyway, but where was it coming from?

'Stand up and walk slowly along the wall to inspect the flowers to your left,' she heard him whisper.

She picked up her basket and did as she was told. The flowers in question were near one of the spyholes in the back wall and Temperance gathered that he must be outside.

'You're taking a huge risk,' she breathed.

'I know, but I had to speak to you. Are you unharmed? I heard Tanaka-*sama* left rather abruptly last night. Did he …?'

'No, no he didn't, but when he returns … I must escape before then! Is there a way?'

Temperance realised belatedly that perhaps she shouldn't have told him anything. What if he was a spy working for Tanaka? It did seem like too much of a coincidence after all, him being here of all places. She also recalled her previous suspicions that he'd been in cohorts with Ryo, hoping she'd go back to the cove so the outlaws could kidnap her. She bit her lip; she definitely should have been more careful. His next words reassured her though.

'I will find a way, don't give up hope.'

'You'll help me?'

'I'll try.'

'You … you hadn't planned for me to be here?'

'No, why on earth would I do that?' She heard confusion in his voice and it sounded genuine, which further quelled her anxiety. 'Come and do your embroidery here as often as you can and I will come again. Now I must go. *Sayonara*.'

Could she trust him? Did she have a choice? He was her only hope really. Temperance bent to smell the delicate fragrance of the flower she had been admiring once more, then turned slowly and headed for the verandah. There was no sign of Ko and she prayed that no one had overheard her speaking to Kazuo. If he was caught outside her garden … No, it didn't bear thinking about. She hoped he was very careful.

As she lay down on the *futon* to rest, a feeling of hope bubbled up inside her for the first time in weeks.

She had an ally.

She had Kazuo.

* * *

Three days went by with no further sign of him and Temperance began to wonder if she'd dreamed the entire episode in the garden. She had, after all, been very sleepy, but surely her mind was not so desperate that it could imagine hearing his voice?

Each morning and afternoon, weather permitting, she went to sit on the little bench by the back wall. As she didn't make any more attempts to wander away from her rooms, her ladies began to relax their vigilance ever so slightly. On several occasions she found herself alone in the garden, but to her chagrin she didn't hear any whispers from outside. She wondered what had happened and fretted in case Kazuo had been caught loitering outside her wall. There was no way she could ask, of course, and she had to suffer the torment of not knowing.

Finally, in the afternoon of the third day, the voice came again.

'Temi-*san*? Nod if you can hear me.'

Temperance nodded slightly and held up her embroidery as if inspecting the work. Then with an exaggerated sigh, she put it down on the bench beside her and stood up, stretching and yawning, before wandering slowly along the wall towards the flowers near the spyhole.

'Well done. Are you as good at climbing as you are at swimming?'

'How do you mean?'

'If you wish to escape, you're going to have to climb this wall.'

Temperance looked at it with dismay. 'But it's at least two feet taller than I am. I can barely even reach the top with my fingers.'

'There is a tree, isn't there? I can see it from this side. If you could pull yourself up, then I will catch you on this side. It's the only way.'

'Now?' She scanned the garden, but Ko and the others remained inside for the moment.

'No. You must make it a habit to rise early. Say you wish to watch the sunrise over the lake, alone. Then on the seventh day from now, you must climb the wall and I'll be waiting.'

'That long? What if Tanaka-*sama* comes back before then?'

'He won't. There has been word. Do you trust me?'

'I … yes.' Temperance still wasn't sure she did, but it was either that or resign herself to a future with Tanaka. She would rather throw in her lot with Kazuo, whatever his motives, of that she was sure.

'Good. Then I will see you seven days hence.'

'Where are you going, lady?' A very sleepy Ko stuck her head out from under the covers and stared at Temperance with a frown. The grey light of dawn was only just creeping into the room and all was quiet save for a dog barking in the distance.

'I just want to watch the sunrise over the lake. I heard someone say it was particularly fine this time of year and I thought I would be able to see it through the holes in the wall,' Temperance whispered.

'Oh. I'll come with you then.'

'No need, Ko-*san*.' Temperance gave a quiet little laugh. 'I'll be fine. It's not as though I'm going far. Nothing can happen to me in the garden, now can it?'

She tiptoed out of the room and made her way down the steps and along the path to the back wall, fairly sure that Ko would be watching her nonetheless. She stayed motionless by the spyhole until the sun rose in all its splendour, then made her way back inside. Ko was in her bed, but her eyes were open.

'Oh, Ko-*san*,' she whispered, excitedly, 'that was indeed amazing. If I'm awake, I'll watch it again tomorrow. What a sight! You must come and watch too if you're not asleep.'

Ko smiled back, then relaxed as she saw Temperance lie down on her bed once more. 'I've seen it before,' she murmured. 'Many times.'

One step at a time, Temperance thought to herself. Please God, let the woman be lulled into a sense of security.

The night before the seventh day Temperance couldn't sleep at all. It had been difficult enough to make herself wake up early the other days, but this time she couldn't take any chances. If she wasn't by the wall at the appointed hour, she knew she'd be lost. Tanaka would come back very soon and she felt sure that everyone would be more vigilant after his return, including her own guards. Then her chances of slipping away would be non-existent.

She tried not to toss and turn, and breathed a silent sigh of relief as the first slivers of light stole into the room at last and she began to make out shapes in the darkness. Ko was snoring and didn't stir when Temperance made her way stealthily out of bed. There was no sound from the room next door where the other ladies slept either. For the last two mornings, Ko-*san* hadn't moved so much as a muscle when her charge went into the garden, and Temperance prayed the woman would remain asleep today as well.

Wearing only a bed gown and *tabi*, the strange socks with a separate section for the big toe, she walked quietly towards the verandah just as she had done every morning for the past few days. She made no less noise than usual; in case Ko woke up she wouldn't want her to think there was anything special about this day's sunrise viewing. Once out in the garden, Temperance made her way to the spyhole, then waited, on tenterhooks in case Kazuo didn't keep his word.

All was silent, save for the chirping of a few birds who appeared to be clearing their throats, ready for the day's singing. As Temperance strained to hear the slightest sound, she caught only the sighing of the breeze and the occasional call of an animal. At last a voice whispered outside, 'Temi?'

'Yes, I'm here.'

'Then climb, and quickly please.'

She didn't need to be told twice. Making her way over to the tree, she cast one last glance towards the verandah, but Ko didn't appear to have moved at all and no one was watching her. She grabbed a sturdy branch and pulled herself up, grabbing the trunk of the tree with her legs as much as possible. Thanks to the self-defence training Midori had given her, she had developed hitherto unused muscles. She sent a silent thank you to her cousin now as she managed to heave herself up to the level of the wall's crest.

She felt as if she'd been making a terrible racket, the leaves on the branch rustling and her feet scrabbling for a foothold against the bark, but when she paused for a moment to listen, there was still no movement from inside the building. With one last enormous effort, she flung one leg over the top of the wall, then pushed herself into a sitting position and looked down. In the semi-darkness below she saw Kazuo with his arms stretched up towards her. 'Jump!' he urged, and she hesitated only briefly before she let go of the tree.

Kazuo caught her, but the impact was such that they fell to the ground together, with him underneath taking the brunt of it. He made a muffled sound then embraced her quickly before pushing her upwards. 'There is no time to talk,' he whispered. 'We must leave immediately, before my absence and yours is noted. Come.'

He took her hand and together they set off at a half-run in the direction of the lake. Temperance let him lead the way without questioning him as to their destination. She didn't much care where they were going, as long as it was away from here. Another wall blocked their way out of the garden, but Kazuo took her to a small back gate which was only manned by a single guard, who was yawning behind a half-raised hand.

'Wait behind this tree,' Kazuo whispered and Temperance nodded, peeking out from behind the trunk to see what he would do. The poor guard was half asleep, and it proved easy for Kazuo to sneak up behind him and hit him on the side of the head with the handle of his sword. The man went down without a sound and Kazuo beckoned Temperance forward. 'Hurry.'

Outside the wall was a moat, but a bridge spanned it nearby and they made their way to it stealthily. Presumably the guards were all on the inside of the closed gate at night as there was no one about here either. They ran on silent feet across to the other side as fast as they possibly could. After that, it didn't take long to sprint down to the edge of the lake and Kazuo led her along the shore a little way to a place where they were shielded from view by trees, before he stopped.

'Now we swim,' he said.

'What?'

'It will throw anyone following us off the trail. If we don't steal a boat nor any horses, they will assume we've left on foot and will look for us along the roads or in the forests. I doubt they will imagine us swimming, so that is what we must do. Besides, if they bring dogs to track us, there won't be any scent for them to follow.'

Sunrise was coming ever closer and the grey sky had turned a paler shade of silver, but over the lake hung little clouds of mist, floating sleepily just above the surface of the water. Temperance realised this would provide excellent cover for them.

'Go on, take your clothes off. This is not the time to be modest,' Kazuo chided, while divesting himself of his own clothing. From behind a small bush he retrieved a large wooden tub, which he must have hidden there previously, and Temperance saw that it already contained a bundle. Kazuo added his clothes, swords and shoes, then picked up the garments Temperance had removed and put them in the tub as well. Shivering in the chill of the early morning, she waded into the water after him, and saw him unfurl a rope that had been tied to the tub, which he looped around his wrist.

'That was well thought of,' she murmured and he grinned at her.

'I didn't want to have to walk around in wet clothes for the rest of the day. Now swim, as fast as you can. It will keep you warm if nothing else.'

The water felt cold and Temperance had to clench her teeth together in order to submerge her body without shrieking. She swam after him with quick strokes, shuddering as the icy water enfolded her, but she knew it wasn't just the cold which was making her body act like that. Part of it was a reaction to the escape and fear that they would be discovered any moment now. She tried to listen for sounds of pursuit, but couldn't hear anything other than the shushing noise of the tiny waves rushing by.

Dear God, please help us now, she prayed. He had helped her once before, would he do so again?

Kazuo knew that Temi was a good swimmer as he'd witnessed this for himself the day they met, but he was still impressed when she managed to keep up with him for a long time without complaining. They both kept their splashing to a minimum, which made it more difficult to swim fast, but they soon settled into a rhythm that took them away from Tanaka's domain in a short space of time. Kazuo kept the shore in sight as much as possible, but stayed as far out as he dared so that the thick mist hid them from view.

He could see the tops of the trees by the lakeside, but hopefully no one there could see them. The foggy tendrils could have been interpreted as an extraordinary piece of luck, aiding their escape, but he believed it was his ancestors' way of assisting them. He had been born on an extremely misty day and his mother told him it was a sign that mist would always be his friend thereafter. He hoped she was right. The swirling mass was certainly helping now. It must mean the *kami* of those who had gone before them had come to give him their blessing. He was extremely grateful.

He glanced at the woman by his side, wondering what it was about her that had captivated him to the extent that he was now risking his mission for her sake. Had he gone mad or had she perhaps cast a spell on him? From the moment he'd set eyes on her, he had been fascinated, and when he saw her at the mercy of Tanaka and the loathsome Imada, he just knew he had to help her somehow. It was sheer madness and he had, as yet, not even a fixed plan as to where they were going. His main concern had been to spirit her away from Tanaka's estate before it was too late. Now what was he to do with her?

As if she'd read his thoughts, she glanced at him, her lips quivering slightly with cold. 'How much further?' she whispered.

'As far as we can manage. We're not far from the shore, so we can stop any time, but the further away we are, the better. Can you continue a while longer?'

She nodded and clamped her teeth together so hard he saw a muscle in her jaw twitch. He could tell that she was trying to be brave, but he was asking a lot of her and he needed to make sure she stayed strong as they weren't out of danger yet. Far from it, in fact.

'We can rest for a moment if you wish, just float. Here, let us share our body heat.' He stopped swimming and pulled her into his arms, treading water, as he'd done in the sunlit bay where they first met. Lake Biwa on a cool early autumn morning was a far cry from that warm haven, but as he held her close the heat between them was, if possible, even more intense in comparison to the cold all around them. He felt her relax her tired muscles, letting him do most of the work of keeping them afloat, and her soft curves moulded themselves to his hard body as if the two were meant to be one. It was a surreal moment, enveloped as they were by moisture of one kind or another on all sides, and with the tub containing their belongings bobbing nearby like a child's toy boat.

Pale slivers of daylight had begun to reach through the mist and when Temi turned her face up to his, Kazuo saw the trust in her eyes and was deeply moved. Acting on impulse, he buried his face in the hollow of her throat, savouring the feel of her soft skin against his cheek and mouth. She responded by leaning into him and he felt her quivering again, although not with cold this time. With an inward sigh he moved his head away, then just held her. This was not the time, he told himself sternly, and he couldn't abuse her trust, no matter how fierce the desire that raged inside him. He knew that she relied on him to guide her to safety and this thought spurred him on.

'Can you continue now?' he asked gently, releasing her from his grip, but not letting go of her arms until her legs started to move.

She nodded and wordlessly they began to swim once more. Kazuo closed his eyes and prayed for strength of mind and help from his ancestors and the goddess of the lake.

He would need all the assistance he could find this day.

Chapter Thirteen

It had been a long and tedious journey and Haag wasn't the only one to heave a sigh of relief when the Dutch party arrived at the inn in Nihonbashi Hongokucho where they were to stay. It was situated not too far from Edo castle, where the *Shogun* held court, but the inn's location didn't really matter because, as always, the foreigners weren't allowed to leave its confines. The only time they were permitted to set foot outside was for their obligatory visit to the castle.

'What's the point of coming all this way if we can't even see the sights?' Haag grumbled, but he knew the rules as well as everyone else. The *Shogun* didn't like foreigners and they were there on sufferance. If they wanted to continue to trade with Japan, they had to accept all the edicts and restrictions put on their movements. There was no other choice.

Haag knew that a few coins could work miracles, however, and he had no intention of staying cooped up here, kicking his heels for weeks on end. As soon as all his fellow countrymen had taken to their beds, he went in search of the innkeeper's son, whom he'd seen earlier loitering in the courtyard. Most youths were always ready for a bit of fun and in Haag's experience they were usually kept short of money by their parents. Hopefully, that would make this one more amenable to a little bribery. This proved to be the case.

Haag's grasp of Japanese wasn't very good, but he managed to make himself understood with a few words and a lot of gestures. 'Women. Drinking. Music.' He mimed enjoyment of these essentials. 'Pleasure district?' He'd learned the word for that early on as there was one in Nagasaki where most of the whores came from.

The youth, who'd said he was called Kenji, nodded with a knowing grin. 'Yoshiwara,' he said. 'Follow me.'

Either he wasn't aware that the foreigners weren't allowed out or the bribe made him turn a blind eye. Haag didn't really care which. He sneaked out of the inn via a back door and stayed in the shadows, happily wearing a strange hat and a belted jacket the youth provided as a disguise.

Once in the pleasure district, he hoped to find others to bribe. Perhaps someone there would know of a *gai-jin* lady with ash blonde hair? If she was in the city, she'd stick out wherever she went. Someone had to have seen her. All Haag needed to do was find that person.

He was still angry at having lost his prize, just when she was so close to being in his grasp. And he dreamed of her every night – tortured dreams where he caressed her creamy flesh, buried himself inside her, made her pay for all the frustration she'd caused him – then woke in a state of painfully unfulfilled lust. It hadn't helped that Noordholt wouldn't let them engage the services of any whores along the way to Edo. Haag couldn't remember the last time he'd been without a woman for this long and it was driving him insane.

It was yet another thing he'd make the Chief Factor pay for eventually.

But first he'd enjoy a night on the town at last.

By the time they waded ashore, Temperance was aching all over from the unaccustomed exercise and her breathing was coming out in short, painful gasps. Kazuo picked up the tub and, looking round to make sure this part of the shore was truly deserted, nodded for her to follow him into the dense forest. Feeling ready to collapse, she stumbled after him and sat down on a large stone as soon as they were sheltered from view by the trees.

'Oh, dear God,' she panted. 'I can't move another step.'

'We can have a short rest, but we'll have to keep going all through the day if we are to stand a chance of evading capture. Here, dry yourself and put some clothes on.' Kazuo held out a piece of cloth and some garments. 'I brought you some men's clothing. It will be easier to walk in. You don't mind?'

Temperance shook her head, too tired to even reply. She lifted her arms to dry herself, but they refused to obey her and in the end she just sat on the rock holding the cloth against her. Kazuo finished dressing himself, then looked up and saw her.

'Here, give me that.' He took the cloth back and pulled her to her feet, then began to rub her briskly. 'We must get your blood moving or you'll catch a chill. Turn around.' Temperance stood meekly while he dried her all over, then helped her into the clothes. There was a strange pair of breeches, similar to the ones Midori had given her, which were very comfortable, and a tunic and belt. Deftly, he dried her hair as much as he could, then twisted it into a knot and secured it on top of her head by tying a piece of material around it. Finally he handed her the broad-brimmed straw hat he'd been wearing at Imada's house, and wriggled a pair of straw sandals onto her feet. 'There, you're ready.'

'Thank you. You are very kind. I see now that I definitely must have been wrong about you.' Temperance sat down on the rock once more as Kazuo handed her some *sembei* and told her to eat it quickly.

'What do you mean you were wrong about me?' He looked puzzled.

'I thought maybe you'd sent those *ronin* to capture me in the bay the week after you left. It seemed like too much of a coincidence that I should meet with two lots of outlaws in such a short space of time. Or am I wrong? Is Ryo a friend of yours?'

'Never heard of him.' Kazuo was frowning now. 'And why would I send someone to kidnap you?'

'Well, for the money I suppose, but it's clear that you are not like Ryo and the others.'

'I most certainly am not. I don't know who they are, but they must have happened to come along just as you were in the bay. Perhaps they were the *ronin* I saw when I turned back to escort you home? Why did you go back there? I would have sent word if I had returned.'

'You would? I didn't know. You said something about a sign ...' It seemed stupid now, the idea of going back to look for him, and Temperance was too embarrassed to admit how desperately she'd wanted him to be there. 'I suppose I wasn't thinking clearly,' she finished lamely.

'What's done is done, now we have to concentrate on evading Tanaka's men. He'll be in a towering rage when he finds you gone, on top of everything else that's just happened to him. It will probably be the final straw as far as he's concerned.'

'Do you know if he found his wife?'

'Of course he found her. She was being guarded by his brother and I was told she was sent back to her family in disgrace. She's probably committed *seppuku* by now.'

'*Seppuku?*' Temperance knew this was a form of ritual suicide only practised by people of the *samurai* class. Her cousin had told her about it a long time ago. 'Surely they wouldn't expect a woman to do such a thing?'

'Why not? It is the only way to restore her honour, although Tanaka might have wished to deny her even that small mercy. He's a cruel man. I know that he went after her lover and he will have killed him and his entire family, but then the slight to *his* honour had to be avenged, of course.'

'Dear Lord! Did he have to kill that many people?'

'Of course. The provocation was great.'

Temperance didn't really understand this concept and shuddered to think it might be directed at her now. 'Where I come from we have a saying, "an eye for an eye, a tooth for a tooth", which basically means that revenge should be the same as the provocation. That doesn't seem to be the case here.'

Kazuo shrugged. 'It is more complicated than that, but there's no time to discuss it now. One day I will tell you about the code of the *samurai*, then perhaps you will understand.'

Temperance doubted this very much, but was too tired to do more than nod in agreement. 'Let's go then. I feel rested now,' she said, although that was far from the truth.

'Very well. Just wait one moment while I dispose of the tub.' Kazuo took it to the edge of the lake and filled it with stones before throwing it as far out as he could. It sank beneath the waves, leaving no trace.

Warmth and movement soon returned to Temperance's limbs and she was able to follow Kazuo towards the mountains. They headed west first, in order to confuse anyone following, as they would probably be expected to head either north towards Edo or south towards Kobe and the coast.

'They will think you're trying to go back to your family. At least I hope so, then they will concentrate their search in the south and thereby give us more time.'

'Where are we going though? I mean, I do want to go back to Dejima eventually, if possible, but I understand that it would be dangerous to try to aim for that immediately.'

'I'll take you to your family, but I'm afraid you will have to accompany me on my mission first. I have lost a lot of time now and I really can't afford to return to Nagasaki until I have accomplished what I set out to do.'

'Can you tell me about your mission or is it secret?'

'I will tell you later, when we have stopped for the

night. It's a long story. For now we have to concentrate on putting as much distance between ourselves and Tanaka as possible. He's a wily old fox and won't miss the fact that we disappeared together. No doubt that will infuriate him even further as it means I have stolen one of his possessions. He'll never rest until he recovers his property.'

Being referred to as Tanaka's 'property' made Temperance shudder and she increased her speed.

She wouldn't be going back if she could help it.

They reached the foothills of the mountains and began to climb, slowly but surely making their way upwards until they could look out over the valley and lake below. Towards the evening the drowsy mist returned, hiding most of the view from sight, but higher up it was mercifully dry and the evening was balmy.

'We will sleep on the ground,' Kazuo said. 'If you can manage it, I think we should take turns to keep watch, at least for tonight.' He knew they were far from safe yet and if he'd been travelling on his own, he would have kept going. For Temi's sake they had to rest though. She'd been amazingly uncomplaining but he was sure she must be exhausted by now.

'Yes, of course. Shall I stay awake first?' she offered. Kazuo hid a smile. He doubted she'd be able to keep her eyes open for more than a few moments, but she was stubborn enough not to want to acknowledge it.

'No, you go to sleep, I'll wake you later,' he said. 'First we must eat something to keep our strength up. I'm afraid I only have dry food, but perhaps tomorrow we can catch some fish in one of the streams and risk a fire.'

'Dry food is fine. I'm so hungry I'll eat anything.'

Indeed, she didn't seem to pay any attention to what it was she was putting in her mouth and finished quickly.

'Mm, it's wonderful to have a full stomach and to be

allowed to rest,' she commented with a contented smile. It made Kazuo glad that he'd been able to provide her with something, even if it wasn't much.

'Here, put your head on my lap and go to sleep,' he told her. He was seated cross-legged on the ground next to her and began to arrange some spare clothing on his lap to act as a pillow for her. She didn't need a second bidding but put her head down and went to sleep in no time. Kazuo watched her incredibly long, dark eyelashes settle on her cheeks like a tiny bird's wings and marvelled at her white skin. The ladies at Imada's establishment had covered her with rice powder, but in truth she had no need of it – her skin was perfect in its natural state.

Without thinking he reached out to stroke it. Tenderness towards this woman swept through him. She was courageous, resilient and strong, but also so very vulnerable. It was up to him to keep her safe now. He'd do his very best, even though it might mean jeopardising his mission.

'Please hurry, son,' had been his father's final words to him.

The old man had been ill, a terrible cough rattling through his lungs at short intervals, and Kazuo wasn't even sure if his father would survive long enough to enjoy the triumph should his son be successful in restoring their honour. There was no time to lose and certainly none that could be spared in order to return Temi to Dejima first.

Somehow he had to combine the two tasks, may all the gods and *kami* help him.

They took turns to keep guard during the night, waking each other as soon as they grew too sleepy to stay properly alert. By the time morning arrived, Temperance felt anything but well rested, but at least she'd had some sleep and it would have to be enough. Kazuo let her have the last rest before morning and as she came to, she realised that her head wasn't in his lap any longer. He was gone.

Instant panic flooded her and her eyes opened wide as she sat up abruptly and began to look for him. Before she'd had a chance to scan the area around her, however, her eyes caught a movement on her left hand side. She swivelled round, letting out a horrified gasp as she came face to face with a snake. Various shades of brown and white, with distinctive markings along its back and head, it looked a bit like a viper she had once seen and was almost as long as her arm. It hissed, the tiny tongue slithering in and out of its mouth, and Temperance froze with fear.

'Don't move or the *hebi* will be frightened.'

She heard the whispered command from behind her and relief flooded her at the thought that Kazuo had returned. At the same time she wanted to break into hysterical laughter. *The snake will be frightened? I'm the one who's terrified here!* She wanted to scream, but clenched her teeth to stop herself from crying out. Hearing Kazuo's voice had reassured her somewhat, but she couldn't take her gaze off the snake, who appeared to be preparing to launch into attack if she so much as breathed.

Dear God, help me, she prayed silently, the words reverberating round the inside of her skull. After everything that had happened, she didn't want to die this way.

Without warning Kazuo suddenly hurled a large stone at the snake, striking it with unerring accuracy, before pulling Temperance to one side. Shaking with fright, she stood up and watched as he threw another stone to make sure the creature was really dead.

'It was a *mamushi*,' Kazuo said matter-of-factly. 'They are poisonous.'

'How comforting,' she murmured sarcastically through chattering teeth.

'What?' He frowned at her, as if realising for the first time how scared she'd been. He came over and put his arms round her. 'You've never seen a snake before?'

'Yes, but not that close up.'

'Don't worry, I wouldn't have let it harm you.'

'Well, you weren't here when I woke up, so how could you have prevented it if you hadn't returned in time?' She couldn't help the slight note of accusation that crept into her voice. It frightened her that she was so dependent on him. If he left she would be lost.

'I was only answering a call of nature.' He stroked her hair which had escaped from the confines of the scarf and was tumbling down her back. 'I would never leave you for long, surely you know that?' He looked at her with a solemn expression and Temperance felt vaguely guilty for doubting him.

'I ... I don't really know you, do I? How can I be sure you're not just using me for your own ends?'

He stroked her cheek with two fingers. 'I suppose you don't, but if I give you my word that I will protect you to the best of my ability, will you believe me?'

'Your word as an honourable outlaw?' She smiled at the feeble joke, but her eyes were riveted to his and she knew that deep down she did trust him, outlaw or not.

He smiled back. 'Yes, of course.'

'Very well, I believe you.'

'Good. Then let us eat something and be on our way. We have far to go today and then, hopefully, tonight we'll be at a safe distance from Tanaka and his henchmen.'

They travelled for several days, heading in a northerly direction through the prefecture of Gifu, a rugged, mountainous area full of lush, dense forests and gushing rivers.

'I'm familiar with this region as I spent time with relatives here some years ago,' Kazuo told Temperance, and it seemed to her he led the way without hesitation.

Occasionally they walked through valleys, dotted with small villages and with fields covering almost every square inch. Temperance kept her head down and her face hidden, following in Kazuo's footsteps without paying too much attention to her surroundings. On the third day they entered an even more densely forested region, with high mountains rising on all sides. Here Temperance felt able to look around her at last and she found it achingly beautiful.

Following hidden tracks through the vegetation that only Kazuo seemed able to see, they came across numerous rivers and streams that rushed by at great speed. To her relief, he proved adept at catching fish for their meals. He had ventured into one of the villages they passed, while Temperance waited anxiously nearby, and bought some rice and a vessel to boil it in, and they now dared to light a fire in the evening to cook their food.

Kazuo also said he no longer thought it necessary to keep watch all night. Instead they slept back to back under a particularly bushy tree with branches that almost touched the ground, and although Temperance revelled in the feeling of security this gave her, she had to admit to a slight disappointment that he didn't so much as attempt to hold her again. It was disconcerting to think that the one man whose touch she might actually welcome, didn't want her. Life was strange.

'Why are we going up into the mountains?' she asked him the following day.

'I have remembered a distant cousin living there who might give us shelter for a while. If we stay with him for a few days, Tanaka might become tired of looking for us and call off the search, then it will be safer for us to continue to Edo.'

'We're going to Edo? Isn't that dangerous? What if someone were to see me?'

'I know it's a huge risk, but it's one we must take and I think we can carry it off. Your disguise is very good and as long as we don't draw attention to ourselves and you keep your eyes downcast and don't look at anyone, we will blend in with the crowds and all should be well. I'm sorry, but we have to go to Edo. There is someone I must see there.'

Temperance thought her disguise far from ideal, but she didn't say anything more even though the thought of going to Edo, the largest city in Japan, was terrifying. Like all such places it would no doubt be teeming with people – *samurai* and their servants and guards, shopkeepers, artisans and common people going about their business – none of whom would hesitate to denounce a *gai-jin* the moment they spotted her. She shuddered and thought longingly of Dejima and her fellow countrymen. Would she ever see them again or was Kazuo leading her to certain death?

No, she had to believe that Kazuo knew best, and if Edo was where he needed to go, she had no choice but to go with him.

Chapter Fourteen

On the afternoon of the fifth day they reached a tiny village clustered around a small valley and surrounded by mountains. The houses clung to the hillsides as if hanging on for dear life, and terraced paddy fields of varying sizes were doing the same all around the buildings. There was an air of tired shabbiness, as if the owners didn't have the time or the wherewithal for regular upkeep, but the houses looked sturdy enough. A bed under any kind of dry roof would be most welcome after sleeping on the hard ground for so many nights, Temperance thought.

'This is where my cousin Hanano-*san* lives,' Kazuo whispered as they made their way towards the largest of the houses. 'He is the headman of the village. Please walk behind me with your head down until we know whether he will receive us or not. Men's allegiances change. I need to make sure before I trust him with our lives.'

They need not have worried. When apprised of their arrival, Hanano gave them a very courteous welcome, and even when he had been told that they were on the run from Tanaka, he only smiled benignly.

'That man needs to be taught a lesson,' he said. 'Even this far from his domain we hear stories of his ruthlessness and greed.' He fixed Kazuo with a shrewd gaze. 'Wasn't he one of the men who signed the warrant for your father's arrest?'

'Indeed, and I had hoped to find some evidence during my stay with him to prove that my father was wrongly accused.'

'Such as?'

'I don't know. Letters, documents or even a loose-mouthed servant, but I'm afraid I wasn't there long enough and never had an opportunity to search properly.'

Temperance had by now been told the story of Kazuo's father's arrest and banishment, so she knew what the men were talking about. She felt guilty for diverting Kazuo from his true mission, and wished that she could help him clear his father's name, but she didn't see how it could be done. If only she could get back to Dejima on her own she would eliminate at least one problem for him, but it was impossible.

A solution suddenly occurred to her, but as Kazuo had asked her to keep her head down, she didn't dare interrupt the men now, so she kept her thoughts to herself. She wondered if perhaps later she could speak to Hanano and ask him if there was anyone from his village who could take her back to Nagasaki. That way Kazuo would be free and there wouldn't be a need for her to face the unknown terrors of Edo.

As a mere woman, however, and a stranger at that, she had no idea how to approach Hanano on her own, and in the end it seemed easier to simply ask Kazuo instead. When she was walking with him towards the tiny guest house where they were to sleep, she tentatively broached the subject.

He looked at her with a frown. 'I doubt Hanano-*san* can spare anyone. Why do you ask?'

'I feel that I'm hindering your plans. You have already risked so much for my sake, I'd like to let you go on your way now. You have more important things to do than play nursemaid to me.'

Kazuo stopped and looked her in the eye. 'I don't regret helping you for a moment,' he said. 'My mission could wait a few days, your life couldn't. Fate brought us together and I couldn't ignore what the gods had decreed. I'm sure there is some meaning with this and we will find out in due course. Until then, we stay together.'

'If you're sure …?'

'I'm sure. Now, let us go to the *onsen* before supper. It is

147

the most wonderful thing in the world and we can't appear before our host without being clean.'

'There is a hot spring here?'

'Indeed, bubbling up straight from the ground. Change into a robe and I'll show you.'

The little guest house had two small sleeping chambers and Hanano's wife was waiting there to see to their needs. She handed Temperance a loose cotton robe and asked her politely to change out of her dirty and travel-stained clothing.

'If you give them to me, I will see that they are washed.'

'You are very kind, thank you.' It would be heaven to be clean again. She felt as if her travel clothes had been welded to her skin for days and it wasn't a nice sensation. Temperance smiled at the woman and handed over the garments, forgetting to keep her eyes lowered. She heard the lady gasp, but before she had time to explain, the woman had fled. 'Damn,' Temperance muttered.

'Are you ready?' Kazuo popped his head round the door frame and held out his hand peremptorily. '*Hayaku*, hurry. Let's go.'

She followed him outside and onto a steep path that led to a grove of trees further up the valley. Soon a small rock pool came into view, surrounded by trees on three sides and with a frothy waterfall pouring down a steady torrent of water nearby, fed by a stream further up the mountain. At the edge of the pool stood a dilapidated wooden building whose roof stretched partway over the water as if to protect it from the elements. In addition there were huge rocks and boulders strewn about the edges of the hot spring.

Hanano's wife had given Temperance a little towel to wash herself with before sliding into the *onsen*. 'Where do we wash, inside the house?' she asked, but Kazuo shook his head and pulled her over towards the waterfall.

'It's a bit cold, but it's bearable for a quick scrub,' he told her. 'Anyway, you'll soon be warm once you enter the bath.' He pulled off his robe and went to stand under the waterfall, rubbing vigorously at his body. Temperance turned away. She wondered how long it would take before she became used to the sight of his nakedness. He seemed to think it natural to shed his clothing in front of her, but although this was now the third time she had seen him thus, she couldn't accustom herself to such uninhibited behaviour. She could still hear her father's strictures on morals ringing in her ears and felt her cheeks heat up with embarrassment.

'Come on, your turn,' Kazuo called. 'It's not that cold, really.'

Temperance took a deep breath and untied the belt of her robe. She waited a moment until Kazuo had his head under water and his eyes closed, then she let the robe fall off her shoulders and made a dash for the waterfall. She gasped at the chill of it, but at least standing under its heavy spray she was partially covered from view. With her back to Kazuo she began to scrub every inch of herself clean with the little towel.

'Would you like some assistance with your back?' The noise from the waterfall was almost deafening at such close quarters and Kazuo had to shout.

'What? No, thank you. I can manage.' Temperance closed her eyes under the stream of water and let it cool her cheeks, trying to ignore Kazuo's nearness.

'Well, I can't. Could you do mine please?'

She opened her eyes and half turned around to find him standing very close, holding out his towel towards her.

'Oh, very well.' Temperance felt it would be churlish not to help him. After all, not everyone was flexible enough to be able to reach round their own back. He presented the broad expanse of it to her and slowly she rubbed at it with the towel. She soon discovered that she enjoyed this task. He had the most incredible skin, tanned by the sun and as smooth as polished marble, and she watched the play of hard muscles underneath taut skin in fascination. In fact, she became quite lost in contemplation of this until he turned round with a grin, asking whether she had finished.

'Uhm, yes, yes I think so,' she stuttered, turning away in confusion.

'Are you sure you don't want me to do yours? It will be faster and then we can get out of this cold water. Here, let me.' He snatched the towel out of her hand and she found herself unable to resist as he spun her round and pushed the heavy mass of her hair to one side before gently massaging her back with the cloth. She almost squirmed with pleasure, but caught herself at the last moment.

'There, that should do. Now come, this is the best part.'

Without giving her a chance to protest, he took her hand, lacing his fingers with hers, and pulled her out from the protection of the waterfall and over towards the pool. Temperance gasped with further embarrassment and scanned their surroundings, in case they were being watched, but thankfully there didn't seem to be anyone else about. Kazuo stopped by the edge of the pool and sat down, tugging at her hand until she did the same.

'Now take it slowly. Ease your limbs in bit by bit, or else you'll scald yourself,' he told her, sliding his feet towards the surface. The water in the pool was steaming gently, and when Temperance followed his advice and dipped a toe in she found that it was very hot indeed, boiling almost.

'Ow!' Midori had told her about this type of spring and the scalding heat, but Temperance hadn't quite believed her. Now she realised it was the truth.

'You get used to it. Just wait.'

Kazuo was right and after a while her body accustomed itself to the boiling temperature of the spring little by little.

He was hardier than her and managed to ease his entire body in long before she did, which left her sitting on the side with nothing to shield her from his view. She crossed her arms over her chest self-consciously. He leaned his head back on one of the stones near the edge of the pool and contemplated her from beneath half-closed eyelids.

'You don't need to feel ashamed of your body, you know,' he said, almost conversationally. 'It is exquisite. Quite, quite beautiful in fact.'

Temperance refused to meet his eye and managed to slide into the water at last. She made sure she sat as far away from him as possible before replying.

'It's not that I'm ashamed of it,' she murmured, 'but it is wrong to show it to a man who is not my husband. At least, that's what I have been taught and it's how we do things in my country.'

'I see. To me it is just a natural state. It is how we are born and most bodies look the same.'

Temperance was fairly sure that wasn't the case, except perhaps in the broadest of terms, but she didn't feel able to argue with him. This was obviously how things were done in Japan and as she was here, she would have to become used to their customs.

Kazuo edged towards her until he was sitting very close, so close his thigh touched hers. 'You do not find it abhorrent to look at me, I hope?'

'No, of course not.' Temperance couldn't tell him just how far from the truth that was.

'That's good. I wouldn't want to scare you.' He grinned at her and touched her nose with the tip of one finger. 'Here, lean on me and close your eyes.' He pulled her head gently down towards his shoulder. 'Isn't this just wonderful?'

Temperance obediently shut her eyes and gave herself up to the pleasure of the moment, too tired to do anything else. He was right again. It was heavenly and her limbs felt completely relaxed, almost as if they were dissolving in the hot water. Her skin was turning rather pink and rubbing her fingertips together she could feel them beginning to wrinkle, but the enjoyment far outweighed such minor concerns and she sighed with contentment. Sitting next to Kazuo like this felt so right. She wanted to remain there forever.

She had no idea how long they stayed in the *onsen*, but eventually they emerged from the pool, as carefully as they had gone in. 'You don't want to rush,' Kazuo advised her, 'or you might pass out.' He helped her into her robe, then put on his own and took her hand in his. Looking slightly sheepish, he added, 'I have a confession to make.'

'Oh? What?'

'I hope you don't mind, but I told Hanano-*san* that you are my mistress.'

'What? Why?'

'Because I wanted to make sure that we were put in the same guest house and also in order to protect you from other men. If I am known to be your patron, they will respect that and keep their distance.'

'I see.' His words made sense, but still made Temperance feel slightly uncomfortable.

'I just thought I'd better tell you in case anyone says anything. It would be best if you pretended to fill that role whenever we are with the others.'

'Very well, if you think it's necessary. But what about my appearance? I forgot to tell you that I inadvertently looked at Hanano-*san*'s wife earlier and I think she was frightened by my eyes.'

'Don't worry. I also told Hanano that you are an albino, hence the pale hair and eyes. I'm not sure he believed me, but he pretended to nonetheless. He will inform everyone else, I'm sure.'

'I suppose that could account for my strange looks,' Temperance grudgingly agreed.

'It is something they understand and at least it's not illegal. They've probably never seen an albino before, so they won't have anything to compare you with.'

'Have you?'

'Yes, as it happens, and he didn't look anything like you, but who's to know? Now we had better dress and join Hanano and his family for supper. It would be impolite to keep them waiting and I'm looking forward to a proper meal.'

Temperance nodded in agreement, but her thoughts were not on food. Instead she wondered if Hanano and his clan would really be fooled by such a simple explanation, but yet again, she had to trust that Kazuo was right.

What other choice did she have, after all?

The evening air was cooler up here in the mountains, and after a well-cooked meal and some time spent with Hanano's family, Temperance knew she would sleep well that night. Her body had had to work extremely hard during the past few days and now she was looking forward to the comfort of a *futon*. Kazuo held her hand again on the way back to their lodgings to keep her from stumbling. The meal had been stiffly formal, and they'd been offered *sake*, the potent rice wine. As it would have been impolite to refuse, Temperance had imbibed as many cups as had been poured for her. Now her head felt rather strange and her legs seemed to have a will of their own. She tripped over a stone and felt Kazuo's hand steadying her.

'Watch your step. It's difficult in the dark, I know.' She thought she heard laughter in his voice, but she ignored it. He had drunk *sake* too, so surely he must be feeling the same?

'Are you sure we'll be safe here?' she asked Kazuo when

they finally reached the guest house. 'Your cousin wouldn't betray you to Tanaka, would he?'

'No, you heard what he said. Tanaka is extremely unpopular hereabouts. Besides, Hanano-*san* would never act dishonourably as he owes my father a debt of gratitude. I should have remembered that earlier.'

'How so?'

'My father helped him out once when he was in dire straits financially. Hanano was never able to repay him, but it didn't matter. They are kin and as such will always protect each other. That includes their families too.'

Inside the guest house Temperance headed for her little room and was surprised when moments later Kazuo followed her in, carrying his bedding. 'But what are you doing?' she asked.

'I think it's best if we sleep together, just in case there is any danger. You don't mind, do you?'

Temperance opened her mouth to protest, then realised she had become so used to sleeping next to him that it would feel wrong not to. 'No, I suppose not. If you think it's best.'

'I do.'

He placed his own *futon* next to hers and lay down. When she did the same, he wriggled over so that his back was against hers, just as he had done every night, but suddenly it didn't seem enough to Temperance. She wanted more. The *sake* humming through her veins melted all her inhibitions and made her feel bold, carefree and utterly daring. Without thinking she turned around and put her hand out to stroke his back, then felt, rather than saw him, move round.

'Temi-*chan*, what are you—?'

She cut him off by kissing him, softly, languidly, and felt his body stiffen before he responded. 'Temi,' he murmured. 'This is not a good idea.'

'It's just a kiss,' she whispered against his lips and used her tongue to entice him into opening his mouth, just as Nyoko had taught her. She felt vaguely guilty and immoral, but smiled when he didn't protest any further. The woman had obviously been right – men liked this and come to think of it, so did she.

It was a kiss that lasted for a very long time, until Temperance's limbs started to feel as weightless and tingling as they had in the *onsen* earlier. Somehow she ended up lying underneath him, which felt completely right, and Kazuo's hands gently explored her body. She made no protest when he slipped the robe off her shoulders so that he could trail kisses down her neck.

'You are so lovely,' he whispered, and she shivered when his mouth touched the sensitive pulse underneath her ear. She felt an answering shudder in him when she put her hands on his warm chest and let her fingers splay out slowly, but when she allowed them to stray further down, caressing the hard planes of his stomach, he captured them with his and held her still. 'No, please, don't tempt me further. I think we had better try and get some sleep now, don't you?'

She knew he was being strong for both of them and a part of her was grateful, but at the same time she felt bereft. She wanted him, all of him, and it no longer seemed important that he wasn't her husband, nor was he ever likely to be. What man in his right mind would want to marry her now in any case? To all intents and purposes she was already a fallen woman, having spent weeks alone in the company of various men. Therefore she might as well behave like one, she reasoned.

It was ironic though that she wanted to give herself to this man when only weeks ago she'd dreaded this very thing happening with Tanaka. What a difference it made to be with the right person.

But Kazuo wasn't the right one for her, not really. How could he be when they came from such different worlds?

So she held back and accepted his refusal for what it was – the act of a true gentleman.

Kazuo lay awake for ages, staring into the darkness. His body was on fire and he wanted nothing more than to turn back to Temi and make her his, but he knew that he couldn't. Shouldn't.

He closed his eyes and relived the kisses they'd just shared. She had shocked him when she put her mouth on his so unexpectedly, then used her tongue to ensnare him further. Those were whore's tricks, something she must have learned while staying at Imada's house, but although no decent man was supposed to want his wife to act that way, Kazuo had enjoyed it immensely. And he was surprised to realise that he didn't think any the less of her for playing the courtesan. He still wanted her for his wife and couldn't see the pleasure in having a spouse who simply submitted meekly night after night. No, he would far rather have someone like Temi, who took the initiative and tried to please him.

He wondered what other tricks she had learned at Imada's tea house, then wished he hadn't thought along those lines as the fire inside him flared up anew. He clenched his fists to stop from groaning out loud. This wouldn't do, he had to stop this madness.

The worst part was that had she been a Japanese girl, he wouldn't have hesitated. However different their status, he could have found a way to marry her later or keep her as his mistress, but how could he possibly do that to a foreigner? Even if he could make his father accept such a thing, where would they live? Wherever they went, she would be in danger from the authorities and he couldn't see a way around it.

Taking deep breaths he tried to calm his body, but sleep was still a long time coming.

Chapter Fifteen

'How long are they going to keep us waiting, for heaven's sake? It's been days!' Haag complained, pacing back and forth in the spacious room the foreigners had been allocated to socialise in.

If he had been Chief Factor he would have insisted they be received much faster. They were, after all, the envoys of a foreign kingdom, not just lowly traders.

'The *Shogun* is probably doing it on purpose, just to show us he's the one with the power.' Noordholt shrugged, seemingly not too bothered. It annoyed Haag that the man was always so unflappable and patient. So superior. *Unbearable!*

Noordholt wouldn't be quite so smug when Haag denounced him to the Japanese authorities and took his place. That was now his plan and he'd find a way to evade Noordholt's watchful eyes in order to do it. It would mean getting rid of the deputy chief as well, but Haag would cross that hurdle once he'd dealt with Noordholt. There were always ways and means. However, he wasn't doing anything until he had Temperance back. Everything else paled into insignificance. The longer he had to wait, the more he wanted her. He *had* to have her, the little bitch.

If only he could find her.

Haag was becoming frustrated beyond measure. He'd had no luck finding anyone who'd seen or heard of a foreign woman and he was running short of funds. At this rate he would have to try to steal some of the silver Noordholt had brought, but he'd rather not except as a last resort. The Chief Factor was cannier than most men and might guess who'd taken his precious funds.

'Well, has there been any word about Mistress Marston from your concubine's relative or the spies he was proposing to hire?' he asked, not bothering to hide his impatience. 'What did she call them, *ninja*?'

Noordholt shook his head. 'I hardly think he'll be using *ninja* just to find out some information. They're trained assassins. But to answer your question, no, I've not heard anything yet. Japan is a big country and no doubt it will take time to find any information.' The Chief Factor hid it well, but Haag could tell he was extremely worried about his young kinswoman and frustrated at his inability to act. He was in an impossible situation, reliant on others to search for her as he couldn't officially be seen to do anything. He sighed as he added, 'Besides, whoever took Temperance won't want her to be found, so perhaps they've disguised her or at least hidden her away. She may even have been spirited off to another country altogether, although God forbid!'

Haag added a silent 'amen' to that sentiment. It would be most annoying if the stupid girl had gone missing for good. He had no idea how long he'd be forced to stay in Japan, but he would much prefer to do so with a European woman to see to his needs, rather than the native ones. And not just any woman, it had to be her. It had become a matter of honour now. No one, but *no one*, got away with making a fool of him. Temperance must be made to pay for that and for trying to escape him. Besides she was the only woman he'd ever wanted with such intensity. He had no idea why, but he simply couldn't get her out of his mind. She was like opium, a drug he'd tried once before realising how it made him crave more.

'You speak the language well. Can't you make some enquiries yourself in secret?' Haag asked.

'I've tried, but I'm getting nowhere. The people here don't seem happy to talk to a foreigner like myself, even one who speaks Japanese. And you know I'm not supposed to.'

'Well, why don't you bribe them? I'm sure a few coins would loosen plenty of tongues.'

Noordholt sent him an irritated glance. 'I did say I was offering a reward for information, but no one has come forward. Bribing people won't work. They'd just pretend to know something and pocket the money. Waste of time.'

Haag disagreed but swallowed his counter-argument. Once Noordholt had made up his mind about something, he was remarkably difficult to shift. There was nothing for it – Haag would have to do the bribing himself. With the Chief Factor's coins.

Temperance and Kazuo left the little village a few days later, taking a circuitous route across the mountains rather than heading straight for the east coast post road between Kyoto and Edo.

'It would have been faster to go straight to the Tokaido Highway, which runs along the East Sea,' Kazuo explained, 'but I don't want to take any unnecessary risks. The longer we stay out of sight, the better I think.' There had been no sign of any pursuit and they surmised that Tanaka had either given up looking for them, or had gone the wrong way and thereby lost their trail, but nevertheless Kazuo was still wary. 'We will join the highway about a day's walk away from Edo, but until then it's safer for us to stay away from major routes.'

'That sounds eminently sensible to me,' Temperance replied. She was quite happy to stay away from civilisation for as long as possible. 'How long will it take us to reach it?'

'Two weeks, perhaps three. It depends how far we travel each day.' He glanced at her, a slightly worried expression in his eyes. 'It is really a question of how strong you are. Walking all day, every day, is arduous in the extreme as you have already found out, and there is nowhere we can stop for a long rest. We have to keep going.'

'Don't worry about me, I'll be fine.'

'We'll take it slowly at first, to give you a chance to build your strength. You must promise to tell me if I am going too fast.'

Temperance nodded, but she had no intention of holding him up. She would walk as fast as he wished, whether her body agreed or not. She felt she had already delayed him enough and after he'd told her of his father's illness, she'd been as aware as he was of the necessity for speed.

Quite apart from all the walking ahead of her, Temperance was sorry to leave the little village. Slumbering in the seclusion of its mountainside hideaway, it had seemed like a haven of tranquillity. She knew she would miss the comfort of the guest house and most especially the daily baths in the wonderful *onsen*. She told herself that this was not because she wouldn't have the opportunity to enjoy the sight of Kazuo's physique, but because the hot water made her feel more invigorated and rested at the same time than she had ever felt before. The less she thought about Kazuo, the better, as she knew nothing could come of it.

He had spared her blushes by not mentioning her daring actions that first evening, and she'd made sure she only took the smallest of sips from her *sake* cup after that. They spent each night back to back as before, neither making any move to touch the other, and Temperance kept her yearning for more to herself. She felt ashamed of having acted in such a wanton way and reminded herself of her father's strictures on loose women.

'The Devil constantly puts temptation in our way, but we must fight him with all our might. We cannot let him win,' he had thundered, when informed of the scandalous behaviour of one of their neighbours. Temperance knew that if he was watching her from heaven, he would be thoroughly disgusted.

Was it possible that he'd been wrong though? The women at Imada's establishment seemed to think that fornication was a natural phenomenon, something humans were made to do. They weren't ashamed of their profession and she'd never seen them being abused by other citizens. Why then was it such a sin? Cousin Midori had told her many times that she didn't believe Temperance's father was right in everything. She said there were always many ways of looking at something, and who was to say which was right or wrong? Midori's father had taught her beliefs that differed fundamentally from those of her English uncle, and Midori always claimed the Japanese way of thinking made more sense. The wonderful feelings Temperance herself had experienced with Kazuo hadn't felt sinful either, unless enjoyment was a bad thing in itself, which surely couldn't be the case?

Temperance was beginning to see what Midori had meant, but couldn't quite subdue her Puritan conscience or set aside her Christian upbringing. She felt that she still had a lot to learn before reaching any conclusions.

The long trek towards Edo was the most physically difficult task Temperance had ever undertaken and the first few days passed in a blur of exertion and pain.

'Are you all right?' Kazuo threw the question over his shoulder every so often, and each time she gritted her teeth and panted out a 'yes', even though she longed to scream 'no!' instead.

She registered steep hills, dense forests and thick climbing ivy vines that seemed to trip her up at every opportunity, but she didn't really take in any part of the scenery. She was concentrating too hard on simply putting one foot in front of the other without flagging.

Kazuo stopped at streams and waterfalls so that they could

drink and replenish their water supply, as well as catch fish for their supper. Temperance was too tired to appreciate their wild beauty and wanted nothing more than to sit slumped against a boulder or giant tree root and close her eyes.

Gradually, however, as the days went by, she found herself less tired and her body began to respond without its previous sluggishness. She was even able to appreciate her surroundings at last. Lush forests, beginning to change into their spectacular autumn hues, enveloped them in a cocoon of vegetation. From time to time they came upon steep mountain ravines and swift-flowing rivers and streams that quite took her breath away.

'You are gaining strength,' Kazuo commented with a smile when she drew his attention to a particularly fine view. 'Good. I was beginning to think I would have to find somewhere to hide for a few days.'

'I was trying my best,' she protested.

'I know.' He grinned. 'And I appreciate your efforts. You've done well.'

His praise made her feel all warm inside, which was ridiculous really, and she told herself not to be so silly, but somehow his appreciation meant a lot to her. More than she'd realised. She had a sneaking suspicion that she could very easily fall in love with this man, but no good would come of it and so she clamped down on such thoughts. They simply had no future together.

There was no reason why they couldn't be friends, however. Although they hardly spoke at all during their long daily walks, she felt that there was a growing bond between them, and they walked in a companionable silence which didn't feel strained in any way. Sometimes Kazuo took her hand to help her over a particularly difficult patch of ground or a stream, and at such times Temperance felt an affinity with him that she'd never had with anyone before.

A wonderful sense of belonging, of rightness. Her hand felt small and cherished in his large, warm one, and she drew strength from this brief contact. She knew he would never let any harm come to her if he could help it and for her own part, she would do anything she could to help him achieve his goals.

If only it were possible.

The weather continued fair for the first few days of their journey, but late in the afternoon of the fifth day, a sudden rainstorm assailed them without warning. Thunder boomed, echoing around the mountain tops, with great flashes of lightning dividing the sky, while fat raindrops began to pelt down mercilessly.

'We must find shelter,' Kazuo shouted above the din. 'Follow me!'

They had been walking along a deep gorge and he grabbed her hand and pulled her along towards the nearest mountain side. As luck would have it, there was a huge overhang of rock and they were able to squeeze in underneath it and thereby escape from the torrents unleashed by the rain clouds. It wasn't a minute too soon.

'I'm half soaked already,' Temperance complained. 'Where on earth did that come from?'

'Storms can come on suddenly like that, it just happens.' Kazuo shrugged. 'Here, let's huddle together for warmth.' He sat down, leaning his back against the hard rock and put his arms around her, pulling her close. 'Our clothes will soon dry, but it wouldn't do to catch a chill in the meantime.'

Temperance was very happy to be held like that and nestled closer, breathing in the scent of him. His clothes smelled of fresh mountain air and greenery, while underlying this was his own unique essence. She closed her eyes, savouring the moment, but soon opened them again to watch the spectacular fireworks of nature going on outside their little hideaway.

'Are you sure we're safe here?' she asked. The crashing of the thunder seemed to be coming ever closer and the streaks of lightning appeared to be almost bouncing off the nearby rock face.

'Perfectly. The lightning could never reach under here.'

He sounded so sure Temperance felt all her fears melt away. Instead she began to notice things like his even breathing beneath her ear, and his steady heartbeat, clearly audible despite the noise going on around them. She closed her eyes once more and, lulled by the comforting tattoo from inside his chest, she felt herself drifting into sleep.

This was where she wanted to stay – in his arms. Perhaps he wanted that too?

But when she woke some time later, to find the world outside a wet, but quieter place, her cheek was no longer resting on his shoulder. He had placed a piece of clothing under her head instead and sat as far away from her as possible, staring out at the softly falling rain.

Nothing had changed.

Kazuo hugged his knees and rested his chin on top of them, concentrating hard on the soft curtain of rain in front of him. He listened to the gurgling of tiny streams, merging into larger ones as they headed down the slope of the hill, and the pattering of raindrops on large leaves nearby. He drew in deep, calming breaths of moist air, heavily scented by the drenched vegetation, and tried his best to cleanse his airways of the sweet smell of Temi. Out of the corner of his eye he caught a movement and knew that she was awake, but he didn't look her way. He couldn't allow himself to do so.

He was finding it increasingly difficult – almost impossible in fact – to be near her all day, every day, without touching her. Holding her in his arms earlier had felt so right, as if that was where she belonged. But how could that be? Surely the gods didn't mean for him to marry this foreign girl?

He would be very happy if that was indeed his fate, but there were so many difficulties inherent in taking such a step that he couldn't see how it could possibly be the right thing to do. No, it was more likely that the gods were testing him somehow. They had been on his side so far during his mission. Even though he had yet to find what he sought, they'd kept him safe, but Temi was a definite distraction so it may be that she'd been sent to test his resolve.

Well, he thought, he was strong-willed and had proved that he could resist the temptation of her soft body once already. No doubt he could do it again.

But only if he stayed well away from her.

And only if she stopped looking at him with such absolute trust in those strangely beautiful blue eyes.

They came at last to the edge of the Kanto plain, the richest agricultural area in the whole of Japan, according to Kazuo.

'Edo lies due east from here,' he informed Temperance, 'and you'll be happy to hear that there are no more mountains to cross.'

'Thank God,' she muttered. Her feet were covered in blisters and her sandals nearly worn out. She sincerely hoped that walking on flat ground would be easier, because she didn't think either her feet or shoes would last much longer.

'You should be saying "thank the gods",' Kazuo pointed out. 'It would be safer for both of us, in case anyone heard you.'

'Oh, yes, sorry.' Temperance knew Christians weren't tolerated and the last thing she'd want to do would be to have anyone suspicious of them because of something she said. 'I'll try to remember.'

'Good. Now we should be joining the Tokaido Highway

in a day or so and we've avoided the worst part of it – the Hakone pass.'

'Why is that so bad?'

'It's very high for one thing, so crossing it is an arduous task, but also there are robbers lying in ambush. And although I'm well able to defend myself, I'm not sure I could take them on if there was a whole group of them. Much better not to go there at all.'

'How long is this highway?'

'It goes all the way from Kyoto to Edo, a journey of about twelve to fifteen days on foot. There are no less than fifty-three so called "stations" along the way, where travellers can stop for a rest at a tea house or inn, but it still feels like it goes on forever.'

'Yes, I can imagine.' Before coming to Japan, Temperance had never left her native Plymouth, so she was eager to see this great road for herself, as well as the people who used it, but Kazuo again reminded her of the need to be careful.

'Please keep your gaze on the ground at all times. If anyone should catch sight of your eyes, we're done for. I don't think our story of you being an albino would be accepted as readily here. The people in the mountains are more ignorant, whereas travellers along the Tokaido Highway will be wiser and more sophisticated.'

Temperance nodded. She would heed his warning.

The roads across the plain were easier to travel than the hazardous routes through the mountains, but it was tiring nonetheless. Temperance breathed a sigh of relief when they reached Totsuka at last.

'This is the rest stop where we join the Tokaido,' Kazuo whispered. 'We are only about a day's walk from Edo now and most people spend the night here before continuing the rest of the journey. We will do likewise.'

The approach to this station was lined with beautifully

shaped pine trees, but Temperance didn't dare more than a glance at them before lowering her gaze again. There were a great many people about and she knew she had to be extra careful from now on. It was a shame, as there was so much to observe, but she couldn't risk jeopardising Kazuo's mission simply because she was curious.

Most of their fellow travellers appeared to be men, although she glimpsed two women being carried in a *kago* each. This was a slightly simpler conveyance than an enclosed palanquin, open on the sides. It looked like a sedan chair or sling that had been suspended from a crossbeam and each was carried by two men. Temperance also noticed a less affluent woman on foot with a small child tied to her back. Her loose-fitting outer garment had been adjusted to wrap around the child as well, so all that could be seen was a small face peering over the top. Temperance thought it looked like an excellent method of carrying a child, seeing as it left the mother's arms free to do other things. The child itself was enchanting, just like the children they'd seen in Hanano's village, with a mop of thick, black hair that stood virtually straight up on top of its tiny head. Temperance wanted to smile at the little one, but averted her gaze instead.

The station itself consisted of a small tea house which really did serve tea and wasn't a euphemism for anything else. It had a thatched roof, dusty and worn, but seemingly watertight, as well as a lodging house and a stable. There were quite a few other travellers, some just resting, some grouped around an officious-looking man who was writing something down in a book.

'What is he doing?' Temperance whispered to Kazuo, curious as always to learn more of this amazing country.

'He is the station official. He arranges for people to have a change of horses or bearers for their palanquins, then he has to record the fares paid in his notebook.'

'That seems very organised.' Temperance marvelled at the way the Japanese did everything in such an orderly fashion. Nothing seemed left to chance.

'But of course, how else should it be?'

Kazuo requested a bed for the night for the two of them and they were soon seated in a quiet corner with a bowl of *soba* each.

'This is heavenly.' Temperance sighed with satisfaction. The steaming hot buckwheat noodles in a clear broth, with large deep-fried prawns in a golden batter on top, tasted better than anything she had eaten for a long time. She finished every last morsel, slurping her noodles the way she noticed everyone else doing.

Kazuo smiled at her obvious enjoyment. 'It is a speciality of this region. You'll no doubt get tired of it soon enough.'

'I shouldn't think so. I feel as if I could live on this for the rest of my life.'

With a full stomach and aching feet, it was a relief to bed down on a thin mattress in the poorer quarters of the inn, and despite the bad quality of their *futon*, Temperance didn't complain. She lay down, facing the wall and making sure that her hair remained well covered, in case anyone should happen to look their way. Kazuo took up his usual position back to back with her and she felt as if she had a human shield, which was very comforting.

'Sleep well,' Kazuo whispered, 'tomorrow we'll reach Edo.'

Temperance hardly dared to believe him. It seemed like a dream, but what would happen when they arrived in the capital? It appeared to her that danger lurked everywhere, waiting to catch her unawares, and only God could keep her safe. She closed her eyes and prayed.

Chapter Sixteen

After another bowl of the delicious *soba*, they set out early the next morning, feeling more refreshed than they had for a long time. The next station after Totsuka was Hodogaya, a small village nestling next to a low hill, which they reached easily, but they didn't stop here. Instead they crossed a bridge over a wide stream and continued on their way.

Soon after, however, there was a great noise from behind them and Kazuo pulled Temperance to the side of the road.

'Get down onto the ground and kneel,' he hissed.

'What? Why?'

Kazuo gave her a little push as she hesitated in confusion and kneeled beside her, his head bowed down. Temperance followed suit, still not understanding what was happening. 'There is a great lord approaching,' he said quietly, 'and we must make obeisance to him as he passes with his retinue. If we don't, we could be severely punished.'

'But you're a nobleman yourself,' Temperance protested.

'Not at the moment, remember? Now hush, please, I'll explain later.'

A long convoy of men came round a bend in the road; a mounted guard first, then the lord himself, and finally an endless stream of attendants on foot, hurrying along at a half-run in order to keep up with the riders. Temperance tried not to breathe in the dust they stirred up while marching by, but it was difficult to avoid it and she ended up coughing several times. The procession appeared to go on forever, with hundreds of feet tramping past, and her knees ached when they finally disappeared and she was able to stand up again.

'What a ridiculous custom,' she muttered. 'We're not slaves, for heaven's sake.'

Kazuo frowned at her, while brushing the dust off his knees. 'Please do not *ever* voice such thoughts in public,' he warned. 'Commoners here know their duty and never question it. We mustn't either.'

'If you say so,' Temperance replied, but she still thought it a very silly thing to have to do. What if it was pouring with rain and the ground was muddy? Or even covered in snow? She shook her head. If the man had been a king or an emperor, she could have understood it, but for a mere lord to expect such reverence seemed wrong. Nevertheless, she had to do as everyone else did, so she told herself it was best to become accustomed to it.

The highway soon became steeper as they approached Kanagawa, which consisted of a street that ran the length of the top of a cliff overlooking the huge sweep of Edo Bay. There were plenty of tea houses here and Temperance was amused by the persistent efforts of serving women outside each one, trying their best to entice travellers into their particular establishment. They beckoned and called, and if that didn't work some even resorted to dragging unwary customers inside. Temperance made sure she kept well out of their way, while Kazuo shook his head at such goings-on.

'Honestly, you'd think they had enough customers without having to use such methods,' he muttered. He too steered clear of the shrill women. 'Look at the view,' he added, 'isn't it magnificent here?'

It was indeed, but Temperance didn't dare admire it for too long until they were well away from the throng of people around the rest station.

By the time they reached Kawasaki, the next stop, Temperance had forgotten about the sea view. Instead she found it difficult to take her eyes off the incredible sight of Mount Fuji which presided over the landscape, majestic in the distance.

'That is simply beautiful,' she breathed, staring in awe at the snow-clad summit and sides which gleamed in the sunlight. It seemed to her almost like a benign being, or perhaps a serene presence watching over them all. She now understood why people often referred to it as 'Fuji-*san*', as if it were a person.

'Yes, isn't it?' Kazuo seemed pleased that she was enjoying the sights of his country, and Temperance realised that he must have missed this view himself if he'd been banished for a number of years.

'How long is it since you were last in Edo?'

'Oh, it must be three years now.'

Temperance frowned. 'And you really think you'll be able to find any trace of the man who ruined your father, so long after the event?'

Kazuo nodded. 'There are always people with long memories. My father is not entirely friendless, despite what happened, and I'm sure we will find something.' He clenched his fists unconsciously. 'We must.'

Temperance admired his optimism, but wasn't sure she shared it. Still, it wasn't for her to say, so she kept her opinion to herself.

There was a large river to cross at Kawasaki, which they did by ferry, but after that the journey seemed to go much faster and they soon reached Shinagawa.

'This is the final stop before Edo itself,' Kazuo told her.

Here the sea came right up to the road and they were able to look out over Edo Bay from its shore. There were ships moored not too far away and that reminded Temperance of the harbour at Nagasaki. A pang of homesickness for the foreign enclave on Dejima assailed her. She wondered what Midori and Nico were doing at this moment and whether they missed her as much as she missed them. She shook her head and concentrated on the view in front of her instead. It would avail her nothing to dwell on such thoughts. If God wished it, she would return there one day. In the meantime, He was fulfilling her desire to experience more of Japan, so she shouldn't complain even if this wasn't quite how she'd envisaged seeing the sights.

A row of houses backed onto the sea, and it seemed as if the whole of Shinagawa was thronged with travellers, all chatting excitedly in anticipation of the end of their journey. The numerous tea houses, eating establishments and entertainment quarters were doing a roaring trade. There were many people making their way to the nearby temple of Tokaiji, presumably to pray for good fortune, but Temperance and Kazuo didn't dare do more than buy a quick meal.

'You don't want to go and pray?'

'No, there are temples in Edo,' Kazuo said, 'and I'm sure my ancestors are watching over us anyway.'

'How much longer do we have to go?' Although exhilarated that they were going to reach their destination that day, Temperance was flagging slightly and her poor feet longed for some rest. She was also becoming nervous about the prospect of being in such dangerous surroundings, her fear of being caught mounting with every step she took. She would have been happy to wait for Kazuo to go and spend some time at the temple so that she could gather her courage before facing the unknown terrors of Edo.

'We'll be there before sundown. It's not far now.' Kazuo seemed to have sensed her feelings, because he added, 'And don't worry, no harm will come to you as long as you remember to keep your eyes on the ground and do exactly as I say.'

This reassured her slightly and she kept any further misgivings to herself. It was late afternoon now and she knew her ordeal would soon be over. Once they were ensconced in lodgings somewhere she would be safe, at least for today. After a short rest and some sustenance, she was able to continue without complaint, despite her fatigue. Admittedly, the last leg of their trek passed in something of a blur, but when they reached the Nihonbashi Bridge at last, Temperance was not so tired that she couldn't look around surreptitiously from under her hat and marvel at the sight of the enormous construction.

'This is where the Tokaido Highway starts,' Kazuo explained, 'and it is something of a meeting place as well.'

She could see that for herself. A large crowd of people milled about, talking, laughing and enjoying themselves. Fish vendors cried their wares, dogs barked, children ran about squealing and playing. The cacophony of noises was almost too much for Temperance's ears since they had been used to nothing but the sounds of nature for the past few weeks.

'Come, we mustn't stay here. It's too dangerous,' Kazuo said in a low voice. 'Follow me.'

'Where are we going? Is there anywhere that is truly safe?'

'Yes, Yoshiwara, the pleasure district.'

'The what?'

'The area where men go for entertainment at night.'

Temperance was aghast as memories of Imada's inn came flooding back. 'But I've just escaped from ... well, that sort of thing. Surely you're not taking me back to a ... a house of ill repute?'

Kazuo flashed her a smile. 'Never fear, I'm not about to sell you to the highest bidder again. No, we are going to see a very special lady, by the name of Hasuko. She was my father's chief concubine, but when he was banished she wasn't allowed to go with him. We had a message from her to say that she was residing in Yoshiwara and that if we ever wanted her help, she was willing to do anything in her power for us.'

'And is she a ...? I mean, does she work there now?'

'Not exactly. I believe she's the owner of one of the

establishments but I don't think she's selling her own services. Even if she is, it's beside the point. The poor woman has to earn her living somehow since I'm sure she received no help from whoever ousted my father. It is not for us to judge her. No doubt she did what she had to. I tell you, she's a good woman. My father was ... is very fond of her and what is more important, trusts her completely.'

'Oh, I'm not judging her, far from it. She sounds like a remarkable lady, and courageous too.' If this journey had taught her nothing else, at least Temperance knew by now that there were indeed women who had no choice in these matters. Having come so close to submitting to such a fate herself, she felt she was the last person to be in a position to look down upon ladies of easy virtue. She merely thanked God that she had escaped, at least thus far.

As they walked through the streets of Edo, Kazuo told her more about Yoshiwara. 'It's a special area of the city, with walls all around it. The people who run businesses there have to be licensed and it's the only place in Edo where everyone is allowed to be out and about at night. There's entertainment day and night and hundreds of women live there, controlled by their owners.'

'They are slaves?'

'No, more like indentured servants. Most are sold into this life as children then trained until they are ready to become fully-fledged courtesans. Once they start receiving clients, I believe they usually have to work for ten years in order to free themselves from their debt to the brothel owner, but after that they are allowed to leave. Wasn't that the case at Imada's place?'

'Yes, except from what I heard, hardly any of the girls ever made it out of there.'

'He was a thoroughly nasty man. Things are better regulated here in Yoshiwara, although it's true the women can't leave without permission. There is only one entrance and it's heavily guarded.'

'How sad.' A thought struck her. 'But how will we get in or out then?'

'I have a special password arranged by Hasuko. She's paid the guards handsomely and they will turn a blind eye.'

'Couldn't those poor women do the same?'

'I doubt they get to keep that much of their earnings. Hasuko had some money put aside from her time with my father and she is an astute woman, which is how she came to buy an establishment.'

'I see.'

Whatever the secret password was, it worked, and they were allowed inside the gate without any questions asked. One of the guards gave Kazuo directions to Hasuko's house, which apparently went by the name of The Silk Room, and they were soon on their way. Temperance tried to keep her eyes on the ground, but couldn't help the occasional peep from under the brim of her hat at the exquisite women that passed them frequently. Mostly in giggling groups, they tottered along on their high *geta*, their brightly hued *kimono* a colourful sight. Of the few she managed to observe, however, Temperance noted that for most of them, their air of gaiety was very forced. There was no real happiness in their dark eyes and it made her stomach clench to think of the dreadful lives they were forced to lead.

Droves of men, some obviously the worse for wear from drinking too much *sake*, passed them as well, and Temperance noted that they all looked fairly prosperous. She surmised that mostly wealthy or upper-class men came to find their nightly entertainments here.

'Here we are, this is it.' Kazuo stopped outside a large establishment and read the wooden sign outside the door, which was open but had a curtain covering the aperture.

Temperance chanced a quick glance and took in the front of the building. There were latticed windows, slightly open, which showed a large room inside, covered with *tatami* mats and with beautifully decorated walls. She knew from her time at The Weeping Willow that this was called the *harimise* – the display room. At least a dozen girls sat on plump silk cushions obviously waiting for clients. To pass the time, some were smoking tobacco, some drinking tea or playing the *shamisen*, a strange three-stringed instrument Midori had shown Temperance. The girls were a mixture of fully-fledged courtesans in splendid robes and younger *shinzo*, apprentices, in their slightly less sumptuous *furisode* with long sleeves. Child servants scurried between them, fetching and carrying. In some ways it was a peaceful scene, but then Temperance remembered what they were all waiting for and a little shudder went through her. This was a market place and the goods on sale were these women's bodies.

'Let's go round to the back,' Kazuo said. 'We don't want it to seem like we are customers.'

He led the way down a small alley to the back of the three storey house, and knocked on a tiny door. After a whispered conversation with the old woman who opened it, they were ushered inside and taken straight to an upstairs room.

'Please, sit down. I will fetch Hasuko-*san* immediately,' the old lady said and bowed to them. They did as they were told and sank down onto a pair of dark green silk cushions on the soft *tatami* floor. Temperance breathed a sigh of relief – they were here at last and so far no one had discovered their deception and denounced her to the authorities.

A small woman came into the room, a wide smile on her face as she glided gracefully across the floor towards Kazuo and bowed deeply. 'Kazuo-*sama*, you managed it. I am so pleased to see you. Welcome to my home.'

'Thank you, Hasuko-*san*. My father sends you his very

best wishes and I am glad to find you in such glowing health. All is well with you?'

'Indeed it is. Naturally, I miss your father, but apart from that I cannot complain.' Hasuko glanced at Temperance, who had kept her head down. 'And you have brought a companion? Someone to help you with your quest?'

If only I could, Temperance thought. Instead she was nothing but a nuisance and no doubt Kazuo was wishing he were rid of her now that he'd reached his destination. It was a lowering thought.

'Not exactly. This is Temi-*san*. She is travelling with me, but I will tell you all about that later. For now we would be very grateful for somewhere to rest and perhaps something to eat and drink.'

'Of course, it is being seen to already. If you don't mind, I think it best if you sleep upstairs in one of the smaller rooms. I am sorry to offer you such humble accommodation, but in view of the circumstances ...'

'We understand and we're very grateful for your help, Hasuko-*san*.'

The little room they were led to nestled under the eaves of the house and was so small it held nothing but a plump *futon*. Since this was all they needed, however, Temperance and Kazuo were very happy with this, and even more grateful when two large trays arrived loaded with various delicious-smelling dishes.

Hasuko herself delivered the trays. 'The fewer people who see you, the better,' she said. 'If there is anything else you need, don't hesitate to ask. For now, I think it best if you stay up here. Then when everyone has left I will come and fetch you so that you can come down to the kitchen and have a bath.'

'That sounds perfect, thank you so much.' Both Kazuo and Temperance bowed to the kind lady, who bowed back, then left them to the bliss of eating a huge and satisfying meal.

'You still want to live on *soba*?' Kazuo teased as Temperance finished off the last piece of *sushi* on the tray, made with fish so fresh it fairly melted in her mouth. She had eaten raw fish many times before, since her cousin insisted on including an element of local food into the otherwise European diet on Dejima, but she didn't think it had ever tasted this heavenly.

She threw him a withering glance. 'I'm not going to answer that. You had the unfair advantage of knowing what Edo cooking is like, I didn't.'

He grinned at her. 'Very well, I'll allow you to eat some *sushi* from time to time.'

She leaned over to hit him playfully on the arm, but he caught her hand easily and pulled her towards him so that she ended up sprawled on his lap. For a long moment, they stared at each other, spellbound. She thought she caught a look of pure desire in his eyes, but then he slowly released her and turned away.

'Let us make plans for tomorrow, while we wait for Hasuko's return. There is much to do, at least for me, Temi-*san*.'

The formal way of addressing her doused any hope that he may relent and at least kiss her. Temperance sat up and slowly made her way over to lean against the wall, wrapping her arms around her bent knees and resting her forehead on top. She listened as Kazuo told her what he hoped to achieve within the next few days, but she wasn't really paying attention. Instead, her troubled thoughts mulled over her precarious position here.

What if anything were to happen to Kazuo? What would become of her? A chill of apprehension ran down her spine as she grasped just how dependent upon him she was at the moment. He was her only buffer, her only advocate. In short, the only person here who actually cared what became of her.

Should he disappear or, God forbid, be killed, there would be no reason for Hasuko or anyone else to keep Temperance alive or assist her in anyway. She didn't even have any money to bribe anyone with. She had nothing.

Only Kazuo. Would that be enough?

Chapter Seventeen

'There's silver missing from my pouch. Do you know anything about that?'

Haag had been summoned to Noordholt's private room and was now on the receiving end of a terrifying glare. If he'd been less sure that he'd done the right thing in using Noordholt's coins for bribery he would have been cowering behind the nearest door. As it was, he stood his ground and tried his best to feign surprise.

'No. Why would I? You didn't ask me to keep watch on your possessions.'

He was sent another shrivelling glare and wondered if that had sounded too insolent, but it was the truth.

'I didn't think there was any need. You're the only man here who knows how much I brought as we left the Deputy Factor back in Dejima.'

'I may know how much there was to begin with, but I have no idea where you've been keeping it or how much has been spent,' Haag protested, although part of that sentence was a lie. He'd spied on the Chief Factor through a hole in the paper partitions and found out that the silver was hidden under a loose stone just outside Noordholt's room in a tiny private garden. It had been child's play to liberate some of it when the man went to the privy.

Noordholt didn't look convinced, however. 'Well, if I find that you're not telling the truth you'll regret it, I promise you. And from now on, I'll keep the damned silver on my person at all times. Whoever is stealing it will have to kill me first.'

'Good idea,' Haag murmured, but inside he was seething. He'd hoped the thefts wouldn't be discovered quite so quickly. Now he regretted not taking more while he had the chance. Somehow he'd have to make the amount he had left last. It would be the very devil of a task. He could only hope they'd be leaving Edo soon.

Temperance and Kazuo eventually fell asleep while waiting to be summoned, and were woken in the early hours of the morning by Hasuko herself and taken down to the small kitchen at the back of the house one at a time.

'You go first,' Kazuo urged Temperance. 'I'll wait up here.'

'Very well, thank you.'

The house was silent and slightly eerie in the first light of dawn, but Temperance hardly noticed. She was still tired after their journey and her brain fogged with sleep.

Their kind hostess and her maid, the older woman who had ushered them in on arrival, had prepared a tub of hot water and a smaller one for washing first. They bustled about making sure there were towels and wash cloths, but when Temperance removed the piece of material that had been tied round her head for so long, the Japanese ladies stopped dead and gasped.

'*Nani?*' Hasuko put a hand up to her mouth and took a step backwards.

Temperance blinked, still befuddled from being woken up so suddenly, then realised Kazuo had never got round to telling Hasuko about his travelling companion being foreign.

'Oh, I'm so sorry, we forgot to warn you. I'm a *gai-jin*, but I'm not a threat to you in any way, I promise.' She glanced at the maid whose eyes were huge with surprise and fear. 'Really, I assure you, I won't harm you.'

Hasuko was obviously made of sterner stuff and lowered her hand, nodding. 'Kazuo-*sama* wouldn't have brought you otherwise.' She frowned at the maid. 'Seiko, stop gawping and let's get started. *Gai-jin* or not, this lady needs a bath.'

The women helped her remove the rest of her clothing

and made sure she was thoroughly washed. Temperance had never been so grateful to be clean in her life. It felt wonderful after the grime of the long journey. As she sank into the near-scalding water in the little bathtub she closed her eyes. 'This is wonderful,' she murmured. 'Thank you so much.' She had missed the daily baths in the *onsen* more than she'd realised and revelled in the feel of the hot water against her newly scrubbed skin. All her aches and pains began to subside.

'Yes, but I'm afraid you can't linger,' Hasuko said. 'It wouldn't do for anyone to find you here and you never know, someone might wake up.'

No sooner had she uttered these words than there came a sharp rapping on the front door of the house. The three women looked at each other in consternation.

'Who could that be? We're not expecting anyone at this hour,' Seiko whispered, wringing her hands nervously.

'Do you think you were followed?' Hasuko asked, concern shadowing her eyes.

Temperance shook her head. Her heart was lodged somewhere near her throat and beating painfully. She had been lulled into a false sense of security by their arrival at Hasuko's house and had momentarily forgotten the very real danger they were in. The knocking reminded her in no uncertain terms. 'Not that we were aware of.' She stood up quickly and grabbed a drying cloth from a nearby stool. 'I'd better go back upstairs though, just in case.'

'Wait, I'll find out who it is. Perhaps I can stall them, if indeed they have come for you. Seiko will show you where to hide if necessary.'

Hasuko made her way towards the front of the house while Temperance dressed hurriedly in a clean sleeping robe which Seiko handed to her. She and the little maid stood still near the door and tried to hear what was happening, but although there were raised voices, Hasuko didn't call out a warning of any kind. Temperance could feel herself trembling and swallowed hard. Had they come this far only to fail? It didn't bear thinking of.

It seemed like they waited for ages, but in fact it was probably only a short while before Hasuko returned, an expression of relief on her face. 'Don't worry, it was only a drunk customer who claimed to have left something behind. I told him we always make sure that doesn't happen, so he must have lost the item elsewhere, but it took a while to persuade him.'

Temperance and Seiko let out their breaths in unison and smiled shakily at each other. 'Right, well I'd better go and fetch Kazuo then,' Temperance said. 'Thank you very much for the bath, *domo arigato gozaimasu.*' She bowed deeply to Hasuko and the maid.

'*Do itashi mashite*, you are most welcome.' Hasuko bowed back. 'If you leave your clothing here with Seiko, she will wash it for you.'

'Oh, but I could do that myself.' Temperance already felt beholden enough to the kind ladies and didn't want to make more work for them.

'No, I think it best if you stay hidden for now, Temi-*san*.' Hasuko glanced at the long, bright hair and strange eyes with a worried expression and Temperance understood her silent message. It was no doubt difficult enough to hide a wanted man, but to keep someone as different-looking as herself secret would prove impossible if anyone else were to see her.

'Of course. Thank you again.'

To her surprise, Temperance fell asleep again after her bath and didn't wake up until the sun was high in the sky. She lay for a moment, staring at the ceiling, before noticing that she was alone. There was no sign of Kazuo or any of his possessions and she sat up abruptly, looking round.

Had he left for good?

She couldn't help a small bubble of panic from rising within her. What if he didn't come back? What if he'd never had any intention of bringing her further than Edo?

'Don't be such a ninny,' she admonished herself out loud. Kazuo would never do something like that without telling her. He was an honourable man, as he had proved several times already. Too honourable on occasion, although she knew she ought to be grateful that he hadn't taken advantage of her in any way. He must have set off early to try and gather the information he needed, that was all.

A knock on the sliding door interrupted her thoughts. Seiko-*san* opened it enough to slide in a tray of food, then bowed and made to leave as quickly as she had come, obviously still uncomfortable with having a foreigner in the house.

'Wait, please.' Temperance seized her chance for reassurance. 'Did Kazuo-*san* say how long he would be gone?'

'No, but I wouldn't expect him to come back before nightfall,' the maid replied. 'It would be too dangerous.'

'Oh, of course. Thank you.' Temperance felt silly for not having thought of that herself. Naturally he'd have to be cautious and it would be a lot easier to be spotted in daylight. Kazuo would never jeopardise Hasuko-*san* by coming and going openly.

She pulled the door to and ate her food slowly. It was, after all, likely to be her only occupation for quite some time so she might as well make the most of it.

Temperance was ready to scream with boredom by the time Kazuo finally returned. It had been dark for several hours. In fact, it was probably nearly midnight and she had seriously begun to believe her own fears that he may never come back.

'At last!' She threw her arms around him in pure relief and he laughed, an expression of surprise on his face as he briefly hugged her back before letting go.

'Was I away that long?' He gave her a quizzical look and she half turned away, embarrassed now by her impulsive behaviour.

'It seemed like forever to me. I've had nothing to do all day and there's only so much sleeping a person can do.'

'Forgive me, I should have asked Hasuko-*san* to give you something to occupy your time with. I will do so tomorrow.' Kazuo sank down onto the *futon* and Temperance followed suit, albeit at a slight distance from him.

'You're going out again?'

'Of course.' His eyes became troubled. 'I have yet to find anything out that is useful. I didn't have any success today whatsoever. In fact, I had a major setback.'

'How so?'

'Yamada-*sama*, one of the three men who signed my father's arrest warrant, is dead. Admittedly, he was the one who was least likely to have been the instigator, since he was a mild-mannered man who hardly ever bothered with the intrigues going on around the *Shogun*, but still ... I should have liked to at least speak to him.'

'How did he die?'

'An illness of some sort, apparently. I don't think it was foul play, although I suppose it can't be ruled out altogether.'

'And didn't he have any relatives?'

'Only a daughter and I doubt I would be allowed to talk to her. She's married to one of Tanaka's cousins.'

'Tanaka's?' The mere name made Temperance's stomach muscles clench with apprehension and her eyes flew to Kazuo's. 'So the man was related to him by marriage? Doesn't that seem suspicious to you?'

'Naturally, which is why I wanted to speak to him. As I

said, neither my father nor I believed him capable of malice so he must have been coerced. Whether it was by Tanaka, through being related, or by the third man, who is very powerful, cannot now be confirmed.'

'But surely it doesn't matter? If he wasn't the instigator then he's not the man you're looking for anyway.'

'No, but he could have led me to him. Now I'll have to try other means.'

Temperance thought for a moment. 'Who is the third man?'

'His name will mean nothing to you and I think it's safer if I don't tell you. What you don't know, you can't reveal.' Kazuo looked serious, which made her stomach flutter again.

'We're really in that much danger?'

'Yes, I'm afraid so. Neither of us should be here and you are now a fugitive on top of everything else. So am I, really, as I was ostensibly Tanaka's servant. But never mind, we'll manage somehow.' He took her hand briefly and gave it a reassuring squeeze, then sighed and drew his fingers through his hair. That action made it come loose from the topknot and tumble down his back and shoulders like a dark waterfall. 'I'm sorry, I really should have taken you straight back to Nagasaki. I shouldn't have been so impatient. My mission could have waited.'

'No, don't say that. What about your father's health? You said time was of the essence.'

'True, but who knows? It might already be too late.'

'You mustn't think that. From your description he sounds like a stubborn old man, a fighter, he'll not give up easily. Either way, I owe you for rescuing me from Tanaka. Really, I don't mind waiting. I just don't want you to get hurt.'

He smiled wanly. 'There was always a risk of that. Even if I do find the right man, I have to actually be able to prove him guilty, otherwise I've achieved nothing. Killing him will not right the wrong done to my father and simply knowing who it was won't help either so a verbal confession from someone is no good. I need hard proof.' He shook his head. 'It won't be easy and may even be impossible.'

She put a hand on his arm. 'Don't give up yet. I'm sure you'll find a way.'

He sighed. 'Perhaps.' He was silent for a while then made a visible effort to talk of other things. 'Have you seen Hasuko today? I spoke to her this morning and she promised to talk to you if she had the time.'

'No, I haven't seen anyone except Seiko very briefly at meal times. I ... uhm, I'm not sure Hasuko-*san* wants to talk to me. It did rather startle her when she found out that I'm not Japanese.'

'Oh, I doubt that would trouble her for long. No, she's probably been busy on my behalf. She's very good at gathering information, which is one of the reasons my father found her so useful. Although naturally he liked her for herself as well.'

Temperance frowned. 'This business of concubines, I don't quite understand it ...' She trailed off, wondering if this was a subject she ought to avoid, having come so close to being one herself. Her curiosity was, as always, nagging at her, however, and she genuinely wanted to know.

'Well, a nobleman has to marry a woman who can bring him wealth and powerful connections to other noble families and allies. But that's simply duty and after presenting her husband with heirs, a wife can introduce a suitable concubine to him in order to lessen her burden.'

'Lessen her burden? But if she loves him, then how can she bear it if he sleeps with another woman?'

'Love? That is something that rarely happens. Only in poetry or stories. No, you marry for gain and if you like each other, so much the better. If not ...' Kazuo shrugged.

'Well, look at what happened with Tanaka's wife,' Temperance protested. 'He's divorced her for loving someone else.'

'Ah, but you were asking about concubines. Wives don't have the same rights. They must remain faithful to their husband, no matter what.'

'How unfair,' Temperance said without thinking, then realised that it was no different from the double standards practised in her own country. If an English girl should happen to become pregnant while unmarried for example, she'd be the one who was ostracised by society, not the man who did the deed. This was equally as unjust, but it was the way of the world.

Kazuo frowned. 'I suppose so. I've never thought about it. It's just how it is.' He shook his head, looking slightly bemused. 'Do the men in your country not do the same then?'

Temperance thought back to snatches of conversation overheard many years before, when her mother and aunt were gossiping in the kitchen, and had to acknowledge that Kazuo was right. She sighed and looked out of the window. 'Yes, but they're not supposed to. If a man was unfaithful he would try to keep it a secret, not have the second woman living openly in his house.'

'That seems more deceitful to me.' Kazuo crossed his arms over his chest. 'Lying is a most dishonourable trait.'

'Well, I … Yes, yes it is. Even so, it all seems wrong to me.' Temperance threw up her hands. She didn't know what to think any longer. She only knew that if she married, she would hate it if her husband strayed.

Kazuo regarded her for a moment then tactfully changed the subject. 'I think we need some relaxation. How would you like to go moon gazing tomorrow night?'

'I beg your pardon?' Temperance thought for a moment she had misunderstood him.

'It will be the fifteenth day of the eighth month of our calendar, the perfect time to observe the autumn moon in all its glory. Lots of people gather to do this every year. It's very popular. They have parties and write poetry about the beauty of the moon.'

'You're joking?' Temperance tried to stifle a giggle. She could see that he was serious, but it seemed a ridiculous pastime to her. 'And it's not the eighth month, it's the tenth – I'm fairly sure it's October now.' She pronounced the word in English and he looked puzzled.

'Ocku-toh-beruh? What's that? No, it is definitely the eighth month here. And I'm not joking. Just come and try it, you might enjoy yourself.'

'Very well, but I'm not writing any poetry. I'm useless at that.'

He smiled. 'I'll do it for you.'

Chapter Eighteen

Escaping from Hasuko's house via the back door the following evening, Kazuo saw Temperance stop for a moment to breathe in the unfamiliar odours of Yoshiwara at night. There were mouth-watering cooking smells assailing them from all directions, as the proprietors of the various establishments made sure they had sumptuous dishes available to serve their customers. Clouds of scent enveloped them whenever any ladies of the night passed them on the street. Fumes of *sake* emanated from the jolly customers weaving their way to one tea house or another, their way lit by coloured lanterns, and in addition there was a tang of brine in the air, borne on the breeze from the ocean. Kazuo smiled to himself as he saw Temperance battle her curiosity and trying her best not to look around too much, but suddenly she stopped and frowned.

'It smells so clean,' she exclaimed. 'How can that be?'

'What do you mean?' Kazuo was puzzled by her question and smiled openly. She was a delight, this woman, constantly surprising him with her opinions or actions.

'Well, where I come from everyone throws their, uhm, rubbish out into the street. Quite frankly, it stinks, but here?' She sniffed again. 'Nothing.'

'That's because there are sewer ducts on either side of the streets and in the back alleys. Anything thrown out will be carried away and waste is usually collected and taken away.'

'How sensible! Is there anything here in Japan that is not done in an orderly fashion?'

Kazuo wasn't sure, but he almost thought he detected a note of exasperation in her voice and he didn't understand why that should be so. 'Well, no, I don't suppose there is,' he replied cautiously. 'Why do you ask?'

'No reason.' She wouldn't elaborate and Kazuo let the subject drop. There were some things about her that he would never understand, he realised. They were just too different.

They were allowed through the gate, the password once more working like magic, and began to walk towards the outskirts of the city. Although it was dark, it wasn't very late yet and there were still people everywhere. At street crossings, in the vicinity of bridges and along the larger streets, people congregated to eat, drink, talk and watch street performers like acrobats or owners of rare animals.

'All this noise is making my head spin,' Temperance confessed. 'It's quite a contrast to our quiet little room, isn't it?'

'To be sure, the noise and bustle takes some getting used to, but soon you won't notice.' Kazuo had spent the last two days out and about and was no longer bothered by the crowds.

They walked until they came to the Sumida river and continued on, past the Sensoji Temple, which was illuminated by lanterns. Temperance wanted to explore this intriguing-looking building, but Kazuo took her hand and tugged her along impatiently. 'Not today,' he said firmly and wondered if there would ever come a time when he could walk around with her openly, without having to worry about being seen. It seemed unlikely.

Soon they reached the outskirts of the city and there, in a nearby field, was a throng of people. They were standing in groups, chatting in hushed voices, or sitting on blankets on the ground, writing implements at the ready.

Kazuo came to a halt on the edge of the field in the shadow of a large tree. 'Let's stay here. If anyone looks our way, I don't think they can see the colour of your eyes in the shadows. Look, isn't it beautiful?'

Temperance gazed up at the moon, huge and round, with a benignly smiling face clearly visible, and sighed with pleasure. 'Yes, it is.' She smiled. 'I suddenly feel very small and insignificant.'

'I know what you mean.'

It was a perfect evening for moon-viewing, with not a cloud in the sky nor any wind. The stillness all around them, as well as the hushed voices nearby, combined to make them feel as if they were in the presence of something exalted.

'It's quite awe-inspiring,' Temperance whispered. 'But what's so special about tonight?'

'It is the full moon and this time of year it's larger than usual, thereby increasing its impact on the viewer. Now let me think, I'll see if I can come up with a *haiku*.'

'*Haiku*?'

'A short poem consisting of three lines – the first one with five syllables, the second one with seven, then a final one of five again,' Kazuo explained. 'There are other rules that apply as well, but that is a simple explanation and as we're neither of us experts, I don't think it matters.'

He closed his eyes, took a deep breath and concentrated. Instead of the moon, he saw only Temi's lovely face in his mind's eye and he frowned. This wouldn't do. He was supposed to compose something about the moon. He concentrated even harder without success, then finally, the solution came to him – he would combine the two. He opened his eyes and smiled at her. 'How about this?

The moon shining bright
Your skin soft, warm and fragrant
'Neath my questing hand.'

Temperance nodded, but looked slightly embarrassed at the image conjured up by his words. He knew he shouldn't have so much as hinted that he wanted to touch her perfect skin, but he couldn't take the words back now.

An impish grin suddenly lit her features as if she had been struck with inspiration. 'I know. What about ...?

Moonshine on your hair
Brightness on darkness reflects
Light on a deep pond.'

Kazuo grinned back. 'Not bad. I thought you said you didn't do poetry?'

Temperance blushed and looked away. 'I don't usually. That one just came to me. Your kind of poetry is different to ours. Easier somehow.'

'Perhaps the way we just did it, but if done properly it's anything but easy, believe me. Come, let's sit down and just enjoy the moonlight for a while before we go back.' Kazuo unfolded a large cloth he'd brought and spread it at the base of the tree. They sat down with their backs to the harsh trunk and gazed upwards, spellbound by the magical light. Kazuo couldn't resist a small measure of contact with her, so he took her hand in his and suddenly everything felt right. It was enough to just sit under the tree and enjoy the here and now.

Temperance was lost in her own thoughts. She could see a small crease between Kazuo's brows and wanted to reach out and smooth it down, but she restrained herself. A warm feeling was spreading inside her simply from holding his hand, but she was sure that he only meant it in a companionable way, nothing more.

He looked so perfect in the moonlight, his high cheekbones

emphasised by the unearthly sheen, his hair like dark velvet. Her poem had been inspired by the sight of it and she'd recited it without thinking. She sincerely hoped the shadows had hidden her embarrassment afterwards.

Neither of them said anything for a long time, there was no need, but after what seemed like ages Kazuo stirred.

'I suppose we'd better go back,' he said, his voice tinged with regret. He pulled her up and picked up the cloth, shaking it out before folding it. Temperance heard him sigh and couldn't resist prying.

'Is something the matter?'

'No, I was just thinking how complicated life can be. At times like this, I wish it could always be as peaceful as tonight. No strife, no power struggles, just harmony and appreciation of the beauty of nature.'

They made their way back to Yoshiwara in silence. Temperance pondered his words, which struck a chill inside her and reminded her of the dangers they had yet to face.

Peace would be a long time coming, if at all.

All *daimyo* had to have a residence in Edo because of the system known as *sankin kotai*. This meant the feudal lords having to spend every second year in Edo and returning to their home provinces for the rest of the time, while leaving their wives and children as permanent hostages in Edo in order to guarantee their loyalty to the *Shogun*. Kazuo knew it was a clever way of maintaining centralised rule, while weakening any opposition or provincial strength. It was also a system Kazuo had counted on to be to his advantage in his quest.

Accordingly, the following day, he made his way to the grand abode of the third man who had signed his father's arrest warrant. It was luxurious beyond belief, consisting of an upper, middle and lower residence, surrounded by gardens, ponds and storehouses. The lord and his family always lived in the upper residence, so Kazuo hoped he would be taken there. Or at the very least, if he was employed by the man, that he would be allowed access to the main house.

The third man, as Kazuo had dubbed him, was a powerful northern lord, astute and careful in all his dealings with others, and definitely nobody's fool. It wouldn't be easy to infiltrate his household, and finding any evidence of wrongdoing would no doubt be even harder. Kazuo had observed the man from across a crowded room some years ago and at that time he had judged him to be both clever and honest. Kanno senior had agreed with this, but they both knew that circumstances could change a man. His having signed the warrant made Kazuo wonder if their appraisal had been wrong or if something had happened to make the man want more power.

The lord's house, which was so opulent it seemed like a palace compound close up, was easily reached. Kazuo had no trouble getting through the main gate either.

'I have a message for his lordship,' he said and was waved through by a lazy guard.

The next step was to go in search of whoever was in charge of appointments in the lord's household, in order to ask for temporary employment, but when he finally managed to track the man down, Kazuo was bitterly disappointed.

'I'm sorry, young man, but his lordship has just finished his stay in Edo. He left for his northern castle months ago, so we don't need any more staff at the moment.'

'Oh, I'd been told it was his year for staying in Edo,' Kazuo said, trying to look crestfallen so that the man would think him merely upset at missing the opportunity of working for such a great lord.

'It is, but his lordship was called away to deal with a border dispute. The *Shogun* himself asked him to go, as the neighbour in question has been a troublemaker in the past and he trusted my lord to deal with the matter swiftly and efficiently. Having to go so far, he said that he might as well stay for a while and deal with estate matters before returning to Edo, so I cannot say for certain when that will be. There's also his daughter's wedding.'

'Wedding?'

'Yes. My lord's wife and oldest daughter were granted permission to travel north as well in order to prepare for the girl's marriage to the son of another neighbour.'

'I see. Well, thank you. You have been most kind.' Kazuo bowed his way out, while swearing inwardly. He couldn't believe his recent run of bad luck. If only he'd gone to Edo first, rather than Tanaka's abode, everything might have worked out better. He could have been in the north by now in the third lord's service. Instead, he would have to follow him and try to bluff his way into employment there, the way he'd done at Tanaka's house in the south. But it would be much more difficult as outsiders were seldom taken on except in the big cities. On his own estates his lordship would have an endless supply of workers and wouldn't need to employ perfect strangers, whereas in Edo that was often necessary.

Kazuo swore again. He couldn't help but wonder if Temi was bringing him bad fortune, since everything had started to go wrong the moment he set eyes on her at the inn where Tanaka bought her. A little voice inside him told him this must be the case, but how could he have acted differently? He'd had no choice but to save her, especially when it was his fault that she was captured in the first place, although he didn't know that at the time. Fate had decreed that he should be at Tanaka's estate in order to rescue Temi, and he couldn't regret helping her. Perhaps this was merely another test of his integrity?

He sighed. It didn't make any difference how he had

come by his bad luck, all he could do was try to salvage the situation as best he could. With a heavy heart he set off to prepare for yet another journey, one he hadn't counted on having to make.

'We're going north? But we only just got here.' Temperance looked at Kazuo, searching his face for a sign that he was joking, but finding none. She couldn't believe that they'd come all this way for nothing. The prospect of many more weeks on the road, sleeping rough and being uncomfortable, wasn't one she relished.

'No, not "we". I'm going north by myself. You will have to stay here. I'm sorry, I may be gone for quite some time, so you'll have to be patient.'

'No! No, I'm coming with you.' Temperance definitely didn't want to be left behind. Even travelling was preferable to spending endless days cooped up in this tiny chamber.

'You can't. I'm going to seek employment with the third lord, the one I was telling you about. That will be difficult enough. There's no way he'll employ you as well. Think about it.'

Temperance swallowed hard. She could see what he meant. 'But I could live in the forest nearby, perhaps? And you can come and see me from time to time. If you just teach me how to catch fish and other creatures and—'

'Temi, it's impossible and you know it.' Kazuo frowned at her, his tone severe. 'And how could I concentrate on my task when I'd be worrying about you all the time?'

'I'd be fine.'

'You might not be. I'm sorry, but I'm not taking you and that's final.' He looked forbidding, every inch the son of a high-ranking *samurai* who was used to having his orders followed and Temi shivered. It was unlike him to speak to her so severely, but perhaps she'd never tried his patience to this extent before. She opened her mouth to protest one last time, but he held up an imperious hand to forestall her.

'No more. I will not change my mind on this.' His mouth was set in an uncompromising line and Temperance could see that further arguments would be futile. Relenting slightly, he added, 'I'll ask Hasuko to find you more to do so that the time passes quickly. Then when I come back, I promise I'll take you straight to Nagasaki.'

Temperance sighed. His words made sense, but the thought of being left behind made butterflies dance in her stomach. How could she bear it?

'But what if you never come back?'

He looked away. 'I will leave money with Hasuko and instructions for her or someone she trusts to hire a boat and take you back to your family if you haven't heard from me in three months.'

'Three months!'

'The third man lives very far north and it might take me some time to even gain employment, never mind find the evidence I seek.'

'Why can't she find me passage right now?'

Kazuo looked away. 'Although I trust you, I cannot risk anyone finding out about my mission.'

'But I'd never tell a—'

He held up his hand again. 'I know you wouldn't, not willingly. But what if you were captured along the way? You could be made to talk. Trust me.'

Temperance wanted to scream and shout and stamp her feet like a spoiled child, but she did none of those things. She understood his reasoning and he didn't owe her anything, after all. On the contrary, she was indebted to him for her very life. Feeling defeated, she capitulated. 'Very well, I'll wait here, but you had better come back or I'll come after you.'

Kazuo smiled wryly. 'You can always try.'

Chapter Nineteen

Falling asleep took Temperance a long time that night as her thoughts were troubled. She couldn't help worrying about her future, as well as Kazuo's safety, and although she knew she could rely on Hasuko to do as he asked, it just didn't feel right to stay behind. She sighed into the darkness. Why did everything have to be so complicated? Perhaps she should have tried to make her way back to Nagasaki on her own, instead of relying on Kazuo, but then she may not even have made it this far.

She would just have to trust him to stay safe, she decided. He seemed to know what he was doing and she felt sure he would never jeopardise his mission by acting foolishly. If anyone could see it through, he could, and no doubt he would accomplish what he'd set out to do. He was right – with no one to worry about except himself, he could perform his task with more speed and concentration and she was sure he would succeed. He had to.

Her eyes were finally closing, when suddenly she became aware of a low rumbling noise and the floor began to move. She sat up, shaking Kazuo who had his back to her as usual.

'Earthquake,' she hissed, shaking him harder as the trembling of the floor became more violent.

'It will pass,' he murmured. 'They come and go. Go back to sleep.'

'No, wake up! This is a big one.' Temperance had experienced slight tremors before, but nothing like this. She began to tremble herself and watched through the window as a nearby roof seemed to sway in the moonlight. It was as if it were a mere toy, being played with by the gods. 'Kazuo, please, I'm serious!'

He sat up and rubbed his eyes, steadying himself with both hands on the floor as he felt the building moving. 'Very well,' he muttered. 'It does seem a bit fiercer than usual.'

He stood up and went to the window, then quickly made his way over towards the door. He opened it and leaned against the frame. 'Come here, you'll be safer.'

Temperance did as she was told and he pulled her towards him, her back against his chest. Together they stood there, waiting for the tremors to subside, which they soon did, but Kazuo didn't move.

'It's not over yet,' he said. 'They usually come three at a time and the last one is the worst.'

'Oh, no.' Temperance had thought the first one was bad enough. 'But what if the walls collapse? We'll be trapped in here. Shouldn't we go outside?'

'No, we're safer here. Even if the house fell down, we'd be fine. The walls are only made of thin wood so we should be able to dig our way out.'

Temperance didn't even want to contemplate such a fate, so she closed her eyes tightly and held on to Kazuo's hands, which were twined around her abdomen. The second quake soon began – first the low-pitched grumbling sound that heralded the earth moving and then the rattling of wood as the house shook on its foundations and loose window frames oscillated. Temperance felt herself quivering with fear, but Kazuo merely tightened his grip around her, whispering, 'Don't be afraid, we'll be fine.'

When the third tremor shook the house violently, the vibrations made a noise almost like muted thunder and Temperance couldn't help a small whimper from escaping. All around them were the sounds of objects falling down, ornaments crashing to the floor, roof tiles shattering on the ground outside and the splintering of wood and plaster which could no longer resist the forces of nature. Temperance had never felt so small nor so helpless in all her life. She was sure that her last moment had come and she turned and buried her face in Kazuo's shoulder, closing her eyes tightly. If she was going to die, she wanted to die like this, held fast in his arms and breathing in the scent of him. She grabbed his robe with both hands and hung on for dear life.

At last, it was over and after waiting for a few minutes, Kazuo let go of her and walked over to the window. '*Chikusho!*' he exclaimed. 'Fires.' He turned to search for his clothes on the floor. 'I've got to go and help put out the fires. They'll need all the assistance they can get. Stay here, I'll be back as soon as I can.'

'But can't I come too?'

'No, someone might see you, remember? You'll be perfectly safe now. The earthquakes are finished and the fire isn't anywhere near us.' He hurried out of the room, leaving Temperance staring after him.

She went over to the window and peered into the night. She heard voices shouting and the sound of running feet, and the sky was lit by an eerie glow from several fires nearby. She knew that all the houses were built mostly of timber and no doubt they went up in flames in no time at all.

'Dear God, don't let the fire come this way,' she prayed quietly. If it did, how would she get out? Just in case she had to leave, she got dressed as well, tied her hair into the piece of cloth she normally used and made sure it was all hidden underneath.

She looked out the window again and noticed for the first time that it overlooked a small roof that sloped towards a similar one on the house next door. Temperance decided to investigate the possibility of escape that way, just in case, and eased herself over the windowsill and onto the roof. It was made of tiles and seemed quite sturdy, but she held onto the window at first to make sure she didn't fall through, then took a few tentative steps. It appeared safe enough so she sat down and looked out onto the street. She had a much better vantage point here and could see the various comings and goings without being seen herself.

In the next few moments, everything happened very quickly and Temperance barely had time to think. She gasped as, without warning, flames shot up from the house next door, and the people inside began to scream.

'*Tasukete kure!* Someone help us, please!'

Temperance watched with mounting horror as terrified ladies of the night scrambled out through windows on the ground floor, as well as spilling through the front door into the street. But there were others still inside on the upper floors and their screams continued unabated.

'Help! We're stuck! The staircase is on fire. Someone please help get us out of here!'

She glimpsed shadowy figures running to and fro on the floor below the one she was at, and when a woman stuck her head out the window, she looked about frantically for some means of helping those who were trapped. She had to do something, but what? At first, she couldn't see any way out for them, but then an idea came to her and she shouted down to the woman, 'Go upstairs and climb out the window. I'll help you get across to this house, then you can use our staircase. *Wakarimashita ka?* Understand?'

The woman was so terrified, it took Temperance a while longer to make her grasp what she was saying, but her instructions finally sank in. '*Hai, wakatta.*' The woman disappeared inside, only to reappear with two other ladies and a small child on the top floor.

The houses were built fairly close together, but it was too far to jump, so Temperance rushed inside to search for something that could be used as a bridge. There was nothing apart from the futons, which were too insubstantial, but then her eyes alighted on the door. It was made of thin wood, but might be strong enough to bear someone's weight for a short while. Temperance prayed this was so and aimed an almighty kick at the side of it.

The wood protested and the door moved slightly. Temperance kicked again and one corner came loose. Hearing the women from the neighbouring house shouting again outside, she began a frenzy of kicking that finally freed the door. Then she stumbled towards the window with it, shoving it through as quickly as she could.

'Wait, I'm coming,' she called to the terrified group. 'Just hold on.'

The door began to slide down the slight slope of the roof, but Temperance held on to one end and stopped it from falling to the ground. Using every last ounce of strength, she heaved it up and across the space that divided the two houses. One end landed with a thud on the opposite roof.

'One of you hold it, to make sure it's not moving,' she ordered. 'Then start crawling. You first.' She pointed at a woman with a toddler. The woman's eyes were huge with fright and she began to shake her head and back away.

The fire was roaring behind them now, its ferocious flames licking every square inch of wood with hungry intensity and moving incredibly fast. Temperance's stomach was doing somersaults at the thought of the fate awaiting the ladies if they didn't escape soon, but she forced herself not to look at the conflagration. Instead she concentrated on the people who needed her help. There wasn't much time left, so Temperance shouted in her most imperious voice, 'Just do it. Now. *Crawl*!' She fixed the woman with an icy glare. Miraculously it worked and she did as she was told, while one of the others held on to the corners of the door.

'Make the child crawl underneath you,' Temperance instructed. 'You can hold her with one arm. Go on, you can do it.'

With some more urging from the others, and a slight push in the right direction, the woman managed to do as she was told. She reached the safety of Temperance's roof within a short space of time. The others followed quickly, scrambling across on their hands and knees, while trying not to look down into the abyss beneath them. As the last woman began to crawl, the door slipped a little and she screamed, but one of the others helped Temperance steady it on their side and the woman made it at last.

'Inside, please, quickly,' Temperance ordered, feeling guilty for telling everyone what to do in such an imperious fashion, but knowing instinctively that they were all too scared to think for themselves at that moment. 'Hurry, let's go downstairs before this house catches fire too.' The ladies needed no further bidding and everyone dragged themselves across the windowsill and began to descend. Two of them were sobbing with relief now while the child whimpered, still shocked.

Temperance grabbed her wide-brimmed hat and followed them after one last glance through the window at the roaring inferno that was now the neighbouring house. She shuddered. It had been a close call and they weren't safe yet; the flames could come their way. When they all trooped into the street, she went to stand behind the others, as far away from the light as possible, trying to stay hidden. The woman with the small child sought her out, however, and whispered hoarsely, 'Thank you, thank you so much. You saved my life and that of my child. I will always be in your debt.'

Temperance shook her head. 'I just did what had to be done. Anyone would have done the same. I'm glad you're safe.'

The woman bowed low to her and smiled, albeit somewhat tremulously. 'I'm Kei and if you ever need my help with anything, you only have to ask.' She bowed again and Temperance bowed back.

'It was nothing. Really.'

Kei leaned closer and whispered, 'And I won't tell anyone about you, I swear.'

'What do you mean?' Temperance felt a chill of fear snake down her back.

'I saw your eyes in the light from the fire. I know you're … not one of us. But don't worry, I won't tell a soul and I'll make sure the others don't either.'

Temperance realised she had forgotten to keep her eyes lowered in the heat of the moment and could only be grateful to Kei for her promise.

'Thank you, you're very kind. I'm, er, not staying very long. Hopefully I should go back to my family soon, but until then, I have to stay hidden.'

'I understand. Don't fret, we'll keep your secret.'

It was a long night and Temperance was bone weary by the time all the fires had been put out and she was able to go back inside. The people fighting the fires had managed to stop it from spreading into Hasuko's house, so Temperance went back to their little room just before dawn. She'd huddled behind Kei and her friends for most of the night and was grateful to escape to the attic where no one could see her.

Kazuo came back some time later, too exhausted to say anything other than that he was fine. He fell asleep as soon as his head hit the pillow and Temperance snuggled down next to him, grateful that he was unharmed. As he was so deeply asleep, she allowed herself to put one arm around his waist and her cheek against his back. She breathed in the scent of him, which was now mingled with the stench of smoke and soot, and thanked God for keeping Kazuo alive, at least for now.

'*Gai-jin-san*, I may have some information for you.'

Haag had just entered the brothel he normally frequented in the Yoshiwara pleasure district, followed by an interpreter he'd taken to using. It made talking to people here so much easier and meant he didn't have to tax his brain with trying out his very limited vocabulary. The man was uncomfortable with having Haag roam the streets of Edo, since it was forbidden, but the promise of a large bribe upon their return to Nagasaki had persuaded him that perhaps it wasn't such a terrible thing after all.

The brothel was one of the seedier ones in a tiny back street, but Haag didn't care. A whore was a whore as far as he was concerned, and from what he'd seen the expensive establishments just charged extra for a lot of unnecessary things like entertainers, raconteurs and hangers-on. He had no need for any of that.

'Information? Really? What have you heard?'

The owner of the establishment held out his hand in a none too subtle reminder. Swallowing a sigh of annoyance, Haag delved into his pocket and pulled out a few coins. The owner made a little face, but accepted them nonetheless. Just as well, since it was all Haag had brought.

'There's a rumour going round that a strange lady with pale eyes was seen in this area last night after the earthquake.'

'Here, in Yoshiwara?' Haag could hardly believe his luck. At last, a sighting of Temperance, for surely it couldn't be anyone else? There were no other foreign women in Japan as far as he knew.

'Yes, apparently.' The owner shrugged. 'I don't know exactly where though. It's a large place.'

That was true. Haag reckoned there had to be at least a thousand people living in the pleasure district, if not more. 'Are you sure you can't be more specific?' he asked. 'Which street was she seen in?'

Again, a shrug. 'No idea. My informant didn't say.'

'Well, can you let me speak to him, please? Maybe he'll tell me.'

'No, he's gone. Left yesterday.'

Haag swore softly, but tried to stay calm. 'Very well, thank you. I appreciate you telling me this much, at least.'

He'd have to roam these streets until he found her, which was a damned nuisance, but how hard could it be? She'd stick out like the proverbial sore thumb.

Kazuo slept all day and didn't stir until early evening, when the rumblings of his stomach woke him and reminded him how late it was. He had a quick bath to rid himself of all the various odours and dirt that had adhered to him the night before, then bid Temperance goodbye after a hasty meal.

'I must go and see about hiring a horse and buying some equipment,' he said. 'I'll be back as soon as I can, then perhaps we can go out together one last time before I leave.'

Temperance nodded and smiled, but he noticed that the smile didn't reach her lovely eyes. He sighed inwardly. He knew it would be hard for her to be left behind here for so long, but there really was no way he could take her with him. It would be impossible.

Thoughts of what was to come and worry about how Temperance would fare in his absence, as well as a lingering tiredness from the long night of helping to fight the fires, made him careless. He forgot to pay attention to where he was going. Consequently, he walked into a man who was coming round a corner with a group of others and only looked up when one of them roughly grabbed his arm.

'Well, look who it is,' the man sneered. 'The fugitive. Just the man Lord Tanaka wanted to speak to.'

Kazuo blinked and realised that he'd had the misfortune to bump into some of the men he had worked with briefly at Tanaka's estate. They surrounded him eagerly and as he took in the triumphant glances and smirks, his stomach plummeted.

He was in big trouble.

Acting with lightning speed, he managed to free himself from the iron grip of the man holding him, then feinted to the left before ducking to the right to try and escape. They were too fast and too many for him, however, and within seconds he was held in a secure grip once more.

'You're not going anywhere until his lordship has had a word with you,' one of the men said and guffawed. The others joined in and the sound of their mirth made Kazuo's insides tighten. He had no illusions as to how Tanaka conducted interviews with people reluctant to speak to him. And one who was suspected of having spirited away his new concubine wasn't likely to receive a fair hearing by any means. He gritted his teeth as he was dragged away towards an even more lavish residence than the one he'd visited the day before.

Just as the group turned the corner to return the way they had come, Kazuo caught sight of Hasuko. She was standing in a nearby doorway watching him, having obviously been out on some errand. One hand was covering her mouth to hide her astonishment, but she quickly schooled her features into an expression of indifference and turned away. He looked away immediately as well, so as not to cast any suspicion on her, but he knew that she'd seen him. He wondered if there was anything she could do to help, but doubted it. If he came out of this ordeal alive, then perhaps she could be of assistance, but for the moment all he could do was pray to the gods to give him fortitude and courage.

He would need both in the hours ahead.

Chapter Twenty

'Temi-*san*, I must speak with you immediately.'

Temperance was woken from a half-slumber by the urgent knocking on the door, which had already been replaced by one of Hasuko's efficient servants. She went to slide it open and looked out at the worried face of her hostess.

'Come in, please. What's the matter?' Dread took hold of her and twisted her insides. She knew by the expression on the woman's face that Hasuko was the bearer of bad news.

'It's Kazuo-*san*. He has been taken.'

'Taken? By whom? I didn't think anyone knew he was here.'

'He was captured by Lord Tanaka's men. It was pure coincidence, I believe. I saw him coming along the street and he was deep in thought. Somehow he bumped into a group of people and one of them recognised him. He tried to escape, of course, but there were too many of them and they took him away. I didn't dare interfere. It wouldn't have done any good anyway.'

Temperance felt cold all over and shivered violently. 'Oh, Hasuko-*san*, this is a disaster,' she whispered. 'What dreadful bad luck. You're sure they were Tanaka's men?'

'Yes, they were all wearing the same clothing with his clan motif. It is very distinctive, I would recognise it anywhere. I'm sorry.' Hasuko hesitated for a moment. 'He is the man you escaped from, isn't he? Kazuo-*san* mentioned it.'

'Yes, and Kazuo will be blamed. They will torture him until he confesses and then you and I will be in danger too. You must leave, Hasuko-*san*. Have you anywhere else to go for a while?'

'Don't worry about me. I have friends who will help me. It

is you who must go. Kazuo prepared me for this possibility and it's all arranged. I know a man with a boat who is willing to take you all the way back to Nagasaki. It will be expensive as well as dangerous, and Kazuo had hoped to avoid this, but we have no choice now. You must hurry and pack your belongings then I will take you to the harbour myself. The fewer people who know about this, the better.'

'But what about Kazuo? We can't just leave him at Tanaka's mercy! In fact, I don't believe he has any.' The thought of what Tanaka might even now be doing to Kazuo made Temperance feel physically sick.

'I will ask my friends. Perhaps there is some way of helping him, but it was his wish that you be taken to safety first.'

'No, I won't go. I can't. There must be something I can do.'

Hasuko put a hand on her arm and squeezed gently. 'It is noble of you, but you are a foreigner and at risk yourself. What could you possibly do?'

'I don't know. I'll think of something.'

Hasuko shook her head sadly and sighed. 'I really think you would help him more by following his orders.'

Temperance wasn't listening though, but bit her lip, deep in thought. Her brain felt paralysed with fear, but she forced it to work, trying desperately to come up with a plan. Thinking out loud, she said, 'We must rescue him somehow. Tanaka has hundreds of men working for him, guarding his house and grounds. How could we get in? Some ruse? Poison the guards?'

'You're sure you don't wish to leave?' Hasuko regarded her with her head to one side. 'I am offering you a means of going back to your family. Is that not what you wanted?'

'Yesterday, yes, but not now. I'm sorry, Hasuko-*san*, but my mind is made up. I simply can't leave Kazuo to his fate. He saved me, now I have to do the same for him.' She didn't add that the mere thought of leaving him, let alone in the clutches of an evil man like Tanaka, was intolerable.

'Very well then, let me think.' Hasuko paced the floor of the little chamber, even though she could only take a few steps in each direction. 'Are you squeamish? I mean, could you kill a man if you had to? For Kazuo's sake.'

Temperance nodded. 'My cousin trained me. I can wield a sword and a dagger. I'll do whatever is necessary to free him.'

'Good. Then I must find a beautiful girl who is willing to go with you. You should both dress in the finest *kimono* in order to dazzle the guards. You can say that you have been sent for by Lord Tanaka himself, but as soon as you are past the guards, you must let the girl go on her way while you search for Kazuo. He will no doubt be kept well away from the main residence. Can you do that?'

'Yes, I think so. What will happen to her though, the girl? I don't want anyone to be hurt unnecessarily.'

'No, she can always say that she had received a summons, but that perhaps the owner of the establishment where she works got the message wrong. I don't think they'll connect her arrival with Kazuo's disappearance until it's too late, provided you can free him of course.' The older woman shook her head, frowning. 'If only there was some way of distracting his guards, the ones closest to him I mean. You can't just walk up to them and stab them. Besides, they are bound to be extra vigilant.'

Temperance thought for a moment, then an idea occurred to her. '*Yuki onna*,' she said triumphantly.

'I beg your pardon?'

'I can pretend to be a snow ghost and try to scare them.' After Ryo had called her those names, Temperance had asked some of the girls at The Weeping Willow what he meant. She'd been told that a *yuki onna* was the ghost of someone who had frozen to death and they were invariably pale and white, just like her, including the hair. Impersonating one shouldn't be too difficult. 'People are so superstitious, especially at night. And if I'm dressed all in white with my hair loose and lots of rice powder on my face, they might think for a moment that I'm a ghost. That will give me the element of surprise and enough time to despatch them quietly.'

Hasuko nodded, a smile beginning to curve her mouth. 'Yes, it might work. I can't think of anything better, in any case. I will ask around and see if anyone has a pure white *kimono* we can borrow.'

'Who will you send with me? It will have to be someone truly stunning so that the guards believe she has been sent for by Tanaka.'

'I will ask Kei-*san* next door. She told me what you did last night and that she is indebted to you. She will do anything to help you, she said.'

'But she has a child. I wouldn't want her to put herself in danger for my sake.' Temperance remembered the way Kei had lovingly cradled her daughter once they were safe. 'Isn't there anyone else?'

'No one I would trust with your secret, and besides, Kei-*san* is truly lovely. I wish she was one of my girls.'

'Yes, you're right. I just hope she won't be hurt in any way.'

'I'll make sure she is careful. Now, let's put our plan into action. You must come downstairs for a bath so that your hair is extra shiny, while I find a suitable garment for you. Just wait here a moment, please.'

'Very well. But Hasuko-*san*? What if we're too late?' Temperance didn't really want to contemplate such a thing, but she knew that Tanaka was ruthless in the extreme and Kazuo might be fighting for his life at this very moment, if he was even still alive.

Hasuko took a deep breath. 'We mustn't think of that. We will do our best, the rest is up to the gods.'

Kazuo was beginning to think that all the gods, as well as his numerous ancestors, had deserted him completely and left him to the mercy of a man who simply enjoyed inflicting pain on others. As yet another blow struck his already swollen cheekbone, he grunted with the pain of it and tried to focus on the man in front of him through eyelids that would barely open any more.

'Stop lying to me. You were seen sneaking about near the women's quarters and you just "happened" to leave on the same day that my latest acquisition fled my protection. It seems like far too much of a coincidence to me.'

'But, my lord,' Kazuo mumbled through bleeding lips, 'I never saw the lady, I swear. Begging your pardon, sir, but what would I want with a foreign woman?' He daren't go as far as to call her ugly, since Tanaka had obviously found her attractive just like he did himself, but his tone implied as much and Tanaka hit him again.

'That's what I want to know, insolent oaf. You must have wanted her for something, although like as not you left her lifeless body lying in a ditch somewhere after you used her as you wished.'

'I never!' Kazuo knew his protests were falling on deaf ears and racked his brain to come up with something more plausible.

Just then, however, a messenger arrived and went over to whisper something to Tanaka. The latter nodded and, sending Kazuo a look that boded ill, strode off towards the door.

'We will continue this later. The *Shogun* requires my presence on an urgent matter. I would suggest you spend the rest of the evening thinking up a better story, for tonight you will tell me the truth.'

In a final act of frustration and evil, he turned back briefly and slashed in Kazuo's direction with his sword, causing a lightning streak of pain to shoot up Kazuo's thigh as a gash opened up, instantly welling blood.

'Imbecile!' Tanaka added a string of swear words, then left without a backward glance.

The two men who had been holding Kazuo upright during the beating suddenly let go and he sank to the floor, his legs floppy and unable to bear him. The men left, slamming the door shut behind them, and Kazuo dragged himself over to a dirty mattress in the corner of the room. Taking a deep breath, he ripped off a piece of his tunic with his teeth to try to bind the wound in his thigh. He knew he had to stem the blood flow quickly or he would become even weaker than he already was.

'Perhaps that wouldn't be such a bad thing,' he muttered to himself. Maybe he should even try to open the wound further in order to bleed to death before Tanaka returned? At least that would spare him any more pain. He swore under his breath. No, he would face whatever Tanaka chose to mete out to him with courage. There was no honour in dying like a weakling. He couldn't shame his family so.

He finished off the makeshift bandage with a tight knot and blessed his gaolers for at least tying his hands in front of him rather than behind, thus giving him slightly more freedom. Then, in order to conserve his strength, he curled up on the mattress in the foetal position, hugging his knees and drawing in deep breaths to try and stem the tide of pain washing through him. He ached all over. In fact there probably wasn't a single part of him that wasn't covered in bruises or contusions.

'Whoreson!' he muttered through aching lips, sucking on a tooth that was decidedly loose. He knew he wouldn't leave this cell alive. But no matter what the man did to him, he would never betray Temi, even though he was sure that Hasuko would have spirited her away to safety by now. If not for Temi's sake, then for the preservation of her own skin. Tanaka would never find her.

If only the ordeal was all over.

Kazuo took a deep breath and concentrated on the image of Temi in his mind. For her and for his family he would suffer anything, but he prayed for courage nonetheless.

'Are you sure you want to do this, Kei-*san*?'

Temperance glanced at her companion with a worried frown creasing her brow and tried to walk slowly and demurely in her lovely outfit. It felt so strange to be wearing female clothing since she'd been wearing men's apparel for so long. She had to make a conscious effort not to lengthen her stride and to hold up the trailing back part of the *kimono* so that it didn't drag in the dust. As always, she was wearing a wide-brimmed hat, but underneath, instead of the usual scarf, she had a borrowed black wig which was making her scalp itch.

'Of course. I'm happy to be able to help you, Temi-*san*. Don't worry, I am a good actress. It's what I do every day, pretend.'

Temperance's curiosity was roused by this ingenuous statement. 'Is it very bad, Kei-*san*? I mean, having to ... be with men you don't like every day.'

'It could be worse. My master is fair. He doesn't force me to work all the time and he lets me choose the men I like best from those that entertain us. If someone was horrible, he wouldn't make me lie with them. Also, he allows me to keep some of the money I make. Not all masters do that. One day, I may be able to save enough to open my own establishment.'

'I see. And is that what you want?'

'It's not a bad life compared to some and I would have

215

something to pass on to my child. If I'd remained a poor farmer's daughter we would both have had hard times.'

'Ah, yes, your little girl. Don't you find it hard to have a child while working the hours you do?'

Kei smiled. 'No, there is always someone to help me with her in a house full of women. She is very spoilt.'

'I wish I had a child.' Temperance sighed wistfully. 'I doubt I'll ever have one now though. I'm not even sure I'll see my family again.'

'If it is your fate, you will have one,' Kei said firmly. 'Now we have to concentrate on tonight.'

'Yes, sorry, you're right. We must do our best to save Kazuo.' *If it's not too late*, she added inwardly, then sent up a swift prayer that it wasn't.

As arranged by Hasuko, there were two palanquins waiting outside the gate into Yoshiwara, and Temperance and Kei approached one each. Just as Temperance was about to enter hers, however, she was grabbed from behind and she heard a deep chuckle which made her stand stock still with shock.

'Well, well, if it isn't the high and mighty Miss Marston. I thought I recognised that determined chin. Fallen on hard times, have you? Having to resort to selling your delectable body decked out like a native, with a silly wig and all? Tut, tut, and to think you could have been a respectable married woman by now, if only you'd accepted my offer.'

Temperance turned slowly, unable to believe her eyes. Pieter Haag was the last person on earth she had expected to see here in Edo and at first she merely blinked stupidly at him before finding her tongue.

'Mr Haag? What on earth are you doing here?'

'I've come with Noordholt and the others to pay our respects to the *Shogun*. Had you forgotten? I seem to remember you were present when he announced his intention of coming here. It was just before you disappeared.'

Temperance's memory stirred and she remembered the conversation about Nico going to Edo for a few months. It seemed like such a long time ago that she found it difficult to take in the reality of the man before her. Slowly she came out of her stupor and noticed that the hateful man still had his arms around her.

'Let me go, sir. I have business to attend to.' She nodded towards the palanquins where Kei was watching with a worried look on her pretty face. 'These people are waiting for me.'

'Well, they can continue to wait. We have unfinished business of our own you and I, and this time, my dear, you're not going to escape me.' Without further ado, he suddenly produced a knife, which he pointed at her side while pulling one arm up behind her in a painful grip. 'Now tell your "friends" that you are not going with them and we'll be off.'

'But I—'

The knife pricked her through the layers of clothing. 'Do as you're told,' he hissed, his voice brooking no argument.

Temperance called out to Kei that there had been an unforeseen delay to their plans, but her eyes beseeched the girl to run for help. Kei hesitated, but Haag did not. Hauling on her arm, he quickly propelled Temperance in front of him, towards the gate and back into the pleasure district. The guards took no notice and she guessed he must have bribed them. Within moments they were lost in the crowds. Temperance tried to fight him, kicking backwards aiming for his shins and doing what Midori had taught her to break Haag's grip, but to no avail. He was a lot stronger than he looked and anger seemed to be lending him additional strength.

'Don't think you can get away this time, you little whore,' he said, pricking her skin once more. 'Just walk, and fast.'

Haag felt triumph coursing through his veins, making his

heart pump faster with sheer joy. He had her at last and now she was going to pay for the merry dance she'd led him.

'Where the hell have you been?' he hissed angrily. 'We've been looking everywhere for you.'

'None of your business,' she snarled.

He didn't like her tone so he tightened his grip on her and heard her draw in a sharp breath of pain. The sound made him smile. He was so close to having her, after all those weeks of painful dreams and lusting after her. Any intentions he'd had of giving her pleasure or making her desire him in return had been forgotten. All he could think about now was taking her, as quickly and roughly as possible, and if she suffered in the process so much the better. It was no more than she deserved.

'Well, no matter,' he said. 'I've found you now and soon we'll be returning to the inn where I'm staying with the others. But first we have a few matters to discuss.'

'I have nothing to discuss with you whatsoever, you bastard. Let me go!'

She tried once more to wriggle out of his grasp but he reminded her of the presence of his sharp knife and she subsided. *Good.* He had her in his power now and he wasn't letting her go until he had her full co-operation in every way.

He was going to enjoy the next hour or so immensely.

Chapter Twenty-One

Temperance was marched along the street, past the turning for Hasuko's house and into a seedier looking area. She realised that Haag must have been here before and had come to seek pleasure, only to stumble on her instead. It was the worst possible luck.

They reached a small two storey house, whose owner sat outside wearing a jacket that was none too clean. An oily grin split his face at the sight of them and he stood up and bowed.

'Welcome back, *Gai-jin-san*,' he said and Haag returned the greeting curtly before reaching into his pocket for some coins. In order to do this, he had to loosen his grip slightly, which gave Temperance the opportunity she'd been waiting for. Somehow she managed to free herself and sprinted off down the alley, colliding with people willy-nilly, but unheeding of their angry shouts. The *geta* on her feet didn't make for a speedy running style, but she was used to them by now and was able to put some distance between herself and Haag. Her clothing was heavy, however, especially since she was actually wearing two *kimonos* – one normal coloured one on top and the pure white one underneath for the intended ruse – and this slowed her down considerably.

As she glanced over her shoulder and saw her pursuer gaining on her, her heart hammered harder in her chest and she drew in heaving gasps of much needed air. Her eyes searched frantically for somewhere to hide or something to throw in his path to stop him. Instead they alighted upon a very unlikely possible saviour. Without hesitation, she called out his name.

'Ryo! *Tasukete kure*, please!'

She had no idea what her erstwhile captor was doing in Yoshiwara – presumably hiding from the authorities like numerous other outlaws or seeking his own pleasure – but she didn't care. Nor did she care that he might try to sell her again. Anything was preferable to spending time with Pieter Haag, who'd looked as though he would relish hurting her and clearly stopped at nothing to get his own way. Well, two could play at that game.

Panting with effort, Temperance reached a startled Ryo and sought shelter behind him, like a child hiding behind its mother's skirts. 'There,' she pointed at Haag. '*Gai-jin* ... evil ... please, stop him I beg of you ... reward.'

Ryo's features lit up with a grin and he called out to some of his henchmen who were loitering nearby, just before Haag came to a halt only yards away, brandishing his knife.

'Stop cowering behind an innocent bystander,' he shouted at Temperance. 'It will avail you nothing for I'll not hesitate to kill him if I have to. You can't escape me.' To his obvious surprise, however, he suddenly found himself surrounded by six men, armed with swords or knives longer than his own. His bewildered gaze swivelled round while he blustered, '*Nani*? What ...?' Then he stammered out in broken Japanese. 'Woman mine, leave, now. Woman wife. Run away.'

Ryo laughed. 'I can't blame her. I'd run too if I was married to you.'

'*Nani?*' Haag's grasp of the language was not sufficient for him to follow such rapid speech, despite having been in Japan for some time. Temperance knew he'd never bothered learning much, preferring to use a translator.

'Should you be out and about on your own, foreigner?' Ryo asked silkily, taking a step towards Haag. Pulling out his sword, he inspected it in the light from a nearby lantern, testing its blade against his thumb and pretending to flinch at its sharpness.

'What's he saying?' Haag's eyes fixed on the deadly sword in front of him, a frightened look in them like that of prey caught in the gaze of a snake. He quickly glanced at Temperance instead for an answer, scowling mightily.

'I believe he is asking what you're doing here,' she replied, feeling calmer now the immediate threat from him was gone. She didn't know what Ryo intended to do, but he seemed to be on her side for now, which was enough.

'I've merely come to seek pleasure, same as everyone else. Tell him!' Haag ordered. Temperance translated quickly, even though she knew that wasn't Haag's aim right now, but Ryo shook his head with another laugh.

'As far as I've heard, the foreigners are all supposed to stay in their cosy little inn on the outskirts of Edo,' he said. 'I should think someone would pay me well if I capture him and turn him over to the authorities. Shall I do that for you, Shinju-*san*?'

'Would you? Please? I would be forever in your debt,' Temperance breathed.

'Let's have no talk of debts. If I do this, I believe it would make us even,' Ryo mused. 'I have been thinking about my behaviour when we met and I probably did the wrong thing. I should have taken you back to your relatives and asked for a ransom. I ... selling you to Imada was a mistake.'

'I did tell you that.' It seemed so long ago now that Temperance didn't really feel angry about Ryo's actions any longer and it was irrelevant in any case.

'I know, but I was in a hurry and there were reasons why I didn't want to go back. So what do you say, shall I even the score?'

'Yes, please. That man is scum and I don't ever want to see him again. I really don't care what you do to him.'

Ryo chuckled. 'So much the better. Then we can have some sport with him first.'

'What's he saying?' Haag was beginning to panic and

Temperance could see sweat running down his forehead. He tried to bluff his way out of the situation. 'I have a right to go wherever I wish.' He tried again in Japanese. 'Woman bad. Wife, go home.'

Ryo shook his head and sent him a pitiful glance. 'Does he think I was born yesterday?'

Temperance glared at Haag and told him what Ryo had said. 'You're not allowed to be out and about on your own. You should be at some inn apparently. He's going to escort you back there, via the authorities of course.'

'You bitch! This is all your fault. Just you wait till I get my hands on you again. You'll live to regret this day, I swear it,' Haag snarled and tried to push his way through the group of men who had come ever closer, but they were upon him in moments. Although he struggled like one possessed, he was no match for the outlaws who were used to fighting dirty, and they soon had him in a secure grip.

'No, let me go! I'm bleeding. Aaarggh ... my stomach, I'm bleeding I tell you. I need a surgeon. Temperance, order these men to let me go or it will be the worse for you. I'll tell Noordholt where I found you, he'll punish you, he'll—'

'Shut up, imbecile. *Bakajaro!*' Ryo slapped the hysterical man viciously, then turned to Temperance. 'Where were you going? Can we escort you?'

Temperance still wasn't sure if she could trust him and now that the threat from Haag was removed she began to wonder if she had done the right thing. She decided she had no choice, however, so she told Ryo part of the truth.

'I was by the gate, on my way to rescue someone from, er, enforced confinement.'

Ryo's eyes lit up again. 'Can we help? It sounds like you need some strong men for that kind of sport. We're spoiling for a fight. Nothing's been happening for weeks and we're bored to tears.'

'Well, I was hoping to use cunning, but I could probably do with some back-up.' Temperance wasn't sure it was a good idea, but the thought of braving Tanaka's den alone was not one she relished. At least if Ryo was there to fall back on, she would feel slightly better. 'There won't be any remuneration though, I'm afraid,' she added apologetically.

'Doesn't matter. I still have some spoils from our last, er, mission. Tell me where you're going and we'll come along as soon as we have deposited this dog turd somewhere. Come, let us go.'

Ryo took the lead and their little procession began to make its way back to the main gate. Along the way, Temperance told Ryo a short version of how she'd ended up in Yoshiwara.

'Are you going to capture me again and sell me back to Tanaka?' she challenged, still not quite trusting him.

But Ryo shook his head. 'No, I told you, I had second thoughts. It didn't sit right with me and I've regretted the whole episode ever since I left Imada's tea house.'

The evening was beginning to have a surreal feel to it and Temperance wondered if perhaps she was dreaming, but they reached the gate and went through without mishap. The guard seemed to accept whatever explanation Ryo offered for the wild-eyed captive they had with them. To Temperance's relief Kei was still waiting outside, wringing her hands. She ran up to Temperance the moment she set eyes on her.

'Temi-*san,* I have been so worried. I couldn't find anyone to help you and I didn't know where he'd taken you.'

'It's all right, I have a saviour already. Or several, actually.' She indicated Ryo and his men. 'They're even willing to help us with our mission. What do you think?'

Kei thought for a moment. 'Perhaps if you ask them to wait outside and if we haven't emerged within a short space of time, they can come to our rescue?'

'Good plan.' Temi went to tell Ryo what Kei had said and he nodded acquiescence.

'You go ahead then. If you're not out by the time we reach the gate of Tanaka's residence, we'll go in after you. Although we'll avail ourselves of the back wall rather than use the main entrance, of course.' He nodded towards Haag. 'Don't worry about him, he won't trouble you again.'

'You're going to kill him?' Although she disliked the man intensely, condoning murder was not something Temperance could do.

'No, just teach him a lesson. Now go, or you'll be too late.'

Temperance hoped they weren't already.

Kei was every bit as good an actress as she had claimed, and she flirted and simpered her way past the guards at the main gate of Tanaka's residence without any trouble. Temperance remained mutely in the background, her head bent as if she were of lesser importance, and the guards hardly spared her a glance. After one last sally, Kei sashayed through the archway, her tinkling laugh making the men smile and stare after her with lovelorn eyes.

'Well, that wasn't so hard.' Kei smiled. 'The difficult part will be to locate the prisoner. Let me have a go first. You wait over there in the shadows while I try my whiles on that big oaf lurking over there.' She pointed at another guard who was standing near a smaller gate leading into an inner courtyard. The man looked bored and restless, and it would seem Kei had picked her victim well because his expression brightened the moment he caught sight of her.

Temperance skulked in the shadows of a large tree and waited. She couldn't hear what was being said, but she could see from the man's body language that he quickly fell under Kei's spell. The girl really was remarkably good at what she did, and Temperance watched and learned. A look from under lowered eyelashes, a slight touch of fingers on the man's arm, a gurgle of laughter – all these things appeared to hold him in thrall. Kei was displaying a mixture of humility and coquetry that seemed nigh on irresistible to the man. And as an added tour de force she showed off her swan-like neck which was exposed by the cut of her *kimono*. The man stared at it with burgeoning lust in his eyes. Kei was of course exceedingly pretty, but Temperance had a feeling that she could have worked her magic even without that asset.

Temperance had grown restless by the time Kei finally returned to her side and whispered, 'This way,' grabbing her arm and steering her to the right. 'The guard said all prisoners are taken to the furthest corner of the grounds. If anyone is being tortured, the rest of the inhabitants won't want to listen to the screams.'

Shuddering violently at the thought of what might be happening to Kazuo, Temperance hurried after Kei. 'But shouldn't you be going to the main residence? I'll have to find my own way now.'

'Not yet, there is still time. I told the guard I needed to use the privy first and, as luck would have it, that's in this direction too. Come, there's not a moment to lose.'

The two women walked as fast as they could without raising anyone's suspicions, and soon reached the gardens beyond all the buildings. 'It must be on the other side of the gardens,' Kei said. 'Look, I see a light over there.'

The faint light of a lantern being buffeted by the evening breeze could be seen through the shrubs and trees. 'Yes, I see it. Now you must go back. I'll be fine from here on.'

'Are you sure? Let me help you off with the outer *kimono* first.'

Together they managed to divest Temperance of the heavy garment and Kei bundled it up and hid it behind a huge boulder. Temperance took a small box out of her capacious sleeve and opened the lid. Inside was a sponge and a mountain of rice powder, which Kei quickly applied to Temperance's face in a thick layer.

'There, that will do. You look very ghostly to me, at least in this light. Try to stay in the shadows.'

'Of course. Now please go and keep their attention. From what I've seen so far, that shouldn't be very difficult for you.' Temperance smiled, then on impulse bent to swiftly embrace Kei. 'Thank you for everything.'

'It was nothing. Good luck and may the gods be with you.'

Kei melted into the darkness, disappearing the way they had come. Temperance pulled off the dreadful wig, shaking out her own hair while her scalp cooled off. She threw the offending item into the nearest bush then set off towards the distant light, praying that she wasn't too late.

'Leave me alone, I tell you! You have no right to—'

Haag never had a chance to finish his sentence as a fist connected with his cheek and a burst of stars exploded inside his skull. More blows rained down on him and although his arms were left free so that he could defend himself, it wasn't much use since his assailants outnumbered him hugely.

'Cowards!' he shouted. 'Six against one? You call that fair? What did that bitch say to you, eh? She's a liar. A liar, you hear?'

But the Japanese men, who were apparently friends of Temperance, seemed not to understand. Either that or they didn't want to. Instead they jeered at him in their own language and although Haag glanced around for his interpreter, the man was nowhere to be found, which wasn't to be wondered at, he supposed. It was a damned nuisance though as it meant he couldn't reason with them.

'I'm a foreigner. Under protection of the *Shogun*. You'll answer to him if you don't—' Another punch stopped his sentence and split his lip.

Haag gave up trying to defend himself at all and eventually the men stopped punching and kicking him. They bundled him away from Yoshiwara and marched him all the way back to the inn, stopping short of it by some fifty yards. The leader pointed at the door and said, 'Go. Don't leave again.'

He also said something else, which Haag didn't catch, but he understood the gist of it – he wasn't to set foot in Yoshiwara again or accost their friend, the *gai-jin* lady.

He didn't reply, just glared at them and headed for the inn, veering round the back to make use of a water trough to sluice down his damaged face.

If they thought he'd stay here meekly though, they were mistaken. He was going right back to Yoshiwara the minute they left. *A pox on them!*

Chapter Twenty-Two

Kazuo had fallen asleep on the filthy mattress, too exhausted to stay awake any longer despite the tension of knowing what awaited him, but the startled exclamation of one of the guards woke him. Blinking into the darkness while his eyes adjusted, he sat up. Then, as pain shot up his leg, he belatedly remembered about the thigh wound. He gritted his teeth and let the pain wash over him until it became more manageable.

Despite the dizziness that flooded his brain, he was able to stand up with the help of a nearby wall and staggered over to the door. With his right eye, the only one that wasn't completely blocked now by his swollen eyelids, he peered outside through a small opening at face height which had been left unshuttered. He very nearly uttered a startled gasp himself before he realised what he was looking at.

A ghost.

Only this particular ghost looked very familiar. Kazuo began to smile at the sight of two grown men trembling at the apparition that was Temi, although he had to stop almost immediately as his cracked lip pulled him up short, eliciting a grunt of pain. Then the full force of what she was doing hit him and his insides turned to ice. *She shouldn't be here at all!* She ought to be miles away, heading for the safety of Nagasaki.

He clenched his fists. Temi was risking her life for him and she was playing a very dangerous game. At any moment the guards might realise that she wasn't a ghost at all and kill her. She wouldn't stand a chance. Kazuo swallowed and put his eye close to the opening again so he could see what was happening outside.

He watched in terrified fascination as the ghost glided closer, moaning faintly, while the guard who had first spotted it – or her rather, as it was clearly a female apparition – clung to his comrade, almost gibbering in fear.

'*Nan da yo?* Who goes there? Halt! Stop, I say.'

The second guard was obviously more courageous, but even he drew in a hissing breath as the spirit moved closer, moaning louder now as if in pain. Then, without warning, she emitted an almost unearthly cry. Both guards jumped and the first one ran off into the night without so much as a by your leave, shouting over his shoulder that he was going for help. The second guard was left to face the spectre on his own and suddenly he wasn't quite as brave any more.

'Wha-what do you want?' he stuttered, backing towards the door, while fumbling with his keys. His hands shook so much Kazuo could hear the tinkling noise of metal upon metal. He quelled another smile.

'Open the door,' the ghostly figure commanded. 'Your prisoner is dead. I have come for him.'

'De-dead? No, surely not, I—'

The ghost emitted a high-pitched moan and glided further forward, holding out her hands as if she wished to strangle the guard. 'Open it I say or I'll take you with me too.' The words were uttered in a harsh voice that demanded obedience, but still the guard hesitated. He took another step backwards and his back was now flush against the door. Kazuo instantly realised that here was a chance in a million and seized it without hesitation. He reached out through the opening with both hands to grab the man's throat from behind, squeezing hard. The ropes that bound his hands gave him just enough leeway.

'Aaarrghh ... no!' The guard tried to struggle, but Temperance leapt forward and drew a knife out of her sleeve, which she pointed at his chest. This kept him still long enough for Kazuo to finish the job and the man slumped to the ground unconscious.

'Is he dead?' Temperance whispered.

'No, so you'd better hurry. The key, quick!'

Temperance did as she was told and retrieved the heavy key ring from the man's limp grip. Kazuo could hear it jangling and realised that she was shaking too, but somehow she managed to slot the key into the lock and open the door. On wobbly legs, he stumbled through, just as a shout came from the path that led to the main house. The first guard was approaching with several men and had apparently realised what was happening.

'*Chikusho!*' Kazuo swore. 'You shouldn't have come. What were you thinking?' He hobbled in the opposite direction as fast as he could, which wasn't fast enough due to the wound in his thigh. 'Run, Temi, save yourself. It doesn't matter,' he panted.

'No, I'm not leaving you.' She grabbed his hand and tugged, making him go a little faster despite the white hot flashes of pain shooting through him every step of the way. He must have groaned without realising it, for she peered at him with concern.

'Are you badly hurt? What have they done to you?'

'Mostly a beating, but my leg … sword wound. It's all right, I'll manage.'

She muttered something in English that he took to be a curse, but she didn't slacken the pace. They made good progress for a while, but just as Kazuo thought they might make it to safety, six figures suddenly appeared out of nowhere in front of them brandishing weapons. He gasped in consternation. To his surprise, however, Temperance ran towards the men, instead of turning around, and hissed that they were being followed.

'How many?' one of the newcomers asked.

'Five or six, I'm not sure.'

'We'll take care of them, you keep going.' The man nodded

towards the wall. 'Over there, rope ladder. One of my men is outside keeping watch.'

'Will I see you again?' Temperance asked the man.

He nodded. 'Yes, at Hasuko's. Now go, follow Yoshi's instructions.'

Temperance said no more, but pulled Kazuo towards the wall where they found a blackened rope ladder like the man had said.

'Are you sure this isn't a trap?' Kazuo asked, slurring his words slightly as he couldn't open his mouth properly. 'Who was that?'

'That's Ryo and I trust him now.'

'Ryo? But wasn't he the man who—'

'Yes, but that's in the past. I'll explain later. Come on. Can you climb?'

'I'll damn well try.'

It wasn't easy, with one leg turning lamer by the minute, but somehow Kazuo reached the top of the wall and saw the dark shape of a palanquin waiting outside. A figure materialised out of the shadows and whispered, 'Jump!' Although it looked like quite a drop, Kazuo did as he was told, landing clumsily on a grass verge. A pain worse than any he had felt before tore up his leg and though he was aware of landing, the world suddenly went mercifully black.

'Kazuo? Can you hear me? Oh, wake up, do!'

Temperance stared at his poor, swollen face in the moonlight and cursed again in English. What she wouldn't give to be able to punish Tanaka for this, but she knew there was nothing she could do. He was too powerful. Dear Lord, but the man was an animal though. How could anyone treat their fellow human being this way?

'Temi?'

The welcome sound of her name dragged her out of her

dreams of revenge and she turned to Kazuo. 'Yes, I'm here. Are you all right? Is there anything I can do?'

'Leg hurts ... perhaps need stitching?'

'I'll have a look at it when we reach our destination. Can you hold on until then?'

He grunted something that sounded like an affirmative, then added, 'Where?'

'Ryo is to meet us at Hasuko's house. I told him that's where we would go if I managed to free you and Yoshi said he's bringing us a horse so we can leave quickly. Hopefully there will be time for me to see to your wound first. Come, you must get into this palanquin. I'll be in the one right behind you.'

They reached Yoshiwara after what seemed like an eternity, but in reality it probably didn't take very long. Temperance listened anxiously for any cries of pursuit, but heard nothing out of the ordinary. Ryo's men got them safely through the gate, no questions asked. Temperance surmised that they were well known to the guards and thanked God for small mercies. In no time at all, they stopped at the back of Hasuko's house and were ushered in as quickly as possible. Kazuo managed to limp inside, leaning heavily on Temperance, while Hasuko's maid kept a lookout to make sure no one was watching them.

'In here, hurry,' Hasuko urged. 'Someone called Ryo sent me a message to say you were coming. By all the gods, boy, what have they done to you?' She shook her head and tut-tutted at the sight of Kazuo, but led him gently to a chair next to a brazier. He was shivering, but whether from cold or pain, or perhaps both, Temperance couldn't tell.

'He has a wound to the thigh,' she informed Hasuko. 'It might need stitching. Do you know anyone who can do it? I've never tried before, so I'm not sure how to go about it.'

Hasuko nodded. 'I'll see to it. Go to your room and gather up your things. You must leave as soon as Ryo returns.

232

There's no time to lose. Tanaka will send out spies and it won't be long before they find out where you've gone. You must leave before they come here looking for you.'

Temperance did as she was told and swiftly changed out of the white *kimono* into men's clothing and a pair of soft boots Kazuo had bought her. They felt strange at first, as there was a separate space for the big toe, but they were comfortable and would be a lot better for walking or running than the *geta* or sandals she had worn before. They were also warmer, now autumn was advancing. She gathered their meagre possessions into a bundle which she tied together securely, then slung onto her back. There were only a few pieces of additional clothing, a cooking pot, two knives and some money which she'd seen Kazuo hide under the floor. The knives she slid into her sleeve, just in case they would be needed in a hurry. She assumed Kazuo's swords had been confiscated when he was taken prisoner, which meant they were virtually defenceless. If they were able to leave in time, however, then perhaps there would be no need for fighting.

When she returned to the kitchen, Hasuko was putting the finishing touches to Kazuo's wound, which looked dark red and angry. She snipped off the thread, then beckoned the maid forward to put a fresh bandage around it after first smearing it with some evil-smelling unguent.

'That's the best I can do,' she said. 'I just hope he doesn't catch the wound fever.'

Temperance knew all about that, having lived through the English Civil War. Several members of her family had been wounded, Midori among them and some worse than others, and she knew the fever that often followed could be fatal. It wasn't something she had hoped to see again. 'What shall I do if he does?' she whispered to the older woman.

'Just bathe him with cool water and make him drink as much as possible.' Hasuko rooted around in a chest near the wall and brought out a small pouch tied with string. 'This is willow bark. Steep that in water if you can and give it to him, then pray to whatever god you worship.' Hasuko shrugged. 'We can but hope for the best.'

'Thank you.' Temperance stowed the pouch with the rest of their belongings.

A sudden loud knocking on the front door made them all look at each other in fright.

'Who's that?' Temperance asked unnecessarily. They all knew it couldn't be Ryo, as he would never announce his presence in such a way.

'Tanaka's spies were faster than I thought,' Hasuko muttered. 'Quick, into the hidden chamber,' she ordered. 'Seiko, get rid of all this immediately!' She indicated the sewing implements and blood-soaked bandages. The little maid set to work as if she had a devil prodding her, feeding the lot into the brazier where it quickly caught fire. Hasuko grabbed one of Kazuo's arms and dragged him off the chair, indicating that Temperance should follow. 'This way.'

In the hallway a cluster of frightened looking girls had congregated, whispering to each other. Hasuko was just about to order them to disperse, when Kei came rushing through from the kitchen, having obviously just arrived back.

'I'll deal with this. Go!' she hissed, then ordered the other girls to stand aside or go back to their rooms. Hasuko didn't wait to see what would happen as Kei seemed to have everything under control. Instead she led the way into a store room at the back, where she moved a couple of heavy-looking barrels, then lifted up a piece of wooden flooring underneath. It was a trapdoor that concealed a dark, gaping hole, and Hasuko wasted no time in pushing Kazuo and Temperance towards it.

'Get down there and don't make a sound. It's your only chance.'

They needed no further bidding, but clambered into obscurity, stumbling down a few steps onto a cold dirt floor. Before Hasuko closed the hatch Temperance had time to see that the space was only big enough for a couple of people to stand up. There was nothing other than stone walls, nowhere to even sit down. Her heart sank. The wood above them slammed shut and immediately they were in complete darkness with not a chink of light to be seen. Temperance shuddered and reached out for Kazuo. His arms went around her and they leaned against each other, hearts thumping in unison.

Temperance took a deep breath, trying to keep the panic at bay. They had come this far and they were still alive. Surely God would help them once again?

Kazuo had no idea how long they stood there, holding on to each other as if neither could stay upright without support. Temperance clung to him, seeking reassurance even though she must know there was none to be had. Kazuo tried not to think about that and just enjoyed the feel of her arms around him. It was surreal being down in the hole, enveloped as they were in a thick cocoon of earth that muffled all sounds. The air in their hiding place was also heavy and slightly dank, making it an effort to breathe. Kazuo hoped they wouldn't begin to choke or cough. The slightest of sounds could give them away.

Kazuo was still shivering, his body aching like the very devil. Temperance seemed to notice and with some effort she managed to manoeuvre them both into a crouching position, leaning against the freezing wall. It wasn't ideal, but it was better than him having to put weight on his bad leg for any length of time.

Blurred thoughts of what lay before them whirled through his mind. He had no illusions as to what would happen to them should they become Tanaka's prisoners. In truth, he didn't hold out much hope that they wouldn't be found. Surely someone like Tanaka would reckon on there being hiding places. He knew the man was nothing if not thorough and he wouldn't leave any stone unturned. Indeed, there were voices shouting above them now, coming ever closer, and the sound of wood breaking. It would seem his men were wrecking Hasuko's house, pulling it to pieces in their efforts to find the fugitives.

Temperance's breathing began to come in shallow gasps that sounded too loud in the enclosed silence of the little underground chamber. Kazuo wanted to calm her and tried to hold her tighter, even though that hurt his ribs. It helped a little as he felt her trying hard to control her lungs.

She took hold of his hand, which was swollen and probably hot to the touch. He hoped it made her feel safer and squeezed her fingers, silently acknowledging their mutual support, then leaned his head on her shoulder. Gingerly, she propped her own on his. Then she moved suddenly and groped for something inside her sleeve. Knives. He could feel the cool metal against his skin as she slid them out and handed one to him. He gripped it with determination while she grabbed the other one herself.

At least they wouldn't leave this hiding place without a fight.

Suddenly, they heard Tanaka's voice clearly and the heavy tread of *geta* on the floor above their heads. Holding their breaths, they listened.

'They must be here somewhere, I tell you,' Tanaka was growling. 'There is nowhere else they could have gone, unless they fled the city straight away, in which case I'll soon hear about it. Break the floor over there, under those casks, there's bound to be a hiding place.'

The sound of shattering wood reached them, frighteningly

close. Something like an axe was making short work of the floor in Hasuko's store room, and there was the rasping of metal against wood as barrels and casks were moved to make way for the axe man.

Any moment now the trapdoor would give way and they would find themselves face to face with Tanaka. Kazuo steeled himself and got to his feet, inch by quiet inch, feeling Temperance do the same by his side. He raised the hand holding the knife, ready to strike the moment they were exposed.

Nothing happened.

They heard Tanaka swear loudly and then the yelp of another man, presumably the one wielding the axe who had failed to uncover the secret chamber. 'Idiot! Incompetent fool.' Tanaka took out his frustration on the hapless servant although he must know full well it wasn't the man's fault that they had failed. 'We will go and see what news there is from the guards I posted. If they're not here, then they must have left immediately.'

Their footsteps receded and silence fell on the hiding place once more. Temperance lowered her arm and let out a breath she'd been holding for much too long. She turned to Kazuo and buried her head in his shoulder, shaking with emotion, and he held her without saying a word.

They waited another eternity, but then at last the trapdoor eased open and the welcome smile of Hasuko appeared at the top, almost blinding them.

'He's gone,' she hissed, 'but I don't know if he'll be back. You must leave this instant. Come.'

Temperance clambered out then turned to pull Kazuo up to stand next to her. 'That was so close,' she whispered to Hasuko. 'How come he only broke the floor over there?' The planking in one corner of the room was completely ruined.

Hasuko smiled. 'Because usually trapdoors are always

hidden under something, as indeed this was when I brought you here, but I moved the barrels so that he would think I was trying to hide something in the corner. He fell for my ruse.'

They followed the older woman back to the kitchen, where they bid her farewell. '*Sayonara* and thank you for everything,' Kazuo said. 'I shall not forget.'

Hasuko bowed to him and smiled. 'It was my honour to serve the son of a great man.'

He could only hope her loyalty would be rewarded one day.

Outside the back door several dark shapes waited in the shadows and Temperance and Kazuo followed them without question. One of them came up to Kazuo and whispered, 'Can you walk a little? The horse is waiting a few streets away.'

'I will manage it somehow.'

Temperance could hear that he was talking through clenched teeth, but to her relief Ryo must have noticed as well. He and one of his men immediately fell into step on either side of Kazuo, propping him up whenever necessary.

They traversed the back streets of the pleasure district, where thankfully not many people were about. At length they came to a run-down house on the outskirts of the area, and Ryo led them inside. Temperance wondered if they were to wait here until it was safe to leave through the main gate, but Ryo didn't stop. Instead he continued to the back of the dwelling, where a man was standing by an open trapdoor in the floor.

'Another hiding place?' Temperance asked.

Ryo shook his head. 'No, a secret passage under the walls and moat that surround Yoshiwara,' he whispered. 'Follow me.'

The tunnel was low and narrow, but by hunching over they were able to walk along it easily and soon reached the outside world once more. Another man guarded the opening and signalled that it was safe to emerge. Nearby, a saddled horse stood waiting patiently.

'This is for you. It looks small,' Ryo commented, 'but it's strong and sturdy enough to carry you both. It won't let you down.'

'Thank you, you've been a great help.' Temperance gripped his arm and squeezed it. 'We will repay you somehow, I promise.'

He shook his head. 'No need. It was my pleasure to thwart the evil plans of Tanaka. It was my fault you ended up with him in the first place. Now go. Yoshi will show you a way out of Edo where Tanaka's spies don't catch sight of you. They are only watching the main routes. We will go and find our own horses and ride a different way, looking furtive, then perhaps some of his men will follow us instead.'

'Wait, please.' Kazuo put up a hand to halt them for a moment and bowed low. 'Ryo-*san*, I owe you my thanks as well. You and your men will always be welcome in my father's house, which is currently on one of the smaller islands of the Oki group. Just tell him I sent you and give him this password.' He bent forward and whispered something in Ryo's ear.

Ryo nodded and bowed back. 'Thank you. We might do that one day. The life of a *ronin* can become a bit wearisome. But hurry now, there is no time to lose.'

Temperance mounted the little horse and someone helped Kazuo up behind her. He put his arms round her waist and leaned his head on her back. She urged the animal into a trot and followed Yoshi, who was on his own horse. She wasn't an expert rider, but she had ridden before so she knew what to do.

Ryo had been right and Yoshi managed to lead them out of Edo without any trouble. Temperance had been prepared to be challenged by guards as they left the city, but Yoshi took them along narrow streets and somehow avoided being seen. She'd been so sure that Tanaka's men would be lying in wait near every road, but there was no sign of anyone and to her relief no shout of 'Halt!' rang out.

On the outskirts of the city Yoshi stopped. 'This is where I leave you,' he said. 'It's up to you where you go from here. The less I know about it, the better. *Sayonara.*'

'Goodbye and thank you.' Temperance watched him go, but not for long. Time was of the essence. 'Which direction should I go?' she asked Kazuo. They had Edo Bay on their left and she instinctively wanted to head south, the way they'd come, as it was the only road she knew. But it was large and well-travelled and it would be far too easy for anyone following them to find them.

'Head south for a little way along this route, then turn off as soon as you see a smaller road and head back north.'

'Double back you mean?'

'Yes. There will be men watching, I'm sure, so we have to try and fool them.'

Temperance did as she was told and they passed the first station on the post road quite openly, making sure that they were seen. She rode the horse hard past the tea houses so as to make it seem like she was panicking, but reined him in as soon as they were out of sight. Shortly afterwards, she turned off to the right on a small track that shone white in the moonlight, but after about a hundred yards, Kazuo stopped her.

'Wait a moment. You must go back and sweep the entrance to this track with branches or something. We can't leave any hoof prints to lead them to us.'

She dismounted and handed him the reins, then she ran

back to where the track met the post road. There were some bushes nearby and she grabbed a handful of branches and walked backwards, all the way to the horse, sweeping the road as she went.

'Do you really think that will fool them?' she asked dubiously.

'Only for tonight, but it might be enough. It will have to be.'

He sounded grim, but determined, and Temperance took her cue from him. She mounted quickly and spurred the horse on at a steady gait, heading north-west towards mountains that could be vaguely seen as dark shapes in the distance. Kazuo slept fitfully behind her and only woke from time to time when she prodded him to make sure she was on the right course. When daylight crept over the horizon, Temperance was exhausted both physically and emotionally, but she knew she had to continue no matter what. They simply couldn't afford to stop now.

Chapter Twenty-Three

Hasuko was not surprised when Tanaka returned after a short interval. This time she opened the door herself and gave him only a curt bow. Besides mistreating her former master's son, he had caused a lot of damage to her property and she wasn't in the mood to humour him. 'Yes?' she asked. 'What is it now?'

'Get out of my way, you old hag.' He shoved her roughly against the wall. 'My guards report that no one has left the city, so they must still be here. You've conned me,'

'Look all you like, you won't find them,' she muttered, but if he heard her, he ignored her words.

Once more her house was searched from top to bottom and this time he found the hidden chamber he'd missed previously. He swore and cuffed Hasuko in his rage. 'I knew you were hiding them. Damn you!' She glared at him, almost daring him to strike her again, even though she knew it was madness to antagonise him.

'I told you you wouldn't find them. They're gone.'

'Yes, but gone where?'

'I'm sure your spies will tell you that, my lord, but I know where I would go if I was a foreign woman.' She waited for the expected pain as he aimed his fist at her once more, but he was interrupted by the arrival of one of his men.

'Lord Tanaka, the fugitives have been seen heading south along the post road at great speed. Shall we follow them?'

'Of course we're going to follow them, you dolt. Go, go!' Tanaka turned to cuff Hasuko one last time for good measure. 'I'll be back to deal with you later,' he promised.

'And I shall lodge a complaint with the city's officials,' she retorted. 'You have ruined my house and you'll have to pay for repairs.'

He ignored her and set off towards the front door, only to collide with someone who hadn't had the wits to move quickly enough. 'Get out of my way, oaf!'

'*Nani?*'

Tanaka stopped in his tracks as he registered that the man he had walked into was another foreigner with pale eyes and what looked like yellow hair in the light from the lanterns. 'What do you want? Foreigners aren't allowed here,' he snarled. He looked the man up and down, curling his lip in disgust. Hasuko could see why. Not only was the *gai-jin* dirty and dishevelled, but he looked like he'd recently been in a brawl and lost. He had one black eye and there was a trail of half dried blood running from his swollen nose and staining his clothing.

The man seemed oblivious to what Tanaka thought about his appearance, however, and turned to his Japanese servant, letting out a torrent of words that the hapless man was obviously supposed to translate. The servant did his best, while glancing fearfully at Tanaka's scowl.

'My master is here looking for his wife, a foreign lady with silver hair. He believes she lives here and if she doesn't return to him of her own free will, he will call out the magistrate.'

'His wife?' Tanaka looked thunderstruck, then scowled at the man. 'What's your name? *Namu?*'

'Haag. Pieter Haag.'

'And your wife, what is she called?'

'Temperance ... er, Marston. She may not be using my name as she seems hell-bent on running away from me. I have also heard her referred to as just Temi by others.'

Tanaka threw Haag a contemptuous glance. 'Well, the lady *I'm* looking for never mentioned having a husband and her name is Shinju, although I suppose that may not be her real one. It's beside the point, however, she belongs to me now. I paid for her.'

The servant translated quickly for Haag, who blanched and grew angry. 'You can't just buy other people's wives, that's barbaric! She's mine, I tell you, and I demand her back.'

'Can you prove that you are married?' Tanaka crossed his arms and glared at the foreigner.

'Well, we haven't exchanged the actual vows yet, but we are contracted to marry. That is to say—'

'So she's not your wife.'

'Betrothed, if you must be pedantic, but really, we're as good as married. The laws of my country say that—'

'Pah! What do I care about your laws? You can't have her. Anyway, she's disappeared and I'm about to go after her. There's not a moment to lose.'

'Then I will come with you.'

'I don't give a damn what you do. Good night.'

Tanaka strode off and after only a slight hesitation the man, Haag, hurried off in his wake. Hasuko was left staring at their retreating backs, shaking her head. 'Strange, very strange,' she muttered.

'That man is evil too.' Kei came out of the shadows. 'He tried to abduct Temi-*san* earlier today, but Ryo saved her. I don't believe he is her husband at all. Should we do something?'

'What can we do? Besides, I doubt Tanaka will let him anywhere near Temi. Not a puny foreigner like that. No, she's safe enough from her so-called husband, but from Tanaka? That's another matter. All we can do is pray.'

As dawn broke Temperance realised that she had strayed from the track and she was riding cross-country. She tried to rouse Kazuo to ask him what to do, but he only muttered something unintelligible.

'Kazuo? Speak to me?' She turned to face him in the growing light, but he wouldn't open his eyes. She put a hand on his forehead – it was burning hot.

'Oh, no! Kazuo, you must wake up. Please, don't do this to me. How am I supposed to get us to safety without your help?'

But she couldn't make him say anything coherent and she realised that he was delirious. There was only one thing to do. She had to stop and make him take some willow bark. But where would it be safe to rest for a while?

She looked for some time, but couldn't find anywhere ideal like the overhang where they'd sheltered on their way to Edo. Instead, she had to make do with a thicket next to a fast-running stream, and there she dismounted and managed to slide Kazuo off the horse. It was akin to hefting a sack of turnips to the ground and she grunted with the effort. He was barely conscious and kept muttering words that didn't make sense. She hurried to tie the horse to the nearest tree and then set to work steeping willow bark in water.

The infusion ought to have been made by boiling the water first, but Temperance didn't dare start a fire in case someone might see the smoke, so she vigorously stirred the powder into cold liquid instead. She had no idea whether it would have as much effect that way, but she could only hope so. Making Kazuo drink it proved almost impossible, however.

'Kazuo, for heaven's sake, I need you to help me out!'

But it was like dealing with a recalcitrant toddler who was determined not to swallow the medicine on any account. In the end, Temperance was forced into holding his nose so that he opened his mouth to breathe, then she tipped some of the concoction down his throat. She hoped that at least a small measure slid down inside him, despite his coughing and spluttering.

Once the drink was all gone, she sponged him with cold water for a while and tried to make him drink some of that too. The water was refreshing, so he took a few sips, but no more and Temperance sighed.

'This is going to be impossible,' she muttered under her breath.

She knew she couldn't stay put, however, so she forced herself to eat a few morsels of the food Hasuko's maid had given her before they left, then drank some water herself and made sure the horse drank his fill. The most difficult part was trying to heave Kazuo back onto the horse, but she managed it in the end by dragging and cajoling him until he co-operated enough for her to push him onto the horse's rump. She thanked the Lord that it was a small and very patient horse and rewarded the animal with a piece of rice cake before mounting herself. She wasn't sure horses were meant to eat such things, but this one accepted it readily enough and it was the only thing she had to give him so she hoped it wouldn't harm him in any way.

With Kazuo in such a state, she couldn't be sure that he wouldn't fall off, so she took off both their belts and tied them together to form one long one, which she secured around both of them. It wasn't ideal, but it was the best she could think of for the moment. She set off once more, making the poor horse wade along the stream for quite a long time in order to throw anyone off their scent in case they had dogs.

She had no choice but to keep going and prayed as hard as she could for assistance from any deity who happened to be listening. There was no doubt about it – she would need divine intervention to evade Tanaka as she was sure he was hot on their heels.

'Well, it seems fairly obvious they didn't come this way. We must retrace our steps and look more closely at the surrounding tracks.'

Tanaka had ridden hard, without any consideration for either his mount or his servants, but after receiving negative replies at post road stations number two and three, he realised that the foreign bitch and his former servant hadn't gone south after all. Even if they had tried to pass by the stations unnoticed someone would have seen them, and there were no reports of them at all except at the first one.

On the way back, they ran into another group of riders who appeared to be exchanging angry words with some of the *Shogun*'s officials. Tanaka drew rein and addressed the company in a loud voice.

'What is happening here?'

'Who wants to know?' one of the officials replied in a surly tone without bothering to turn around. He and the others were staring at the foreign man, Haag, whose servants they had been arguing with.

'I am Tanaka, chief adviser to the *Shogun*, and I suggest you look at me when you're addressing me,' Tanaka barked. That succeeded in drawing everyone's attention and the officials blanched slightly when they noticed Tanaka's clan motif on the banners held by some of his men.

'My lord, forgive us, we didn't know,' one of them stammered, while they all flung themselves down onto their knees and tried to bow as low as possible.

Tanaka scowled at them. 'Very well, I'll overlook it this once. Now kindly inform me what is going on here.'

'This man claims he is searching for his wife, but he doesn't have the necessary permission to roam the countryside at will. Foreigners are not allowed, as I'm sure you know, my lord. And they're not supposed to bring their wives in any case. We were just about to apprehend him when you arrived.'

'I see.' Tanaka regarded Haag critically. He didn't look like a trained warrior, but he had to admire the man's tenacity. Perhaps he could come in useful at some stage during the search?

'What are you doing here? I told you the woman is mine,' he said to Haag in order to test his mettle.

'"What God has joined, let no man put asunder,"' Haag

intoned in a superior sort of voice and his servant cast him a confused glance, then translated the sentence roughly for Tanaka's benefit.

'What utter rubbish! What have the gods to do with it? I paid in silver. The woman is mine, it's as clear as day.'

'It is against God's law to buy another man's wife,' Haag insisted. 'Our marriage will be blessed by the church just as soon as I find her.'

'You see, my lord?' another of the officials put in. 'Not only is he a *gai-jin*, but a Christian as well. He must be put to death.'

'Yes, I know.' Tanaka rubbed his beard, deep in thought.

'Shall I kill him, my lord?' Tanaka's closest retainer whispered. 'That would solve the problem immediately.'

'No, not yet. I may have a use for him,' Tanaka hissed back. He turned to address the officials once more. 'I will take this man into my custody and if he proves difficult I can always get rid of him. I wish him to assist me on a mission.'

'My lord?' The officials looked confused, but none of them dared question Tanaka directly.

'Go back to Edo,' Tanaka ordered. 'I can deal with one measly foreigner by myself. I'll not let him out of my sight, you have my word on that, and when I have finished with him, he'll be taken to the proper authorities.'

'Very well, my lord, if that is your wish.' The officials bowed once more, and reluctantly set off for Edo, murmuring amongst themselves.

'What do we want with the *gai-jin*?' Tanaka's chief retainer dared to ask, looking thoroughly puzzled.

'I'm not sure yet, but I don't want to risk him escaping from those fools. I want him where I can see him. Now let's go, we have wasted enough time.'

Just then, a shout went up ahead and Tanaka rode up to his scout, who was pointing at the ground. 'There is a small track here, Tanaka-*sama*, showing signs of having been swept recently.'

'Swept, eh? Do they really think they'll fool us that easily? Honestly, this will be like child's play. Lead on.'

Temperance was lost. She knew that she had veered off the track ages ago, long before they even reached the stream, but she had thought that by keeping an eye on the sun she could follow roughly the right course without it.

She was wrong.

She'd been worrying about Kazuo and had stopped several times to try and make him drink a little. Occasionally he would co-operate, but more often than not he would simply turn his head away and no amount of cajoling could persuade him to drink. As the day wore on, Temperance became increasingly disorientated, and every time she looked up the sun had moved yet again and she was heading in completely the wrong direction.

'Damn it all!' she shouted in English, wanting to hurl something in frustration, but she didn't dare to move in case she dislodged Kazuo from his precarious position. It was difficult enough to support him as it was. Her back muscles ached with the strain of trying to keep him upright, as well as herself. 'Now what do I do?' she asked of no one in particular.

But there was nothing to do, other than continue, so she plodded on.

The mountains had come steadily closer all day and by dusk the weary horse was heading up a fairly sharp incline. She was certain it wasn't the north-western mountain she'd been heading for originally, but by now Temperance didn't care. At least there were plenty of trees to shield them from view and there must be somewhere they could stop safely for a rest.

In order to spare the horse, who was beginning to sound rather wheezy, she dismounted and walked beside it. She retied the belt so that Kazuo was strapped to the horse's back instead. He lay like a sack of flour, slumped forward, still muttering from time to time, but she knew that she couldn't tend him now, much as she would like to. Instead, she scoured the countryside for any sign of a good stopping place. She had to find shelter for them before nightfall.

At first there was nothing and as the light faded she began to despair. Then she spotted something in the distance, far up on the side of a rocky ravine on a wild, pine-clad mountain. It looked like a building, albeit uninhabited and in bad repair, and she wondered if it was the answer to her prayers. Heading in that direction, she soon found an overgrown path leading up towards it. As she came closer she realised that it was an old temple. The steep roofs with tip-tilted corners had been finely crafted once upon a time, although now there were alarmingly big holes in most of them. The place must have had a fine view before the nearby forest began to encroach upon the temple grounds. She wondered why it was no longer in use, and whether there were other buildings nearby, but couldn't see anything in the gathering darkness.

Trees surrounded her as she walked, so thick and high they made the fading light even more obscure, and she shivered. There was an eerie stillness about this place that made her want to turn and run, but she knew she had to go on. Even if the temple was haunted she would have to brave the night there. She simply must find Kazuo a place to rest that was warm and reasonably dry or he would die. She ruthlessly ignored the annoying voice inside her that said he might die anyway.

As she came closer, she saw that the little temple, which was clinging to the hillside, was in even worse repair than she'd thought. With mounting despair she took in the dreadful state of it. There was a smell of decay and rotting timber all around and she wondered if any part of it would be habitable. It may even be dangerous. She was in two minds whether to try and find somewhere else to go, but just then Kazuo groaned and thrashed around restlessly on the horse's back. She came to the conclusion that she didn't have any choice but to make the best of this place.

Some of the trees outside the temple had old bits of paper fastened onto their branches, most of which were in tatters and flapping forlornly in the breeze. Temperance knew they were prayers, tied there by hopeful supplicants wanting assistance from the gods. She wondered if they had received what they asked for? Perhaps she ought to tie one up herself?

'No, it will have to wait.' And besides, she didn't have any paper.

Leaving Kazuo and the horse at the foot of a steep stone staircase that led up towards the main entrance of the temple, she went off to reconnoitre.

'Stay there for a moment, I'll be right back,' she murmured, although she was fairly sure he couldn't even hear her.

She took the steps two at a time and, as daylight was disappearing fast now, she hurried round the buildings, inspecting each and every room, looking for one that might keep them dry for the night. All the main rooms were in a sad state, the floors rotten and slippery, and the only thing that was virtually intact was a stone figure of a god. It grinned inanely at Temperance, scaring her half to death before she realised what she was looking at.

'I don't know what you're laughing at,' she told him. 'You don't have anyone to look after but yourself.'

Naturally the god didn't reply, but she thought for a moment that she saw its bronze eyes glance to the left and she felt compelled to walk in that direction. She came first to two rooms with a magnificent view overlooking the valley, and a long balcony outside that must have caught the last rays of the sun each evening. It was lighter there than in the rest of the temple, but Temperance didn't dare go outside, as it was sure to be unsafe. Instead she turned right and ended up in a tiny room that had to be behind the statue of the god. Although it was very dark since it had no window, the roof was mercifully sound.

'Oh, thank the Lord!'

Temperance got down on her knees to feel the floorboards and was relieved to find them dry. Just to be on the safe side, she walked round the room, jumping on some of the planks to make sure they weren't about to break, and then, satisfied that they would hold, she rushed back outside to fetch Kazuo. She had to go slowly down the stone steps, which were slippery with moss and lichen, but she made it to the bottom without falling and Kazuo was still where she'd left him.

'Now then, how are we going to get you up there to the temple?' she murmured to Kazuo. This was indeed the next question. Temperance decided that her only hope was to try to cajole the horse up the steps, as she couldn't possibly carry or drag Kazuo all the way herself, but it wouldn't be an easy task. The horse was an extremely good-natured animal, however, and when offered a bribe in the shape of bits of rice cake, he followed her up without protest. Temperance held on to Kazuo's jacket with one hand so that he wouldn't fall off, while bribing the horse with the other.

'Good boy! You're a wonderful horse, absolutely marvellous,' she encouraged the little steed, and he seemed to respond to her voice and continued steadily up. At the top, outside the entrance to the temple, there was a small paved area with grass sticking out between the slabs, and the horse stopped there, starting to munch happily on whatever he could find.

Temperance half dragged, half carried Kazuo into their temporary abode. Once she had him settled on a horse blanket in the corner furthest away from any draughts, she collapsed next to him, panting for breath. She had never been so tired in all her life.

'Can't sit here all day though,' she muttered. She still needed to find some water for herself and the horse, and the animal would need rubbing down as well, or he would catch a chill. Wearily she rose to her feet and set to work.

It was full dark by the time she'd finished everything she needed to do, but she was pleased with what she had achieved. The horse had been watered and cared for and left outside with a blanket for cover, and she had enough water for her own needs as well. In one of the rooms near the balcony she had found a stone trough, which she'd pushed and pulled into the back room and then filled with sticks and bits of wood. After much effort, she managed to get a fire going and the little room immediately seemed more cheerful, if a tad smoky. Soon the tendrils of smoke found their way out through cracks in the roof though, which helped. She manoeuvred Kazuo closer to the fire, then made him sip some more willow bark, properly prepared with boiling water this time.

For the first time that day she felt in control and although she knew that Tanaka might catch up with them at any moment, at least she had done her best. All she could do now was pray for time and for Kazuo to recover, then perhaps all would be well.

Chapter Twenty-Four

All the hard work took its toll and Temperance soon fell asleep lying close to Kazuo. Several times during the night she was woken by his shivering or muttering, and each time she got up and put more wood on the little fire before sponging him with cold water. He talked a lot of nonsense, but she paid no heed to it. He obviously didn't know who she was, so she was sure he wasn't talking to her.

After a while it began to rain and Temperance rushed outside to bring the little horse into the main temple chamber where she found a reasonably dry corner for him to shelter in. She thought that this might possibly be sacrilege and glanced at the statue of the god which gleamed faintly in the darkness.

'Please forgive me, but needs must,' she murmured to the god, but really she didn't care if she offended him. It was more important to keep the horse healthy than to worry about superstitious nonsense. And yet ...

'I do hope you understand?' she whispered to the statue, before hurrying back to Kazuo.

As the wind began to howl around the corners of the temple and the rain fell in great torrents, drumming on the roof and running in through the various gaping holes, she began to wonder if perhaps she should at least have asked the god's permission before bringing the horse inside. The wind made an unnatural noise, as if a thousand voices were complaining about her behaviour, and she cowered in the back room, holding tight to Kazuo and closing her eyes.

'Don't be a ninny,' she admonished herself. 'Ghosts can't hurt you, only the living.' But it only made her feel marginally better.

Towards morning, Kazuo's breathing calmed slightly and

she lay with her arms wrapped around him, waiting for the dawn. When the rain and wind eased off a little to make a more soothing noise, she fell into a dreamless sleep at last.

The sun was high in the sky when she finally woke again and all was quiet apart from the sounds of nature all round them. The rain had stopped completely, but water was still dripping into the building and onto the ground off the nearby trees. The air was moist and fresh, with a tang of clean vegetation which had replaced the odours of decay. Through the doorway, Temperance could see tendrils of mist floating lazily outside, caressing the old buildings.

She lay still and listened, soothed by the peace, then sat up suddenly as her ears caught another sound, one she'd been dreading. She could hear footsteps. Someone was walking around inside the temple.

Extracting her knife from the sleeve of her jacket, she stood up and tiptoed over to lie in wait by the door opening. The quiet footsteps were coming closer now and any moment the intruder would spot Kazuo. She waited, and at the last minute threw herself over the person entering the room, causing a surprised yelp from her victim.

'Peace! I come in peace,' she dimly heard, but it wasn't until she had gripped him round the throat from behind and forced him onto the floor that she realised she'd caught a monk, not one of Tanaka's henchmen. Slowly she released the man and stood up, knife at the ready despite his statement. There was no knowing who they could trust.

'I beg your pardon, but we were not expecting anyone,' she said curtly.

'I was, but you startled me,' he replied, standing up and fingering his throat while grimacing with discomfort. 'I saw the smoke from your fire last night and thought I would come and see who was here.'

'You saw the smoke?' This was bad news. If the monk had seen it, then so could others. Temperance bit her lip.

'Yes, but only briefly. I live in a hut further down the hill. Hardly anyone comes here any more, but I have retreated to this place for solitude.' He bowed to her. 'Please, put your knife away, *gai-jin* lady. I swear I mean you no harm.'

'How do you know I'm a woman?' The *gai-jin* part was easier as he must have seen her eyes when she released him. She cursed herself for not being more careful.

'I, er ... felt your curves against my back when you were trying to throttle me.' The monk raised his hands in an apologetic gesture as if he was at fault, when really she should have thought of that herself.

'Ah, how stupid of me.'

He shook his head. 'No, understandable if you had other things on your mind. Now will you trust me? I really do come in peace.'

She nodded, convinced by his sincere tone of voice, and put the knife back inside her sleeve. She swept a hand to indicate Kazuo and said, 'I'm sorry if we're trespassing, but my friend here was too ill to go on. We had to stop for the night.'

'So I see. May I have a look at him? I have some skill at healing.'

'Please, feel free. Nothing I do seems to help. I've given him willow bark and sponged him repeatedly with cold water, but the fever refuses to leave him.'

'Do you know what has caused it?'

'He is wounded in the thigh. I must change the dressing I think.'

'Let me. I have some clean bindings here.' The monk took some things out of a leather satchel, which Temperance hadn't noticed until then. With gentle hands he uncovered Kazuo's wound, which looked angry and raw and was oozing pus. 'Hmm, that doesn't look too good. I think we need to do something about that or he'll never recover.'

'Like what? It has already been stitched.'

'I know, but I believe we ought to open it again and cauterise it. It's the only way. If not, he may lose the leg, if not his life.'

'Oh, no! But the pain?'

'Is better than dying, surely?'

Temperance nodded mutely and watched as the monk set about the task, laying out what he needed on a clean piece of cloth ready to hand and putting a small iron rod into the still hot fire. While they waited for it to heat up he said, 'What is a foreign lady doing here of all places, if I may ask?'

'It's a long story and one it's probably best you don't know. If you must tell anyone about me, it might be safer to say that you met an albino.'

He raised his eyebrows at that, but nodded acquiescence. 'If that is your wish.'

Temperance continued to watch as he carried on with his preparations, impressed that he seemed very sure of what he was doing.

'Are you being followed?' the monk asked suddenly, taking her by surprise.

'What? Oh, er ...'

'Don't worry, I won't tell. It's just that what we are about to do will probably make your friend scream, and if anyone is following you they may hear him.'

'Then what do you suggest?'

'We have to gag him.'

It seemed an extreme measure, but Temperance couldn't afford to take the chance of Kazuo's screams reverberating around the mountainside. She nodded and the monk deftly fashioned a gag which he bound round Kazuo's mouth. 'There, that should do. Now, could you sit on him, please, facing away from me, and hold down his shoulders with all your might. I'll be as quick as I can.'

What followed must have been a nightmare of pain for Kazuo. Temperance suffered with him every step of the way, but although he opened his eyes and tried to scream through the gag, she could see that he wasn't in his full senses. His eyes were wild and frantic, but there was still no spark of recognition when he looked at her and she could only pray that if he came through this ordeal, he wouldn't remember it.

She hung on for dear life, using all her weight to keep Kazuo still, and the monk worked as quickly as he could. She could smell burning flesh and hear the hissing of the hot iron against the wound. She gagged at the thought of it, but somehow she managed to swallow her bile. At last, she heard the monk say, 'There, that will do. You may let go now.' She breathed a sigh of relief and noticed that Kazuo was dead to the world.

'I think he's fainted.'

'Just as well. He will be hurting at first, but I think I have stopped his wound from festering now, so if we can just keep him alive for another day or two, he should start to recover. Although I must say, someone's done a very thorough job of beating him up which probably isn't helping.'

'Yes.' Temperance thought it best not to say who had done this to Kazuo. 'We can't stay here,' she added. 'We have to move on.'

'How far behind were your pursuers?'

'I have no idea. We were supposed to be heading north-west, but I'm afraid I lost my way yesterday, so that might have made it harder for them to follow our tracks. They can't be that far away though, certainly no more than half a day's ride.'

'Hmm. Might I suggest something?'

'Please do.'

'If I could borrow your horse for a few days, I will ride back the way you came and then continue in a different direction, stopping at the villages along the route. I know the people hereabouts and I can ask them to say that they've seen you heading south-west. It might help. Then I'll sell your horse and buy another one and return to you.'

Temperance didn't know what to do. On the one hand, it sounded like an admirable scheme and would give Kazuo a chance to recover and have some much needed rest. On the other, how did she know she could trust this man, despite the fact that he was a monk? Were there not greedy monks as well as ordinary men? What if he sold their horse and never came back? Or even led Tanaka to them?

She sighed and glanced at Kazuo. One thing was clear, he couldn't go any further for the moment, so she decided she would have to take the chance that the monk was honest. 'Very well, I accept your suggestion with thanks. It is very kind of you to put yourself out on our behalf.'

He shook his head with a smile. 'I do it gladly. I enjoy helping my fellow men. Come with me, I want to show you something.'

Slightly bemused, Temperance followed him to the front room of the temple, where the stone god was now clearly visible, a shaft of sunlight streaming down onto his bald head.

'This is Musubi-no-Kami, the god of love, and over there is the lovely Kannon, the goddess of mercy.' The monk pointed to an alcove Temperance had missed the previous night, where a smaller bronze statue of a beautiful goddess stood. 'I swear by both these deities that I will return to you with all haste, as soon as I have carried out my tasks, and I will pray to them to keep you safe while I'm gone.'

'Thank you.' Temperance looked around her once more, the neglect even more noticeable in daylight. 'What happened to this place? Why is it deserted? It must have been breathtakingly beautiful once.'

'It's been empty for many years, long before I came here, but I've been told that it is haunted by a former priest. The unlucky man happened to fall in love with a beautiful lady who came to pray to the god of love. Knowing that he could never marry her, he threw himself off the balcony. His soul still roams this place.'

Temperance shivered. 'That's all I need,' she muttered, but the monk smiled.

'Don't worry. I have slept here many a night and I have never seen or heard anything untoward. I'm sure it's just a story. Now, I'd better be on my way. Keep on giving the young man the willow bark and make him drink as much water as you can. I will pray for you both.'

The day passed slowly and although Temperance was kept busy with her patient, the hours still seemed to drag on ad infinitum. By nightfall Kazuo appeared no better and she was beginning to despair of him ever recovering. She was exhausted from fighting with him each time she tried to give him the willow bark as he was stronger than her even when ill. To hold him down and make him swallow the bitter tasting concoction was a struggle. She persevered, however, and in between she occupied herself by collecting more firewood and making herself eat a little.

To her relief there were no sounds of pursuit and she began to hope that the monk's cunning plan had worked. The heavy rainfall of the night before should have helped to obliterate their tracks as well, which was all to the good. If their pursuers were using dogs to track them, hopefully the water had obscured their scent.

If only Kazuo would get better, but there seemed little hope of that.

The night-time brought more strange noises and creaking timbers, but without the howling wind Temperance was able to think rationally and refused to let it frighten her. She lay down next to Kazuo as before, but was woken during the darkest part of the night by him thrashing around and shouting something about 'injustice'.

'Kazuo, calm down. Listen to me, there's no one here. Please, shush,' she begged him, but it wasn't until she began to sponge his face with cold water that he stopped ranting and lay still again. He was, however, drawing in shallow breaths that rasped through the silence in a way that chilled Temperance to the bone. Was this it? Was he going to die now and leave her here, stranded in the middle of a strange country with no idea where to go? It didn't bear thinking of.

With renewed determination she began to sponge him down, even pulling open his tunic to dribble the cool water onto his chest, which was as burning hot as the rest of him. Over and over again, she repeated the process, until at last he felt cooler to the touch, and appeared to have gone back to a more peaceful sleep. Temperance wrung out the cloth one last time and laid it across his brow, then wrapped them both up inside the blanket and held him in her arms.

'Please, my love, don't die. I couldn't bear it if you did,' she whispered, and she realised that it was the truth. She loved this man, despite all the barriers between them and despite the fact that she knew they were not destined to be together.

Love took no notice of such things, however, and had crept over her without warning, insinuating itself into her heart without giving her a chance to resist, and now it was too late. For a crazy moment, she wondered if the little god in the main temple chamber had had a hand in this madness, but in truth she knew that she had loved Kazuo almost from the first moment she'd seen him. She would only be deceiving herself if she thought otherwise.

She closed her eyes and waited for sleep to claim her, but instead she felt Kazuo's arms come around her waist, pulling her closer, and then his mouth nuzzled her cheek. 'Temi?' His voice was rough, but sounded more lucid than before, and Temperance blinked in the darkness and put a hand to his brow. It was still cool.

'Kazuo? Are you all right? Can you hear me?'

'Yes, a bit too loudly actually.' A small chuckle rumbled through his chest and she felt it through his tunic.

'Sorry,' she whispered. 'I've been so worried about you. Are you really better?'

'Mmm, tired … thirsty …'

'Wait, I will give you some water. And please, can you drink some willow bark? I haven't the strength to fight you again.'

'Don't want to fight … will drink.'

'Thank God!' She hurried to give him the infusion while he was still awake enough to accept it without protest, and although he made a noise of disgust, he drank it all. Temperance was so relieved, she lay down and hugged him tightly, wanting to laugh and shout with joy. 'Well done, that ought to help.'

'Ouch! My ribs …'

'Oh, sorry, I forgot.' She loosened her grip on him and would have removed her arms altogether, but he protested.

'No, hold me. Feels good.' He snuggled close, wincing slightly, but then coming to rest with his head on her shoulder.

Temperance smiled into the darkness. Perhaps all would be well.

She woke just after dawn and sat up with a gasp, wondering if the happenings of the night had been a dream. Was Kazuo really better? She put her hand up to his brow and drew a sigh of relief when she found it cool to the touch. Before she could remove it, however, it was covered by another hand and pulled down towards Kazuo's mouth. He kissed each finger tenderly and opened sleepy eyes.

'My saviour,' he whispered hoarsely.

'Not really. I just did what I had to.' It was such a joy to find his eyes actually looking at her, clear and intelligent once more, that she couldn't help but smile broadly.

'Why didn't you go back to your family when you had the chance?'

Temperance avoided his gaze. 'I wanted to help you first.'

'You could have been killed.'

'I still could, but I'm here now, so there's no point thinking about that.'

'Where are we? Are we being pursued?'

'I have no idea. In a temple somewhere.' She went on to tell him a little of their journey, but after a while he stopped her by putting his finger on her mouth.

'Never mind. Later you can tell me everything. For now, let's enjoy the peace.'

To her surprise he replaced the finger with his mouth and kissed her slowly, as if savouring something he had thought gone forever. Temperance was stunned at first, but soon became lost in the kiss and returned it in full measure. It was a gentle kiss, without any of the urgency of true desire, but there was desire in it nonetheless, conveyed by the reverence with which each caressed the other's lips. Having lived through what she considered hell, Temperance thought she had died and gone to heaven.

All too soon, however, he broke off, too weak to continue. 'I'm sorry,' he murmured. 'Later. Must rest.'

'Of course. Close your eyes, there's no hurry.'

And she knew they had all the time in the world.

As long as Tanaka didn't find them.

Chapter Twenty-Five

'I can't believe it could be that difficult to find one clumsy girl and a weak man on a horse. A foreign girl at that!'

Tanaka surveyed the countryside around them with an angry scowl and noticed that several of his retainers cowered in fright whenever his glance came anywhere near them. No doubt they knew from experience that if their master couldn't find the true target for his wrath, they were likely to be substitutes. Tanaka couldn't care less. He had to vent his frustration on someone and that was what servants were for in his opinion.

'The villagers said they'd seen such a couple pass this way,' his second-in-command reminded him diffidently.

'I know, I know, but how can they travel so fast? That horse must be half dead by now.'

'At least we know we are going in the right direction, my lord.'

'They're leading us a merry dance, I tell you, and I'm tiring of it. You should have—' But the hapless man was spared the rest of this sentence, as the foreigner, looking petulant and disgruntled, chose that moment to ride up to Tanaka and ask through his interpreter why they were dawdling.

'Dawdling! How dare you?' Tanaka felt a vortex of rage swirl inside him and pinned the *gai-jin* with an angry glare. Out of the corner of his eye he heard his retainers draw a collective sigh of relief as they realised that their master had found an outlet for his temper other than them. Several of them smirked behind raised hands. 'I'll give you dawdling, you good for nothing, *gai-jin* son of a whore!'

Tanaka whipped his sword from the scabbard and jumped off his horse, grabbing the bridle of Haag's mount and tugging violently. The sword swished through the air in an angry arc, too close to Haag's ear for comfort. The foreigner squawked indignantly and scrabbled for his own much smaller sword. For a while he put up a spirited fight, but he was never going to beat someone like Tanaka with such a puny weapon.

'What are you doing? I have a right to know what's happening. She's my wi– ... betrothed!' he shrieked and jumped off the horse on the other side, giving up on trying to defend himself with the sword. 'You said I could come along. I'll report you to the *Shogun*! You can't treat a foreigner this way, I'll ...'

Tanaka didn't reply, merely pursued Haag on foot growling furiously. He only understood the word *shogun* among the rest of the foreigner's unintelligible words, but he had no intention of letting the fool tell anyone anything. Without further ado he knocked the man unconscious with a heavy blow on the back of the head from his sword hilt. That wasn't nearly enough to rid him of his frustrations, however, so he proceeded to pummel the defenceless foreigner into the ground for good measure, raining blows on the unconscious man without stopping. No one intervened as they knew full well it would mean instant death.

When at last his fury was spent, Tanaka returned to his horse and mounted in one fluid motion, giving the order to set off immediately.

'And bring that son of a foreign whore. I may wish to hit him again when he wakes up. As for you,' he pointed at the men who had come with Haag, 'I tire of seeing you whispering with the *gai-jin*. Either go back where you came from or follow my orders from now on. Understood?'

They all nodded and bowed without a moment's hesitation.

Another day passed and towards evening Kazuo was sufficiently rested to sit up and partake of a little food. He was still as weak as a kitten and winced every time he had to move his leg, but when Temperance uncovered it in order to clean it, there seemed to be a marked improvement and no further infection. She sent up a silent prayer of thanks.

'That monk obviously knew what he was doing,' she said. 'I do hope he's not fallen foul of Tanaka. It was so kind of him to offer to help and to think I didn't even ask him his name.' She had told Kazuo the full story of their journey by now and he nodded agreement.

'Indeed. He has bought us valuable time, but we really ought to move on soon.'

'You're in no state to go anywhere yet,' Temperance protested.

'By tomorrow I'll be fine. We can't stay any longer than that. It would be too risky.'

'But where will we go? Back down south?'

Kazuo shook his head. 'No, north. I have one more man to investigate and somehow I have to do it.'

'The third man you were speaking of? Surely you can't continue your quest now. It will have to wait.'

'No, I must go on or else it will be too late. I'm more than half sure that my father's downfall was all Tanaka's doing. From what I've seen of him so far, he is ruthless and ambitious in the extreme and I have no doubt he would have coveted my father's position and influence. If he couldn't gain it by fair means, he wouldn't hesitate to use foul play. Still, it could be that the third man was his accomplice and I have to make certain. Besides, I still have no proof.'

Temperance sighed. 'Wouldn't it be better if you went back to your father's house to recover fully first?'

'No. This way I can pretend to have been injured by outlaws and perhaps I'll be taken into the lord's household and given shelter for a while. That will give me a chance to observe him.'

'And what about me? Where will I be?'

Kazuo frowned. 'Could you survive a few days on your own in the forest? If I leave you with enough food and build you a shelter? It would only be for a very short while.'

'I suppose so, but what if you don't return?'

'I will.'

They were interrupted by the sound of horse's hooves and Temperance's stomach performed an uncomfortable somersault. When she peered out into the dusk, however, it was to find the monk tethering a new horse to a nearby tree and as she went out to greet him, he smiled at her.

'You're back so soon?' Temperance picked her way down the treacherous steps carefully and smiled back.

'Yes. I think I succeeded in my mission and I persuaded a farmer's son to ride the other horse a bit further, pretending he'd been sent on an errand. He should be leading your pursuers well away from this area.'

'Thank you, you've been most kind. In fact, I don't know how to thank you enough and what's more, I don't even know your name.' Temperance felt like hugging the little man, but thought that probably wasn't allowed, so instead she bowed deeply to him in a gesture of pure respect and gratitude.

'My name is Daisuke and no thanks are necessary. If I have saved two lives, then I am content. Speaking of which, how is the patient?'

'Much better. The fever is gone and although he's still weak, there is nothing wrong with his brain. Come and see for yourself.'

Together they mounted the steps and walked into the back room. Temperance performed the introductions and when Kazuo struggled to stand up to greet the monk, the latter put a hand on his shoulder and pushed him back down. 'No, please, don't get up on my account. I will sit next to you instead.'

He repeated his tale for Kazuo's benefit and was thanked once more. 'I will see that my father rewards you if at all possible,' Kazuo said. 'Your help has been invaluable.'

'Oh, I want nothing for myself, but if you really want to do something, then perhaps you could ask him to restore this temple to its former glory? It's such a shame it has fallen into disuse.'

'I agree.' Temperance nodded. 'It must have been lovely once.'

'Then that is what I will do,' Kazuo agreed.

'Good. Now how about some fresh food?' the monk asked. 'I bought some in the last village I passed through.'

The monk chose to spend the night sitting in the balcony room, deep in contemplation of all that had just come to pass. His presence reassured Temperance so that she was able to sleep deeply all night. She woke feeling much refreshed and after checking on Kazuo, she packed up their few belongings and made everything ready for their departure.

'I hope we will meet again one day, Daisuke-*san*,' she said to the monk when he came to help her with the horse.

'If not in this life, then in the next,' he replied. Temperance knew he didn't mean in heaven, but she let this pass. She respected the fact that he had different beliefs and felt certain that somehow she would meet him again. Such a good person would surely be rewarded by God whether he was a Christian or not. His actions were certainly those of a deeply honourable and compassionate man.

Kazuo was able to hobble slowly down the steps, with the help of the monk who was surprisingly strong. Temperance could see that it pained Kazuo to mount the horse, but his jaw was set with determination and she didn't say anything. It would have been better if they could have rested one more day, but she knew that he was dead set against this.

'Time is of the essence,' he'd insisted, and she had to admit that the thought of fleeing as far away as possible from the evil Tanaka was a comforting one.

'*Sayonara!*' the monk called after them as they rode slowly down the hill. They waved for as long as they could see him, but soon they were swallowed up by the mighty forest and his tiny figure disappeared from view.

For days they travelled north, then north-west, passing through great cool groves of cedar, across fertile valleys, around the rim of freezing cold lakes and skirting great mountains. Emerging from dense woodland they would suddenly come upon the glorious sight of a high waterfall, thundering down a mountainside, its damp spray chilling them as it hovered in the air in the shape of misty clouds. Or a still pool in the middle of an emerald grove, so calm as to be almost unreal.

'This is breathtakingly beautiful,' Temperance marvelled, and Kazuo agreed. Such reminders of the beauty of nature only made them feel even more grateful to be alive, and for her part Temperance couldn't regret having made the decision to stay with Kazuo. She may have lost the opportunity to return to her family, but it made no difference – she was with the person she loved and for now they were safe.

At first they had to stop frequently to allow Kazuo to rest, but as the days went by his strength began to return and he was able to ride for longer periods each day. He still had a limp whenever he tried to walk, but he practised for a while each evening in order to strengthen his leg. Temperance's heart soared every time she looked at him and she thought she saw an answering glimmer in his eyes. To her chagrin he had reverted to his previous rule of sleeping back to back with her though and didn't attempt any more kisses. She wondered if he had only done so out of gratitude that first night, but she sensed that he'd undergone some sort of change and that he was battling with himself as to what he should do.

She decided to give him time to think it over. She knew her own heart and it belonged firmly to Kazuo, but she wanted him to feel the same before she handed it over unconditionally.

'There's been no trace of them for two days now. That peasant boy must have been lying.'

Tanaka paced the floor of the inn he and his men had taken shelter in during a sudden rainstorm, feeling as ready to burst as the thunderclouds they had just escaped. His men tried to make themselves invisible, huddling in the corners, speaking in hushed voices, and he noted that no one dared reply to his comments. His gaze swept round the room searching for inspiration, and alighted instead on the foreigner, who was slumped on a bench near the window. He was a sorry sight after the recent beating Tanaka had administered. But despite the numerous bruises that ought to have reminded him of the folly of crossing such a powerful man, the *gai-jin* stared back almost insolently now, a half-smile of derision playing on his lips.

'And what is it you find so amusing?' Tanaka demanded, marching up to stand in front of Haag with his hands fisted at his side, ready to inflict more damage at a moment's notice. He knew it wouldn't take much to ignite his fuse right now and he would welcome the opportunity to beat the fool to a pulp once more. 'You think it's funny that my concubine is roaming this country with a thief whose company she apparently prefers to that of her master or the man she is supposedly betrothed to?'

The translator, who was sitting nearby, quickly told Haag what Tanaka had said, but the foreigner continued to smirk.

'What I'm enjoying is the sight of such a great man being led a merry dance by a mere woman, even if she is a cut above the rest.' The translator looked aghast at Haag's words and stammered out a shortened version, obviously not daring to render them in full. 'Besides,' Haag added, 'I know where she's gone.'

'*Nani?*' Tanaka moved forward until he was towering over Haag, but the latter kept calm, as if sensing he had the upper hand for once. 'You will tell me at once.'

'Why should I do that? You've treated me disgracefully so far. I don't owe you anything.'

Tanaka raised a fist and had the satisfaction of seeing Haag flinch ever so slightly. 'You will tell me what you know because if you don't you will never speak again. Is that clear enough?'

Haag blanched, but hung on to his composure somehow. He glared at Tanaka. 'If I tell you, will you promise to return me safely to Edo after we find the fugitives?'

Tanaka lost what little patience he had left and grabbed Haag around the neck with both hands. 'I will promise you nothing other than that you may live, cretin,' he snarled. 'Now spit it out or else ...' He shook his victim as if he were a sack of rice and although Haag tried to fight back at first, his bravado deserted him completely when Tanaka tightened the grip around his windpipe and began to squeeze.

'No! Let me *go!*' Haag tried to prise away the strong fingers clamped round his throat, but rage lent Tanaka additional force. Swearing under his breath, Tanaka banged Haag's head against the wall behind him.

'Where. Have. They. Gone?' Each word was emphasised by the satisfying thump of skull on wood.

'All right, all right.' Haag's teeth were beginning to rattle audibly. 'North,' he gasped. 'They must've gone north.' Tanaka let go at last and stood panting in front of the infuriating *gai-jin* while Haag put his hands up to massage his sore neck.

'Why on earth would they go north? It's getting colder by the day and if they're hoping to find help from other foreigners it's completely the wrong way.'

'Ah, but they're not seeking help from foreigners. I think they know someone who lives in northern Japan. The Chief Factor of the Dutch has a concubine whose relative is secretly helping in the search for the woman. I can't recall his name at the moment but I know they said he lived up north. And Temperance was very friendly with that concubine so she's bound to have heard all about the lady's relatives and where they live.'

Tanaka hit himself on the forehead. 'Of course, Lord Ebisu! Why didn't I think of that? Isn't that the name?'

Haag shrugged. 'Could be. As I said, I don't know.'

'It must be. The thief had a letter of reference from the old man when he first sought employment in my household. No doubt he'll seek shelter with him. Hah! That will avail him nothing. Old Ebisu is mortally afraid of me and he'll hand them over without the slightest protest. Excellent, let's be off then. Make haste everyone, we're going north.' The day seemed suddenly brighter and he strode off towards the door.

'But, my lord, the rain ...?' one retainer protested without thinking.

Tanaka cuffed him hard. 'What's a little rain? Now cease your whining and saddle the horses.'

'I'm coming too. She's *my* woman.' Haag stood up, swaying slightly.

Tanaka threw him a pitying glance. 'Go where you like. I don't care. And whether she's your woman or not, I paid for her, so if you want her back when I've finished with her, you'll have to pay me a ransom. That's *if* she agrees to return to you at all.' He chuckled. 'She doesn't seem very keen to be reunited with you and if she has even half the brains you credit her with, she'll stay in my household for good.'

Haag glared after Tanaka's retreating back. The man was a complete maniac. In fact, he was inhuman and the sooner they found Temperance, the better. The moment they did, Haag vowed to put a knife in the mean bastard's back. If he thought he was giving up *his* woman to someone like that, he was much mistaken. He'd rather see her dead.

Not that it wouldn't be what the idiotic girl deserved, to be punished by Tanaka, but if anyone was going to make her pay, it was Haag. He felt he'd earned that right after all he'd been through. And he still wanted her, even if she was soiled goods, because the hunger inside him must be appeased. The dreams of her had only intensified with time and he constantly woke with his body on fire with lust. He'd damn well have her for as many times as it took to put that fire out.

Tanaka may have the upper hand for now, but Haag would find a way to defeat him, by fair means or foul. At the moment he needed the man to help find the fugitives, but as soon as that happened, his usefulness would be at an end.

He just had to be patient a little while longer.

Chapter Twenty-Six

The journey seemed endless and turned into a blur of impressions while the horse plodded steadily onwards, but Kazuo knew he had to continue or his mission would have failed completely. He couldn't risk Tanaka sending a message to the third lord, if indeed they were co-conspirators. His only chance was to reach the man first and see whether he could find any evidence of guilt.

When he had first woken up in the temple to find that Temi was still with him and had in fact saved his life instead of returning to her family, he'd experienced a mixture of emotions. Foremost of these was a sense of fate or inevitability. No matter what he did, it seemed the two of them were destined to remain together. And as he had to acknowledge that that was his own wish, were he given a choice, it wasn't difficult to accept. Now that he knew this was so, he felt calmer. He was also more sure of where his future lay, should he succeed in clearing his father's name.

If he failed, however, there would be no future for either of them.

'Are you warm enough?' He looked over his shoulder to where Temi was sitting on the horse's rump, lightly holding onto Kazuo's waist but lost in thought.

'Hmm? Oh, yes, thank you. I'm fine. And you? Would you like me to guide the horse for a while?'

They had been taking turns so that the person on the back could close their eyes and doze a little if they wished and thereby save energy. However, Kazuo found that after a week and a half of travelling, his strength was returning at last and he no longer needed as much rest. 'No, I'm not tired.'

The weather had grown colder the further north they

came, and Kazuo had had to stop at a small village to buy them warm, padded jackets and some more blankets. The villagers had been only too happy to part with these items in exchange for silver, and for a slightly larger sum had sworn not to mention having seen the two strangers should anyone enquire. Kazuo had his doubts as to whether they would keep this promise, but there hadn't been any signs of pursuit so far and he could only hope that Tanaka had at last given up. Surely the man must have better things to do than hunt for two fugitives, no matter how much it galled him?

Thinking out loud, he said, 'It was a good thing Tanaka never thought to question me as to the real reason why I requested employment with him. I'm sure he would have thought of that sooner or later, but you managed to rescue me in time.'

'Did he only ask you about me then, during your, uhm, interrogation?'

'Yes. Being the sort of man he is I don't think he could stomach losing any part of his property, be it human or otherwise, in such a way. He seemed intent on getting you back, probably to punish you severely before casting you aside.' He felt Temi shudder behind him.

'Hateful man,' she muttered. 'To think I had almost talked myself into believing that I could give myself to him without a fight.'

'Really?'

'Well, yes, what choice did I have? But when it came down to it, I simply couldn't do it. I was just about to fight back when that messenger arrived to tell him about his wife's infidelity. I've never been so relieved in all my life.'

'It was fate yet again,' Kazuo mused.

'Fate?'

'Yes. It wasn't your destiny to be Tanaka's concubine.'

'Perhaps it's not my fate to be anyone's mistress or wife.'

Temi sounded so forlorn that Kazuo twisted in the saddle to look at her. '*Nani?* What's this? Self-pity from the bravest woman I've ever come across? Surely not?' He smiled at her and she reluctantly smiled back.

'I'm not at all brave.'

'Yes, you are. Don't argue with your liege-lord.' He was still smiling to show that he was joking.

'My what? You're not my lord anything.' Playfully she hit him on the shoulder, only to put a hand over her mouth as he grunted. 'Oh, sorry! I forgot again. You seem so much like your normal self now it's hard to remember the bruises are still there.'

'It's all right. I'll live.'

Without warning they came upon a clearing in the forest where a small waterfall tumbled into a dark pool. It seemed like a magical place and Kazuo stopped the horse to sit in silent contemplation of the beauty around them for a moment. Then, making up his mind to do what he'd been wanting to do for days, he jumped off the horse and held out his hand to Temi. 'Come, let us stop here for a moment.'

'But, do we have time?'

'Not really, but there's something I want to ask you.'

Looking intrigued, Temi followed him to an old tree trunk near the mysterious pool and didn't protest when he pulled her down to sit there. 'This is incredibly peaceful,' she commented, staring at a tiny rainbow shining in the midst of the spray from the waterfall. 'Like something out of a fairy tale.' All was quiet, apart from the occasional chirp from a bird and the gurgling of the water.

Kazuo nodded, but didn't reply. He was silent for a moment longer, then asked, 'Temi, would you like me to be your lord?'

Temperance turned to frown at him slightly. 'For me to be your vassal, you mean? I don't think I could. The *Shogun* would never let me stay in Japan.'

'I meant as my wife.'

Temi gasped and blinked in surprise. 'Your wife? But, how could I? I mean, I'm a *gai-jin,* you're a *ronin* ... we'd never be allowed ...'

When he looked at her again, she was shaking her head and her eyes were suspiciously shiny, as if she was trying to hold back tears. He didn't know if they were tears of happiness or sadness, but she was clearly lost for words. He leaned forward and kissed her on the mouth to silence any more protests. 'If it's what you want too, we'll find a way, don't worry. If not in Japan, then somewhere else.'

'Are you serious? You truly want to marry me?'

'There's nothing I would like more. As long as you want me, that is?'

'Yes, yes, of course I do.' Her eyes shone at him, making him feel as though he was drowning in the clear blue therein, and she smiled broadly. She wrapped her arms around him more closely and squeezed hard. 'I just can't believe you would go against all your family's expectations. Aren't you the eldest son?'

'Yes, but I have brothers. My father is a wise man. He'll not deny me anything if I succeed in my quest.'

'Ah, yes, the quest ...' Temi's mood became instantly more sombre. 'And if you don't succeed?'

'Then I'll be dead, so it won't matter. We've made a pact. Our spirits will be together now whatever happens.'

Temi didn't look convinced, but she didn't say anything else.

That night they found a cave to sleep in and made themselves as comfortable as they could, fashioning a single bed out of moss, blankets and clothing in order to keep warm. When Kazuo lay down with his back towards her as usual, Temperance thought about their earlier conversation and came to a decision. She put a hand on his shoulder. 'Kazuo?'

'Yes?' He half turned towards her, but instead of replying she leaned over and kissed him.

It started as a mere touch of mouth on soft mouth, like the kind of kiss they'd shared in the temple when Kazuo was too weak to do anything else. But now he was feeling better, it was no longer enough for her. She wanted more and instinctively she deepened the kiss and caressed the nape of his neck, pulling him closer in the process.

'Temi, are you sure—?' he began, when they had to pause for breath, but she put a finger across his mouth and shushed him.

'You said you wanted me to be your wife. And just in case anything happens, I want us to have this moment to remember. It can't matter, surely, whether we wait or not? We have made a commitment to each other already, right?'

He nodded in wordless agreement and turned fully to draw her into his arms. Outside the little cave the night was so cold a frost was settling on every living thing, but inside their cocoon the temperature rose steadily as Kazuo kissed her again. Tentatively at first, as if he was unused to it, then slowly giving in to her questing tongue and joining in the age-old game.

During another pause for breath he whispered, 'Temi, I know that you spent some time at Imada's establishment, and no doubt many unpleasant things happened to you there, but I want you to know that they don't matter to me. Only the future is important.'

Temi looked at him and understanding dawned. 'You think they made me earn my living while I was there?'

Kazuo looked away. 'As I said, it doesn't matter. I can feel that you have some experience of these things, so ...'

'No, no, you have it all wrong, my love.' She cupped his cheeks with her hands and turned him back to face her. 'It's true that they taught me much, but I only ever had to watch and learn in theory. I never actually took part. That's why I found it so hard to contemplate submitting to Tanaka.'

'*Honto*? Then you were very fortunate. I've heard dreadful things of such places.'

'They were just training me so that I would please whoever bought me. Imada was hoping for a large sum for me, although as you know Tanaka drove a hard bargain.'

'Now I understand. And you managed to escape Tanaka before he …?'

'Yes, I told you. So you'll have to be gentle with me.'

'Perhaps it's the other way round?' he teased. 'Show me what else they taught you and we'll see.'

Temi smiled and kissed him again, while letting her hands roam. At first she followed dimly remembered instructions from Nyoko, but as her fingers found the contours of his lean body, they took on a will of their own. She forgot everything except the feel of his skin under her fingertips. She marvelled that anything could be so perfect and couldn't get enough of touching him. If this did indeed turn out to be their only time together, she was determined to remember every last detail. She'd have this memory to carry with her forever.

Kazuo allowed her free rein for a while, then took his turn at exploration, calling forth shivers of delight with his feather-light caresses. Somehow their garments were shed until there was nothing but warm skin against skin. His strong hands cradled her softly rounded curves with infinite gentleness at first. Then subtly the pace changed and their mutual caresses became more demanding, urgent, until at last Temperance couldn't stand it anymore and boldly guided him to her.

'I want you, Kazuo,' she whispered. 'I love you.'

'As I love you.'

Although there was a sharp pain at first, she forgot it the instant he started to move as waves of exquisite sensations began to engulf her. She finally understood that love-making between two people who loved each other could be magical and she was infinitely grateful to have been granted this night with the man she loved.

'How far is it now?' Temperance asked, as they prepared to continue on their way the following morning, somewhat later than the previous days. They had allowed themselves some extra time in the cave for more love-making, neither one of them able to resist the desire that welled up anew. Consequently the sun was already high in the sky.

'Not much longer. In fact, I think we may be quite close. It might be a good idea if I leave you somewhere safe for a while and go off to scout the layout of the land.' He caught sight of her expression and hastened to reassure her. 'It won't be for long and I'll be very careful, I promise.'

'Can't I come with you?'

'I'll be able to move more quietly on my own, and faster too. Besides, it will be less tiring for the horse.'

'I suppose so.'

'This cave is as good a place as any, really,' he added. 'What do you say, shall I leave you here or do you want to look for somewhere else?'

'Let's see how close to our destination we are first, then you can bring me back here if we can find the way.'

'Very well. Don't worry, I'll leave a trail that only I can see.'

Their plans all came to naught, however, because just as they were ready to leave, they caught the sound of movement nearby. The crack of a twig, snapped in half by a heavy foot, made a bird fly squawking out of a bush and an unnatural silence ensued. It was as if the world was waiting for something to happen, holding its breath, and a feeling of foreboding shimmered down Temi's back. Kazuo froze and gestured for her to return to the cave. Moving slowly, together they backed towards the safety of the darkness, all the while scanning the edges of the clearing.

'Was it an animal?' Temi breathed. She couldn't see anything, so whatever it was had to be hiding. On purpose? 'Are there bears here? Wolves?' She hadn't thought to ask him before as she'd felt so safe in his company.

Kazuo shook his head, looking grim. 'We need to leave. Now.'

But it was already too late. The moment they took one step towards the horse, Tanaka and his men burst into the clearing and surrounded them on all sides.

'I knew we'd catch up with them,' Tanaka crowed, a grin spreading over his features. 'Didn't I tell you? Now kill him, but don't harm the girl. I have other plans for her.'

Temperance felt as if she had just swallowed a huge quantity of lead. How could this be? How had Tanaka found them? She'd been so sure that they were safe from him now and the only threat to them would come from the unknown man they were heading towards. For a moment her body refused to move and she gazed around wide-eyed at Tanaka's men. As if in a dream, she heard Kazuo draw in a hissing breath and swear quietly. They still had their backs towards the mountainside where the opening to the cave gaped, and both instinctively reached for the knives inside their sleeves. As one, they drew them out and Kazuo moved slightly closer towards her as Tanaka's men advanced.

'No,' Temperance called out. 'You'll have to kill me too. I'm not going with you. Never!' The men hesitated.

'Don't be a fool,' Tanaka snarled, then turned to his men. 'Well, what are you waiting for? Go to it!'

Four of his men rushed forward, their swords raised, but they hadn't counted on fighting more than one man and were therefore taken by surprise when Temperance joined in the fray. Although the knives she and Kazuo carried were puny in comparison to the long *katanas* of their assailants, they were both quick. By ducking and feinting, they each managed to hurt one of their opponents. Temperance had a feeling that in her case it was pure luck as she was surely no match for a trained warrior, despite the practice sessions with Midori. Fear rose within her and she tasted bile.

Kazuo was a different matter. He had been born into the same life and no doubt trained from birth. He quickly sank his knife into one man's sword arm, while grabbing the assailant's weapon swiftly and turning to fight another man with that. Having shortened the odds thus, he quickly despatched the second attacker.

Temperance was heartened by this and told herself she wasn't helpless either. She *had* been taught to defend herself and she'd show these bastards their task wasn't as easy as they'd thought. She danced out of reach of one deadly sword coming towards her, and managed to avoid the other by meeting it with her knife. The clang of steel against steel reverberated all the way down her arm to her shoulder. She bit her teeth against the pain, but she had no time to think about it, because the men were advancing once more and had now been joined by several others.

'Here, Temi, catch.' Kazuo had picked up the sword of the second man he'd killed and threw it to Temperance, hilt first. She caught it deftly and the feel of it in her hand gave her the confidence to go on the attack herself, thereby astonishing the men who were coming towards her. She let out a blood-curdling yell and charged at them, hurting one more.

The element of surprise only helped her briefly, however, and she soon realised that she couldn't fight these men. They were simply too good. She stayed out of their reach as much as possible, hiding behind Kazuo who was fighting like one possessed. The battle became a blur of slashing steel, blood and cries of pain or exertion. Temperance could never afterwards quite recall the exact details of what had happened. All she knew was that Kazuo was fighting for their lives and she couldn't do anything other than help him to the best of her ability. The fact that she was prepared to die rather than surrender to Tanaka kept her from giving in to the pure terror that was coursing through her.

'By all the gods, make short work of him!' Tanaka yelled, frustration clear in his voice.

Temperance could see that Kazuo was an excellent swordsman, but in the end the sheer number of their assailants inevitably began to get the better of him. She also noticed that he winced whenever he had to put too much weight onto his bad leg. No matter how hard he fought, there was always someone else to take him on, and Temperance knew that he couldn't hold out much longer. Her own arm ached from her exertions, her breath was coming out in short bursts, and she was worried that Kazuo simply didn't have his usual stamina.

I can't bear to watch him die!

The words reverberated around her mind and, thinking furiously, she came to a decision and suddenly shouted at the top of her voice, 'Stop! Wait!' To her surprise, everyone obeyed, and she launched into speech before she could change her mind. 'I will agree to give myself up to Lord Tanaka, if you let my husband go first. If not, I'll kill myself here and now.' As if to prove that she meant every word, she put the small knife into her right hand and positioned the lethal blade of it against her heart.

Tanaka frowned and stared at her. 'Your betrothed, you mean? You want me to let the foreigner go?' He shrugged and glanced at someone behind him. 'He can go any time he wants. He's not my prisoner. In fact, I'd be happy to be rid of him.'

Temperance blinked and realised for the first time that on top of a scraggy horse behind Tanaka sat a very dishevelled Pieter Haag, scowling at everyone. He must have arrived later than the others and in the heat of the moment she hadn't noticed. She shook her head in exasperation at his tenacity. Was she never to be free of him?

'No, not *him*. I wouldn't marry that disgusting toad. This,' she pointed at Kazuo, 'is my husband. We were married five days ago by a monk.' She had no idea if monks performed such rites here, but it was the only thing she could come up with on the spur of the moment. It seemed important to her that if she was to die, she would do it as Kazuo's wife. If not in actual fact, then at least with everyone believing it.

'I'm not letting *him* go,' Tanaka snarled. 'He's a thief and probably more besides. Kill him.'

'Then I die too. Is that what you want?' Temperance cried, feeling more desperate for each moment that passed.

Tanaka's men hesitated, looking from her to their master and back again.

'She won't do it,' Tanaka stated confidently.

'I wouldn't be too sure if I were you,' Kazuo put in. 'But I won't let her. If anyone comes so much as a step nearer, I will kill us both.' He looked Temperance in the eyes as if for the last time. 'Remember what I said, Temi-*chan*? Our souls will be together for eternity.'

She nodded, believing him now. Taking a deep breath, she leaned over to give him a hard kiss and whispered. 'Do it, my love, for Tanaka is right. I don't have the courage to kill myself.'

Kazuo nodded and raised his sword.

Chapter Twenty-Seven

Temperance closed her eyes and swallowed hard, hoping that death would come swiftly. Before Kazuo had time to do anything, however, a new voice suddenly rang out in the clearing. 'Halt! What is happening here?'

Temperance's eyes flew open and she saw at least twenty men, all dressed in identical black outfits with a clan motif embroidered on each shoulder, appear from behind the trees like wraiths. They moved silently and with deadly intent in their eyes. Their leader was mounted on a black horse and rode forward to face Tanaka. Temperance found her legs paralysed with fear once more and all she could do was stand and stare at them as they came closer. To her surprise they hardly glanced at her and Kazuo. Instead they seemed intent on Tanaka and his men.

'Who are you? What do you want here? This is private land.' The leader spoke in clipped tones.

'I am Lord Tanaka and these are my men. We are in the process of apprehending two fugitives, one a thief and the other a concubine who belongs to me.'

'Well, you can't do that here. You're trespassing. Anyone found in this forest is to be apprehended by us. Now leave or we will be forced to attack you.'

'How dare you? Do you know my rank?' Tanaka's voice rose an octave, his patience obviously at an end and his choler almost at boiling point judging by his complexion. 'This woman belongs to me and I'm taking her back. There's an end to it.'

'She doesn't belong to him at all. She is this man's betrothed.' Haag's interpreter piped up, having been prodded by his employer. 'Lord Tanaka is refusing to return her to him.'

'For the last time, I am *not!*' Temperance shouted, anger making her forget her own fear temporarily. '*This* is my husband.' She indicated Kazuo, who nodded agreement.

Tanaka began to protest and everyone was suddenly speaking at once until the leader of the black-clad men lost his temper. '*Enough!*' he bellowed. 'I don't care who belongs to whom. You,' he pointed at Tanaka, 'will leave this area instantly or we'll have to kill you and your men, and you,' he nodded at Haag, 'can come with us as our prisoner. Foreigners are not allowed in this country. I'm sure the lord of these domains will be very happy to turn you over to the authorities.' He turned to look at Temperance and Kazuo. 'As for you two, you're coming with us as well.'

'We are but travellers, lost in the wilderness,' Kazuo said, sounding calm, although Temperance could feel a slight tremor run through him when he took one of her hands into his. 'Please, couldn't you let us be on our way? We promise to leave the area as fast as we can.'

'No. Your wife, if that's what she is, looks like a foreigner as well. We cannot let you pass.'

'My wife is not a foreigner. She's an albino. It's not against the law, is it?' His voice was still even, but had a slight edge to it.

'Hmm. Albino, eh? Well, we'll let our lord decide that for himself.'

'Is it really necessary to trouble him with such a trifling matter?' Kazuo asked. 'We're just passing through. We mean no harm to anyone.'

'I'm sorry, but I have orders to apprehend any strangers, harmless or not. Now are you coming willingly or do we have to coerce you?'

'Very well.' Kazuo gave Temperance's hand an imperceptible squeeze and then went to mount their horse, pulling her up behind him.

Tanaka, who had remained silent during this exchange, suddenly joined the fray once more. 'They are lying and I'm not leaving without them. The woman is mine, bought and paid for.' He turned to his men. 'Attack!'

Temperance gasped at her former master's foolhardiness. Following the skirmish with herself and Kazuo, Tanaka was down to only seven men, including himself, and to pit them against twenty seemed the height of idiocy. To her surprise, Haag joined forces with Tanaka. She could only surmise that they had some sort of pact or perhaps fighting on his side seemed more appealing than being apprehended and given over to the Japanese authorities. She watched from behind Kazuo's left shoulder as the black-clad men made short work of Tanaka's retainers. As for Haag, he was rendered helpless even faster, with a thrust from a sword followed by a thump on the head, although to Temperance's surprise, he wasn't killed.

When only Tanaka himself and one other man remained, apart from Haag, the villainous lord appeared to come to his senses and instead of continuing, suddenly turned and fled, his retainer hot on his heels. 'I'll get her back yet, see if I don't. You haven't heard the last of this!' he shouted over his shoulder before disappearing out of sight.

'Shall we follow them, sir?' someone asked the leader of the black-clad men, but he shook his head.

'No, let them go. I know who he is and our lord wouldn't want that man's blood on his hands unless it's absolutely necessary. Let's be off.'

Silence fell on the clearing, but Temperance's ears still rang with the sounds of fighting. She leaned her head on Kazuo's shoulder, wrapping her arms round his waist, and hugged him close. A shiver went through her and she closed her eyes.

They were still alive, but for how long?

* * *

'You're making a mistake. I have permission to be riding about your country. All I want is my woman. She's not an albino, that's nonsense. I can take her off your hands, return her to where she belongs ...'

Haag couldn't believe he was once again a captive, although this time no one was paying him the slightest attention. He wasn't even sure they understood him, since his interpreter had stopped translating his words, the coward.

He'd contemplated hiding behind a large tree trunk during the fight in order to stay unnoticed and to perhaps have an opportunity of snatching Temperance while everyone else was occupied so they could leave together at last. But he had thought his only chance lay in joining forces with Tanaka, who had seemed invincible up until now, so he'd followed his instinct and fought the black-clad men. Unfortunately for him, this turned out to be the wrong choice.

His head throbbed with pain and he could feel blood running down his torso and arm from a wound to the shoulder. He needed a physician, not being dragged through the countryside to who knew what godforsaken place. '*Godverdamme*,' he swore, adding a few more choice epithets to help battle the pain shooting through him at regular intervals.

'Where are we going? Who do you work for? Does your master know that foreigners are under the protection of the *Shogun*?'

He knew that wasn't true but reckoned these men might not know this.

'Shut up.' Someone smacked him on the back of the head, making it ache like the very devil. 'You can talk later.'

He understood that much and decided that perhaps it was better to save his energy. Hopefully he'd be given an opportunity to put his case and when he did, he would need all his powers of persuasion.

With a bit of luck, the lord of these domains was a more reasonable man than Tanaka. He could hardly be worse.

As they followed slowly behind the cavalcade of men, who had retrieved their own horses a short distance away, Temperance leaned forward to whisper in Kazuo's ear. 'Now what do we do? Are these men servants of the lord you were hoping to speak to?'

'Yes, I recognise the clan motif on their clothing.'

'But how will you find anything out if they are suspicious right from the very beginning? They'll soon realise I'm not an albino at all.'

'We'll think of something. This may even be to our advantage. Without being captured like this it could have taken me weeks to approach his lordship. This way we might find what we're looking for much faster.'

He sounded confident and calm, but Temperance still had her doubts. She thought it best not to voice her fears. Instead, she just asked him to tell her what to say if she was questioned.

'Stick to the truth as much as possible. You are from Nagasaki, you met me when I came south on an errand for the lord I was employed by, we fell in love and I persuaded you to marry me and move north with me. Simple. The rest of the time we have been travelling.'

It sounded easy enough, but Temperance still began to pray. She had a bad feeling about this.

Just before dusk the castle appeared suddenly in front of them as they came out of the forest and looked down upon a large valley below. An impressive sight, it made Temperance gasp with the sheer beauty of its white walls and distinctive roofs, but the menacing power of the central tower, the *tenshu*, also made her insides clench with fear.

This was it. They had arrived.

Clattering down the hill, the poor tired horse picked up his pace as if scenting the end of his journey at last. It didn't take long before they were crossing a drawbridge over the wide moat and into the first of many courtyards. Their captor spoke quietly to some of the guards on duty before beckoning for everyone to follow him further into the castle compound. The party passed through several more gates, and across increasingly smaller courtyards, until they came to a halt in front of a large staircase with wide steps leading up to huge double doors covered with hammered bronze decorations. Temperance stared at it with equal measures of awe and fear swirling around inside her.

'Stay calm,' Kazuo whispered. 'All will be well,' he added, but as if to disprove his words immediately two of their escort grabbed hold of him from either side as soon as he set foot on the ground and began to drag him off in a different direction. 'Hold on a moment! I demand to see your lord. You can't just—'

'Shut your mouth. You'll get your chance to speak to him soon enough. Now come on.'

The guards began to pull him away once more and although he tried to break free of their grip it proved impossible and he had to give up, at least for the moment. 'Let my wife come too. It's my duty to protect her.'

'That's for our lord to decide. Now cease arguing and do as you're told.'

Temperance panicked, suddenly convinced that this was the last time she would ever see him. 'No! Where are you taking him? I want to go with my husband.' She jumped off the horse and rushed over to the leader of their captors and shook his arm, but he took no notice. Instead he grabbed her wrist in a painfully hard grip.

'You are to come with me. His lordship may wish to speak

to you as well, but either way, he won't want to see both of you at the same time. He'll want the truth.'

'But we will tell the truth,' Temperance protested, trying to dig in her heels, which was difficult as the courtyard was paved with smooth stones that left her no grip. 'Please, just let me stay with my husband.'

'No. Now be quiet or it will be the worse for you. Come along.'

Temperance felt as if all the air went out of her in one sudden whoosh and she knew then that resistance was futile. They were up against a whole castle full of armed men. What could two people possibly accomplish against such a force? Throwing one final glance in Kazuo's direction, she saw that he had made the guards halt one last time as well, and they exchanged a look of longing and despair. Regret for what might have been swamped her mind and Temperance's eyes filled with tears.

Was that to be her last ever glimpse of him?

Temperance was taken to a guardroom which, although reasonably clean, was ingrained with the smell of hard working men and also somewhat damp. A single brazier stood in one corner, but it wasn't enough to heat the entire room. As Temperance was led to a bench in the opposite corner, she felt only the chill of the wood beneath her and the dank walls at her back.

'Stay there,' the man commanded, then went to give orders to the two other men whose duty it obviously was to guard her. She didn't hear his words, but it made no difference. Nothing mattered any longer.

She pulled her legs up and curled into a ball of misery, shivering from a combination of cold, fear and sheer exhaustion. The last few weeks had taken their toll on her and she had very little resistance left to whatever fate chose to throw at her, least of all any more setbacks. That morning she'd been so happy after their wonderful night together. She had felt like Kazuo's wife in every sense except for trifling legal details and perhaps eventually the blessing of the church if he agreed, but now her dreams were all shattered. She stared reality in the face.

She and Kazuo had no future. It was as simple as that.

She had no idea how long she remained in the little room. At one point she was offered something to eat and she accepted it automatically, although she didn't register what it was that she ate. Her mind was turned inwards, treasuring the memories of the night before, storing them up as a shield against the unpleasantness to come. She had no illusions as to her fate now. Somehow she or Kazuo would be made to tell the lord exactly what they were doing there and then that would be it.

'What's your name?'

Temperance vaguely registered that someone was speaking to her, but she had dozed off by this time and didn't hear the words. The person shook her shoulder. 'Your name?' he repeated, slightly more forcefully.

'Name? I'm Temi,' she muttered. 'Kanto Temi *desu*.' She and Kazuo had decided to use the surname Kanto if anyone should ask, as they dared not use his real name.

'Very well, Kanto-*san*, come with me. His lordship wishes to speak with you in person.'

'Really?' Temperance blinked, suddenly awake. She wondered if the man simply meant that his lordship wanted to be present while she was being interrogated, but as she followed the guard along corridors that grew increasingly opulent she concluded that might not be the case. Surely a *daimyo* didn't torture people in his private quarters? She frowned.

The walk seemed endless and they didn't meet anyone apart from the odd guard, stationed at strategic points where corridors met or where there were outside doors set into the walls. It was almost eerily quiet and Temperance realised that it must be very late at night. Thick candles on tall stands were positioned at intervals along their route and the flames flickered as they walked past, but nothing else stirred.

As they continued on, Temperance began to take in her surroundings. When she compared them mentally to Tanaka's residence, she noticed that this place was both older and less ostentatious, but still much more elegant in an understated way. There were none of the effusive paintings that had adorned Tanaka's house everywhere, nor as much gold leaf and hammered bronze. Instead there were delicate painted silk screens, spaced out so as to draw the eye, and wooden carvings decorated with just enough gilt or bronze to highlight the exquisite workmanship. Temperance came to the conclusion that whoever owned this castle had far more discernment and taste than the boorish Tanaka, who obviously just wanted to draw attention to his high status with vulgar displays.

At long last the guard stopped outside beautifully painted screen doors and knocked softly. Temperance was ushered in and, just before announcing her name, he pushed her to her knees right inside the door. Her time with Tanaka had taught her to do this without being asked, so she didn't protest, only shook off the man's hand surreptitiously. She bent her head down as low as she could without actually touching the *tatami* mat beneath her and hoped his lordship hadn't seen the slight tussle. Breathing in the fresh scent of the mat, she knew without seeing that it was fairly new, and it felt soft and springy under her legs as well. She tried to calm her breathing and concentrated on the summery fragrance.

'*Dozo, irrashaimase.* Come and sit over here where I can see you.' A low-pitched voice, calm and measured, rang out and Temperance raised her eyes to look at her host.

He was dressed all in black and at first Temperance found it difficult to make out his shape in the fairly dim light cast by a few lanterns scattered around the room. As her eyes adjusted, however, she could see that he wasn't as old as she had expected. Perhaps in his mid to late thirties as his body appeared to be well honed under the layers of clothing. Something about him made her think of a large sleek cat, its latent power only visible when intent on pouncing, but he exuded no immediate menace and she felt at ease for the moment.

He had an air of neatness about him, as if he liked everything to be just so, and although his clothing looked sombre she could see that the silk was sumptuous. It shone with the same lustre as his dark hair, which had been expertly bound into the customary topknot so that not a wayward strand escaped. His expression was bland, his features unremarkable, albeit even and not unattractive, but her gaze was drawn to his eyes, which were fixed on her with interest.

'Here, sit.' He indicated a large, crimson silk cushion not too far from the small dais where he sat, his back ramrod straight and his hands folded neatly in his lap. She did as she had been asked and shuffled forward to kneel on it. He nodded as if pleased that she had obeyed, then looked her over before speaking again.

'I have been told that you are an albino, Kanto-*san*. Would you be so kind as to remove your head gear? I wish to see the colour of your hair. Just out of curiosity, you understand. I mean you no harm.'

The words reassured Temperance a little, although she didn't know if he was telling the truth. He looked sincere enough, but looks could be deceptive. In any case, she took off her hat then unwound the scarf from around her head. Her hair tumbled out, a silver cascade down her back. It had grown during the last two months and most of it was in a tangle after being confined for so long. She thought it probably wasn't too clean, but didn't really care.

'My lord.' She bowed to him to show that she'd done his bidding.

His lordship regarded her for a long time, but made no further comments about her looks. Briskly, he asked her some questions, firing them off at a rapid rate.

'Where have you come from?'

'Nagasaki.'

'What is your business in this part of the country?'

'My husband and I had decided to move north.' Temperance related the story she and Kazuo had concocted, then fell silent, waiting with trepidation to see what would happen next.

His lordship sighed, then chuckled, a sound that made Temperance raise her eyes to stare at him in astonishment. What could possibly amuse him about her tale? He shook his head, as if in exasperation.

'You will have to forgive me.' He tried to compose his features, but she could still see mirth twinkling in his eyes. 'I'm afraid you lie no better than any of your countrymen and I can't help but find it amusing.'

'My ... my countrymen?' Icy slivers of fear shot through her once more. He knew.

'Kanto-*san*, I may live far from the rest of the country, but that doesn't mean I don't travel and I'm not an imbecile. I go to both Edo and Nagasaki regularly and I have met *gai-jin* before. None so pretty or quite so fair-haired, I'll admit, but nevertheless similar. You may be able to fool simple peasants, but not me I'm afraid.'

Temperance was silent while this unwelcome news sank in and she tried to think of some way of turning his knowledge to her advantage. Nothing came to mind and she grasped at straws. 'Well, as I'm married to a Japanese man, doesn't that make me a citizen of your country now?' she asked.

'As to that, I have no idea. I don't believe the *Shogun* has changed his mind yet about wanting to be rid of all foreigners, but I may be wrong.'

Temperance hung her head, feeling even more defeated than before. She was just about to ask him what he planned to do with her, when there was a knock on the door.

'Enter.'

The leader of the group of men who had brought Temperance and Kazuo to the castle came into the room and bowed low. 'Forgive the interruption, my lord, but the foreigner we captured this morning claims to have information that will aid your interrogation of this lady.' He glanced at Temperance, his eyes widening slightly as he took in her dishevelled blonde hair. 'I thought it best to tell you.' He bowed again to his master.

'Thank you, Watanabe-*san*. Perhaps you had better bring him in so that we may hear what he has to say. Does he speak our language?'

'No, my lord, but we captured his interpreter as well and the man has agreed to help in exchange for a small remuneration.'

'Good. Show them in then.'

Chapter Twenty-Eight

Temperance's spirits sank even lower as she watched Haag being ushered into the room. He was looking very pale and wan, his clothing dirty, torn and bloodstained. Temperance saw him wincing from time to time as if he was in pain, but he still sent her a look that promised retribution for all the inconvenience and frustration he obviously felt she had caused him. She suppressed a sudden urge to shudder. He groaned loudly and protested as his escort pushed his head down onto the floor and growled, 'Bow to his lordship, *gai-jin.*'

'Mind my head! It hurts.' But the guard ignored him and Haag reluctantly did as he was told, then straightened up and shook off the man's hands. He remained kneeling on the floor, but sat up straight to look at the lord of the castle, then began to speak before he had been invited to do so. The translator, who had sidled into the room behind the others, started to translate his words as fast as he could.

'My lord,' Haag began, 'I thought you ought to know that this woman is not an albino as she claims, but a foreigner like myself. We hail from the island of Dejima, where we are part of a Dutch trading contingent. She is, in fact, my betrothed, but she ran away with the man she currently claims as her husband and has led me a merry dance all over your country.'

'Is that so?'

Temperance glanced at the lord, whose voice had a distinctly frosty tone as if he didn't believe a word of Haag's story. She wondered why that should be. Haag sounded eminently truthful to her, possibly because he must believe his tale himself by now. She could see an almost insane hunger for her in his eyes whenever he glanced her way and his need to justify his obsession had obviously overridden his common sense.

'Yes, my lord. And what's more, I know where they were heading.'

'Really? And where was that?'

'To someone called Lord Ebisu. Lord Tanaka, with whom I was travelling for a while, said that the man had presented him with a letter of reference from Lord Ebisu when he came to ask for employment on Tanaka-*san*'s estate. Therefore, he must be a friend of his.'

The lord of the castle was silent for a while, as if deep in thought. Finally he said, 'Do you have any proof of your betrothal to this woman?'

'Proof? Er, yes, yes of course. Well, not with me, naturally.'

'Why not? I would have thought that if you were following on her trail, trying to have her returned to you, you should have brought some proof of your claims. And as far as I know, you're not allowed to roam this country without express permission from the *Shogun*. I should know, as I am one of his chief advisers. Do you have such permission?'

Haag blanched and began to stammer. 'I … it was, I mean, it all happened rather suddenly. I didn't know where she'd gone and thought her lost, but then I happened to run into her in Edo and naturally I had to follow her. I couldn't just let her go. And … and then I was, er, coerced by Tanaka-*san* into going with him. He said he had the authority to keep me at his side.'

The lord turned to Temperance, who had remained quiet during this exchange since she saw no point in arguing with Haag in front of their captor. 'And what have you to say to these allegations, hmm?'

'I utterly refute them, every last word, my lord. I am *not* betrothed to this man, nor would I marry him if he was the last man on earth. He has no rights over me whatsoever. He has tried to force me into marriage with him several times, but without success and this is his way of wreaking revenge on me. He has a twisted and devious mind, in my opinion.'

'I see. And were you on your way to Lord Ebisu?'

'I have no idea who he is and have never even heard the name. We had no fixed destination for our journey as far as I know.'

'She is lying!' Haag snarled, as soon as the interpreter had relayed Temperance's words. He tried to lunge towards her, his fist at the ready. The interpreter managed to restrain his master and reluctantly translated for him again then shrugged, as if distancing himself from this madman and his beliefs. 'She is simply frightened of facing me and the other foreigners because she knows she'll be punished for what she did,' Haag added, while the guard in his turn grabbed him from behind to further control him.

'Do you wish me to remove him from here, my lord?' the guard asked.

'Yes, please. I don't think he has anything more constructive to say.'

The interpreter was still in full flow and automatically translated these words for Haag's benefit. Haag began to struggle against the guard's hold on him, shouting imprecations in English. 'She's my woman, I tell you! Why won't anyone believe me? Do you not have laws about these things in this godforsaken country? Heathens! Barbarians! Sons of she-dogs ...'

The flow of words continued as he was dragged from the room and he could be heard all the way down the corridor outside. The guard returned briefly to ask what he was to do with the prisoner, while the interpreter bowed himself out, having been dismissed by a gesture from the lord.

'Just leave him in the dungeon for the moment, please,' the

lord said. 'It sounds to me as though he needs to cool down a little.'

Silence descended on the room and Temperance took a deep breath. She was having a hard time comprehending that the man in front of her had taken her side against Haag, even though the story he'd been told had sounded so plausible. On top of that, she still didn't know what was going to happen to her and Kazuo and her fears returned in full force. Unable to wait any longer, she blurted out, 'So what do you plan to do with me then, my lord? With us?' The question came out in a hoarse whisper as she had to keep swallowing hard to keep the tears at bay.

The lord didn't reply immediately, so she plunged on even though she knew she was probably asking in vain.

'Could ... would it be possible for you to let my husband go on his way, uhm, before you hand me over to the authorities? It's not his fault. I mean, my husband isn't responsible for me being foreign ...' She tailed off, realising how lame a defence she was presenting.

When she looked up again, however, the lord was smiling broadly and looking at her with something like admiration in his eyes. 'I can't fault you for trying and your loyalty to your husband is commendable,' he said, 'but the answer is no.'

Temperance opened her mouth to ask why, but he startled her into stunned silence by adding in perfect, albeit slightly accented English, 'He is not going anywhere until I find whole truth, but now you, Temperance-*chan*, are going to bed. It is very late.'

He had spoken English and he'd called her by her real name. Shock reverberated through Temperance and she stared at him in disbelief.

'How did you ...?' she began, then the truth dawned on her and she almost fainted with relief. 'You are Ichiro-*san*,

Midori's brother,' she said, hardly able to believe her luck. 'I beg your pardon, I mean Lord Kumashiro, of course. This is Castle Shiroi, my cousin's former home?'

'Indeed, and I apologise for testing you in this manner, but it was necessary. Had to make sure you were not held by your so-called husband Kanto against your will. It would seem not, so I cannot accuse him of abduction. But ...' Here he gave her a faint smile. 'I doubt my sister will be too pleased to hear you married a Japanese man without asking permission.'

'Midori, is she all right? I mean, have you heard from her?' Temperance still couldn't believe this was happening. She was here, in the very castle her cousin had told her about so often, the one place in Japan where she was truly safe. It was incredible.

'Many times recently,' Lord Kumashiro replied in a somewhat caustic tone. 'She has been in panic because her cousin disappeared and did not leave a message for her.'

Temperance heard the unspoken disapproval in his voice and hastened to defend herself. 'But I *was* abducted. How could I have left a note? I have worried so much about what Midori and Nico would think, but I've had no way of letting them know I was safe.'

He frowned. 'You just said you were not abducted. This was not true?'

'No, you don't understand. I was, but not by Kaz— ... er, my husband. It was a band of outlaws led by someone called Ryo who grabbed me. Although they're now my friends, but that's another story. Anyway, they sold me to a despicable man who owned a tea house, and after that—'

'Hold on a moment.' Lord Kumashiro held up his hand. 'Slow down, let me understand clearly. You were taken. Where?'

'In a small bay where I went swimming near Nagasaki.'

'Yes, Midori said that what probably happened. And outlaws who abducted you had a leader, one Ryo, who is now your friend?'

'That's right. He sold me to Imada-*san* first, a horrible man who trained me to be a *shinzo* so that he could sell me to a rich man as a concubine.'

Lord Kumashiro's brows had risen as he listened to this. 'And this came to pass?'

'Unfortunately, yes. He found a man who was willing to pay for me, but he was even worse and I just couldn't ... I didn't want to ... well, I've never been so happy in all my life as when he was called away to Edo before ... before anything happened to me.'

'And do you know this man's name?'

'Of course. It's Tanaka. He is a very powerful man, I understand, but evil if you ask me. I had to escape.'

'*Ah, soh.* Of course.' Lord Kumashiro's mouth was twitching again, as if he found her tale more fantastic than anything he had ever heard before. 'And how you accomplished this?'

'Well, that's where K— ... uhm, my husband comes into it. You see I had met him before, while swimming in that bay on another occasion. Unbeknown to me, he was working for Tanaka-*san* too and when he saw me, he knew at once he had to rescue me, so that's what he did. We ran away early one morning while Tanaka was in Edo.'

Lord Kumashiro shook his head. 'This is very complicated story and you must be tired. If you like, we continue tomorrow? Please tell me. I don't mind waiting. At least I know you are safe and can send messenger to my sister.'

'Well, if you don't mind, I would really prefer not to go on without speaking to my husband first. You see the rest of it concerns him more than me. I merely tagged along, as it were, until he could find the time to take me back to Nagasaki.'

'So you planned to go back?'

Temperance felt herself blush. 'Uhm, yes, until we discovered that we wanted to marry. I mean, of course we would have gone back anyway, but until that point I had thought to return by myself once he found a way of getting me there.'

'I see. Well, you have some rest now and we will speak more in the morning. Guards will bring your husband to you at dawn and you can speak with him first if you wish. No doubt he's asleep already, so we won't disturb him now.'

'Thank you, you are very kind. I'm so happy to have met you at last.'

'And I you, Temperance.'

He managed to pronounce her name quite well, but she could tell it wasn't easy for him, so she said, 'Please, just call me Temi. Everyone else does.'

'Very well. Goodnight, Temi-*chan*.'

As she arrived some moments later at a suite of rooms almost as grand as Lord Kumashiro's own, Temperance pinched herself hard to make sure she wasn't dreaming. It was such a far cry from the miserable prison cell she had been imagining would still be her fate this night that she couldn't believe it. But if it was a dream, she never wanted it to end.

In a cold, dark and damp little cell, Haag sat on a straw mattress and watched as drops of moisture chased each other down the walls. All the fight had gone out of him. He realised that he had burned all his bridges by shouting imprecations at the lord of this domain.

He had lost.

His last sight of Temperance had been of a woman in full control of herself, not cowed in the slightest. She had sounded believable and the lord had been taken in by her lies.

She had won.

He couldn't believe it. Didn't want to. But all hope had

died inside him. No one except her knew that he was even here. There was no chance of escape, no chance of rescue. And he was sure she'd never tell a soul of his whereabouts. Why would she?

It was so unfair. So unnatural. She should have known her place and done as she was told. Women weren't meant to decide anything. They were weak. Meek. Biddable.

Most of them.

Why did he have the misfortune of coming across the only one who wasn't? *Damn it all to hell!*

But it looked like he was the one going to hell. Or rather, he was already very nearly there.

He felt faint now. His head ached, feeling as though someone was pounding on his brain with a mallet, whereas his shoulder had gone blessedly numb. He'd tried to staunch the flow of blood earlier with torn-off bits of his shirt but could feel it oozing slowly still. His life force was ebbing away, drop by red drop in little rivulets down his torso, and no one cared. They didn't even know because he hadn't mentioned his wounds. He'd been too intent on gaining his freedom and getting his hands on that infernal woman.

'Help!' he called, remembering how to say it in Japanese. '*Tasukete kudasai!* Please, someone, I need a surgeon ...' But the guards didn't come and he knew it was his own fault. He'd shouted too much earlier, when they'd first put him in the cell and now they had stopped paying attention to him. It was doubtful if anyone was even within earshot as they'd probably left him to cool his temper.

Darkness enveloped him and he felt as if he was falling, even though he was still lying down. Then everything went quiet and he suddenly saw a white light coming towards him, beckoning, inviting.

He welcomed it.

* * *

Kazuo was woken early.

'You're to come with me,' the guard said. He sounded gruff and Kazuo braced himself for a cuff on the head or some such, but it didn't come. The guard just waited patiently until he was on his feet, then led the way into the castle.

To Kazuo's amazement he was taken into the luxurious domain that must be the *daimyo*'s own part, with long corridors of polished floorboards and huge suites of rooms along one side. The guard stopped outside one and nodded towards the door. 'In there,' he said.

Kazuo frowned and steeled himself. It would seem the lord of the castle himself – or at least someone very high-ranking within his staff – wanted to speak to him. He only hoped he could make whoever it was believe his story.

The guard opened the sliding door and Kazuo entered on his hands and knees, but when the door hissed shut behind him, there was no sound from within the room. He chanced a quick upward glance and drew in a hasty breath. Before him, on a thick *futon*, lay Temi, seemingly asleep. Kazuo rushed over to her and put a hand on her shoulder, shaking gently.

'Temi? Temi, my love, wake up.'

She sat up abruptly, looking completely disorientated as she took in the sight of him and also the opulence of the large room she'd been sleeping in. Kazuo knew exactly how she felt – totally bemused – because he felt the same.

'Kazuo!' She smiled, but then frowned and reached out a hand to touch his cheek. He knew it was grubby and he probably had several fresh bruises. 'Oh, what happened? Did they mistreat you again?'

He shook his head. 'Not really. It was mostly my own fault because I tried to escape. I should have known there wouldn't be a way out of a castle like this, not without inside help. But please, tell me what's going on? I don't understand.

Why are you here, in such a room? Why am I here? What happened last night? Did he ... did he touch you?'

'Who, Ichiro? No, of course not.' Temperance laughed and Kazuo stared at her, confused. She put her arms around him and pulled him closer. 'He is my kinsman,' she explained. 'Well, sort of anyway. My cousin Midori's half-brother. Do you see?'

He pulled away to stare at her, having a hard time taking this in. 'You are related to Lord Kumashiro?'

'Yes, strange isn't it? If you had only told me the name of the third man, I would have known immediately that you were on a doomed quest. And I could have obtained entry for you to this castle without any need for subterfuge.'

'Why doomed? He is still the third man, whether he is related to your cousin or not.' Kazuo scowled, not at all convinced.

'Yes, but don't you see, I know him through everything Midori has told me about him and there is no way he would act dishonourably. Never! He is firm, but just, and he wouldn't stoop to anything as low as ousting another man from power to promote himself. Especially not in such an underhand manner. It's just not possible.'

'How can you be so sure? You don't know him.'

'Midori lived with him for nineteen years and they were very close. She knows him inside out and he simply wouldn't do such a thing. Please, talk to him and explain your quest, then perhaps he will help you? He can at least tell you why he signed that piece of paper.'

Kazuo stood up and paced restlessly to and fro. He just couldn't sit still as a jumble of thoughts chased each other round his brain. 'This is all very strange,' he muttered. 'Too strange. I can't take it in.' He stopped before her. 'Why should I trust him? He might have changed since your cousin left. She's been gone how many years?'

'Seven, eight, I don't know, but—'

'You see? A man can change and there's no denying how powerful he is. Look around you.' He swept a hand to indicate the costly surroundings.

'He was born with all this. His father was very powerful too. That doesn't make him a bad man. Please, will you not trust me?'

Kazuo ran his fingers through his hair, almost dislodging the already unruly topknot. He wanted to believe her, but it seemed too easy somehow. A trap? He sighed. 'I don't know. I suppose I have nothing left to lose. There's no way I'll find any evidence of his guilt now, unless he invites us to stay on as guests for a while and I can snoop around.'

'No, Kazuo, I can't let you do that. If you don't want to tell him, you had better just leave. Go now, while you are free. I assume you are allowed to roam the castle or is there a guard waiting outside?'

'I don't think so. They merely brought me here and left.'

'There you are then. If you want to continue your quest elsewhere, you can, but personally I think you'll find the answers you need right here.'

Kazuo felt torn and began to pace again. 'And if I leave, what about us?' He knew deep down that Temi meant more to him than the quest now, but he still hoped he could finish that first. He would hate to disappoint his father, if he was still alive, and lose face before his clan. He'd been brought up to put honour before all else, especially personal feelings, emotions. How could he go against that?

'You know where to find me. Ichiro has sent a message to Midori and somehow I will be taken back to Dejima. You can come there when you are finished.' She held out a hand to him. 'You know I'll wait as long as it takes, if only you promise to come for me.'

He stopped and took her hand, then pulled her close and

kissed her hard. 'Oh, Temi, I was out of my mind with worry last night. I thought I'd never see you again. I imagined all sorts of things ...' He buried his head in her shoulder. He'd had nightmares about what might have been happening to her.

'Me too. I was so scared, but as soon as I realised who the lord was, I knew everything would be all right. Why not come with me to speak to him at least, on other matters? You'll see that he is very amiable and perhaps you'll find you might be able to trust him after all.'

'Perhaps.' He kissed her again, then just held her close for a long time before pulling away. 'Well then, do you think we ought to ask if we could make ourselves a bit more presentable first? I can't think that Lord Kumashiro wishes to speak with two dirty fugitives.'

Temperance smiled at him and nodded. 'I'll call the maid and ask.'

Chapter Twenty-Nine

The bathhouse at Castle Shiroi was every bit as wonderful as Midori had described it to be. After a lengthy session in the hot water, as well as a welcome change of clothes, the two of them were ushered into Lord Kumashiro's presence. Temperance still thought of him as Ichiro, since that was how Midori had always referred to her brother, but she knew that she ought to use his more formal title. She also followed Kazuo's lead in bowing low and staying down until he told them to rise.

'Please, come and join me for a meal. You must both be famished.' Lord Kumashiro indicated a low table groaning with all manner of delicacies and surrounded by three plump cushions upon which they took their places. He squeezed Temperance's hand as he helped her to be seated and she thought he gave her a reassuring nod, but couldn't be sure.

Kazuo was wary at first and the conversation very polite and stilted, but as the meal progressed he relaxed slightly, although he let Temperance do most of the talking. Lord Kumashiro tactfully refrained from asking Kazuo any questions and instead concentrated on Temperance, making her give him her impressions of Japan.

'Well, I have to say I never thought I would travel through your country quite this extensively,' she said, 'but what I have seen so far is wonderful for the most part. There are one or two places I could have done without, like the tea house of The Weeping Willow for instance, but on the whole, I love it here.'

'Your Japanese is very good,' Lord Kumashiro commented. 'You must have a quick mind.'

'There was nothing else to do on Dejima, so I spent a lot of time practising with Midori. I was most disappointed when I discovered that I couldn't enter your country, but had to stay cooped up on that tiny piece of land.'

'And that is why you decided to go, er ... exploring?' Lord Kumashiro asked with a smile.

'Yes, although I'm sorry I caused Midori so much worry. I never meant to and I suppose it was naïve of me to think I could leave Dejima without anyone being the wiser. Having already met Kazuo the first time, I don't know why it didn't occur to me that I might meet other people too, like the outlaws.'

'As you say, you were perhaps a bit naïve, but you were not to know.' Lord Kumashiro turned to Kazuo. 'So what did you think the first time you came across Temi-*chan*?'

Kazuo looked vaguely embarrassed and gave a sheepish smile. 'I thought she was a water sprite.' As Lord Kumashiro chuckled, Kazuo defended himself. 'Well, who wouldn't? Look at that hair and imagine her swimming in the sea like a dolphin. She's a great swimmer, you know.'

'Indeed, I can see exactly why you would think her a *kami*. I think it's a miracle you've managed to pass her off as Japanese for so long.'

'Well, we had a little assistance. There was a lady in Edo who hid us while we were there and also Ryo and his men, who were extremely helpful.'

'You really went to Edo? You didn't come straight here?' Lord Kumashiro looked mildly horrified. 'By all the gods, that was risky, wasn't it?'

Kazuo's expression turned grim. 'Yes, entirely too much so and I take full responsibility for that stupidity. Really, I should have taken Temi home before continuing with my ... er, before carrying out a certain task. I should never have put her in such danger.'

'Tanaka found us, or Kazuo at any rate,' Temperance put in quietly. 'Completely by mistake too, which was such bad luck, but we managed to escape again even though Kazuo was badly hurt. A kind monk helped me to heal him and so here we are.'

Lord Kumashiro was silent for a while, then he looked Kazuo in the eyes and said, 'I cannot force you to trust me, young man, but if I tell you that I have guessed your true identity and I am still willing to let you leave this place any time you wish, would that help, Kanno-*san*?'

Kazuo stared back. 'How did you guess?'

'You look a lot like your father did as a young man. I met him many times, as you probably know. We were friends.'

Kazuo sighed, then after a moment he nodded, as if he had come to a decision. 'Very well, I will tell you why I'm here, but only if you swear that no harm will come to Temi whatever happens.'

'Of course, that goes without saying. My sister is probably even now on her way, if I know her. She would flay me alive were I to harm a hair on Temi's head.'

Kazuo nodded again, then haltingly at first, and later with more force, he told his story. Lord Kumashiro didn't interrupt a single time and when Kazuo had finished he waited a moment before commenting, 'It is as I thought.'

'You knew why I had come?'

'No, but I guessed why you were on the mainland when you're not supposed to be. Any son worthy of the name would do the same and I can't blame you for that.' It was his turn to sigh. 'You say my name was on the document that condemned your father?' Kazuo nodded. 'Yet I wasn't present when he was sent away.'

'That's what my father told me, yes.'

'And do you know why I wasn't there in person to see him on his way?'

'No.'

'Because I was here, up in the north. I didn't go to Edo

311

until several months after your father was exiled and I remember making enquiries into what had happened because I thought it strange. I was never told that I had signed that document though.'

'Told? You mean you didn't sign it personally?'

'Of course not. How could I, if I wasn't there? Someone must have faked my signature, not too difficult a feat, and with me so far away they probably thought I would never come to hear of it. In fact, it never occurred to me to ask who had ordered the investigation. I was only told what had been found and the evidence seemed irrefutable.'

'Ah, yes, the *Shogun*'s precious object,' Kazuo said. 'I believe it disappeared again before the authorities had a chance to return it to the *Shogun*. Someone must still have it, and although I can now guess who, I could never prove it.'

'What exactly was it that was stolen?' Temperance asked, overcome by curiosity.

'A jade ornament in the shape of a lioness and her cub, with a large pearl in between them. Both were mounted on a golden plinth,' Lord Kumashiro said. 'I saw the item myself on many occasions. It was one of the *Shogun*'s favourite things and it was old and very valuable.'

Temperance gasped. 'Did you say lioness? I don't believe it ...'

'What's the matter?' Two pairs of eyes regarded her, one with curiosity, the other with concern.

'I think I've seen it,' Temperance whispered. 'It was in Tanaka's bedroom when he ... There were some shelves built into a recess and he had many beautiful things displayed upon it, but the little lioness caught my eye because I thought ... Well, it sounds silly now, but I felt as if she was laughing at me, mocking me in my predicament.'

'You are sure?' Lord Kumashiro frowned at her, his gaze penetrating.

'Absolutely. It's the kind of object that you can't help admiring and so it stays in your mind, although I suppose it's possible that he merely has a similar one.'

Kazuo shook his head. 'There was only one ever made. It is centuries old and no one would dare copy it.'

'Kanno-*san* is right,' Lord Kumashiro said. 'I can't believe Tanaka would display a stolen object openly though, that seems like sheer lunacy.'

'He wasn't displaying it really. The cupboard was only half open, as if someone had forgotten to close it. Besides, I don't suppose anyone goes into his bedroom unless they have permission.' Temperance shuddered at the memory of what had so nearly happened there. 'It was like the inner sanctum of a temple where only the chief priest is allowed.'

'You could be right.' Lord Kumashiro looked thoughtful. 'The question is, what do we do about it and how can we prove that Tanaka engineered your father's downfall, Kanno-*san*?'

'There is only one way,' Kazuo said. 'To send a strong force of men to Tanaka's house and search it, with or without his leave. There would have to be officials present, of course, to see that all is done lawfully, but Tanaka mustn't be given a chance to escape or to hide anything. It has to be a complete surprise.'

'I have enough men and, I believe, enough power in official circles to order such a search. It might be wise to send some of my *ninja* ahead though, to make sure the item is still in place and to keep guard. Otherwise we will look like complete fools if nothing is found. Tanaka is a wily old fox. He may have moved it by now.'

'Good idea. So you will help me then?' Kazuo asked, looking more hopeful than Temperance had seen him do for weeks.

Lord Kumashiro smiled. 'Try and stop me. Tanaka has

been a thorn in my side for years. Indeed, I believe it was his interference that caused me to almost lose my sister. I have long suspected that he conveniently reminded the authorities of her existence and the fact that she was half *gai-jin*, although I could never prove it. She nearly died before I managed to smuggle her off to England. The man needs to be stopped.'

'There were others in Edo who muttered the same, but no one dared do anything openly,' Kazuo said.

'I know, I've heard rumours too. Well, now we have a way of proving his guilt. Let us make plans.'

Temperance listened to the two men plotting their enemy's downfall as if they had been the best of friends for years, and she smiled. The moment she'd realised who Lord Kumashiro was she had known they would get along famously, but it had taken them a while to acknowledge it, at least on Kazuo's part. It made her very happy though, as she now felt she had an ally in Lord Kumashiro, should Midori prove difficult when it came to the question of Temperance's marriage. Come what may, she was determined to go through with it – if Kazuo still wanted her of course – and nothing would stop her. Still, it was always good to have someone on your side and Lord Kumashiro could, she felt, be a formidable force when he wanted to be.

All in all, it had been a very pleasant morning.

Kazuo couldn't believe his luck. It seemed the gods were smiling upon him once again and they'd sent him the best possible co-conspirator. Although he'd been doubtful at first, he could see why Temi trusted Lord Kumashiro so completely – he seemed to be a man of honour and integrity in every way.

Their plotting finished for now, Kazuo and Temi rose to return to their own quarters for a rest, but before they could leave there was a knock on the door.

'Enter.'

One of Lord Kumashiro's servants came in and bowed in the customary fashion. 'I'm sorry, my lord. I bring news of the foreigner.'

Kumashiro stood up. 'What of him? Is he making more trouble? I would have hoped his temper had cooled somewhat by now.'

The servant raised his head, his expression serious. 'I'm afraid he won't be making any more trouble at all. He's dead, my lord.'

'What? How?' Kumashiro frowned. 'I thought I ordered him not to be harmed.'

The servant cringed visibly and seemed to be swallowing hard. 'I ... that is, no, he wasn't. It would appear he had sustained an injury and as far as we can see he simply bled to death.'

'Why did no one tend his wounds?' An angry Kumashiro was not someone Kazuo would want to deal with and he felt for the hapless servant as his lordship scowled at the man, although he was sure Kumashiro would never take out his fury unjustly, the way Tanaka had done.

'We didn't know he had any, I swear! He never said. When we checked on him during the night, we just thought he was sleeping ...'

'I see.' Kumashiro sighed. 'Well, then, I can't blame anyone for his death. He brought it upon himself.'

Kazuo glanced at Temi, who had paled at the news. 'Are you all right?' he whispered to her. Perhaps she'd been more attached to the *gai-jin* than she'd let on? The thought made jealousy surge through him, but she took his hand and squeezed it which reassured him.

'I'm fine. It is sad that he should die like that when perhaps it wasn't necessary, but it was his own fault. He shouldn't have come here at all chasing after me like that. What a waste.'

Kazuo could only agree, but looking at his lovely wife he could understand the other man's obsession – she was a prize worth following to the ends of the earth.

A week went by and then all was ready and the time had come for farewells. 'Are you sure you don't mind staying here?' Kazuo asked Temperance, looking worried but excited at the same time.

'No, of course not. I've had more than my fair share of adventures recently. This is one I'm happy to leave to you and Lord Kumashiro, but please be careful and come back in one piece! I wish you the best of luck.'

He pulled her close and gave her one last kiss, urgent and full of desire despite a whole week filled with love-making. Lord Kumashiro had taken them at their word and given them a suite of rooms as if they really were married.

'I will come back for you, believe me,' Kazuo whispered.

'I believe you. Just watch out for Tanaka, he'll be dangerous when cornered.'

'I know. Don't worry, I won't let him hurt me again.'

Temperance watched the huge retinue ride off up the hill and into the forest and sighed deeply. She had tried to show Kazuo a brave face, but inside the worry was already gnawing at her. She knew she had to suppress it, however, or go mad. With determination she turned her steps back to the women's quarters. She'd made friends with Lord Kumashiro's wife and daughters and knew they would keep her occupied as best they could.

Anything to take her mind off what was happening to the men.

Chapter Thirty

Kazuo had hoped never to set foot on Tanaka's estate again, but as he crept stealthily through the gardens from the lake side an unexpected surge of exhilaration fired his blood at the thought of what lay ahead. This was what his mission had been all about – the moment of retribution and justice he'd been wishing for throughout the years of exile. He wouldn't have missed it for the world.

Kumashiro's *ninja* had somehow managed to verify that the little ornament was still in Tanaka's possession. They'd also confirmed that he was at this moment sound asleep in his bed, having returned a few days previously. He had, by all accounts, been in a foul mood since he came back and his servants went in fear of their lives since he had already administered several beatings and ordered no fewer than three executions. Kazuo clenched his fists – he was going to enjoy giving the traitorous cur a dose of his own medicine.

He looked to his left where Kumashiro moved silently through the early morning gloom, his black-clad body barely visible. Kazuo was very glad that he had listened to Temi and confided in her kinsman. Kumashiro had been as good as his word and moved swiftly to dispatch both his *ninja* and a secret messenger to the *Shogun*. The ruler had sent back his permission for the dawn raid.

'I will be waiting anxiously for news of the outcome,' the ruler had personally added at the end of the missive. Kazuo sincerely hoped the *Shogun* wouldn't be disappointed.

Another messenger had also been despatched to inform Kazuo's father of their plans, but as yet there had been no reply. Kazuo worried that the old man might have succumbed to his illness already. It would be the worst of luck if he didn't live to see his honour restored, now that this seemed a distinct possibility. The Oki islands were further away, however, so he tried not to worry unduly. No doubt Kanno senior would make his way to the mainland as soon as possible if he could. The *Shogun* had promised that he would be given free passage throughout the country.

Approaching the main residence from behind, Kumashiro's men fanned out to cover all exits, while their master and Kazuo made their way to a back door. The guard waiting there had already been bribed to turn a blind eye and was only too happy to help, overjoyed at the prospect of being rid of Tanaka. He slid open the door with the slightest of swishing sounds and motioned for them to follow him inside.

The three of them tiptoed along a corridor and Kazuo held his breath, waiting to hear the telltale squeaking of a nightingale floor, built specifically to warn the lord of the house of anyone's arrival. Most influential men would have such flooring installed as there were always those who sought their downfall. To his surprise, the floor made not a sound though and he looked at the guard with raised eyebrows and pointed downwards.

'Tanaka thought himself sufficiently powerful not to need a singing floor,' the man mouthed and grinned at them. 'More fool him.'

Kazuo shook his head. This seemed foolish indeed, but it didn't accord with what he knew of the man. Tanaka may believe that he was powerful enough for such extra precautions not to be necessary, but he was nothing if not wily and Kazuo couldn't help but wonder if there was some other reason why Tanaka felt safe in his lair. This worried him and he decided to be extra vigilant.

At the end of the corridor they came to an extravagant door, liberally covered in gold leaf and over-ostentatious decorations, and the guard stopped and put a finger to his mouth. He pointed inside and held up four fingers to indicate that there were four other guards immediately inside. Kazuo and Kumashiro both drew their swords as quietly as possible in readiness for action.

The guard counted silently to three, then slid open the door with one swift movement as they all launched themselves into the room simultaneously, taking the men inside by surprise. The resultant melee was short-lived and the guards despatched into the hereafter without too much effort. As expected, however, they had all made a lot of noise in order to raise the alarm, and other men came running from adjacent rooms and in from a small private courtyard garden. They filled the room with a seemingly endless stream of warriors prepared to die for their lord. Kazuo, Kumashiro and the first guard fought them doggedly and succeeded in killing most of them without too much damage to themselves by standing back to back in a loose triangle and helping each other whenever possible.

Kazuo was worried that it was all taking too long as Tanaka would have to be deaf not to hear the commotion. There was no doubt he would try and escape and therefore Kazuo had to find him as soon as possible and prevent this. He had agreed beforehand with Kumashiro that he would be the one to face the traitor. 'Where is Tanaka's bedroom?' Kazuo hissed at their assistant.

'Over there.' The man nodded towards the far corner.

Kazuo glanced at Kumashiro to see whether he had matters in hand and received a nod in confirmation. 'Go,' he urged Kazuo. 'There's not a moment to lose.'

Kazuo hurried over towards the far corner, but had to battle his way past another two men before he reached his goal. At last he was free to slide open the door and he drew a silent sigh of relief when he came face to face with Tanaka. The man was standing by an open cupboard on the other side of the room shoving something into his capacious sleeve. The bird hadn't yet fled the coop.

'Stop right there,' Kazuo ordered. 'I arrest you in the name of the *Shogun*.'

Tanaka laughed. 'You'll have to catch me first,' he hissed and drew his sword.

Kazuo leapt across the room, his own sword raised, but just as he was about to strike the first blow, Tanaka moved to one side and opened a hidden door in what had seemed to be nothing but a part of the wall. He stepped inside a cupboard and slid the door shut before Kazuo had time to reach him. There was a loud click to indicate that the door had been locked from the other side. Kazuo growled with frustration and threw himself at the wall, shoulder first.

'I knew it!' he cried. It had been just as he feared. Tanaka had another exit strategy which explained why he hadn't needed the nightingale floor. 'Damnation!'

The wall hardly budged, but Kazuo wasn't about to give up so easily. He began to kick at the place where he assumed the lock of the door to be on the other side, and shouted for Kumashiro to come and help. Together, they rained down a frenzy of savage blows on the hapless door and it wasn't long before the wood splintered and Kazuo was able to make his way through. To his dismay the hidden door led not to another room, as he'd thought, but to a trapdoor in the floor and from there through a tunnel that presumably led outside.

'Damn it all!' he swore. 'This tunnel could end anywhere. How do we know where to go from here?'

'Which direction is it pointing?' Kumashiro asked, peering down into the hole.

'West, but no doubt it changes course several times. He wouldn't have been fool enough to build a tunnel in a straight line.'

'Well, my men are waiting outside and should catch him wherever he comes out, but just in case, I'll follow him through this tunnel while you go outside and see if you can find him. Hurry, before it's too late. We can't let him escape.'

Kazuo clenched his jaw and set off at a run without another word. He knew that it might already be too late and their quarry had managed to evade capture. It was precisely the outcome he had feared the most and he ground his teeth in frustration while swearing again under his breath.

He ran round the outside of the entire house, alerting Kumashiro's men to what was occurring along the way, but there was no sign of Tanaka. Kazuo made himself stop and think. What would he do if he wished to escape? Where would be the most logical place to have the tunnel come into the open if it wasn't immediately adjacent to the house?

'Of course,' he muttered. 'The lake!'

Beginning to run once more, he took off in the direction of Lake Biwa as fast as he could, his eyes searching the gardens ahead of him as he went. The gloom of the pre-dawn was starting to disperse and there was slightly more light now, making it easier to see into the distance. Kazuo thought he detected movement over by the far wall and headed that way.

He reached the gate he and Temi had slipped through all those weeks ago, but he didn't stop. The guard was long gone, having been taken care of by Kumashiro's men earlier. Kazuo noticed that the door was slightly ajar and he pushed through as fast as he could. Down by the lake, he could just make out a fleeing shadow, and he forced his legs into even greater efforts, sprinting towards the water.

The mist was once again swirling around the marshy ground, but out of the bushes to his right, Kazuo saw Tanaka emerge with a boat in tow, pushing it into the lake with a mighty heave.

'Stop!' he cried out as he came closer, and to his surprise

Tanaka did, turning to face him with tendrils of mist curling round his legs.

'You don't give up easily,' he stated matter-of-factly. 'But you have come in vain. You'll not catch me.' He drew his sword from its scabbard and awaited Kazuo, looking sure of himself, but with a slightly mad glint to his eyes that was unnerving. Kazuo drew in a deep breath to steady his heart, which was beating rapidly from the exertion of his long run, and wiped his hand on his trousers before grabbing his own sword.

'I *will* catch you,' he said quietly with conviction. 'You deserve to be punished for what you did to my father, and others too no doubt.'

'Your father?'

'Kanno-*san*.'

'Ah, now I understand. I thought you looked vaguely familiar. I should have listened to my instincts as always, but you fooled me with your letter from Lord Ebisu. Very well, come and punish me then, if you can.'

The time for talking had come to an end and Kazuo launched himself at his opponent. Although he was tired from running, he was by now fully recovered from his wound and back in shape. He had trained with Kumashiro's men every day in order to improve his strength and he knew that being at least twenty year's Tanaka's junior was a huge advantage.

Tanaka was an expert swordsman, however, and Kazuo found it far from easy to get past his defences. It was clear that the man had been trained by a master of the art, and although older and not as agile, his technique more than made up for this. It would seem they were evenly matched.

Back and forth across the shore of the lake they went, first Kazuo gaining the upper hand, then Tanaka clawing it back by foul means or fair. The old fox had several tricks up his sleeve and wasn't above using tactics such as hurling rocks and sand at his opponent to throw him off his stride. After one such incident, when Kazuo was furiously rubbing grit out of his eyes, Tanaka struck him a blow on the side of the head with his fist, which sent him reeling.

'Hah! Thought you could best me, cur?' Tanaka taunted. 'It would take a better man than you, I tell you.'

A flame of fury shot through Kazuo, electrifying his limbs and propelling him to his feet in one lithe movement. 'No, it wouldn't,' he grunted. 'I *am* the man who is going to beat you.' The certainty of this flowed through him, giving his tired sword arm added strength, and he rained down a flurry of thrusts which had Tanaka retreating towards the bushes.

'This is all in vain, you know,' Tanaka panted as he parried the blows, steel meeting steel with jarring clangs of metal, tiny sparks shooting off to either side. 'Even if you best me, you'll never prove that I was the man to oust your father.'

'Why is that then?' Kazuo didn't waver once in his attack, but continued on relentlessly, not giving Tanaka another opportunity to bend and pick up more sand or devise any other diversionary tactics.

'Because the proof is going to disappear.' Tanaka smiled and stopped suddenly, pulling the little jade ornament out of his sleeve. 'Like this,' he continued and threw the object into the lake before Kazuo had time to react.

'No!' Shock reverberated through Kazuo as he realised that Tanaka was right and he stopped dead. Without the proof of the man's treason the *Shogun* might not believe in his guilt, much as he may want to. The two men stood facing each other, Tanaka's face split by a huge grin now while Kazuo's brain raced to try and find a solution. A calm voice cut through the morning air, making them both turn.

'I think you're forgetting something.' Kumashiro was standing not ten yards away, his arms crossed and a calm expression on his face.

'You!' Tanaka scowled at the newcomer. 'I should've known you'd be behind all this. Kanno and his idiot offspring would never have the guts to try and take back their position and you were ever jealous of my influence with the *Shogun*.'

'That's where you're wrong,' Kumashiro said mildly. 'Young Kanno thought of this all by himself and I have only lately been apprised of the situation and asked to lend him aid. Furthermore, I have never coveted your so-called influence, as it is enough for me to count our ruler as my friend. Not everyone in this world wishes for as much power as you do.'

'Fine words,' Tanaka sneered, 'but you don't fool me.'

'Be that as it may, shall we return to the matter in hand?' Kumashiro approached slowly. 'What you forgot was that I heard your words to young Kanno here, so I can testify to the fact that you were the man behind his father's downfall. Furthermore, I saw the *Shogun*'s ornament in your hand just now and watched you throw it into the lake. The mere fact that you had it in your possession is proof enough. Several of my men have infiltrated your household in the past few days and they can also testify that the lioness and her cub were in your room.'

Tanaka looked from one man to the other, then unexpectedly lunged at Kazuo. 'Well, you'll not take me alive,' Tanaka averred.

Kazuo jumped out of the way at the last moment, but felt the sting of Tanaka's blade cutting his upper arm. He drew in a hissing breath, but let the hatred he felt for the man in front of him supersede the pain that jolted through him. Whether he had proof or not, he *would* rid the world of this scum.

Afterwards, he never quite knew how he accomplished it, because the red mist in front of his eyes obscured everything but the need to kill the evil man before him. Shouting out the war cry of his clan, he bombarded Tanaka with sword thrusts, kicks and blows from his left fist in such rapid succession, that the older man had to retreat towards the lake. Kazuo vaguely noted a look of alarm in the other man's eyes as he came to realise that perhaps he had misjudged his opponent. But before Tanaka had time to retaliate, he stumbled on a small rock and this gave Kazuo the opportunity to finish him off. Without hesitation, he slashed his sword across Tanaka's exposed throat as the man lost his concentration for a moment, and in the next instant, the lifeless body fell into the water with a huge splash.

Kazuo followed, ready to continue if the man wasn't truly dead, but as he stood panting over Tanaka, his sword still raised in readiness, the mist cleared from his sight. He could see the man's eyes staring unseeing into the sky while a huge red stain spread through the water all around him.

'Well done,' he heard Kumashiro say from behind him. 'Your father will be proud of you.'

Kazuo turned and nodded, too tired to even feel triumphant yet that he had succeeded. 'Thank you for not interfering,' he said. 'I know that together we could have beaten him sooner, but I wanted to do it myself.'

'I know,' Kumashiro said with a smile. 'And you had no need of me, I could see that.'

Kazuo wasn't so sure as it had been touch and go for a while, but he was grateful to Kumashiro for his understanding. Despite his earlier words, however, there was one thing Kazuo felt he had left to do. He held out his sword towards Kumashiro. 'Here, please can you hold this for a moment?'

'*Nani*? What are you doing now?'

Kazuo didn't reply, just stripped to his loincloth as quickly as possible and ran into the lake, diving head first into the water. He shuddered as the icy cold hit his skin, but he blanked out the discomfort and concentrated on his task.

In his mind's eye was an image of Tanaka throwing the ornament as far as he could, the object glinting in the early morning light because of the golden plinth. Its trajectory had created a bright arc that pinpointed the exact spot where it had sunk. Following his instincts, Kazuo took a deep breath and headed down into the murky depths.

Visibility was almost non-existent as, this close to the shore, the water consisted of a thick soup of seeds and mud all mixed together, although a few rays of light penetrated the gloom below. At first Kazuo couldn't see anything at all, other than blurry shadows of vegetation and the vague outline of boulders that were strewn across the bottom of the lake. After coming up for air, however, and trying a second time, his sight began to adjust and he could make out more details. He tried a third, then a fourth time, without success, then stayed on the surface for a while to get his bearings. Moving slightly to the left, he tried again and this time he caught a glint of something in the mud below as a beam of sunlight penetrated the darkness. Kicking out with all his might, he propelled himself towards the spot and reached out. His fingers closed around a small animal body and he let out a whoop of delight, causing air bubbles to swirl all around him while he swallowed a goodly amount of water. He shot up to the surface and coughed until he thought his lungs would burst.

'Did you find it?'

The shout came from the shore and in reply, Kazuo held the lioness aloft. The plinth she was standing on glinted in the rays from the rising sun, as did the pearl her cub was playing with, and her mouth was split into a huge grin. Kazuo grinned back.

'Well, I never …' Kumashiro began to laugh and as Kazuo waded ashore, he enveloped him in bear hug. 'Well done. I have to say I thought you were on a wild goose chase there.

Here, dress yourself before you die of cold. Temi would have my guts if I let any further harm come to you.' He glanced at Kazuo's arm which was oozing blood from a nasty looking gash. 'We'll have to have that seen to.'

'I think the cold water took care of the worst of it. It's enough to freeze your blood.' Kazuo's teeth were now chattering with a combination of cold and relief that it was all over. 'Are you unscathed, my lord?'

'A few scratches, that's all.'

'Good, I'm glad. Thank you for everything. I couldn't have done this without you, I realise that now.'

'Do you know, I think you could,' Kumashiro replied with a smile. 'But I'm very happy to have been of assistance in bringing down that madman.' He glanced at the dead man still floating near the edge of the lake. 'He deserved to die and I'm only sorry his death was so swift.'

'Me too, but at least we can breathe easily now. How soon can we go back north? I want to tell Temi.'

'Soon, but first, I believe there is someone who wishes to see you.'

Chapter Thirty-One

'Kanno-*san*, I am pleased to see that you are in good health.'

The *Shogun* inclined his head and waved a hand to indicate that Kanno senior, Kazuo and Kumashiro no longer had to remain with their foreheads on the floor. They knelt on cushions placed in front of the ruler, who was seated slightly above them on a small dais.

Kazuo's father had arrived only the day before and to his son's relief appeared to have made an almost miraculous recovery from the illness that had plagued him for weeks.

'My joy at hearing of your success was a large factor in the healing process,' Kanno senior had told Kazuo, but the latter thanked the gods and his ancestors as he was sure it was more down to their influence than his own efforts on the clan's behalf. Either way, he was extremely happy to see his father again.

They had all been summoned to attend the ruler at their earliest opportunity and were now alone with Tokugawa Iemitsu, the third person of this powerful family to occupy the exalted position of *Shogun*. It was a singular honour accorded to very few. He sat stiffly before them, his face a polite mask. He was dressed in the most sumptuous of robes and flanked by two guards who were as immobile as statues. Kumashiro was one of his most trusted advisers, however, and Kanno senior had been a childhood friend of Iemitsu's, which had helped to secure him favours prior to his spectacular fall. Kazuo was sure he detected a certain warmth in Iemitsu's eyes as they rested upon them each in turn.

The room they had been ushered into was small and intimate in comparison to most of the *Shogun*'s other chambers, but still vast by anyone else's standards. Decorated with the most exquisite of silk screen paintings and with several shelves filled with decorative ornaments of various types, as well as exquisite *ikebana* flower arrangements, it was a haven of tranquil beauty. Chief among the objects on the middle shelf was the little lioness and her cub, now restored to their rightful place. It seemed to Kazuo that Temperance had been right – the animal was laughing, but this time he could discern no mockery. She was simply happy to be back where she belonged.

'Kumashiro-*sama* has told me what has transpired and I am pleased to hear that Tanaka is dead. The rest of his family will soon follow him to the grave. I have given orders for you to be reinstated in all your former positions and for your possessions to be returned to you, as well as a small additional gift – that of the Oki island you have so recently inhabited.'

'You are most generous, Your Excellency.' Kanno-*san* bowed low once more and Kazuo followed suit.

'There is one matter upon which I would seek clarification, however,' *Shogun* Iemitsu said. 'I have been told that a young *gai-jin* woman was instrumental in the success of your son's mission. Is this correct?'

'Indeed, sire. She had been captured by Tanaka and was being held against her will, and when my son helped her to escape, she agreed to assist him in return. It was her cunning plan that freed him from Tanaka's torturers so that he could complete the mission. And when given the choice of whether to return to her own people or save my son's life, she selflessly and courageously opted to aid him.'

'That is indeed commendable.' *Shogun* Iemitsu nodded gravely and looked thoughtful.

It was a well-known fact that he feared and disliked foreigners and wanted to have as little to do with them as possible. It had been at his instigation that all *gai-jin* and their offspring had been expelled from the country some ten years before and the Dutch traders, the only ones he tolerated, were relegated to the island of Dejima. Kazuo held his breath to see what the *Shogun* would say about Temperance.

'I have further been informed that your son wishes to take the *gai-jin* woman to wife,' *Shogun* Iemitsu said, frowning slightly. 'Is this so, young man?' He looked directly at Kazuo, who tried not to show any emotion whatsoever, although inside he was quaking.

'Yes, sire. I owe her my life and wish to repay her in this manner.'

'Would not a gift suffice?'

'I'm afraid not, sire. The foreigners consider her honour compromised because she has been in my company for so long and the only way to redeem it would be by marriage. If it pleases you, my lord, we propose to go and live on the Oki islands and will not set foot on the mainland without your express permission. I will withdraw any claim I have to my father's other titles and lands. I have several brothers, all of whom are capable of succeeding him in my stead.'

Shogun Iemitsu pursed his mouth while pondering the matter. He was no longer a young man and Kazuo wondered if perhaps some of the fervour of his early years had left him, but he was still a force to be reckoned with. Should he decide to humour Kazuo, he and Temperance would be safe, if still virtually banished from the mainland. On the other hand, if he didn't give his consent, Kazuo could find himself an outlaw once more.

Shogun Iemitsu chuckled suddenly. 'Ah, the impetuosity of youth,' he said. 'I remember feeling passionate about a woman to the point of madness and I can see in your eyes, young Kanno, that this is the case with you. For your sake, I hope that it is not a passing fancy, since you are taking a very serious step, but I wish you well. Thanks to you I have one of my most treasured possessions returned to me, as well as my old friend, a man I always believed I could trust. You have proved my instincts right.'

Kazuo and his father both bowed low, the former with relief and gratitude. With the *Shogun*'s permission his father could no longer voice any objections to his marriage and he was free to live his life in peace.

'You are most gracious and kind, my lord *Shogun*. I shall be forever in your debt and will do my utmost to serve you in any way I can.'

'I shall bear that in mind.'

And Kazuo knew he would, for *Shogun* Iemitsu was as cunning as they came and he had a long memory. Somehow Kazuo would be made to serve the ruler, but he didn't mind, as long as he could have Temperance by his side.

'What could be taking them so long? Surely it doesn't take a whole month to ride to Tanaka's estate and back,' Temperance complained, standing up to stretch her cramped legs and aching back. Although she was used to sitting on the floor by now, it still made her stiff if she did it for too long and she had to stand up at frequent intervals to move her muscles.

The lady Chie, Lord Kumashiro's wife, and his oldest daughter, Megumi, who was sixteen, both smiled at her impatience. 'They will come when they are ready,' Lady Chie said in her soft, melodious voice. 'I'm sure my lord husband would want to do everything in the best possible way and that might take time. In fact, everything takes time in Edo, including meting out justice.'

Temi had been told that strictly speaking, Lady Chie and her daughter ought to have been in the capital as well, because of the laws of *sankin kotai*, but they had been given special permission to return to the north for a few months in order to prepare for Megumi's forthcoming wedding. Temperance was very happy to spend time with them as she liked them both immensely.

'But surely it doesn't take this long?' Temperance paced the floor in order to give her frustrations some kind of outlet. She felt like going for a long, brisk walk, but she was wearing an exquisite *kimono* borrowed from Lady Chie and matching silk slippers, neither of which were conducive to walking fast. With a sigh, she flung herself back down onto the cushion and took up her embroidery.

'At least we know they succeeded in their mission,' Lady Chie reminded her. There had been one rather short message to let them know all had gone well, but that had been weeks ago now. Temperance wanted to see for herself that Kazuo wasn't harmed in any way.

Just then there was the sound of running feet in the corridor outside Lady Chie's rooms, and a swift knock on the door soon after.

'Enter, please.'

'My lady.' The servant kneeled on the floor and bowed to his mistress. 'The Lord Kumashiro has been sighted and should be here soon. I thought you would wish to know.'

Lady Chie inclined her head gracefully and thanked the man. 'There, you see?' she said to Temperance, who had jumped up once more. 'There was no need for impatience.'

'There was every need,' Temperance retorted with a smile.

Lady Chie shook her head in mock exasperation. 'Off with you. Go and see your husband. I shall follow at a more decorous pace. Megumi, you may go with Temi-*san*.'

'Thank you, Mother.'

As soon as the two of them were in the corridor and the door closed behind them, they picked up their *kimonos* and half ran, half shuffled as fast as they could towards the main courtyard, giggling like little girls.

'Father would say you are a very bad influence on me,' Megumi panted.

'He would be right.' Temperance laughed.

Coming to a halt on the steps just outside the main doors, Temperance waited impatiently until the row of riders began to file into the courtyard in front of her. She scanned the crowd of men and horses anxiously, trying to locate the one person in the world she most wanted to see. At last she caught sight of him, but just as she was about to set off towards him, a familiar voice rang out from the right.

'So this is where you've been hiding, eh? I should have known you'd go off by yourself if I didn't arrange a visit fast enough.'

Temperance stopped in mid-stride and turned towards the owner of that voice. 'Midori? Midori! I don't believe it. What are you doing here? And Nico!' She saw her cousin's husband standing next to his wife, a protective arm about her shoulder as always.

'Why, we've come to take you home, of course. I think you've done enough gallivanting about. We waited ages for you to return to us, but despite Ichiro's assurances that he would send you south soon, nothing happened. So here we are.'

'Right, of course, but I ... oh, it's so good to see you.' Temperance embraced them both, grinning from ear to ear. 'I thought at one point I would never see you again.'

'*Temi!*'

At the sound of her name being shouted above the din in the courtyard, they all three turned and watched as Kazuo came running towards them. He had eyes only for Temperance and didn't even see her companions as he swept her into a fierce embrace with one arm, his other one being encased in a sling. She returned it, forgetting her cousins for the moment, and clung to him, happiness bursting through her.

'Temi, my love, are you all right?'

'Yes, yes, I'm fine. But what happened to you? Are you much hurt?'

'No, a mere scratch. It's healing nicely.'

They stared at each other, oblivious to their surroundings, before embracing once more. Kazuo kissed her like there was no tomorrow and she gave herself up to the enjoyment of it, forgetting everyone around them.

'Ahem. Is there something we should know about?' Nico said loudly, reminding Temperance of their presence. She felt her cheeks grow hot and let go of Kazuo, although she held on to his hand almost defiantly.

'This is Kazuo Kanno, my, er … my husband to be. If you don't mind. And if his father agrees. Although if he doesn't, we'll marry anyway. Isn't that right, Kazuo?'

Kazuo nodded and squeezed her hand, but before he had time to reply, Midori interrupted. 'But what about Mr Haag? I thought you were promised to him?'

'What? Pieter Haag? Never! He would have been the last man on earth I'd want to marry, you know that,' Temperance protested. 'And anyway—'

But Midori laughed and didn't allow her to finish the sentence. 'Just teasing. In fact, you couldn't marry him even if you wanted to because he seems to have gone missing. He apparently set off in pursuit of you, as far as we understand, but never returned.'

'Yes, well, I'm afraid there's a reason for that – he's no longer alive.' Temperance shuffled her feet slightly. 'He was wounded in a skirmish, fighting on Lord Tanaka's behalf, but no one knew so he was put in your brother's dungeon without having his cuts seen to. The guards found him the next day and … it was too late. I'm sorry. I feel bad because I asked Lord Kumashiro to keep him there for a while in order to teach him a lesson and he very kindly agreed. Only we had no idea he was hurt so badly. He never said.'

Nico shook his head. 'A shame, but you weren't to know. Haag wasn't the easiest of men and I'm sure he didn't help matters. I'll talk to Ichiro, think no more about it.' He abruptly changed the subject. 'Now then, about this marriage ...?'

Midori and Nico were still looking at Kazuo, who bowed to them formally, his expression serious now. 'I apologise for not introducing myself, but I didn't realise Temi was with someone.'

'Are you indeed her husband-to-be?' Nico asked, looking merely curious to Temperance's great relief.

'Yes. I have spoken to my father and he has agreed, so I hope we can go ahead with the ceremony as soon as possible. In fact, here he comes now, so he can confirm it himself.'

They all watched as what looked like an older version of Kazuo approached across the courtyard, smiling broadly. 'There you are, my son. I wondered where you disappeared off to, but now I can see what drew you in this direction.' He bowed to Temperance, staring at her blonde hair and blue eyes in fascination, before recalling his manners and bowing to Midori and Nico in turn. They all bowed back.

Temperance felt her cheeks heat up. 'I am pleased to meet you at last, Kanno-*sama*.'

'Father, I was just telling Temi and her relatives that you have agreed to our marriage. Is that not so?'

'Indeed. How could I refuse after the young lady saved your life?'

'Really, I did nothing special ...' Temperance felt embarrassment stain her cheeks an even deeper red.

'That's not what I have heard,' Kanno senior smiled again, 'but I like your modesty. A good trait in a wife. Still, my son has the permission of the *Shogun* himself, so who am I to gainsay such an exalted man?'

'The *Shogun*?' Temperance gasped and stared at Kazuo. 'You told him about me?'

'But of course. He would have found out anyway, he has spies everywhere you know.'

'And what did he say?' Temperance hardly dared believe this.

'Well, although he doesn't like foreigners in general, he gave me his special permission to marry you because of your bravery. I could see it went against the grain, but I have promised him we won't live on the mainland and he seemed satisfied with that. We will be going to the Oki islands as soon as possible. Will you mind?'

'No, I'll live anywhere, as long as I can be with you.' Temperance turned to her future father-in-law. 'And you, my lord, are you staying on the mainland?'

'Oh yes, nothing could induce me to set foot on those accursed islands again.' He chuckled. 'Unless I have the incentive of visiting a grandchild, that is.' His eyes twinkled at Temperance and she smiled back at him. She had a feeling he would be a frequent visitor, grandchildren or not, and she looked forward to spending time with him as she already liked him immensely.

'Sounds like you have everything in hand,' Nico said. 'Congratulations.'

'Nico, you're supposed to be acting as her guardian,' Midori protested, glaring at her husband.

'And so I am. Didn't you hear me asking the young man his intentions?'

Midori hit him on the shoulder. 'That was very half-hearted and you know it. You don't even know who he is.'

'Well, what would you have me do? Look at our dear cousin. She doesn't exactly seem as though she'll brook any interference from me. Likely, she'd run away again. I'm satisfied that Kanno-*san*'s intentions are honourable and anything else can be discussed later.' He winked at Temperance, who threw her arms around him and gave him a bear hug.

'You are a wonderful man, Nico. I've always said so. You are so lucky, Midori, but now I'm lucky too.' She took Kazuo's hand in hers once more and smiled at him. 'Come, you must be in need of a bath and clean clothes.' She beckoned to Midori and Nico. 'You as well. Please, come and meet Ichiro's wife and children. It must be years since you last saw them. Lady Chie is a gem, I adore her.' Chattering on, she led the way into the castle.

'You should have been sterner,' Temperance heard Midori hiss at her husband. 'Temi's brother will blame us when he hears about this.'

'Daniel is a very intelligent man, he'll do no such thing,' Nico replied. 'He would want his sister to be happy and have you ever seen anyone happier than that girl right now?' Temperance turned to see him nodding in her direction and she exchanged a glance of pure delight with her husband-to-be.

Midori sighed. 'Only one person – me, the day you asked me to marry you.'

'Well, there you are then. Now lead the way to our room, my little termagant.'

Temperance rolled her eyes at Kazuo as her cousin once more punched her poor, long-suffering husband on the arm, but he didn't look as if he minded in the slightest. In fact, quite the opposite. They were perfectly matched and Temperance knew that she and Kazuo were too. Whatever life threw at them from now on, they would weather together.

Having come to Japan to find excitement and adventure, she felt sure that despite everything she had been through, the adventure was only just beginning.

Epilogue

April 1650

Temperance and Kazuo stood on the newly strengthened balcony of the little temple in the forest, where they had hidden from Tanaka, and looked out at the magnificent view across the valley. It seemed a long time ago now, that desperate journey from Edo, but the intimacy of their brief moments together here remained vivid in her memory and made Temperance give her husband's hand a squeeze. He looked at her and smiled, no doubt thinking about the same thing.

Daisuke, the monk, came to stand in the doorway behind them. 'All is ready for the purification ritual,' he announced. 'And I think my namesake is getting slightly fractious so we'd better hurry. Perhaps it is soon time for his meal?' As if to concur with this, the sound of a baby's grizzling could be heard from inside the temple.

'No, he's just impatient, like his mother.' Kazuo bent to kiss his wife to show that he was joking.

Temperance shook her head at him. 'Or maybe he's always hungry, like his father?'

'Well, I have to eat a lot. I'm still recovering my strength after the ordeals I went through.'

Temperance just snorted. Her husband had recovered ages ago and was as fit as any man – probably fitter since he spent so much time training with his men. Although they had made their home on one of the Oki islands, Kazuo assured her the *Shogun* might one day call on his services and he intended to be ready.

'I simply cannot risk him taking his wrath out on my family ever again,' he'd said and Temperance could see his point. But she was very happy with the way things were right now and secretly hoped the ruler would forget all about them so they could continue to live in peace. She knew Kazuo's father was doing his utmost to help in that respect, offering the services of his other sons whenever anything needed doing. Kanno senior had assured her she need not worry and she believed him.

They had decided to name their little boy after the monk because without him Kazuo might not have lived to sire him at all. It seemed an auspicious choice. Little Dai, as he was usually called, was a strong and healthy baby with a huge set of lungs, a delight to his parents, grandparents and Temperance's relatives. They met up whenever possible and had all gathered here today for the monk to perform a purification of the recently refurbished building.

'It's normally done for newly built structures,' Daisuke had written to them, 'but I feel as though this temple has begun its life anew and therefore it seems fitting to do this. I would be honoured if you could be present.'

'It will be our pleasure,' Kazuo had replied, even though it would be a risk for Temperance to travel across the mainland. She'd once again dressed in men's clothing, hiding her hair as before and keeping her eyes downcast. But this time she'd had Nico and Midori by her side, also in disguise, which made things easier, as well as Ryo and the other outlaws who had tired of their nomadic lifestyle and pledged their allegiance to Kazuo and had now made their home on the Oki islands.

'We're not missing out on this,' Midori said with a smile when they met up on the coast. 'Ichiro told me what was happening and said he was going, so just you try and keep us away. Besides, his men will protect us if necessary.'

'So will Kazuo's,' Temperance replied, glancing at Ryo who had overheard and was smiling and nodding at her words. She knew he would lay down his life for her and her family, which was a comforting thought.

'I'm so grateful to your father for restoring the temple,' Daisuke murmured now to Kazuo as they made their way to the inner room of the temple, which was no longer gloomy and damp. 'It's as beautiful as I always imagined it could be.'

And indeed it was. All the rotten timbers had been replaced, the holes in the steep roofs repaired, pillars painted a bright fiery red and everything polished, cleaned and spruced up. The building smelled of paint and beeswax mixed with cedar wood and various types of incense. Temperance breathed in these fragrances and stored them in her memory. Outside, the forest had been cut back and the temple grounds tamed and pruned to show nature to its best advantage. Temperance felt it was a magical place, the site where she had finally begun to hope that her love for Kazuo might be reciprocated.

A new red-painted *torii* – a traditional Japanese gate made of two sturdy upright pillars and two crossbars, with curved ends on the top one – had been erected at the bottom of the stairs leading up to the temple. It added a wonderful splash of colour to the surrounding greenery, where trees were bursting into their light green spring colour. Just outside the temple itself stood two *sakura* trees in full bloom, one either side of the path, and the white blossom petals floated on the breeze like thistledown, ending up in little drifts in various corners. It was a sight Temperance would never tire of, she was sure.

'Here, you'd better hold the little varmint.' Midori, with Casper and Emi trailing in her wake, came over to hand Dai into his mother's arms where he snuggled contentedly as the monk began his rituals. He remained quiet through the ringing of a bell, clapping of hands and chanting, as if he understood the importance of this day and the part this wonderful place had played in his life.

One day Temperance would tell him about it and she vowed to bring him back when he was older so he could see it for himself. To her, the temple represented hope and new life, and as they all left the building she lagged behind to perform one final task. She stopped before the little stone god by the entrance. His bald head gleamed in the sunlight while his bronze eyes glittered. She bowed low, holding Dai close, and smiled at him.

'Thank you so much for your help. I shall be forever grateful,' she whispered, and was almost sure she saw a twinkle in response.

'As will I, thank you.' Kazuo's voice was slightly louder and she looked up to find him bowing to the god as well before putting his arm around her and their son.

Musubi-no-Kami, the god of love, hadn't just shown her the way to the inner room, to safety, that cold October day, he'd outdone himself since. He had given both of them the greatest treasure they could ever have – a perfect soulmate.

Author's Note

Although I try to stick to known historical facts as much as possible, as an author I sometimes have to use a little bit of 'artistic licence' to make the story more exciting. In the case of this novel, I have described the Yoshiwara pleasure district of Edo as it looked slightly later than during this period. It existed at the time this story is set, but didn't actually become a separate walled-in area until 1657.

The foreign traders were restricted in the ways I describe. I have been to Dejima myself where you really do get an understanding of how claustrophobic it must have been for them and how frustrating not to be allowed on the mainland. I would thoroughly recommend a visit for anyone going to Japan as it's a fascinating place!

I have not used real people in this story, apart from the *Shogun,* preferring to make them up, and I hope my portrayal of him is fair.

About the Author

Christina lives near Hereford and is married with two children. Although born in England she has a Swedish mother and was brought up in Sweden. In her teens, the family moved to Japan where she had the opportunity to travel extensively in the Far East.

The Jade Lioness is Christina's tenth novel with Choc Lit. She also has a number of novellas published under the Choc Lit Lite imprint, which are available online.

Christina's novels have won many awards, including the Big Red Reads Fiction Award for *The Scarlet Kimono* and Historical Romantic Novel of the Year awards for both *Highland Storms* and *The Gilded Fan*. *The Silent Touch of Shadows* won a Best Historical Read award and Christina's debut novel, *Trade Winds*, was also short-listed for the Pure Passion Award for Best Historical Fiction.

To find out more visit:
www.christinacourtenay.com
www.twitter.com/PiaCCourtenay
www.facebook.com/christinacourtenayauthor

More Choc Lit
From Christina Courtenay

Shadows from the Past series

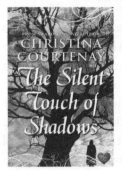

Kinross series

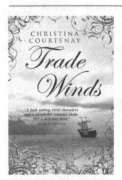

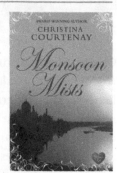

Kumashiro series

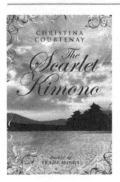

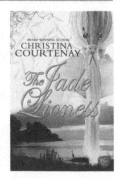